The Four Horsemen

Also by Gregory Dowling

Ascension

The Four Horsemen

GREGORY DOWLING

Thomas Dunne Books
St. Martin's Press
New York

THOMAS DUNNE BOOKS.
An imprint of St. Martin's Press.

THE FOUR HORSEMEN. Copyright © 2017 by Gregory Dowling. All rights reserved. Printed in the United States of America. For information, address St. Martin's Press, 175 Fifth Avenue, New York, N.Y. 10010.

www.thomasdunnebooks.com
www.stmartins.com

Library of Congress Cataloging-in-Publication Data

Names: Dowling, Gregory, author.
Title: The four horsemen / Gregory Dowling.
Description: First U.S. edition. | New York : Thomas Dunne Books, St. Martin's Press, 2017.
Identifiers: LCCN 2017023766 | ISBN 9781250108548 (hardcover) | ISBN 9781250108555 (ebook)
Subjects: | GSAFD: Suspense fiction. | Mystery fiction.
Classification: LCC PR6054.O862 F68 2017 | DDC 823/.914—dc23
LC record available at https://lccn.loc.gov/2017023766

Our books may be purchased in bulk for promotional, educational, or business use. Please contact your local bookseller or the Macmillan Corporate and Premium Sales Department at 1-800-221-7945, extension 5442, or by email at MacmillanSpecialMarkets@macmillan.com.

First published in Great Britain by Polygon, an imprint of Birlinn Ltd

First U.S. Edition: October 2017

10 9 8 7 6 5 4 3 2 1

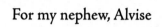

For my nephew, Alvise

Foreword

After the publication of Alvise Marangon's adventures in *Ascension* a number of people asked me where I had come across this story. The answer, as so often in Venice, is in the archives. The Archivio di Stato, housed in the ex-monastery of the Frari church, has over seventy kilometres of shelving, containing documents pertaining not only to every aspect of Venetian history but also to the history of every part of the world with which the Venetian Republic ever had dealings – and that really means most of the Western world and a goodly portion of the Eastern. It seems nothing ever got thrown away.

The archives contain all the reports drawn up by Venice's legions of confidential agents and spies. These documents have, of course, been extensively consulted and studied by historians, since they throw extraordinary light not only on to political matters but also on to aspects of Venetian daily life. Everyone, it seems, was under observation, and unflattering comparisons have been drawn to life in East Germany under the Stasi.

We have come to know details about the lives of some of the more diligent or observant spies, such as the ever-watchful Giambattista Manuzzi, who reported, among other things, on the suspicious dealings of a certain Giacomo Casanova – who would himself join the ranks of Venice's secret agents later in life.

However, not all the files and folders have been scrutinised. I found on one shelf a folder that had been pushed to the back, bound with a leather strap that seemed never to have been loosened. When I finally managed to open it I found not the usual short reports, intended for immediate scrutiny by the Inquisitors or by the Missier Grande, but long detailed narratives of certain otherwise unknown events in the history of the city. The fact that the folder was included among the other reports of secret agents suggested that the Inquisitors had got hold of the manuscript, even if it had not originally been intended for them. Alvise Marangon wrote in reasonably correct Tuscan Italian, although a number of Venetian expressions crop up, and most of the dialogues are reported directly in dialect. He also uses the occasional English words, testifying to his own bilingualism. Given the nature of the stories he tells, it seems possible that he wrote these accounts later in life, when it might have seemed to him that no harm could accrue from their publication; the fact that the manuscript was catalogued among the secret reports suggests that the Inquisitors, learning of its existence, clearly disagreed with the author and confiscated it. Alvise wrote as if for a general audience, drawing on his experience as a *cicerone* to explain certain matters of Venetian life that might not be familiar to a non-Venetian.

I have done my best to maintain the tone and spirit of the original document. I have not attempted to translate it into a version of eighteenth-century English prose, since I feel it would be impossible to do so without sounding stilted and artificial. I have, however, striven to avoid anything too obviously anachronistic in the language. To avoid confusion I have modified all time-references to conform with current practice; in eighteenth-century Venice zero hour (or the 24th hour) corresponded to the Angelus, the ritual prayer recited half an hour after sunset.

This is the second of Alvise's adventures. I have not yet explored the entire contents of the folder, but it seems fairly clear that it does contain a number of other stories, which I will continue to translate so long as readers continue to be interested in them.

Gregory Dowling
Venice
July 2017

Venice, under the Dogeship of
Pietro Grimani (1741–52)

The Four Horsemen

I

I didn't like the man who approached me at the Malvasia del Remedio. Unfortunately I made the mistake of making it clear that I didn't.

It wasn't entirely my fault. He should not have interrupted me while I was reading. And he should not have been so offensively slimy.

A fault-finder, had there been one in the tavern at that hour, might have hinted that perhaps I could have been a little more sober. But it had been a long day, it was cold outside and the Malmsey wine provided by the tavern was both comforting and reasonably priced. And like so many of the tavern's clients, I liked to indulge myself in the fancy that the very name of the place indicated that it offered a remedy to life's ills, even while I knew that Remedio just happened to be the proprietor's surname.

"Sior Marangon?" said this individual.

I looked up from my volume of Pope; it was a beautiful edition of the first two books of *The Iliad*, which had been given to me by a grateful client with good taste. The shift from Achilles' wrath to this man's fawning tone was jarring. His excessively tight clothes, over-powdered wig and fixed smile all added to the contrast, and to my irritation.

"That's my name," I said, in as civilly neutral a tone as my annoyance would allow.

"You work as a *cicerone* principally with English travellers, I believe," he said, and sat down at the table opposite me. He never stopped smiling; or, to be more accurate, he never stopped displaying his teeth, which gleamed in the light from the candle-bracket above my head. His eyes, which flittered around the room as he spoke, were entirely unaffected by the smile.

"That is the case," I said. Although Venetian by birth I had grown up in England, thanks to the intermittently nomadic life led by my actress mother. Being able to speak both English and Venetian fluently was an undeniable advantage in the fiercely competitive world of the professional tour guides or *ciceroni*. "Are you proposing a new client? Because at the moment I am already engaged with a young nobleman."

"Yes, I am aware of that," he said. "And it is precisely on that subject that I have come to speak to you. On behalf of my master, Sior Molin. Sior Lucio Molin."

"Ah," I said.

His eyes fixed on me for one moment. "I gather you know of my master?"

"I've heard of him," I said, my tone remaining neutral. I lifted my book in as obvious a fashion as possible.

He ignored the hint. "Then you will know he has one of the most sought-after gambling establishments in the city."

"Yes," I said.

"And he has asked me to propose a business arrangement with you."

"Please thank your master, but tell him—"

He lifted his hand. "You have not yet heard his very generous offer."

"No, and I don't wish to hear it," I said, deciding to abandon all semblance of civility. "When my clients ask me for advice on gambling establishments, I recommend the state *ridotto* and nowhere else. I have no wish to be blamed for any losses they might sustain."

"Who is to say that they might not win?" he said, and somehow managed to reveal a few more gleaming teeth on both sides of his mouth.

"Who indeed?" I said. "But the answer remains no."

"I understand that you accept pecuniary rewards from some of the artists that your clients visit."

"Well, that's different. When my clients buy a portrait from Sior Nazari or a *veduta* from Sior Marieschi, it's possible that they may be so lacking in taste as to be dissatisfied with the work, but the painting does exist. In real terms they are no poorer than they were before."

"Visitors to Sior Molin's establishment, of course, do not always win, but they certainly pass a pleasant and sociable evening in the best of company . . ."

"And long may they continue to do so," I said. "I certainly won't prevent any of my clients from visiting it. I just don't wish to be the one who sends them there."

"If I may say so," he said, "you are turning down a considerable source of income, and one that is perfectly legitimate."

It was here, perhaps, that I made my mistake. "I have little more than my reputation to keep me going," I said, "and so I have no wish to jeopardise it for a few easy bribes."

Suddenly his display of teeth became unambiguously menacing. "I will inform Sior Molin of your refusal – and also of your insult. He will not be pleased."

It might have been more dignified on my part simply to dismiss him at this point with a wave of my hand and to return to the epic struggles of the Greeks and Trojans, but rather late I remembered that Lucio Molin, like so many managers of gambling establishments, had a number of burly henchmen, or *bravi*, in his employ, and so I mumbled a few words to the effect that I certainly had no wish to offend anyone. However, my interlocutor was already getting to his feet and paid no attention.

As he left me I caught the eye of Siora Remedio, who came over to my table.

"Another cup of wine, Sior Alvise?" she said.

"I think I'd better not," I said, although the temptation to drown my misgivings in Malmsey was strong. "Oh, by the way . . ."

"Yes?"

"Did you happen to notice if the man who was talking to me just now was with anyone else?"

"Anyone else?"

"Yes. Like a *bravo* – or two."

3

"Oh dear," she said. "Have you been getting into trouble again, Sior Alvise?"

"Again?" I said.

"Well, for a quiet young man who likes reading you do seem to have a few, um, unusual friends," she said.

I knew who she was thinking of. My second job, slightly more lucrative though considerably less respectable, was as a confidential agent for the Missier Grande; this occasionally involved my meeting with one or more of the city's *sbirri* or law-enforcers; "unusual" was probably the most flattering adjective that had ever been used to describe them. I had clearly made the mistake of using the tavern as a meeting-point rather too often.

"You know how it is as a *cicerone*," I said, and hoped my vague arm-sweeping gesture would suggest all sorts of reasonable explanations. "Do you think you could just look outside and see if the man is still out there? Without making it too obvious?"

She picked up my empty tankard and moved towards the door. There were too many other customers for me to see what happened, but I suddenly heard her voice raised with the authoritative tones only possessed by the women who manage Venetian taverns (the husbands are never so imposing). "Be off with you! We don't want your sort hanging around here!"

The clientele of the tavern looked towards the door with interest. It was a dull evening in November and her tone suggested a break in the monotony at least.

She came back to me. "Well, I sent them packing."

"Who were they?" I said, trying to make my voice sound casual, and probably not succeeding.

"That smarmy type who was talking to you and two rough fellows carrying cudgels. Not the sort you should be mixing with, Sior Alvise."

"No," I agreed. "Definitely not. In fact, I'll take your advice and have nothing to do with them. Could I leave by the kitchen door?" I could not imagine that they had gone very far from the tavern. They were probably waiting on the *fondamenta* alongside the nearby canal.

"The kitchen door?" she said. "It gives on to the canal."

"Ah," I said, just briefly toying with the idea of swimming home. "Well, maybe not, then ..."

"But we've got a boat there."

This was to be expected, since their supplies would arrive by boat; however, lending it to me seemed to go beyond what was expected from our hostess–client relationship. I said, "I see," in a puzzled tone.

"All you have to do is swing it out and you should be able to reach the *calle* on the opposite side. We can pull it back."

"That would be very kind," I said, wondering if this was a regular occurrence with some of her more obstreperous customers.

"No problem, Sior Alvise." Then a thought struck her. "You'll settle the week's bill, will you?"

I did not find this apprehension on her part in any way encouraging, but I dug into my purse and paid what she told me was due, wincing just a little when I realised quite how much Malmsey I must have consumed over the last few evenings.

I wrapped my cloak around me (the first really warm garment I had ever possessed, even more expensive than my weekly *malvasia* bill) and put on my tricorn hat. A pity I had come unequipped with a mask; it was already the middle of the month and half the population was indulging in the freedom offered by anonymity. However, I only used masks in those places that required them, like the city's gambling houses and theatres, and this evening I had had no intention of engaging in any such activities.

I followed Siora Remedio towards the kitchen. I think this tame conclusion to the evening disappointed one or two of the clients, although they raised a salutary tankard in my direction.

It proved as simple as Siora Remedio had suggested. The kitchen had a door right on to the canal, and there lay the tavern's simple *sandolo*, moored at both ends. I untied the rope at the prow and pushed off against the brick wall of the tavern; the boat swung out, its prow pointing towards the dark alley between two high buildings on the opposite side of the canal. I glanced to the right, and at the far end of the canal, where it veered leftwards, I could dimly make out the bridge that led into the little square beneath the Querini palace. I thought I saw a figure on the bridge but paid no attention.

The alley had steps down to the canal and I managed to scramble out of the boat and on to their seaweedy surface without slipping straight back. Maybe I was not so very drunk after all, I congratulated myself.

I turned round and waved to Siora Remedio, who stood stalwartly framed against the light of her kitchen. She indicated that I should push the boat back, and I managed to do that too without falling into the canal. I should probably offer to give lessons in sobriety and deportment to the city's youth.

I then applied my keen brain to the question of where I was. "Casselleria," I said to myself, after just a second's calculation, and with a touch of self-congratulation on my geographical expertise. If there had been anyone around I would have told them that it was the street of the chest-makers, who had their own little shrine in the nearby church of Santa Maria Formosa. "And they helped to rescue the Venetian brides kidnapped by Istrian pirates back in the tenth century," I informed a passing rat. Sometimes *ciceroni* can be rather tedious.

I now made my second big mistake of the evening. It would have been perfectly easy to follow the Casselleria northwards and head towards the Rialto, comfortably distant from any lurking *bravi*, and then take a circuitous route back homewards. Instead, feeling complacent in my knowledge of the city's geography, I took the first turning left, which led, after another sharp left, to the Ponte de l'Anzolo, Bridge of the Angel. I had come this way just a few days earlier with an earnest English clergyman to show him the fine sculptured angel on Palazzo Soranzo that looks towards the bridge, and I had told him the quaint story of the monkey and the devil associated with it. He had thought the story a foolish example of Papist superstition, and I had said nothing in defence of the angel (or of the Catholic Church). So maybe now I was coming back to make amends. And perhaps I also felt I needed an angel's protection.

But it didn't work. As I passed the first turning left after the bridge I heard an urgent clatter of approaching footsteps from somewhere along the gloomy depths of the alley – and I realised that it led straight back to the tavern. If that figure I had glimpsed on the bridge earlier had been one of Molin's *bravi*, then they could easily have guessed that I might come back this way. Especially if they knew that I was drunk and stupid. And my conversation earlier had perhaps given them an inkling.

2

Without even stopping to send a word of reproach or of supplication to the angel I broke into a run myself. I guessed that my safest bet was to make towards the lights and bustle of Saint Mark's Square. If nothing else, there would be a troop of *arsenalotti* stationed by the bell-tower.

I was not running as fast as I should, I dimly realised, being hampered by my cloak, which had come unbuckled and was slipping off my left shoulder. I could discard it, I thought – and then rebelled at the idea. Why should I lose the first warm cloak I had ever had (a month's wages) just because a few *bravi* had taken it into their heads to thrash me? I would go down fighting but warm . . .

I could hear their clunking footsteps getting closer as I swivelled right into the broad street at the end of the alley. As I grabbed at the flapping encumbrance I darted one glance back and saw two dim but large shapes lumbering along, one of them already raising a menacing object above his head.

Well, the only alternative to discarding my cloak was to transform it from hindrance to help. And the same applied to the darkness, which seconds ago I had been yearning to emerge from. I ran down the broad street, heading towards the next turning left, which led towards the Square of the Little Lions; I knew I had little chance of reaching the square before they caught up with me, but I did think I could make it to the dark alley itself. And as I ran I loosened the cloak with one hand and with the other clutched at a corner of my tricorn hat. I could already hear the snorting breath of the first man, apparently inches behind me.

I twisted left into the alley, and as I did so I flicked the cloak free from my shoulder with my left hand and with the right jerked off my hat, and then I thrust them both out to one side. I was relying on vague memories of bull-fights I had seen in Campo San Polo; the men were not bulls, but darkness and surprise might at least momentarily rob them of any human intelligence they might possess.

The first man thudded into the alley and swung his cudgel down upon the black shapes of the hat and cloak. The blow was so vicious that my hat was jerked from my fingers. However, meeting an unexpected lack of solid resistance the man staggered forwards, tumbling on to the cloak. Letting go of it, I was able to jerk the cudgel from his hands as he fell, and as the second man loomed into the alley, I was already swinging it in as menacing an attitude as I could assume.

But then the first man, from his sprawling position, grabbed my legs and I staggered, dropping the cudgel as I instinctively put my arms out to break my fall. I didn't see what happened next, but I can only presume that the second man tripped over his colleague, or perhaps got entangled in my loose cloak, because a second later we were all three on the ground, the two men letting out a series of blasphemous imprecations. If they were *bravi*, they were not very good at it.

Another voice made itself heard, one that I recognised. "Come on, give him what he deserves." It was the slimy man I had been speaking to in the tavern, who was standing at the entrance to the alleyway, at a prudent distant from our floundering figures.

I had managed to get hold of the cudgel I had dropped, which had rolled towards the side of the street, and was able to smash it down on the fingers of the man who was now clutching at my waist. At that point, however, a great blow came down on my shoulder, presumably from the second man, who had somehow got himself upright enough to wield his own cudgel forcefully. I lost hold of mine again and squirmed round to face him. He had struggled to his feet and was looming over me, ready to deliver another blow. I sensed he was still unsteady on his feet and with one hand I scrabbled at my tangled cloak, one corner of which he was standing on. I gave it a sudden jerk and he reeled backwards.

I somehow managed to yank the cloak free from both of them

and with a gait that was midway between a crawl and a stooping run I headed towards the hazy lights of the square at the other end of the alleyway. They were not far behind me, with the slimy man screaming furiously at his two inept henchmen. I emerged into the reassuring open space of the Square of the Little Lions, along the northern flank of the basilica of Saint Mark, and cast just one glance at the comforting red-marble figures of the little lions, their backs rendered shiny by three decades of contact with children's bottoms, as I tore past.

The great expanse of Saint Mark's Square, lit by numerous lanterns, lay ahead of me. As usual the coffee houses were busy and there were still a number of people parading on the Liston, the area between the Merceria and the waterfront Piazzetta. I headed straight towards the great solid mass of the bell-tower, where there was always a cluster of *arsenalotti* on hand to quell any trouble.

I was now yelling at the top of my voice, "Thieves! Murderers! Help!" I had definitely caught people's attention, but it did not yet look as if anyone was going to come to my assistance; most people's reaction seemed to be to shrink away. And I could hear the pounding footsteps of my pursuers getting closer.

I was now among the people parading in their finest clothes on the Liston. Perhaps I should have added "Ragamuffins!" or "Scoundrels wearing clothes from last year!" to my list if I wanted a sharp reaction from this crowd.

But then, just as a hefty hand grabbed my shoulder, I heard the reassuring pounding of urgent feet from the direction of the bell-tower and a clamour of gruff Castello accents.

A few seconds later the two *bravi* and I were surrounded by thickset men, all carrying pikes and all looking even more menacing than the two henchmen. The strolling crowd of the Liston had all drawn back; most of them were in masks, but I could sense an air of disdainful curiosity as they gazed upon this intrusive episode of low-life rowdiness. The slimy man was nowhere to be seen.

Things happened very swiftly after that. We were escorted briskly away from the Liston so as not to cause any further disruption. By the corner of the basilica's treasury we were disarmed (well, I was frisked, and my volume of Pope's *Iliad* was confiscated, presumably on the grounds that something had to be taken from me, given that the others had had their cudgels removed). Then we were forced to stand with our backs to the crowds and our hands behind our heads, staring at the four mysterious porphyry figures set into the corner of the treasury, while we waited for the *sbirri* to come.

I wondered whether this was standard procedure with felons, with the notion that we would brood on the grim fate of the men depicted by those statues. Legend had it that these curiously conspiratorial figures, each with one hand on a sword and the other on the shoulder of a companion, were Saracens who had attempted to rob the treasury and had been transformed into stone for their pains. As the minutes passed and I felt the steady throbbing of my shoulder where the cudgel had hit me, I began to think that turning into stone wasn't so bad a fate, though I doubted I would attain the dignity of porphyry. And then at last the *sbirri* arrived and the *arsenalotti* handed us and our belongings over to them. I recognised one of them, a thickset bearded man named Piero, who stubbornly refused to acknowledge me. Things are definitely bad when you find yourself being snubbed by a *sbirro*.

About five minutes later I was in a cell, fortunately by myself. Despite my pleas my *Iliad* had not been returned to me, which meant I had nothing better to do than brood on my situation, rub my throbbing shoulder and prepare my story. The fact that I had clearly been running away from the two cudgel-bearing men ought to tell in my favour, I thought. But against this there was the fact that I had brought disruption into the most prestigious place in the city; I should have allowed myself to be discreetly cudgelled senseless in a side street rather than disturb the elegant pomp of the *passeggiata* on the Liston. The authorities would care little which of us was the aggressor and which the victim; quite simply none of us should have been there. The only spectacles allowed in the Piazza were celebratory ones.

Much would also depend on how influential Sior Lucio Molin

was. The very fact that his employee had decided that an insult should be instantly punished with violence suggested either that the slimy man had simply lost all sense of judgement or that he and his employer had little fear of any denunciation I might make. I rather suspected the latter was the case. If so, then the very least that would happen was that I would lose my licence as a *cicerone*.

Would my role as confidential agent be of any help? Probably not; the very last thing the Missier Grande needed was agents who got involved in street brawls. I would not be able to remind the authorities of my former services to the city (minor things, like thwarting an assassination attempt on the Doge), since my role in that whole affair had never been officially recognised, due to the delicate game of power-balancing that was always being played out between the Missier Grande and the Council of Ten. The Missier Grande effectively ran the city's *sbirri* and was responsible for all matters of common criminality; the Council of Ten – or more specifically the three Inquisitors, who were appointed by the Council – were responsible for all matters that involved the security of the state. The Missier Grande had to be very careful not to venture into such matters himself – or, at least, not to let it appear that he was doing so. In particular he had to be very wary about investigating any matters that involved noblemen, since the very fact of so doing could be thought of as a subversive activity, undermining the foundations on which the Venetian Republic was built. I knew, too, that he was reluctant to let the Inquisitors know that he had an English-educated agent on his payroll; it could suggest he was going beyond his area of competence and involving himself in foreign affairs.

It did make me wonder sometimes whether I was worth all the trouble to the Missier Grande; for the last few months I had had little to do for him beyond drawing up reports on some of the gambling houses where foreigners were regularly fleeced (which was how I had come to know about Sior Molin). It had not been difficult work, and, until today, it had never seemed particularly dangerous either. My gloomy feeling now was that the moment my role as agent proved more problematic than useful, the Missier Grande would simply strike me off his books. That moment looked like being now. And with that I would also lose my licence as *cicerone* and any possibility of supporting myself in Venice.

"Farewell, Lucia," I said, when I came to this conclusion. I had not seen Lucia, daughter of Fabrizio Busetto, bookseller and friend, for some weeks now; our relations, formerly warm, had become somewhat strained ever since it had become clear that I was continuing to act as a confidential agent. It was not unreasonable on her part; everyone knew that agents played an important role in the way the city functioned, but nobody wanted to have much to do with them; the same, after all, was true of those who raked the shit from the city's drained canals. The fact that I was only allowed to keep my licence as *cicerone* on condition that I also did some confidential reporting for the Missier Grande had clearly not proved a persuasive enough argument for Lucia.

Until a few weeks ago I had continued to call in occasionally at the bookshop, hoping that my insouciance might help to make her forget the unsavoury side of my life, but although she was courteous enough a certain wariness in her eyes told me that she could never completely keep from wondering whether every word she said was going to end up in a confidential report to be read by inquisitive functionaries of the Missier Grande. And so in the end I had ceased to visit. I will not deny that I continued to foster the secret (and never consciously acknowledged) hope that my absence would stir a spirit of remorse in her; I even occasionally (and wildly) dreamed that I might wake up in the middle of the night to find her by my bed murmuring that she could no longer live without me.

3

There was a rattle of chains at the door, and then it scraped open. I gazed at the dark shapes, wondering for one wild moment whether the two *bravi* had been sent to join me so that we could make friends. Then the lamplight allowed me to distinguish two of the *sbirri* who had brought us to the prison, one of them being black-bearded Piero, who continued to refuse to acknowledge me.

I stood up. "So now where—" I began.

"Shut up," said the *sbirro* who wasn't Piero, "and come with us." As with most *sbirri* his voice had the rising intonation of western Dorsoduro.

I had had the experience before of being escorted along the labyrinthine corridors of the prison and the Doge's palace, and as on the previous occasion I suspected that the bewildering route we followed was deliberately not the most direct. I realised at one point that we had crossed the Bridge of Sighs and were now inside the innermost parts of the palace, above and away from the splendid halls and chambers with their vast canvases by Veronese and Tintoretto. In fact, I suddenly recognised where we were going. "This is the Missier Grande's office," I said, as we issued into a narrow windowless room, lit by a single chandelier with four candles.

"Shut up," said the *sbirro* automatically.

The Missier Grande's principal offices were at the far end of Saint Mark's Square; it was there I delivered my reports (usually to his secretary, Sior Massaro, rather than to the great man himself). However, as was only fitting, he also had this small space within the seat of government itself, so that he could be on hand to talk to his superiors in the Council of Ten. The familiarity of this place (I had been here on a couple of occasions) was slightly reassuring.

Even more reassuring was the little figure who now scuttled into the room and took his place behind the desk, which was placed on the opposite side of the room. This was round-cheeked, bespectacled Sior Massaro himself.

"Sior Massaro," I said, "it's very good to see you."

"Shut up," said the *sbirro*.

Sior Massaro waved a deprecatory hand at the *sbirro* but didn't actually countermand his order. "We had better wait until the Missier Grande arrives before we start discussing the situation." He sat down at the desk and began fussily to prepare his quill. Once he had done that he began to sort through various papers. He had the clerk's skill of always appearing to be extremely busy, even when there is nothing to do.

As usual the Missier Grande managed to make his arrival seem both non-emphatic and dramatic. He came in silently, his jet-black robe with white trimmings billowing out in the draught created by his own sweeping movements. He sat down without a glance at Sior Massaro and fixed me with his icy blue eyes.

I knew better than to speak first. There was silence for about ten seconds, with just a nervous scratching of the quill by Sior Massaro. Then the Missier Grande spoke.

"So you have been brawling." As always his voice was quiet and almost totally uninflected.

"I was the victim of an assault, Illustrissimo," I said.

"Which began after you had gratuitously insulted a citizen of the Republic."

"Illustrissimo, I would have thought that by now you know me better than that."

"I judge from the evidence before me."

"And this would be the statements of two cudgel-wielding *bravi*?" I said.

"They are the personal servants of a certain Sior Marco Boldrin, who is in the employ of Citizen Lucio Molin. Sior Boldrin reports that you slandered the reputation of his employer in a public place and that he felt called upon to defend it."

"He sent his *bravi* to beat me up," I said, "and all I had said was that I wouldn't take my clients to his gambling house."

"He claims that you used extremely offensive language against his employer," he said. His tone remained as flat as ever. It was impossible to know whether he believed what he was reporting or not.

"Illustrissimo, again I ask you to remember my service to the Republic. Is it likely I would compromise myself in such a fashion?"

"You had obviously been drinking," he said. "Indeed, the effects are still obvious."

I did my best to enunciate my next sentence as clearly as possible. "I may have had a cup or two of *malvasia*, but I can assure you I was not drunk." I had been about to add the usual "Illustrissimo" to this sentence but realised in time the perils of its polysyllabic complexity.

"Indeed. An unusual occurrence, by all accounts."

"That is unfair, Illustrissimo," I said, forgetting all caution in my indignation; even as I spoke the last word I was all too aware of the slushiness of its sibilants. I instantly felt my cheeks flaring with embarrassment. I hoped it would not add to the overall impression of vinous befuddlement.

He said nothing for a few seconds but just continued to gaze at me. The iciness of his stare paradoxically seemed to kindle the fiery glow of my face. I decided my best strategy at this point was to maintain a long silence as well and hope that it would appear to be a dignified one. Finally he said, "I know who Citizen Molin is and I know what weight to give to anything said by those in his employ. However, I have made it clear to you and to all my confidential agents that your constant aim must be that of total inconspicuousness. This means you must resist all provocations and all temptations to indulge in absurd heroics or dramatic gestures. If you cannot do this, then your usefulness as an agent is severely compromised."

"I realise that, Illustrissimo, and I have never called attention to myself—"

"Even if we overlook the altercation on the Liston this evening, there remains the matter of your habitual inebriation."

"Illustrissimo, I may have over-imbibed on the occasional

evening, but I have never made a spectacle of myself," I said. I felt it was true enough; the worst anyone could have said about me was that I might not have always walked as steadily away from the *malvasia* as I did towards it. I had certainly never broken into rowdy behaviour or raucous singing. I wondered who had been reporting on my drinking habits, and felt a touch resentful; I was supposed to spy on other people, not be spied upon. The instant this thought formed in my mind I realised its absurdity: nobody is ever unobserved in Venice.

"You must cease to over-imbibe, however unspectacularly you do it." He pronounced the adverb with just the faintest hint of irony.

I felt vaguely encouraged by this. It was not only that it was the first time I had ever caught any inflection in his voice; there was also the fact that it seemed to indicate the chance of my continuing in the service. He was not likely to have given the advice out of concern for my health.

"Of course, Illustrissimo," I said, and felt proud that every consonant had come out with crystalline clarity.

"This matter can be dealt with swiftly and discreetly."

"Are those *bravi* going to be punished? And Sior Boldrin?" I asked.

I should have known better than to ask a direct question. Sior Massaro looked up from his papers and darted a slightly reproachful look at me.

"That is not your concern," said the Missier Grande.

"Well, I was the one about to be cudgelled," I persisted.

The Missier Grande stared coldly at me for a few seconds and then, surprisingly, gave me a direct answer. "For the moment we consider it expedient to issue a simple warning. You can feel assured the two men will not threaten you again."

Well, that was something. Of course, I would have felt more reassured if he had told me that all three of them were going to be exiled permanently to a remote Greek island, but that was an unreasonable expectation. I guessed that Sior Molin must have powerful friends, but I was sensible enough not to mention this intuition.

"By the way," said the Missier Grande, "you can thank Piero there for this outcome." He gestured towards the hairy *sbirro* standing behind me.

I turned in surprise. It was never easy to read this man's expression, since so few of his features were visible; however, I thought I could detect a faint smirk somewhere behind the hair. I murmured a few words of suitable gratitude and he gave a quick nod and then relapsed into his customary hirsute inscrutability.

"He sent word to me that you were involved in this disturbance, and so I decided to intervene directly. It so happened I was working late in the palace, as was Sior Massaro."

"Thank you, Illustrissimo," I said, feeling unexpectedly touched by this.

"Your particular gifts can still be useful to the Republic, I feel, so it seemed wasteful to allow them to be dissipated."

"It is good of you to say so," I said, just a shade uncomfortably, imagining that he had chosen that last word with his usual deliberation.

"In fact, I have a specific task that I wish you to carry out. It is one for which your gifts seem highly suitable."

"I see," I said. He was presumably not referring to my drinking habits but rather to my linguistic skills and my talent for theatrical improvisation. Those were certainly the qualities that had led to my first being hired as an agent.

"You can consider it a last chance to prove your worth," he said.

"I see," I said.

The Missier Grande looked towards the two *sbirri*. "You may leave us," he said.

They both gave quick bows and turned and left the room. The Missier Grande made a beckoning motion to me. "Come closer. What I am about to say is highly confidential." He glanced at Sior Massaro. "In fact, I will ask you not to make any record of this part of our proceedings."

Sior Massaro looked startled. Such a thing clearly unprecedented. He looked at the quill in his hand for a second and then carefully laid it down, as if afraid of offending it. He then put both hands on the desk nervously, apparently wondering what to do with them now.

The Missier Grande went on in a lower voice: "It might have been better in some ways to conduct this conversation in my own private office outside the palace, but perhaps talking about it here will serve to allay suspicions."

Sior Massaro's face was almost comical to watch, in its mixture of perplexity and dismay.

"First of all," the Missier Grande went on, "can I assume you are sober enough to follow what I am saying and to remember it?"

I presumed he was now talking to me. "Yes, Illustrissimo." I resisted the impulse to prove it with a particularly tasking tongue-twister.

"Very well. I must take your word for it. I am also assuming you are able to take in the full seriousness of what I am telling you."

I nodded.

"You may be aware, Sior Marangon," said the Missier Grande, "of the extremely delicate position I occupy in the matter of the security of the Republic. I am, of course, subordinate to the Council of Ten and more specifically to the three Inquisitors."

Sior Massaro's face now took on an almost sardonic expression, but he knew better than to say anything. I just nodded.

"My area of competence concerns matters of everyday criminality. If I come across anything that concerns larger questions of security, such as internal sedition or threats from external forces, I have to forward the matter to the Inquisitors, who then use their own agents to investigate."

And here Sior Massaro seemed on the point of snorting contemptuously. I knew what he thought of these people: the Inquisitors, who in theory had vast powers (they were even allowed to order secret executions of people considered a threat to the Republic), were, as far he was concerned, little more than bumbling amateurs. Since they only held power for a year at a time, they had little chance to grasp the intricate workings of the machinery of the state before they were replaced by the new set of appointees. Sior

Massaro clearly considered the real reins of power to lie with his master, even if he would never declare such seditious opinions explicitly.

"That, for example," the Missier Grande went on, "is what I have done with the reports of attacks on Turkish citizens over the last few weeks."

I vaguely knew what he was talking about. There had been a succession of not especially violent but humiliating assaults against Turkish merchants and visitors: one or two had had rotten eggs thrown at them in public places; another had had his turban snatched off his head as he stepped into a gondola. Crude slogans had been daubed on walls near their warehouse on the Grand Canal, proclaiming revenge for Cyprus and Crete . . .

"They are certainly acts of common criminality," he said, "but as the target appears to be a foreign community, the Inquisitors feel it is within their area of investigation." His dry tone left hanging in the air the suggestion that their investigation had not been especially fruitful so far.

"However," he went on, "I now find myself in something of a quandary in quite a different matter. I have come across evidence of a crime that seems to have larger implications; I have reported my suspicions to the three Inquisitors and have been told to leave it in their hands. But I have become aware that they are proceeding no further in the matter."

I was listening with growing curiosity and perturbation. Things must be seriously awry for the Missier Grande to express openly such subversive opinions on the highest authorities in the Republic. I glanced around, nervously checking there were no nooks or crannies where a spy might be lurking; of course, it was foolish to think that the Missier Grande would not have foreseen this possibility himself, but it is an occupational hazard of a confidential agent to be permanently wary.

"The story began with the death of one of my agents," said the Missier Grande. Then he put his fingers together and said, "Or rather, that is when my suspicions began. The story, of course, began earlier than that. This man had come to me with a tale about a mysterious secret society, which he referred to as the Four Horsemen.

It seemed just like one of so many such stories. Venetians, as you know, have a fondness for creating small societies for the most varied purposes: gambling, literary discussion, scientific exploration, whoring . . ." He spoke as if these activities were all equally pointless, if not actually reprehensible. "Usually we just infiltrate an agent into the group to check that nothing seditious or criminal is going on and then let them get on with things. My agent had not been able to find out the purpose of this particular group, only that it was highly secret and met on regular occasions. He also mentioned that he thought that some of the members belonged to noble families, but did not specify which.

"Because of this circumstance I passed the information on to the Inquisitors, who told me I need trouble myself no further about it. They also told me that the agent himself was unreliable and should be dismissed from my service. I had little choice but to do so."

I gave another nod but also felt a twinge of anxiety. That was how simply things could happen. I could certainly not expect any strenuous defence of my role by the Missier Grande.

"Just a few days later, word was brought to me that the man had died, falling from the roof of his house. Apparently he had been hanging out the washing on an *altana* and the railing had given way. However, I am convinced his death was not an accident."

"You mean . . ." I said, and then did not know how to complete the sentence.

"I mean no more than what I say. His death was not an accident. I want you to find out how it happened."

"I see," I said. I thought of adding, "That's all?" but realised it would sound flippant.

"However, this investigation must remain absolutely secret. No one must know what you are doing. Above all, no one must know on whose behalf you are doing it."

"I see," I said again.

"And if you are caught and questioned I will deny all knowledge of your proceedings."

"I see," I said for the third time. After a moment's pause I said, "Thank you."

He narrowed his eyes and was probably about to issue a sharp rebuke for insubordination when I added, "For being so clear."

"I think we understand one another," he said. "I am giving you one final chance to prove yourself as a confidential agent."

"What further information can you give me about the man who died?" I asked.

"Sior Massaro will fill you in on all essential details. His name was Paolo Padoan and he lived near Sant'Isepo. I'm afraid we no longer have his report on the Four Horsemen, since we forwarded it to the Inquisitors; they insisted on taking the copy we had made of it as well. Unfortunately, nobody had read it all the way through by the time my suspicions were aroused by his death. All I can tell you is that there may be connections with a literary *salotto*; I have no further information than that. This was simply one passing reference that caught my attention when I first glanced at the report."

"A literary *salotto*?" I said with some curiosity.

"Exactly. That is another reason why I thought you might be suitable for this job. Few of my other agents would have the intellectual qualities required to investigate a *salotto* of this kind."

"Thank you," I murmured. For once it did seem like a genuine compliment. On the other hand, there was the fact that most people with such qualities would never have dreamed of becoming a confidential agent.

"It is not clear whether the Four Horsemen were part of the *salotto*, but it does seem that he acquired his first information about the society while attending it."

"I see," I said. I was beginning to lose track.

"I will now leave Sior Massaro to fill you in on all technical details. Oh, and one last point I should perhaps make."

"Yes, Illustrissimo?"

"Agent Padoan was clearly terrified of the Four Horsemen, whoever they were."

There was little I could say to that, other than a final "I see". Certainly another "Thank you" would have been out of place.

4

"Well, now," said Sior Massaro, after a few seconds of silence. "Well, now."

His tone combined sheer surprise with a certain gratification. The surprise was presumably at the wholly unorthodox notion of an encounter without any written record, while the gratification came from the fact that he had been privileged to be part of this novel event. I imagine there must have also been disapproval there somewhere, but he had clearly managed to push it well down below the other feelings.

"Well, now," I said. "So it's just you, me and the Missier Grande against the world."

He looked a little disconcerted. "We are not against anyone," he said. "We are working in the interests of the Republic."

"Only we mustn't let the authorities of the Republic know," I said.

He waved a hand. "Discretion is always an essential feature of our work. In this case we are just going to have to be a little more discreet than usual." His voice hushed even as he spoke so I had to lean forward to hear him. If anyone had opened the door at that moment we would have looked like sinister conspirators in a bad opera.

"Perhaps we could talk at the other office," I suggested. It would certainly save me from getting a crick in my neck. "Tomorrow morning?"

He looked brighter at this suggestion. I could imagine he was finding it a little difficult to cope under the stress of knowing that in this building we were surrounded by people who would be shocked at what we were up to. "A good idea," he said. "And I have Padoan's files over there as well. At least all his files up to this particular case. And it is getting late now."

He gathered the papers on the desk together, looking with a

slightly pained expression at the virgin blankness of the top sheet. "I suppose I don't need to file it," he muttered.

I didn't say anything. This was a personal crisis he would have to face on his own. In the end he shoved them all into the large leather bag he always carried.

I spoke up. "I don't suppose I could have back the book that was taken from me?"

"Ah, well, we will have to speak to the *sbirri*. I don't know if they have a regular procedure with confiscated objects."

"I think that's very unlikely," I said. "Mind you, it's not going to be much use to them: it's in English."

"Well, we can hope they will have filed and docketed it," he said. "And then you need simply submit a written application for its restitution."

"Yes, of course," I said. What a comfortingly well-regulated world Sior Massaro lived in. I would keep an eye out for the book in the nearest pawn shops.

The next morning I arrived early at the Missier Grande's offices at the north-western corner of Saint Mark's Square. I pronounced the current password to the young man in the outer room and was admitted to Sior Massaro's office, with its view over the square. I did my best to look bright and cheerful, so as to dispel any suspicion that I might be suffering any effects from the previous night's dissipation.

Sior Massaro welcomed me with an extra touch of conspiratorial furtiveness, glancing around before inviting me to follow him into the next room, where he had already laid out the necessary files.

I gave my usual nod to the array of saints in dark craggy landscapes that bedecked the walls and then sat down to read Agent Padoan's reports. Sior Massaro left me to it, clearly finding it hard to restrain himself from putting an admonitory finger to his lips before closing the door.

It was not the first time I had immersed myself in the reports of another agent, and as always the effect was both intriguing and dispiriting. The intriguing part lay in the insight it gave me into the mind of a fellow human being (not to say fellow worker), inducing me to make guesses about what motivated this person to observe and report what he did. The dispiriting part lay in the revealed narrowness of vision – and, more particularly, in the worrying comparisons with my own way of life.

Paolo Padoan, I learned from the information sheet that accompanied his reports, had died at the age of sixty-five, leaving a sister two years younger than him and no other family members. The report on his death said simply that he had fallen from the *altana* (a wooden platform on the roof of the house) where he had been hanging clothes to dry; there seemed to be no evidence of anyone else's being involved. His sister, with whom he lived, confirmed that it was always his job to hang out the washing, as she was very unsteady on her feet now. The wooden railing around the platform had given way and he had plunged fifty feet to the street below and died instantly.

He had worked as a schoolteacher, having failed to win a permanent position at the university in Padua as a lecturer in classical studies. I could sense a certain seething resentment running through his reports, particularly those that concerned people in academic positions, who were invariably shown up as cheats and hypocrites. Padoan's prose was precise, sometimes to the point of pedantry; there was sometimes a distinct note of sour sarcasm as he commented on the unsavoury actions of his fellow citizens. His reports were certainly far more literate than most of those I had seen, but they did not make for comfortable reading.

Alongside the usual animadversions on noblemen who wore *tabarri* instead of the obligatory nobleman's cloaks, on priests who seemed blithely unaware of their vows of chastity, and on foreign ambassadors who entertained too lavishly, he was especially observant (and critical) of people's reading habits, noting those noblemen (particularly the impoverished *barnabotti*) who seemed too fond of French freethinkers like Voltaire or English natural philosophers like Newton. I imagined he must have kept a close eye on bookshops and literary circles and wondered if my friend Fabrizio had known him. I got the impression that Padoan did not really approve of any writers who had not the decency to have been dead for at least a millennium and a half. Newton was possibly less offensive than Voltaire because at least he had the good taste not only to be dead but also to write in a dead language.

His classical learning was on rather ostentatious display, as he frequently dropped in little Latin mottoes (*Corruptissima re publica plurimae leges, Docendo discimus, Ignorantia legis neminem excusat, Publica fama non semper vana*) and even the occasional Greek one, which I couldn't read. I had the feeling that the behaviour of the people he was observing was always being compared to that of some mythical time in the early days of the Roman Republic.

His last report bore a date of three months earlier. It mentioned, in a tone of detached distaste, as if he were reporting the misbehaviour of a class of schoolboys in a classroom adjacent to his own, the new fashion for artistic and literary *salotti*, "where all matters are discussed freely, sometimes by women as well as men, by noblemen as well as citizens and ordinary people". I had the feeling that he had only just refrained from adding "and other animals". He noted, in a curious parenthesis: "Further observations in my diary."

I went through to Sior Massaro, who, as usual when I opened the door on him unexpectedly, gave a nervous start and immediately started writing busily. "Excuse me," I said, "do we have Padoan's diary?"

He raised his eyes from his work and looked at me as if trying to tear his mind away from a thousand other matters. Then he suddenly remembered the need for conspiratorial secrecy and looked all around the office before answering in a hushed voice, "No diary was found. The *sbirri* looked everywhere, and interrogated his sister."

"What did she say?"

"Not very much. It seems she is not entirely right in the head and was hardly any help at all."

"I see," I said. "And presumably all reports since the beginning of September have gone to the Inquisitors."

"Yes, that's right." He gave a resigned shrug at the sheer senselessness of this.

"Do we know what *salotti* he was referring to in his last report? Have we any idea if he was attending one in particular?"

"Unfortunately not," he said, shaking his head with a kind of mortified dismay. He clearly considered this gap in their knowledge of Padoan's movements inexplicable.

"So that is somewhere to begin," I said. "And perhaps I should go and see this sister of his. Did they live together?"

"Yes," he said. "I believe she is still in the house, although the neighbours are a little worried about how she can cope by herself."

"Well, she'll certainly have problems hanging the clothes," I said, and then felt a twinge of guilt at my flippancy.

5

Sior Padoan had lived near the church of Sant'Isepo in eastern Venice, very near to where my gondolier friend and co-worker Bepi lived. So it seemed sensible to start with Bepi. Our working relationship had altered over the last few months. As my little jobs (*lavoretti* was the conveniently vague term I used for them when talking to Bepi) for the Missier Grande became more frequent I had encouraged Bepi to consider himself as no longer exclusively bound to me as a working companion. Fortunately he had accepted this with his usual composure; my self-esteem might have been more flattered if he had shown clear signs of dismay, but I forced myself to take comfort from his adaptability. We now worked as a team from Monday to Wednesday, and the rest of the week he did other jobs, sometimes with other *ciceroni* and sometimes just at the regular ferry stages. I had also worried that my clients might fret at not having the same person on permanent beck and call, but found that they too accepted with equanimity the notion of having a different *cicerone* and gondolier (friends of Bepi and myself) cater to their needs for half the week; it was all a good lesson in humility.

It was Thursday morning and I found Bepi at his usual place at the gondola station near San Moisè. He was playing dice with his fellow gondoliers and looked up in mild surprise at seeing me during what he usually referred to as "the other half of the week".

"What's the matter?" he said. He rarely asked me about my other work, presumably from a sense of delicacy.

"Nothing the matter," I said. "I'd just like to ask you about a neighbour of yours, if you've got a moment."

He glanced at his two companions, who both gave a half-shrug. Although perfectly civil, they were rarely very forthcoming in my presence. Bepi got up from his bench and walked towards the bridge, where we paused and watched a colleague of his helping a large and nervous German visitor into a gondola.

"Who's the neighbour?" Bepi asked.

"Well, ex-neighbour. He died a week ago. Fell from his *altana*."

"Oh, the old teacher," he said.

"That's right," I said. "Did you know him?"

"Well, not to speak to," he said. "Never had a long chat with him."

I thought that there were probably very few people Bepi had long chats with, but quite probably he considered long stretches of companionable silence as an integral part of a chat. "But you knew who he was," I said.

"Oh, everyone knew old Padoan," he said. "One of the local characters."

"What sort of person was he?" I asked.

"Funny old man," he said. "Loner. Children used to make fun of him."

"You mean his students?"

"Oh, he gave up teaching some years back. I mean the local street boys. Nothing too nasty. Just used to imitate the way he walked."

And Bepi himself strutted a few steps, with his head pushed forward, bobbing like a pigeon.

"I can imagine children finding that funny," I said. "What are people saying about his death?"

Bepi looked sharply at me. "This is for your other job?"

"Yes," I said. "I've just been asked to look into it." I deliberately kept things vague. I knew better than to mention the Missier Grande, both because his name tended to scare people into silence and because telling people I was working directly for him could sound like boasting.

"What do they want to know?" he asked.

"Well, has anyone suggested there was anything suspicious about it?"

"Not that I've heard," he said. "It was a fairly old *altana*. Rotten wood. And he was not very steady on his feet."

He was obviously uncomfortable at being involved in my "other job" but was too polite to say so. I went on regardless. "Nobody ever suggested that he was anything other than an old teacher?"

"You mean like – like you?"

"Well, yes," I said.

He shook his head, perhaps in dismay that there could be other people who had fallen so low. "No," he said. "Nothing like that."

"All right," I said. "I just wondered. Sorry to bother you."

"No bother," he said, obviously lying through his teeth.

"See you Monday morning then," I said.

"Yes, of course," he said. This return to the normal Monday-to-Wednesday world of our real work was clearly a relief. "See you then."

He returned to his two friends, and I crossed the bridge in the direction of Saint Mark's Square.

I had other acquaintances in eastern Castello and decided to garner their opinions too. These were three boys aged between ten and twelve, often to be found in the boatyards at the eastern end of the Riva. They had been of great help in my earliest investigation as confidential agent, and I knew them to be quick-witted, resourceful and highly observant. During the mornings, they worked in the boatyards with their families, but they were usually left free in the afternoon to play; their games nearly always seemed to involve mud.

I made my way down the Riva in the early afternoon. A mist had descended on the city, so that when I turned round to look towards the bell-tower of Saint Mark's the golden angel on its peak was wispily unreal. I was glad I still had my cloak, and I wrapped it more closely around myself. I had not replaced the tricorn hat that had been lost in the night attack, so that one or two people gave me curious glances. Well, maybe I would start a new fashion: hatless in autumn.

I found the three boys playing with fishing nets by the water's edge near the boatyards; the aim of the game seemed to be to retain as much mud as possible in one's net. I suspected that at a certain point it would turn into a mud-hurling competition, so I remained at a prudent distance.

"*Bondì, fioi,*" I greeted them.

They recognised my voice and greeted me with their usual mixture of curiosity and wariness. I had rewarded them for performing some minor tasks of surveillance in the past, taking care never to ask them to do anything risky and never to pay them amounts that would arouse undue suspicion among their families.

"What do you want?" said Lucio, a sharp-looking boy who always wore a red Castello cap. He was usually their spokesman and had a refreshing tendency to get straight to the point.

"I just wanted to ask you about a man who died recently," I said, responding in kind. I had found that any attempts to approach matters circuitously were not appreciated.

"Who?"

"A man called Padoan. He fell from his *altana.*"

"Oh, him," said Lucio, and instantly performed the same pigeon-strut I had seen done by Bepi. Lucio's parody was more emphatic and caused his fishing net to spatter mud in a generous radius all around him. I stepped back a pace or two.

"Yes, him," I said.

"What about him?"

"I just wondered if you knew of anyone who had visited him, any strangers who had been seen around this area."

"You mean like you?"

"Well, maybe," I said, a little disconcerted. "What do you mean, like me?"

"A *foresto*," said Lucio, using the Venetian word for a foreigner.

I was a little uncertain how to take this. Had they detected an English intonation in my Venetian? Or did they just consider anyone not from the parish of Sant'Isepo as a *foresto*? I said, "I was just wondering if Padoan had been seen with anyone you didn't know."

Lucio looked at his two companions, who both gave quick shrugs. "He was always alone. No friends. And he used to talk to himself."

"Did you ever hear what he said?"

"Just once," said Lucio. "Sounded foreign to me."

"Foreign? You mean he had a non-Castello accent?"

"No, strange words." He suddenly imitated an old person's feeble tones: "Amamamamus . . . Hababababamimus."

"Ah," I said. I wondered if he had overheard Padoan rehearsing one of his Latin proverbs. "What happened after he died?"

"The *sbirri* came. They say there was blood everywhere."

"All right," I said. I didn't want to encourage them to dwell on this part of the story, although I suspected they were hardy enough to have got over any shock they might have experienced at the time. "And what did the *sbirri* do? Who did they question?"

"Everyone. My aunt's friend's cousin told them she'd seen him fall, but they soon found out she couldn't have: her house faces the opposite way. But she still insists she heard the thump."

I winced. "And did anyone see it?"

"Don't know," said Lucio.

Marco, the smallest of the trio, with a high-pitched eager voice, spoke up. "My aunt did."

The other two boys made contemptuous sounds of disbelief, but Marco insisted, lifting his mud-filled net, ready to give battle if necessary. To avert this I said hastily, "Go on, Marco. Tell me what she saw."

"Well, she lives in a house over by Sant'Antonio, right on the top floor. She's often at the window. She says she saw him on the *altana*."

"And then?"

"And then he wasn't there any more."

The other two boys snorted with contempt at this feeble anticlimax.

"So she didn't see him actually fall," I said.

"No, because she had to pick up my cousin, who had fallen off the table. He was screaming. He can scream really loud." He seemed quite proud of his cousin's abilities in this area.

"So did she tell the *sbirri* about this?"

"No. She doesn't like them."

That was far from unusual. Perhaps only their mothers had any fondness for them. "And they didn't question her?"

"No, her house wasn't nearby. They only talked to the neighbours: people in the same building or the ones next to it."

"Like my aunt's friend's cousin," said Lucio, reasserting his leadership. "She lived right next door."

"But she didn't see anything," said Marco. "She just heard it."

"Yes. A great crash, she said. She thought another chimney-pot had fallen. Then she heard people screaming."

"We all heard that," said Marco.

"Yes," said Piero, the middle boy, not wanting to be left out. "I reckon everyone in Castello heard it."

"Yes, but my aunt's friend's cousin was one of the first. And then she started screaming as well. And she probably has the loudest scream."

"Bet it's not as loud as my cousin who fell off the table. And he's only four."

"Bet it is. She can scream like this . . ." Lucio put his head back and sent forth an unearthly wailing noise.

"My cousin's much louder," said Marco. And he leaned forward and let out a high-pitched screech, which did sound very much like that of a distressed four-year-old child.

I could see men at the nearby boatyard turning to stare at us. "All right, all right, boys, that's enough," I said quickly, seeing Piero preparing to join in the crazed cacophony, presumably in imitation of some vocally gifted relative of his own.

They left off, the two rivals looking defiantly at each other.

"Can you tell me your aunt's name?" I asked Marco. "And where she lives?"

"Anna Biasin," he said. "A big palazzo next to Sant'Antonio. But don't tell her I said anything about her. And don't tell the *sbirri*."

"Of course not," I said. "You know me."

They all gave a slight shrug at this. They were only being honest; there was no point in either my or their pretending that we were on close terms. As the conversation was clearly coming to an end, and I didn't want the men at the boatyard to become any more inquisitive, I pulled out a *lira* and gave it to Lucio. I knew that the other two acknowledged his role as treasurer. They nodded their thanks and returned to their muddy game, letting out an occasional competitive scream as an added feature.

I walked towards the church of Sant'Isepo, their clamorous shrieks getting fainter behind me in the mist. As I walked I began to plan my investigative strategy. My pace quickened as I mulled over different possibilities; as usual the challenge of having to invent a new role for myself was a welcome stimulus. There was no denying that Lucia had a point when she accused me of enjoying the opportunities that my work as a confidential agent provided to put on a performance. Sometimes I had found myself inventing a character for myself when there was no reason for it at all and the questions I was asking could perfectly well have come from Alvise Marangon, *cicerone*. But just as I had divided my week into two separate halves, so I seemed to find it necessary to further divide my personality into multiple fractions.

If I thought hard about it I might find in my past all sorts of reasons for this constant tendency to self-division: there was the fact that I had grown up in England, son of a Venetian actress, and I was now living in my mother's city and using my English background to get work as a *cicerone* for English visitors. I was always Venetian to English acquaintances, and English to Venetian ones. And I had been a performer since childhood.

But I rarely did think hard about it; it was too much trouble.

I reached the house where Sior Padoan had lived. It was in a side street off the *fondamenta* on the other side of the canal from the church of Sant'Isepo. In the second of these streets lived Bepi with his formidable mother and numerous siblings. I walked swiftly past this one, just glancing at the usual row of old women in black shawls keeping a beady eye on their grandchildren. No one called out "*Foresto!*" to me, or asked me why I continued to prevent their Bepi from getting a lucrative position as gondolier for a noble family.

I reached the last street. This was quieter than Bepi's, with just one old man sitting on a stool outside one of the houses, smoking a pipe. I looked at the buildings on either side. They rose to four storeys. I examined the pavement and was relieved to see no sign of lingering bloodstains.

I approached the old man and greeted him with a courteous "*Bondì.*"

He shifted the pipe in his mouth and made an incomprehensible noise, which could have been a reply or just a throat-clearing gargle.

"I'm looking for Siora Nela Padoan," I said.

He eyed me up and down. Then he said, "*Sbirro?*"

I shook my head. "No. From the Scuola dei Marangoni da Case." For once I could exploit my own surname by claiming to be a representative of the guild of house-carpenters. Maybe I could even admit to being called Alvise, if pressed.

He continued to look me up and down. Perhaps he was looking for my tools.

"It's just an enquiry," I said. "We heard of the accident because of the *altana*, and so we thought we should find out who the carpenter was, whether he officially belonged to the *scuola.*"

He took his pipe out and eventually spoke. "I was a carpenter," he said. "Forty-seven years."

Oh, wonderful, I thought. Now he's going to test me.

"At the Arsenale," he said.

Well, that was a relief at least. Ship-carpenters had a different *scuola*. "A great profession," I said respectfully. "You must be proud of what you did."

"Worked on the railings," he said. "For the decks."

"Wonderful," I said.

"Forty-seven years."

"Yes, so you said." I tried not to show my impatience.

"I never saw a railing give way like that one."

My feeling of impatience vanished. "Really?" I said.

"If that's the way house-carpenters work they should be ashamed of themselves." He stared aggressively at me.

"Well, yes, that's what I'm here to investigate . . ."

"Lock them up. Just make sure the jail doesn't have doors made by them."

"Did you see the broken railing?" I said.

"Just the broken bits that came down with him."

"And how had they broken?" I said. "Was it a clean break? Jagged edges?"

"I didn't get a chance to look. The *sbirri* took them all away with them."

I wondered whether these had been the regular *sbirri*, or *confidenti* sent by the Inquisitors. Well, there was no way this old man could tell me that. "So can you tell me where I'll find Siora Nela Padoan?"

He pointed at a house towards the end of the street. The door was slightly ajar. "Top floor," he said. "She's still there, though they're trying to get her to move."

"Who is trying?"

"The other people in the building. They're worried she's going to burn the house down or something. She's not all there." He tapped his head with his pipe.

"Did anyone call on the Padoans before the accident?" I said. I was not sure I would be able to justify this question in my role as representative of the guild of house-carpenters but decided it was worth a try.

"Nobody that I saw," he said. "But I'm not always out here, you know. It was windy that day."

Fair enough. Presumably a good day for drying clothes.

"Why do you want to know?" he said suddenly.

"Well, thank you for talking to me," I said with equal suddenness, pretending not to have heard his question. I walked briskly towards the door, just giving one glance back before entering it. He had put his pipe back in his mouth. I doubted he was really concerned with the oddness of my question.

The staircase was stone and almost completely dark. The ground floor, as so often in Venetian houses, was given over to storage; there were separate storerooms with padlocked doors. I could smell the earthy mustiness of beetroots, cabbages and onions, the tang of vinegar, and the clamminess of various long-forgotten rotting objects. I started up the stairs. On each floor I could hear domestic noises within: children crying, the clattering of pots, a buzz of conversation. Then I reached the top floor; here too there were faint sounds of life. I stood still and tried to work out what I was hearing. Then I realised: it was a single female voice emitting an unbroken sequence of muttered words. I couldn't actually hear any distinct sentences.

I knocked and the muttering voice broke off for a second or two, and then resumed, coming towards me. I began to distinguish words. "Why don't they leave me alone. Who can that be. What do they want now. Why don't they leave me alone. Who can it be. Now what do they want."

Then the door opened. I found myself facing a small woman in black clothes. Her hair was grey and straggly and her face in continual twitchy movement. "What is it now? Who are you? What do you want?"

"Good afternoon, siora. I'm here from the Scuola dei Marangoni da Case."

"I don't want anything. I'm all right. Just leave me alone."

"I'm not trying to sell anything, siora," I said reassuringly. "I offer condolences on your loss. I hope it's not a bad time . . ."

"Of course it's a bad time," she snapped. "You know it is. Just leave me alone and don't come back."

This was not a promising beginning. It looked as if I would have to fall back on the unfailing if undignified persuasive power of money. I pulled out three *lire* from my pocket. "Siora, on behalf of the Scuola dei Marangoni," I said, "I would like to offer you some compensation and a contribution towards your expenses."

Her face stiffened for a moment as she gazed at the coins. "How much is it?"

"Three *lire*," I said. "I realise this is inadequate, but I hope it will compensate for the disturbance I am causing you."

"It is inadequate. Ten *lire* at least." And then she resumed her muttering litany: "Why don't they leave me alone. What do they want. Why don't they leave me alone . . ."

I decided that haggling would be unsuitable, and I pulled out a *filippo*, worth eleven *lire*. "Siora, you're right. Here's a *filippo*. But if I could come in and ask some questions I would be very grateful."

Her hand shot out and grabbed the coin. Whatever else, there was nothing wrong with her hand–eye coordination. Still muttering, she stood to one side and allowed me to enter the apartment.

I hadn't known what to expect: scholarly confusion, scholarly precision, dignified penury, squalid clutter? What I had not expected was what I found: almost complete emptiness. There were shelves and cupboards, but they were all completely bare. There were some plain wooden chairs, a table with nothing on it, and a bare floor with Venetian marbling. I almost expected our voices to echo cavernously as we spoke. A door on the right gave on to a bedroom that looked equally stark.

"Have they taken things away?" I said, looking around in amazement.

"Everything," she said. She spoke with no apparent emotion. This was a simple fact of life.

"Who?" I said.

"Them. The people that came. His people."

"His . . . ? You mean your brother's people? His employers?"

She shrugged and made a vague muttering sound, which could have been an answer to my question or just a reversion to her resentful litany.

"Did you know these people?"

She gave a contemptuous shrug.

"Siora," I said, trying to sound solicitous, "I would like to help you. If these people have gone beyond the boundaries of their authority we can force them to return these things." I hoped what I was saying was true; I could certainly put in a word with the Missier Grande, I told myself.

She continued to mutter, but she did cast one suspicious look into my face, as if to see whether I was serious.

I insisted: "I'm sure they had no right to leave you destitute like this. I speak as someone who knew your brother." Well, my morning's study had made me feel uncomfortably close to him.

She looked at me again, more penetratingly this time. "How did you know him?"

"We were colleagues," I said.

"I thought you were a carpenter," she said at once.

She was more attentive than I had imagined. This would require some inventiveness on my part. "Yes, I'm from the Scuola dei Marangoni. It's actually my surname." I gave a little laugh, in a rather feeble attempt to lighten the mood. "But I'm not a carpenter myself; I'm responsible for the administrative side of the *scuola*. And I also occasionally work for the Missier Grande." This was a risky leap into unknown waters. It would all depend on whether her brother had confided to her about his role as *confidente*. And also on whether she had approved . . . and on countless other unguessable factors.

She stopped muttering and stared at me. "Prove it," she said eventually.

I stared back with equal intensity. I imagined that asking her how I could prove it would not help to establish my authenticity. Instead, I said, "I've read your brother's reports." I was thinking very hard; what was he likely to have told this eccentric but obviously close relative? Well, unless he was grossly irresponsible he would only have given her unimportant snippets of gossip, probably about people she was likely to know. That would limit it to people who lived nearby, I guessed. On a venture I said, "I know about Sior Vianello, the man who works at the Marciana library, and his habit of smuggling books by Voltaire home with him." Sior Vianello lived just round the corner from this house.

She cackled. "Yes, they soon put a stop to that. Lucky to have kept his job."

I was beginning to feel a little less sympathy for this woman, but none the less I kept my tone benign. "Your brother wrote a very balanced report on him. Judicious but not too damning."

"I told him he was too soft. Could have had him locked up for good. Always so smarmy and sneering. And his wife, who does she think she is? Giving me her condolences. I soon put a stop to that. Told her a few home truths."

"Yes, I expect you did," I said, feeling distinctly uncomfortable now.

"Paolo was always telling me not to mention anything he'd found out. Nothing to stop me now, is there?"

"Well," I said, "I still think you should be careful. Even just out of respect for your brother."

She let out another cackle. "I'll just be telling people the things Paolo would have liked to tell them himself but couldn't."

"Because of his vows to the Missier Grande. He" – I uttered the pronoun with a hushed awe so that it would be clear I was referring to the Missier Grande and not to her brother – "would not be pleased to hear that his rules are being flouted. And remember that his reach is extensive."

This did unsettle her slightly. There were few people bold enough to dismiss the Missier Grande airily. "Well, I won't be saying anything against the Republic."

"No, I'm sure you won't," I said. It appeared that I had at least convinced her of my role as a colleague of her brother. I suspected that any investigators who had questioned her before this had not broken down her defences in similar fashion. So now I could start probing with some hope of obtaining fresh evidence.

"Do you happen to know anything about a diary he was keeping?" I asked.

"Ah," she said, and assumed a knowing expression.

"You do know about such a diary, then," I said. "Did the *sbirri* take it away with them?"

She looked contemptuous. "Not them. They had no idea."

"Well, I wouldn't be so sure," I said. "He mentioned the diary in the reports he wrote for the Missier Grande."

"Oh, they knew there was a diary," she said. "And they kept asking me about it."

"And what did you tell them?"

She looked smug. "I didn't tell them anything. I know how to keep my mouth shut."

I doubted that that was literally true. I suspected that on the contrary she had baffled them by indulging in her meaningless sequential muttering. They had probably concluded that she was too deranged to be worth interrogating at length; that had certainly been my initial reaction.

"So where is the diary?" I said.

She continued to look smug. I could see that there was a risk of this becoming an endlessly protracted game unless I played it correctly. She might not be deranged, but there was undeniably something infantile about her. I would just have to treat her as one would an irritating child.

"Oh, I see; you don't know," I said, and turned as if to go.

"Oh, don't I?" she said at once.

"Well, I imagine not," I said, "or you would have told me. Anyway, I have more important matters to attend to." I put my hand on the door handle.

"Wait just one moment," she said. "I *could* tell you . . ."

"Could you?" I said, making my tone as flat as possible.

"Yes, I could."

I waited.

"But my memory isn't always as good as it should be."

I continued to wait. If she wanted another bribe she would have to spell it out clearly.

"Another *filippo* might help." She said it without any embarrassment.

"Another *scudo*," I countered firmly. That was seven *lire*. I did not take it from my pocket yet.

"Well," she said, as if trying to dredge some recalcitrant fragment of memory from the murky depths of her mind, "I might be able to remember. Let me think."

I began to gaze around as if wondering whether I might spot the diary in some previously uninspected hiding place, like the table in the middle of the room.

"Let me see now, let me see now . . ."

"Take your time," I said drily.

"Well, I never actually saw the diary," she said.

41

"Ah," I said. This was unexpected.

"No. But he told me about it. He thought it better to keep it somewhere safe."

"I see," I said. "The *scudo* will be for useful information, you do understand?"

She looked decidedly irked. "Well, I didn't tell you I had it, did I?"

"You led me to understand that you knew where it was," I said. "For that information I promised you a *scudo*."

"Well, I do know."

"Good."

"More or less."

I waited.

"It's here in the city."

"Good," I said. "That will save me dredging the lagoon."

"In recent months he had started visiting the monks on Sant'Elena," she said.

"Oh, really?" I said. There had been no mention of this in any of the files. "Why?"

"He was devoted to Saint Helena," she said. "She discovered the True Cross."

"Yes, so I believe," I said.

"And she was the mother of Emperor Constantine."

"Yes," I said again, still a little puzzled. Then I remembered something from the files. Padoan had had occasion to mention Constantinople a few times, with reference either to merchants who had dealings with the city or to Turkish ambassadors from the city residing in Venice. On each occasion he had referred to it rather curiously as the "Holy City of Constantinople".

"Well, there you are then," she said, as if that explained everything.

I realised I might cast a doubt on my position as a close colleague of her brother if I expressed further puzzlement, so I said slowly, "I see."

"You know what he thought of Constantine," she said.

"Yes," I said, "founder of the Holy City."

That clearly reassured her. "Exactly."

"And so he kept his diary there, with the monks?" I asked.

I think she was trying to calculate whether anything would be gained by another bout of "I *could* tell you". She clearly decided that she had exhausted that particular line of bargaining, for she said after a pause, "I think so." She gazed pointedly at my pocket.

"Did you ever hear him mention a *salotto*?"

"A what?"

"A *salotto*. A place where people meet and discuss literature, politics, the arts ..."

"My brother would never have gone to a place like that," she said without hesitation.

"Are you sure?"

"He didn't like talking. Sometimes he wouldn't say a word for days on end."

I suspected he had never been given much chance. "And did he ever mention a group of people called the Four Horsemen?"

She shook her head. "He didn't talk much. Only sometimes, when I asked him specially, telling him I hadn't heard any news from anyone all day ..."

I could imagine her voice, needling him insistently until he dropped a few gobbets of gossip to keep her happy. I began to feel sorry for her again, as well as for him. I pulled out the *scudo* and passed it to her. She immediately buried it deep in her clothes.

"Could I see the *altana*?" I said, not sure whether I needed to return to the pretence of representing the Scuola dei Marangoni.

"Why?"

"We need to make a report on the accident. Is it certain your brother was alone on the *altana*?"

"Yes, of course he was. I don't go out there."

"Has anyone else been there? Did the *sbirri* inspect it?"

"Of course they did. In and out, up and down, didn't even have the goodness to bring in the washing till I asked them."

"Did they say anything about it?"

"About what? The washing?"

"No," I said patiently, "the *altana*. Did they say what had happened?"

"Just that it had broken. I knew that already. I was always telling Paolo to be careful. It's what I told the landlord's man as well."

"Who?"

"The man who came to inspect it the other week."

"You mean before the accident?"

"Yes, of course. The landlord then told me he hadn't sent anyone, but that's what he would say, isn't it? He said the *altana* was nothing to do with him. He hadn't put it there."

"Is that true?"

She shrugged. "I don't know. Can't remember things like that. Perhaps Paolo put it up years ago. Or someone."

"And you're saying that the other week, before the accident, a man came to inspect it, claiming he had been sent by the landlord?"

"Yes."

"And did you tell the *sbirri* about this?"

"No. No one asked. I told the landlord, said he should be ashamed, and that's when he started saying he hadn't sent anyone."

"What was he like? This man who came to see the *altana*?"

She shrugged again. "Don't know. Pulcinella."

"Pulcinella?"

"That's what he reminded me of. I remember calling him Pulcinella. Didn't seem to mind."

"In what way did he remind you of Pulcinella? His clothes? A long nose? Was he hunchbacked?"

"Can't remember." She was beginning to grow cantankerous. "I've had enough of your questions. Go and have a look at the *altana* if you like, then leave me alone." She resumed her incantatory muttering. "Why can't they leave me alone. Why doesn't he go away. Why can't I be left in peace . . ." I had the idea that this was a habit she had taken up deliberately years ago to keep neighbours away, and now she hardly knew when she was doing it. Maybe it had begun purely as a defensive strategy, but it had become so much part of her character that it was hard to draw a line between pretence and real derangement. I guessed I was not going to get any more sense out of her. It was not surprising that the *sbirri*, who were not famed for subtlety or patience, had not questioned her in any meaningful fashion.

She pointed to a window in the corner of the room. I walked over and stared out. It was a dormer window, and I was looking straight out on to the *altana*, which had been built just outside.

I looked back at her. She was now just staring at the front door, her face twitching and her mouth engaged in the same endless litany. I imagined this would go on until I left by that same front door. I had better carry out my inspection quickly.

There was a stool nearby, clearly kept there to provide easy access. I climbed on to the stool and opened the window. Crouching down, and saying a nervous prayer to myself, I stepped out. There was still a lazily drifting mist, but it was not thick enough to conceal the long drop to the ground. This was one of the tallest houses in the neighbourhood, so there was an unimpeded view of the city. I could see the nearby towers of San Domenico and Sant'Antonio, the dome of San Nicolò and, further off, the slender tower of San Francesco della Vigna; westwards the mist blurred the solid shape of the great campanile of San Marco; gazing out to the lagoon I could see sails and masts swaying slightly – or was it the *altana* that was swaying? I gripped the window-frame more tightly and looked carefully at the structure.

It was a simple square platform, made of wooden planks, and it projected horizontally from the sloping roof. Presumably it was supported at the front end by small columns of bricks, which I decided not to inspect. Around the three sides of the flat square was – or, at least, had been – a simple railing supported by wooden poles at the corners, with X-shaped cross-poles beneath it. However, the railing opposite where I stood was broken in the middle, and just looking at the gap made me feel queasy. Across the middle of the platform, just to the left of where I was standing, ran a single washing line supported by two poles, one close to the window and the other by the gap in the railing. I imagined that while hanging clothes on that side of the platform Padoan was likely to have rested against the railing, and then . . .

I forced myself to approach the gap, and peered over the edge. There was a sheer drop to the street below, and although my feet remained on the platform, my eyes and mind swooped down with a sickening plunge to the grey stones beneath. I examined the broken edges of the railing. The wood looked fairly rotten, and it was perfectly feasible that it had simply given way. With infinite care I knelt on the very edge of the platform and peered down at the guttering; I thought I could see, amid the dead leaves and pigeon-shit, a powdery substance which could well be sawdust. It had not rained in the last week or two, and so if anyone had sawed away at the wood it was quite likely that the evidence would still be there.

"What are you doing?" The woman's voice came suddenly and loudly from behind me, nearly sending me over the edge.

I looked round. Her twitching face was framed in the window, and she was staring at me suspiciously.

"Just inspecting the quality of the wood," I said as calmly as I could while I got to my feet. I walked back towards the window.

"Did you see what the man you call Pulcinella did on the *altana?*" I asked.

"Of course not. I've got better things to do. Anyway, I told you I've answered enough questions now."

Before I re-entered the house I had one last look around. There was just one house on the same level as this one in the neighbourhood; I thought I saw the pale shape of a face at a window, gazing in my direction. It was not far from the church of Sant'Antonio; possibly this was Marco's aunt.

I bade farewell to Siora Padoan, who was obviously glad to be rid of me. As I descended the staircase I could hear the steady patter of her toneless muttering. I wondered whether she stopped for meals.

As I stepped out into the street, the man with the pipe looked at me and tapped his head with the pipe meaningfully. I nodded and set off in the direction of the church of Sant'Antonio.

It took me a few minutes to find Anna Biasin's house, but I was soon knocking on her door, another top-floor apartment. It was opened by a harassed-looking woman in her thirties. A small child was clinging to her skirts and whimpering. I could see that I would have to be brisk and business-like. Probably in this case I should rely on the authority of the Missier Grande to expedite things.

"Yes?" she said.

"Siora Anna Biasin?"

"That's me."

"I've come from the Missier Grande."

Her expression grew more harassed than ever, and she pushed the child away. "Let go," she said to him. Then to me, "What's this about?"

"A very simple question. Is it true you saw Sior Padoan fall from his *altana*?"

She was immediately flustered. "No. Who told you that? I never did, I didn't say that . . ."

I at once assumed a reassuring tone. "Now please don't worry. We are not going to ask you to testify. This is quite unofficial. But you must tell me the truth."

"Yes," she said. She still did not invite me into the apartment, and I did not insist. I guessed that the best way to get results was to rely on a tone of official briskness. Our position in the doorway would help.

"So just tell me exactly what you saw."

"He was there on the *altana* with some clothes. I often saw him hanging things out. Then Pierino called me" – she pointed at the child by her side, who took the opportunity to wail plaintively – "and I bent down to pick him up. When I looked back he wasn't there any more. And I knew he couldn't have climbed back through the window in that time. And anyway the clothes were all there still, in a heap. I didn't know what to do. Then I heard people screaming and yelling, and so I guessed what had happened."

"He was definitely alone on the *altana*," I said.

Her eyes grew wide. "Of course he was. He always hung the clothes out by himself. And took them back in."

"Had you ever seen anyone else on the *altana*?"

Her face grew more agitated, and now she picked the child up, as if for comfort. Pierino stopped whimpering and stared at me in smug triumph. "Why do you ask that?" she said.

"Just answer the question."

"Well, just now I saw . . ."

"Yes, that was me."

"And about a week ago, or a bit longer. A man I'd never seen before."

"Can you describe him?"

"Well, it's a long way away."

"Show me."

She let me into the apartment. Small, with sloping ceilings, simple furniture, a few toys on the floor. She gestured to a window, and I gazed out. It was easy to spot the *altana* in question, as it was a prominent feature. At this distance, though, it might be difficult to identify a particular person.

"Well," I said, "just tell me what impression he made."

"He was probably a bit shorter than you. Dressed in black. And I thought he limped."

"Did he remind you of Pulcinella in any way?"

"Pulcinella?" she said in bewilderment.

"Yes. Was there anything that might have made you think of Pulcinella?"

She shook her head. "I don't remember a hump or anything like that. Just the limp."

"What did he do?"

"Do?"

"Yes. Was he hanging out clothes? Was there any reason for his being there?"

Again she shook her head. "I didn't look that long. I remember he was against the railing there for a bit. I thought he was looking at the view." She clutched Pierino closer to her. "Why are you asking these questions?"

"Don't worry," I said. "Just routine. We want to get an overall idea of what happened. We won't disturb you again. But please do not mention this interview to anyone. This is an order from the Missier Grande."

She was too nervous to reply but just nodded several times. I could tell she was dying for me to leave, so I took pity on her. I patted Pierino on the head, provoking her to squeeze him even more tightly to her breast so that he started wailing again; Marco was right about the force of his voice. I took my leave, trying to look as imposing as possible, but slightly spoiling the effect by getting my cloak caught in the door-jamb.

As I walked down the stairs I felt more displeased with myself than usual, and not only because of the awkwardness of my departure. It was not an interview I would recount with pride to anyone. I would certainly not tell Lucia about it. And I hoped Anna Biasin would take seriously my final warning and not tell her nephew about it; otherwise I guessed I would never be able to ask those boys for help again.

With that thought in mind I made my way back to the boatyard. The three boys had given up the game with their nets; if the aim had been to spatter one's opponents as thoroughly as possible, then Lucio, whose face was still recognisable, was probably the winner. They were now just sitting on an upturned boat throwing pebbles out into the lagoon.

"*Fioi*," I addressed them, "just a quick question."

The usual curious but wary stare in response was visible on Lucio's face; it was impossible to discern any expression on the faces of the other two behind their mud masks.

"Do you remember seeing a man dressed in black with a limp in this area? About a week ago, or maybe a bit longer?"

"Where from? Another *foresto*?"

"Could be," I said. My only real hope was that the man was from outside the parish; if so, it was possible he would have aroused remark. Venetians are fairly territorial and outsiders tend to be noticed, at least in the parts of the city usually unfrequented by visitors. I wondered whether to mention the Pulcinella link, but as I had no idea what feature of Pulcinella had caught Siora Padoan's eye or ear, I thought this might only muddle the issue.

Lucio jumped off the boat and started walking with a pronounced limp around it. "Like this?"

"Probably," I said.

"You remember what Giacomo said," he said to his companions, "about the man he saw in the *malvasia*."

"*Guagliò, aspetta . . .*" said Marco, in a thick parodied accent, slurring the "s" into a "sh" sound.

I suddenly had an illumination. "A Neapolitan!" That was what Siora Padoan had meant by Pulcinella. She had recognised the accent and bestowed the nickname, even if she had then forgotten why.

"Maybe," said Lucio.

"Did you see this man yourselves?" I asked.

"No," said Lucio. "Friends of ours. They were in the *malvasia* over by San Domenico and they heard him talking."

"What about?"

Lucio shrugged. "Nothing special. They just thought the accent was really funny. Like Pulcinella."

Street theatre was probably the only encounter they had ever had with Neapolitan culture, let alone with actual Neapolitans. Lucio had told me he had never been to Saint Mark's Square, so it would be absurd to expect any of them to be acquainted with the world beyond the lagoon itself.

"Thank you, boys, you've been very helpful," I said. "Do you think you could find a boatman for me tomorrow morning? I want to go to Sant'Elena."

"My uncle will do that," said Lucio.

We agreed a time and place, and I thanked them again.

"Do we get another *lira*?" said Marco, bolder than usual.

Feeling guilty at how I had treated his aunt, I drew out a *lira* and tossed it towards them. As always Lucio caught it expertly in one muddy hand.

It had been an expensive day out, but not an unfruitful one, I thought.

6

The lamps were being lit in Saint Mark's Square when I crossed towards the Missier Grande's office. They shone with hazy yellow glows in the mist. I looked up to the first-floor windows and saw that the chandelier was alight up there as well.

Sior Massaro looked at me inquisitively as I entered his room. "Have you found out anything?"

"Do we have any information on a Neapolitan with a limp?" I asked without any delay. It was not a hopeless question. All non-Venetians were supposed to register their presence with the authorities.

He looked doubtfully at me. "Have you got a name? Date of birth? Profession?"

"Well, profession I suspect would be hired killer."

"Dear me," he said. "I'm sure we wouldn't allow anyone like that to be wandering around the city."

"Well, it's possible he didn't register under that title. But does it ring a bell?"

"You might want to study those files," he said, pointing to a shelf with a number of thick dossiers. "That is where we keep information on suspicious *foresti*."

I took the files with me into the inner office. The chandelier was lit for me, and I started another session of depressing research, one that could have led an impressionable reader to the conviction that all foreigners were swindlers, thieves or drunken brutes.

Eventually, after trawling through a hundred cases of pilfering, cheating, wife-beating and house-breaking, peppered with the occasional stabbing and cudgelling, perpetrated by Romans, Florentines, Sicilians, Albanians, Greeks, Germans and Croatians, I found an entry on a certain Antonio Esposito, from Naples, suspected of having been involved in a possible murder case several months earlier in the town of Mira on the mainland. He was described as being short and stocky with dark hair and beard; he walked with a marked limp in his left leg. His date of birth was indicated as 1705, which made him forty-four years old. A report from Naples said that he had apparently been involved in a case of suspicious death there as well. In both instances murder had never been proved; the victim in the Mira case had fallen into the River Brenta and in the Naples case had been crushed by a passing carriage. Antonio Esposito was, according to the description furnished by the authorities, a trader in dried fruits. He had spent some time in Asia Minor, it seemed, where he apparently had associates in the dried-fruit business. It was hinted that this harmless activity might be a cover for various smuggling activities, although no specific details were given.

I could find no clues as to his present whereabouts in the documents. The latest report dated from two months earlier and suggested he had left the city for Genoa, where they were presumably crying out for dates and figs. Or possibly for discreet assassinations.

I took the files back to Sior Massaro's office. He looked at me inquisitively. "I think I have a trail," I said, and rather foolishly tapped my nose in a knowing gesture.

"Aha," he whispered, revelling in this shared secrecy.

"Tomorrow I'll visit the island of Sant'Elena," I said. "The monks might be able to help."

"Aha," he said again, clearly wishing that he knew what I was talking about.

"All details when I return," I said with ruthless reticence.

The next day the mist had grown thicker. As I left my apartment Siora Giovanna from the *osteria* on the ground floor asked me why I didn't have my hat.

"I lost it," I said, "and I haven't had time to buy a new one."

"Well, you be careful. If fog like this gets into your hair you'll probably spend all winter in bed."

She had not yet forgiven me for having given up my wig over the summer months, allowing my hair to grow long. She clearly considered the prestige of the house greatly diminished by the presence of a wigless tenant, and she never failed to find a way to refer to this.

"I'll be very careful, Siora Giovanna," I said. "And I'll buy a hat as soon as possible."

"You be sure you do," she said. "You can never be too careful."

"No, you can't, that's very true."

This was a fair example of our usual conversational manner: sententiously solicitous, carefully courteous and tediously tautologous.

I made my way eastwards, passing by the Arsenale, where the marble lions flanked the great entranceway like ghostly guardians in the mist. The statue of Santa Giustina above the gateway was barely visible. I crossed the angular drawbridge over the canal and made my way down the opposite *fondamenta* towards the lagoon. When I reached the boatyards Lucio was already there with his uncle Biasio, a burly man, who just nodded to me and told me to get into his *sandolo*. It looked as if I had found a rival to Bepi for taciturnity.

We slid out into the featureless grey of the lagoon. I wrapped my cloak more tightly about myself.

It was a ten-minute journey, with Biasio effortlessly propelling us forward and humming some unidentifiable tune to himself. Eventually the tall shape of the church of Sant'Elena grew more and more solid ahead of us, with its steep triangle-topped façade. I had never actually visited the island, although I had passed it many times in Bepi's gondola.

There was a simple landing stage by the grassy patch of ground in front of the church, and I disembarked. Biasio agreed to come back in a couple of hours. Within a minute or so he had disappeared into the fog.

One could almost have believed that the rest of the world had been silently eliminated and that only this small island, with its gaunt brick church and quiet monastery, was left. There was no visible sign of life, but listening hard I heard a plaintive chanting from the church. The monks were at their devotions.

I approached the entrance; there was a fine fifteenth-century statue over the door, which I remembered from my preparatory reading was by Antonio Rizzo, representing a Venetian sea-captain kneeling before a tall stooping figure of Saint Helena.

I pushed the door, which opened easily. The monks were in the stalls around the apse of the church, and their service was clearly coming to an end. I stood in reverent silence until the last echoes died away. They trooped out by the sacristy door, just one of them leaving the group to walk down the central aisle towards me.

"Can I help you?" he asked. From his accent I guessed he was from the mainland, not Venice itself. He was an elderly man, small, but with a natural dignity of bearing.

Time for me to adopt today's role. Concerned neighbour.

"I'm sorry to disturb you, Father; I've come on behalf of the sister of a man who died recently in tragic circumstances."

"Who is that?"

"His name is Paolo Padoan. He fell from the roof of his house."

"I know the man."

"Well, his sister has been looking for a diary he was keeping. She seemed to think he may have left it here."

"Here?"

"Well, perhaps in the monastery. I understand that he regularly visited the island."

"He had a particular devotion to Saint Helena." He gestured towards the chapel that opened off the right aisle.

"Do you have many visitors?" I asked.

"People come to our evening Mass," he said. "And some people are granted permission to consult the books in our library."

"Was he one of them?" I asked.

He gave a stately nod of the head.

"Do you happen to know what he was studying?" I asked.

His sharp eyes looked hard at me. "Can I ask you why you wish to know?"

"His sister is trying to understand what he was doing in the last days of his life. It seems he was a very reticent man. I think it would just be of some comfort to her to feel a little closer to him." I felt almost ashamed at how easily these lies came to me. The one thing

I knew was that a mention of the Missier Grande would be fatal to my inquiry with these people.

"He was reticent with us too. And perhaps his reticence should be respected."

"But I presume that he must have given you some reason for wanting to use your library."

He gazed at me without speaking for a few moments. Then he sighed and said, "It seems he was not happy with the life he was leading. Or the life he had led. He wanted – well, the only word is redemption."

"Redemption?" I said.

"You understand the word?" he said.

"Yes, I know what it means – in abstract terms. But in Sior Padoan's case in particular . . ."

"In all our cases," he said. "There is not one of us who does not need redemption."

"No, of course not," I said. "But given that it is so universal a need, I wonder what made it so particularly pressing with Sior Padoan that he voiced it here."

"He did not do so explicitly," said the monk. "I am to a certain extent interpreting his actions. But I'm not sure I have the right to express my reading of a man who was so naturally private."

"It is his sister's special wish," I said, firmly squashing the inner voice of my conscience. I knew that he was not likely to suggest she came in person to talk to him, since women were probably not allowed to enter the monastery. "It would greatly help her in her grief."

He frowned. "And what is your relationship to his sister?"

"I'm just a neighbour and a friend."

"I see." He stood a moment in contemplation and then said, "Have you visited the shrine of our saint?"

"No," I said.

He led the way into the richly decorated side chapel. Over the altar stood a splendid polyptych, with saints against a gold background. Underneath the altar-table lay a chest with two gratings, through which a gleam of gold could be discerned.

"Brought from Constantinople in the thirteenth century," said the monk. "The body was transported in that chest." He pointed to another large chest, alongside the altar, which bore painted images of four saints. I recognised Saint Mark and Saint Helena.

I said hesitantly, "I remember reading that the church of Aracoeli in Rome also claims to have the body of Saint Helena."

He gave a contemptuous wave of his hand. "And Hautvillers in France, and Verona too. It's possible they have a finger or a toe, but only we have the body. When the ship bearing the chest came into the lagoon, they were intending to take it into the city itself, but the ship was unable to sail past this island, making it clear that this was where the saint wished her relics to remain."

I nodded with pious acceptance of the tale. I may have grown up in sceptical Protestant England, but my mother had been fervently (if intermittently) Catholic.

"And Sior Padoan felt a special bond with Saint Helena," I said. I studied the predella of the polyptych. There were five small scenes, which I thought I could identify as stories of the discovery of the True Cross.

"Yes," he said. "He always said a prayer in the chapel both when he arrived and before leaving. He was also devoted to Saint Helena's son, Constantine. Or Saint Constantine, as our brothers of the Orthodox Church call him."

"Did Sior Padoan consider him a saint?"

"I think so," he said, after a pause. "He certainly considered Constantinople a holy city."

"Yes," I said. "I've heard him say that."

He darted a shrewd glance at me. "So you have spoken to him on these subjects?"

I hoped my blushing was not visible in the flickering candlelight of the chapel. "Not long conversations. He was not a great talker."

"No," he said. "From the few remarks I heard I understood that he was interested in the strong ties between our city and Constantinople. He seemed to feel that these ties were somehow – well, again the word is redemptive."

"Redemptive? For whom?"

"For Venice."

I stood in silence, gazing at the intricate depictions of the mother of the ruler of the greatest empire on earth engaged in the task of excavating planks of ancient wood from the earth.

"As I understood it," said the monk, "Sior Padoan worked for the government of our city but was not entirely happy with some of the things he had to do. He wanted to believe in a nobler and holier city than the one he saw every day. Venice should be the new Constantinople."

"Should be," I said, not sure whether I was asking a question or expressing scepticism.

"That is how he wished he could see the city," said the monk. "After 1453 it was our duty to take on the mantle of the new holy city of Europe."

"After Constantinople fell to the Ottomans," I said, not so much because I wanted him to see that I knew my history but rather because I was reflecting on this desire for a divinely approved geopolitical role for our city – and, as a consequence, for himself.

"Exactly," said the monk.

This was not getting me any closer to the diary. "Do you remember him writing in a diary?" I said. "Or doing any writing at all while here?"

"He may have done so in the library," he said. "I never observed him there."

"Could I ask someone who might have done?"

"You could ask, but you won't get an answer," he said.

"Oh, and why's that?"

"We have a vow of silence outside our hours of prayer. As abbot I am allowed to break it in order to talk to outsiders such as yourself. But my brothers must remain silent during the day."

"So the only person Padoan can have talked to is you," I said.

"That is correct."

"Well, Father Abbot, would you allow me to see the library in any case?"

"That seems a reasonable request," he said. "Do you wish to spend a few moments in contemplation first?"

I realised that yes was the only possible answer to this and knelt down before the shrine. I said a brief prayer; if anyone could help me find this missing object, surely it must be the saint who had found the True Cross buried deep underneath a pagan temple. As I knelt there I allowed my eyes to wander around the chapel. There were fine carved choir-stalls around the apse, more devotional paintings on the side walls and a small bookcase in one corner containing what were presumably hymn-books and devotional readings. Next to it was a wooden board where people had affixed individual prayers and ex-voto paintings with crude but touching depictions of Saint Helena leaning from Heaven to help a child in a bed, a fisherman who had fallen from his boat, a ship grounded on rocks ... They did not inspire confidence in Venetian seamanship.

After a suitable lapse of time I got to my feet and followed the abbot, who led the way out of the chapel. He locked the door of the chapel after we had left it. "You may have heard of some of the recent thefts in churches," he said. "It seems nothing is considered sacred now."

"Yes," I said. "Very worrying." Over the last few months there had been a spate of thefts of precious objects from churches and guilds. The items reported stolen were all, as far as I could remember, of Greek or Eastern origin, which perhaps explained the abbot's concern for the relics of Saint Helena.

He now led the way to a door on the opposite side of the church. This opened straight into a cloister, with a well in the middle. We walked around two sides of the cloister, entered the monastery and climbed to the first floor. The library was relatively small, with windows looking out on to the lagoon. My secular eyes were drawn to that view rather than to the books. All that could be seen was the drifting grey fog, but I knew that across the water lay the green expanse of the Lido. It must be quite a distracting view in clear weather, with the many-masted sailing ships, the simple fishing boats and the barges of the Republic making their way to and from the open gap that leads into the Adriatic. I thought I could discern the ghost of a three-masted vessel proceeding cautiously towards the city.

I looked around the room. Bookcases lined all the walls, with imposing volumes bound in dark leather. Three desks were set out one behind the other; there was just one monk sitting at one of them, and I had the impression that, rather like Sior Massaro, he had given a guilty start as we opened the door and immediately devoted himself with fierce concentration to his work; the scraping of his quill was the only sound.

"Can I look around?" I said, feeling a little daunted by the sheer number of volumes surrounding me.

"If you really think it will be of benefit. You will excuse me, but I have other duties to attend to."

I was very glad to see him go but expressed my understanding in rather more courteous terms. The other monk continued to scribble. Although I could not see his face as he bent industriously over his work, I could sense his annoyance, possibly at having to keep up the pretence of unstinting labour. I did my best to reassure him by immediately turning to the bookcases and focusing all my attention on them.

I perused them shelf by shelf, looking for any object that appeared out of place, scarcely taking in the titles as I did so. I was conscious of the quill continuing to scrape and scratch behind me; it was possibly only my imagination, but I had the distinct impression that if I were to swivel suddenly I would catch the writer glaring hostilely at me, while his quill executed meaningless doodles on the paper. I resisted the temptation to do so, and after a while I forgot all about him.

My eyes grew accustomed to the dim gold writing on the spines as my eyes ran over shelf after shelf, and my body alternately strained upwards, crouched downwards and leaned sideways according to the shelves I was scrutinising. Lives of saints, devotional tracts, collections of sermons, histories of the Church, in Italian, Latin and occasionally Greek. Nothing that I felt tempted to pull out and read. And no modern intruders.

I had completed my inspection of one entire wall when I heard footsteps approaching along the corridor outside. I turned towards the door. My companion did not look up.

The door opened and the abbot stood there with another man, dressed in sober dark clothes, wearing a neat powdered wig and holding a silver-topped cane. I recognised him. It was Marino Basso, a trusted *confidente* of the three Inquisitors. He was not tall, but somehow, by lifting his sharply pointed chin, he managed to give the impression that he was looking down on the world. He prided himself, I knew, on his polished manners, confidential agents of the Inquisitors being a cut above the riff-raff that worked for the Missier Grande. He gazed at me disapprovingly.

"May I ask what you are doing here?" he said, in his smooth Tuscan Italian.

I knew I still had to be very careful not to mention the Missier Grande, even though Basso knew that I worked for him. "I'm here entirely for private personal reasons," I said. "My gondolier friend Bepi was a close neighbour of Padoan, the man who—"

"I know that Padoan worked for the Missier Grande," said Basso. "And that you do too."

I heard the quill pen behind me halt for the first time. This had clearly caught everyone's attention. The abbot was gazing coldly at me too.

"Yes, but that has nothing to do with it," I said. "This is purely a private matter. I'm trying to find something important for Padoan's sister."

"You are referring, I presume, to the man's diary," he said.

"Yes," I said. There was clearly no point in denying it.

"Well, you may stop doing so. The Inquisitors wish to take possession of it."

There was nothing I could say to this. "Very well," I said anyway. "Would you like me to help you look for it?"

"Are you deliberately trying to be impertinent?"

"No, just helpful." I pointed to the wall behind me. "I've searched that bookcase. There's nothing there. You might as well start with that one." I gestured to the opposite wall.

"Thank you. I don't think we need any advice." He didn't add "from a crony of the *sbirri*", but the implication was clear enough from his tone.

I gave a shrug. "Well, I'll leave you to it," I said. "Try not to disturb this poor fellow at his writing. I've been very discreet."

"As I said, I require no advice from you. Oh, before you go, do me the courtesy of showing your pockets to me."

This was decidedly beyond the bounds of his authority, and I toyed for a moment with the thought of refusing. But it struck me that I would not be helping the Missier Grande by allowing the Inquisitors to think that he might have obtained the diary. So I allowed him to inspect my person, limiting my reaction to an expression of haughty disapproval as he patted my jacket and cloak.

"Very well," he said. "You may go."

"Very kind of you," I said in my coldest manner.

"Father Abbot," said Basso, "I would ask you to conduct this person to his boat. I will continue my search here by myself."

"Very well," said the abbot.

"You may inform the Missier Grande," said Basso, "that the diary will be perfectly safe under our protection. He need not trouble himself further with it."

"I'll say nothing at all," I said, "since the Missier Grande has expressed no interest in it."

He merely sniffed and then turned to the nearest bookcase, a smugly triumphant expression on his face; I was reminded of little Pierino after he had got his mother to pick him up.

The walk back down the staircase and through the cloisters was an uncomfortable one, the abbot emanating disapproval and disappointment in his every step and sniff. As we reached the door into the church I said, "Father Abbot, will you forgive me if I take a moment to pray again to Saint Helena? My boatman hasn't arrived yet, in any case."

He didn't answer for a moment. Then he said, "If working for the Missier Grande means what I imagine it means, then perhaps I can understand why Sior Padoan felt the need for redemption."

"Father Abbot," I said, "it probably does mean what you are imagining. But not everyone is drawn into this work for base reasons."

He gave a sigh. "The road to hell . . . I need not continue. But I can certainly understand why you might wish to say another prayer." He gestured towards the chapel of Saint Helena. "Go. But please understand if I ask you not to return to this island."

"I do understand, Father Abbot."

The abbot unlocked the chapel door and returned to the nave of the main church.

I went straight towards the little bookcase I had seen. A few words spoken by Sior Basso had given me a sudden idea. *Under our protection . . .*

All that I had heard of Sior Padoan suggested his strong desire for protection, for himself and for his words. So if he had written something and wanted it to be preserved, he would presumably have left it as close as possible to the saint he had elected as his protector. Ideally he might have wanted to slip the diary into the casket with the body itself, but that would have been problematic; it seemed likely, however, that he would have chosen to conceal it somewhere in the chapel dedicated to her. And the abbot had told me that he always visited the chapel both when he arrived and before he left the island.

I ran my eyes over the books lined up in the little case. As I had supposed earlier they consisted of hymn-books and devotional readings; they were a little more battered than the almost pristine volumes in the library, but they still did not suggest any regularity of use. I ran my eyes and my fingers over them – and then I spotted a black leather wallet-like object, less firm and less bulky than the other books, in a corner of the lowest shelf. I pulled it out and flipped it open. It contained hand-written pages. I gave it just one glance and then thrust it into the inner pocket of my jacket and went to the altar and knelt down for a few seconds, whispering words of suitable gratitude to Saint Helena.

Now if only I could leave the island straight away. Unfortunately when I stepped out of the church, giving a courteous bow to the abbot, who stood at the entrance door and returned it with equal courtesy but considerably more coldness, there was no sign of my boatman. A gondola was moored at the landing stage, and the gondolier was walking up and down by the water's edge, presumably to keep warm. I was tempted to try to bribe him to take me over to the city but realised it would create more trouble than it was worth.

So there was nothing to do but wait for my man to return. I did not dare to take out the package from my pocket, lest the gondolier should see it and mention it to his passenger. I had the distinct impression that it was swelling inside my jacket to monstrous proportions, and I pulled my cloak more firmly around myself to conceal the bulge.

I strolled towards the gondolier in as casual a fashion as possible.

"Good morning," I greeted him.

He looked suspiciously at me. He was a thickset man with an impressive moustache and eyebrows. He gave a grunt which might have been a clearing of the throat prior to expectoration, but as he didn't actually expectorate I chose to interpret it as a response.

"Are you Sior Basso's private gondolier?" I asked. It was unlikely that a mere agent could afford his own gondolier, but I thought it worth asking, if only to torment myself with the discrepancy in pay between myself and him.

"No," he said after a pause, as if wondering whether answering this question would be in any way self-incriminating. Gondoliers are generally wary about volunteering information about their working circumstances. It's probably something inculcated into them from their earliest lessons, discretion having always featured highly among their required skills.

"Hired for the day?"

"Why do you want to know?"

"No reason," I said, giving an airy wave of the hand. I realised I was not going to get any information from this man, so after a few desultory remarks about the fog I moved away from him.

It was a painful wait. I was longing to inspect the package and at the same time I was dreading the sound of footsteps coming from the church. I doubted that Basso would order another search of my person, but I now had the distinct impression that the package was visibly throbbing under my jacket to the beat of my heart.

Eventually, however, I discerned the boat appearing through the mist. Biasio and the gondolier exchanged a couple of salutatory grunts, I boarded, and we set off towards the city. With my back to Biasio I drew out the notebook and carefully opened it.

It was written in Greek.

I flipped all the way through it. There was no break in the neat angular script.

"Pretentious poser," I said to myself. I could make out a few repeated names here and there: Sanudo, Querini, something that looked like Phanariot, whatever that might be. Constantinople appeared here and there and Hagia Helena a couple of times; I also thought I saw a reference to the Komnenos dynasty of emperors. Perhaps he had just been scribbling notes on the history of the Eastern Roman Empire.

So how was I going to get an idea of what was written here? Well, the Missier Grande would undoubtedly know how to find an interpreter, but he had been quite explicit about this investigation's being my business; he might not welcome my running straight to him before I had concluded my inquiries.

There was only one person I knew who could read Greek and could be relied upon to be discreet: my friend the bookseller, Fabrizio Busetto. Lucia's father.

Lucia, of course, would not be keen on their becoming involved in my "other job". So perhaps the best course would be to visit the shop when she was out.

This was clearly the most sensible solution; it was foolish of me to wish otherwise. But then I always was a fool.

7

I knew that Lucia as a rule went to the Rialto market late in the morning, in order to benefit from the bargains on offer when the stall-holders often halved their prices prior to closing for the day. As it was now getting on for midday, I made my way from the point of disembarkation directly to Calle dei Fabbri, where the shop was situated.

Fabrizio looked up at me from his desk opposite the door, where he usually sat reading unless bothered by some importunate person who wanted to buy something from him. His mild face broke into a smile as I entered: "Alvise, very good to see you."

"And you too, Sior Fabrizio," I said warmly. I meant it too. I looked around the shop.

"Lucia is at the market," he said. "She will be sorry to have missed you."

"And I her," I said, only half mendaciously. I wasn't sure how mendacious Fabrizio was being; I hoped not at all. "I'm sorry to have stayed away for so long, but you know how it is . . ."

"Of course, of course," he said. "And now, what can I interest you in? I myself am re-reading Suetonius. Wonderful gossipy stuff."

"So I've heard," I said. I continued to look around the shop. It was the same as ever: the same enticing smell of leather and old paper; the same dark bookcases with curious carvings, their shelves curving under the weight of thickly crammed, darkly gleaming, leather-bound volumes. Although I had spent much of the morning amid books, it was good to be back here.

"Do you just wish to browse?" he asked, already glancing back at his enticing volume of Suetonius. That was one of the reasons why the shop was so welcoming: Fabrizio put the customer under no pressure to buy, or even to chat; he perhaps preferred his gossip to be at least a thousand years old. Lucia, I knew, occasionally became exasperated when a customer left the shop without having exchanged a word – or, more to the point, a *lira* – and she would let her father know it.

"Well, I'd like to do that too, but I'd also like to ask for your help, if you don't mind."

"No, delighted if I can be of assistance."

"I had better warn you that this is for my – my other job, so to speak."

"I see," he said, in as neutral a fashion as possible. We had never talked about this "other job" at any length, although he knew what it consisted of.

"I don't want to put you in an embarrassing position," I said. "All I'm asking for is some linguistic assistance."

"I see," he said again. "What language are we talking about?"

"Greek," I said. "I learned Latin as a child but never any Greek."

"Oh, a great pity," he said. "Of course, it's never too late to start."

"No, of course not, but this is rather urgent." I pulled the notebook from my pocket and handed it to him.

"*Cospetto,*" he said, his usual expression when mildly – or indeed violently – surprised. "And where does this come from?" He started leafing through it.

"This belonged to a man called Paolo Padoan, who was a schoolteacher and occasionally filed reports for the Missier Grande. He was very interested in the classics, and it struck me that you might have come across him."

"Paolo Padoan . . . Padoan . . . Let me see. Was he a small man, about sixty? Didn't I hear that he had an accident recently?"

Sior Fabrizio rarely left his shop and didn't seem to gossip much, but none the less most of the city's news seemed to reach him; I sometimes thought of him as a benign spider, alert to every minor shock in the outreaching threads of the city's web.

"That's right. He was killed falling from the roof of his house. Did you know him, then?"

"He did occasionally visit the shop. In fact, now that you mention it . . ." Clearly he had suddenly thought of something. He sat pondering for a while and then said, "Yes, of course, of course."

"What is it?"

"Well, you know that some of my stock is second-hand?"

"Yes, of course." The second-hand books were the only ones I could ever afford.

"Well, I always take especial care to ascertain the provenance of everything that is offered to me. And occasionally I just have to refuse to buy some books, even though the price being asked would be clearly advantageous to me."

"You mean they're stolen goods?"

"I never know for certain, but I would rather not run the risk. Well, just a few days ago I was offered a set of volumes which were vaguely familiar. And now that you've mentioned his name I realise that they were probably all books that I had sold to Sior Padoan over the years."

"Who was selling them?"

"Well, let's say he clearly was not a bibliophile."

"Could he have been a friend of Padoan? Or a relative?"

"I'm fairly sure he was a *sbirro*, who had removed the books from the dead man's home. Oh, and that reminds me –" But he interrupted himself. "I'll come back to that. As I say, I think he was a *sbirro*."

"Very likely," I said. "Do you remember what the books were?"

"Oh, some standard Greek and Latin classics, but also some works on the history of Constantinople . . ."

"Yes!" I said involuntarily.

Fabrizio looked at me with mild curiosity. "Does your reaction indicate a shared interest in the history of the Eastern Roman Empire or does this just confirm something you had suspected?"

"The latter," I said. "The suspicion is that Padoan was killed and I've been asked to look into the circumstances of his death – discreetly. This is not an official investigation."

"No," said Fabrizio, "I imagine not." Then, as if realising that the implications of his assent might seem invidious, he added, "That is, I presume an official investigation would be up to the magistrates."

"Exactly," I said. "It's just that they don't seem very interested in investigating any further. As far as they're concerned it was simply an accident."

"But you think there's more to it."

"I don't know," I said, "but there are certainly some oddities about it all." I gave him a brief explanation of how Padoan had died and the fact that a mysterious Neapolitan had visited the *altana* a few days before the tragic incident. "So really I'm trying to build up a picture of who Padoan was and why someone might have wanted him dead. And part of the mystery seems to be his interest in a strange secret society called the Four Horsemen."

Fabrizio raised his eyebrows. "A name designed to unsettle, I would say."

"Yes, quite. Mind you, I haven't found anything apocalyptic as yet. What I have found is this diary which he had concealed in the chapel of Saint Helena. Everything seems to go back to his interest in Constantinople."

"Saint Helena, mother of Constantine," said Fabrizio.

"Exactly," I said.

"Although she never visited the city her son founded, as far as I know."

"No, perhaps not, but there's a link."

"The painter Cima da Conegliano seemed fond of her," he mused.

I thought about that. "You're right. There's a painting in San Giovanni in Bragora of her together with Constantine . . ."

"And she is represented in his nativity scene in the church of the Carmini," he said. "I've always thought it wasn't perhaps the height of tact for her to appear with that cross just when the child was being born. But I'm being irreverent. My apologies."

"Anyway," I said, "this is the diary Padoan was keeping – and he clearly wanted to be discreet about it. He had hidden it in the chapel, as I say, and it's written in Greek."

"Well, that is not exactly an impenetrable language," he said, as he gazed at a page of the notebook.

"Let's say it would keep it safe from most people's eyes," I said. "Including mine. And that's why I'm here."

"Yes, I see. So what do you want me to do? Translate the whole thing?"

"If you could just look through it and give me an idea of what he's talking about . . ."

He continued to peruse the page. "His Greek is not exactly perfect . . . And he seems to have some recurring topics."

"Can you give me an idea? It would be extremely helpful."

"Well, let's take the first page, shall we? Why don't you take a seat?"

I took the other chair from against the wall and sat down and listened to him. He skimmed through the page, humming as he did so (a constant habit of his). Then he started again from the top, speaking aloud.

"Date, April 30th.'I will keep this diary in Greek both out of my respect for the language and its culture and in order to preserve my thoughts from – from', well, I suppose, 'prying eyes' would be what he means, even if he's got the adjective wrong.'It will also serve to raise my thoughts above the common level and to strengthen that bond I feel with the Holy City founded by Saint Constantine . . .' Oh, I see he's canonised him, or he's just borrowing the appellation from the Orthodox Church.'. . . founded by Saint Constantine, son of Saint Helena, who discovered the True Cross.'"

Fabrizio raised his eyes and looked across at me. "I suppose Constantine knew Greek, but as I understand it Latin continued to be the official language of the empire until the Emperor Heraclius, in the seventh century."

"Yes," I said, "but I suspect that Padoan is primarily interested in the ties between Venice and Constantinople. And by the time Venice was thriving, a trading partner of Constantinople rather than just its vassal, Constantinople was definitely a Greek-speaking city."

Fabrizio returned to the notebook. "Yes, I think you're right. In fact he goes on to say:'The splendour of my own city is greatly due to the eternal links with the Holy City. It is to Constantinople that we owe so many of our artistic splendours, our golden mosaics, the treasures of Saint Mark's . . .'"

"Only because we looted them," I said.

Fabrizio looked up reproachfully. "I think he would consider it tactless to mention that."

At that moment a customer entered the shop. I stood up and said, "Perhaps I could come back later."

"Yes, of course." Fabrizio greeted the customer, an elderly stooping man. He was clearly an old acquaintance and needed no assistance; he went straight to the nearest bookcase and started browsing. It was enough, however, to interrupt our translation session. Fabrizio said, gesturing to the notebook, "Shall I keep hold of this?"

"That would be helpful; perhaps you could see if you find anything particularly unusual."

"What are you looking for?"

I glanced at the customer, who was paying no attention to us. "Well, what I mentioned about the, um, society. Anything that might suggest he had discovered something new. Something that might explain what, well, what happened."

"I see," he said. "Come back when Lucia is here. She'll be happy to see you."

"Yes, of course," I said.

Clearly he could tell I was not convinced. "She really will be," he said gently.

"I'm glad to hear it," I said, and realised my voice was slightly husky.

He gave a sigh. "Of course, I won't pretend that she is happy about – about –"

"About my other job," I said.

"Yes."

"You realise that's why I chose to come at this time."

He nodded. "I did suspect as much."

"Perhaps it would be better not to mention . . ." I gestured towards the notebook.

"No," he said. He put it into a drawer. "Maybe you're right."

"So if I want to talk to you about it, perhaps it will be better to come back again when she isn't here."

He gave another sigh. "I suppose so. But do come back some other time as well and see her."

"I will," I said. "Thank you." I meant it. I had never been sure what Fabrizio thought of my acquaintance with his daughter. In the past I had tended to suppose that he had never thought of me as a suitor, perhaps because if I began to think of his considering me in that light, I would be forced to realise just how unsuitable he would find a *cicerone* with links to the *sbirri*. But these remarks suggested that he realised that Lucia and I did have a bond, and that he did not resent it.

"Oh, and there's something else," he said suddenly. "Something for you, I think." He reached into the drawer again. "Another *sbirro* this time. Just yesterday afternoon. That was what I suddenly remembered earlier."

I realised he was holding my edition of Pope's translation of Homer. "Oh, goodness me," I said, just managing to restrain myself from making a wild snatch at it.

"Again I suspected that the man selling it might not have had a perfect right to ownership, but this time I took the risk of concluding a deal based on a hunch – which appears to have been correct." He handed it to me with a smile.

"Yes, it's mine, it's mine. I thought I'd lost it for ever."

"Actually the hunch wasn't mine," he said with a faint smile.

"Oh?"

"No, it was Lucia who had the idea. She nudged me while the man was in the shop trying to sell me the book, and she whispered your name."

"That was – that was clever of her."

"She knows your reading tastes. Of course, I don't suppose there are a great many people in this city who are likely to be reading Homer in English."

"Nor who are likely to have got into trouble with the *sbirri*," I added wryly, as I examined the book for damage. "Perhaps that was what suggested it to her."

"Well, she didn't say that," he said a little awkwardly.

"I was set upon by *bravi*," I said, "and the *arsenalotti* came to the rescue."

"*Cospetto*," he said with an air of good-humoured tolerance for the high spirits of the young. "Anyway, look after it. It is a beautiful edition."

"And it's a beautiful translation," I said.

"I hope you'll be able to enjoy the original one day. Beautiful language – as our friend here clearly agrees." He gestured to the drawer where he had placed the notebook.

On this note of general appreciation of the beautiful I left him. He was clearly happy to return to his Suetonius, and his customer did not look as if he was going to disturb him.

8

I spent a pleasant afternoon and evening renewing my acquaintance with Achilles' wrath; I imbibed with restraint over dinner, allowing myself to become intoxicated only with the music of Pope's couplets. When I returned home that evening I think Siora Giovanna, standing at the doorway of her tavern as so often, was surprised to see me approaching with a steady gait; she even omitted to make a remark on my persistent lack of hat and wig.

In the morning, enjoying the unusual sensation of a bare head that was as clear as the weather was not, I strolled through the mist-damp streets to San Moisè and got a report from Bepi on the young English nobleman to whom we had been showing the city earlier in the week. It turned out that he had independently discovered the amenities offered by Sior Molin's gambling establishment and had spent the last few evenings there, happily squandering a goodly part of his family's fortune, to the dismay of his well-meaning but ineffectual tutor. Bepi had now heard about my affray with Molin's *bravi* and the slimy Marco Boldrin. He told me I was a fool to set these people against me, but I detected a hint of slightly surprised approval in his tone. We made arrangements for our next meeting at Fusina on Monday morning to pick up new clients.

"Be careful," were his last words to me. "I've heard that Boldrin doesn't forget a grudge."

"I will," I said, trying for a tone of nonchalant breeziness to match the new image that I hoped Bepi had of me but failing miserably.

Around midday I arrived at Fabrizio's shop. He put down his Suetonius as I entered and shook his head.

"Something wrong?" I asked. I looked around to check that Lucia was not in the shop.

"Your friend," he said.

"Who?"

"This Padoan person. Mad."

"Ah," I said.

"I mean, completely mad. As mad as a horse."

From a Venetian who only knew bronze horses I presumed that was extremely mad. "How did this madness manifest itself?"

"Well, you heard that little fragment I read out yesterday."

"Yes. An eccentric reading of history, I would say."

"No, it was more than that. He was living in a completely imaginary world."

"I see."

Fabrizio pulled out the notebook from the drawer and opened it. "I've been thinking about the man as he presents himself here, and as I knew him."

"Did you know him?"

"As I said yesterday, he had been a customer. And we exchanged a few words over the years."

That sounded likely. Five or ten words every few months, over twenty or thirty years: they would all add up. And the extraordinary thing, I had come to realise, was that Fabrizio had an almost perfect recollection of every little scrap of conversation he had ever had, just as he did of almost every page he had ever read. This was partly why, despite his sedentary lifestyle, he had such a keen awareness of what was going on in the city – and in the world beyond.

"You see," he went on, "when he was younger I remember that he had definite academic aspirations. He very much wanted to become a member of the faculty of the university at Padua. He studied the classics assiduously, and he bought most of his editions from me. Like you, he had a great love for Homer. But unfortunately he did not succeed in this endeavour."

"No. I believe it made him quite bitter."

"Exactly," said Fabrizio, looking at me just a little quizzically. I realised he must be wondering where I had acquired my knowledge of Padoan's history and probably not liking where his wonderings took him. He continued, "He became a schoolteacher and, from all

I heard, not a very successful one. He was not popular with his pupils and did not have the gift of communication. I think it was after some years of teaching Virgil and Homer to boys who did not want to learn Virgil and Homer that he began to buy books on the Roman Empire of the East. I think at first he just wanted a new field of study to explore, uncontaminated by the displeasing associations of his old field: no superior rivals in learning refusing to allow him into their academic precincts, no mean-spirited children laughing at him behind his back. The world of learning and refinement in the Empire of Constantinople had none of these disadvantages. So he began to read such works as *De Administrando Imperio* by Constantine VII, *The Alexiad* by Anna Komnene, the *Chronographia* of Psellos . . . And he clearly began to fantasise that Venice itself was in some way the continuation of that empire."

"How did the sack of Constantinople by the Crusaders under the leadership of Venice fit into this vision of things?" I asked. "After all, if Venice is filled with artefacts from Constantinople it is because of that."

"Well, that I don't know," said Fabrizio. "Remember, as I said, the man was mad. There is no point in looking for complete logic from him. What was clearly important for him was to find a way of . . . well, it's complicated . . . a way to save, or to sanctify, something of the world he lived in, a way to make it seem, well . . ." He seemed lost for words.

"A way to redeem it," I said, recalling the abbot's words.

"Exactly," said Fabrizio. Again he darted a quizzical look at me.

"That was the word the abbot at Sant'Elena used," I said, "when I asked him about Padoan."

"Very apt. And of course the religious dimension to all of this is very important. That also helped to distinguish his new studies from the old. The authors he was now studying were glorifying God, not pagan heroes or pagan deities. Venice, too, was a city devoted to the Madonna, founded on the feast day of the Annunciation, protected by one of the Evangelists. This meant that when he found himself constrained to take on the, um, demeaning job – as he saw it – of a confidential agent" – Fabrizio's eyes were lowered as he said these words – "he could justify it to himself because he was doing it for the sake of this holy city."

"I see," I said, trying to sound coolly objective. "And this is in the diary, is it?"

"Well, let me give you a random example." He turned the pages and started reading, with just a few pauses as he sought for the right word: "June 5th. 'Again I start the day with a prayer to Saint Mark and Saint Helena. Who knows if today my enquiries will be divinely inspired and lead me towards the revelation I am seeking; perhaps among these men and women, frivolous though they seem, I will find the illuminated spirit, the – the soul that has caught a spark of the fire that was not extinguished in 1453 . . .'"

Fabrizio glanced up at me. "Yes," I assured him, "the year Constantinople fell to the Ottomans."

He resumed his reading with an apologetic cough: "'and who knows but that one of these people holds the key to the location of Constantine's tomb . . .'"

"Is that a mystery?" I said. "Wasn't he buried in Constantinople?"

"Yes, in the church of the Holy Apostles. However, our friend is not referring to Constantine the Great but to his distant descendant Constantine XI, the last Emperor of Constantinople."

"Ah," I said. "He was killed when the city was taken by the Turks, wasn't he?"

"Well, that is the mystery, which has given rise to countless legends. He is said to have fought to the bitter end, leading a final desperate charge against the invaders. However, his body was never identified for certain, and so stories abound about his having escaped with a band of trusty followers, some even going so far as to claim that he was spirited away by an angel and is now waiting in some mysterious hiding-place for a trumpet call to summon him to retake the city from the infidels. Your friend seems to be a believer in many, perhaps all, of these legends, even when they contradict one another. He seems to have seen this as his ultimate mission: to locate the tomb – or the resting-place – of Constantine XI. He had been asked to make a report on the Venetian-Greek community for the Missier Grande . . ."

"Ah," I said. That was perhaps a little beyond the Missier Grande's area of competence, since he was not supposed to interfere in diplomatic matters.

". . . and he took this as an opportunity to pursue his fantastic dream of, well, reviving the emperor, finding his legendary sword, and perhaps then leading the charge into the city to drive the Turks out of it."

"I see," I said. "Perhaps a little unrealistic." I was remembering the man's dutifully petty reports for the Missier Grande, his bare apartment in the eastern corner of the city, his resentful muttering sister.

"Well," said Fabrizio with a half-smile, "I invented the part with him leading the charge. But that is certainly the spirit that fires most of the writings in this diary."

"So perhaps those who dismissed his account were right," I said.

"I certainly would not like to make an accusation against anyone on the basis of this man's words."

"No," I said. I realised that Fabrizio had said this last sentence with special precision and deliberation. "My job isn't to accuse anyone. Just to draw up a report."

"Which could be used in an eventual accusation."

This was becoming awkward. I suddenly remembered something. "There remains the fact that someone disliked what Padoan was doing so much that he – or they – had the man killed."

Fabrizio gazed at me. "You are quite sure of that?"

"Yes," I said. "I am. And crazy though he may have been, the least we can do for the poor man is try to find out who did it."

"Well, perhaps you're right. But it's difficult to get a clearly coherent picture of who or what he was dealing with."

"Please try, Sior Fabrizio," I said. "I am relying on you."

"That slightly worries me," he said.

"My job is not to act as a tittle-tattle or a spy," I said. "You know me better than that, I hope. The Republic does face dangers and you'll remember that in the past I helped to avert them. I don't know what is behind this story but I suspect there is some similar peril and it would be better to find out the truth. You can see that, can't you?"

He sighed. "Goodness knows I have no right to judge," he said. He gestured towards his edition of Suetonius. "I have indulged in the vice of gossip myself, and without the excuse that I was creating something of literary value. So what do you want to know?"

"Well, who are these people he's referring to here? The frivolous souls? And has he mentioned the Four Horsemen anywhere?"

"All right. Let's take things in order. When he starts this diary he has just been asked to investigate these Greek Venetians by the Missier Grande, whom he refers to simply as MG throughout." He glanced up at me, perhaps wondering whether to ask if this breezy familiarity was common among agents. But then he went on, "He seems pleased that his philhellenic propensities have been noticed."

"Just one moment," I said. "When you say Greek Venetians do you mean Greeks living in Venice? Or . . . ?"

"Primarily the attention seems to be on members of Venetian families who have, or have had, properties in the Greek-speaking world. That is to say, both those parts that are still under Venetian rule, such as Corfu, Zante, Cephalonia, Cerigo, and those that spent some time under Venetian rule before being lost to the Ottomans, such as parts of the Peloponnese, islands in the Cyclades, Crete . . ."

That would make sense, I thought, since such people were definitely Venetian, and so there would be no risk of the Missier Grande's going outside his area of competence.

Fabrizio went on, "But the, um, MG probably also wanted to hear about Greeks in Venice – and, more particularly, contacts between them and Greek Venetians. And it seems that Padoan's first contact is with a Greek, a man he met at Sant'Elena: apparently another devotee of the saint. Much to Padoan's delight, he finds that the man's name is Constantine: or rather Kostantinos Komnenos."

"Ah," I said, "I thought I had seen that name. I wondered whether he was just writing about history."

"Yes, I can see your puzzlement. It is of course the same name as that of one of the most important dynasties of emperors of Constantinople. The man in question, however, claims to be only distantly related to the imperial family. And it seems he is a poet and a philosopher with quite a following here in Venice. He has been in Venice for some months and regularly attends the *salotto* of Isabella Venier-Querini."

"Ah," I said again. "Another name I spotted."

"The Venier family still rules the island of Cerigo, or Kythira, and so has constant links with the Greek world. Isabella Venier married into the Querini family. You may know that the Querinis were banished from the city back in the fourteenth century, after the attempted Tiepolo uprising..."

"1310," I said in automatic *cicerone* (or know-it-all) fashion.

"... and they established themselves on the island of Stampalia, or Astypalaia, in the Aegean. They ruled there until the early sixteenth century, when the Turks expelled them and they returned to Venice; that branch of the family is now sometimes known as the Querini-Stampalia. And so the marriage between the Venier and the Querini brings together a family that still has possessions in the Greek world and one that looks back nostalgically to the days when they too ruled there. A potent mixture, it seems. Isabella Venier has set up a *salotto* in her palace – or rather her husband's palace, near Campo Santa Maria Formosa – which is attended by many other Greek Venetians and one or two Greeks, like this Komnenos."

"I see."

"Padoan's account of his visits to this *salotto* – it seems he had to overcome a natural timidity – are rather confused. And this is where your horsemen seem to come in. At first it seems he was simply overwhelmed. Rather like, I don't know, an opera enthusiast who finds himself in the same room as Farinelli . . . or a whole roomful of Farinellis. There he was, surrounded by other people from that world he had only read about and dreamed about: the

Greek-speaking world of the eastern Mediterranean; the former Eastern Roman Empire, whose inhabitants still describe themselves as Romans, or *Rhomaioi*. Remember, he has never been further from Venice than Padua. Then he begins to discover that these people are not as touched with the divine fire as he had hoped. Indeed, many of them seem simply frivolous. And then we begin to get hints of danger. He is afraid of something."

"What?" I said.

"Well, that's where the problem lies. His writings become more and more confused, so that you can't tell whether he is reporting what he has really seen and heard, or what he has imagined . . ."

"What does he say?"

"He begins to talk about the Four."

"The Four," I said. "No mention of horsemen?"

"No. Just the Four. Among the people attending the *salotto* are the Four, he has discovered. He has heard people whispering about the Four. And what they have done."

"And what have they done?"

"Things unspeakable. Indescribable. Unutterable. He uses all these adjectives."

"Unspeakably bad or unspeakably good?"

"It's never clear. At first he just seems awed by the fear that the Four inspire, and then he clearly begins to feel the fear himself. He is afraid he is being followed on his way home. He's afraid that someone is watching his house."

"Does he give any indication who belongs to the Four? This Komnenos, for example?"

"He never says so explicitly. We do get a clearer picture of who Komnenos is, however. He tells us he is a Phanariot."

"Yes, I noticed that. What is it?"

"I too was unfamiliar with the term. Fortunately my books" – he gave a vague gesture, which encompassed not only the volumes that surrounded us but also the even greater quantity in his private apartment on the floor above – "supplied the answer. Phanar is the quarter of Constantinople where the Greek patriarchate is situated.

It's where the most prominent Greek families reside. You may be aware that a good part of the Ottoman administration is run nowadays by Greeks; most dragomans – the ambassadors of the Ottoman court – are Greek, since the Muslim Ottomans are often not willing to learn the languages of non-Muslim peoples. The Phanariots are thus people of great prominence in Constantinople and in the Ottoman Empire as a whole, working for the Sultan while remaining proudly Greek. A curious situation. Komnenos grew up in this world and, I think, occupied a position as interpreter. At some point he seems to have given up his official role and become a travelling poet or thinker or whatever he is . . . his current role is not entirely clear."

"Hm," I said. "Perhaps I'll have to try to visit this *salotto*."

"That might be an idea," said Fabrizio.

"What might be an idea?" said a voice behind us, a voice that, as ever, gave me a feeling of sudden elation.

I turned round. Lucia was standing in the doorway with a laden basket.

"Sior Alvise," she said with a smile. It was also the same smile as ever, and it still hit me like a swig of succulent Cypriot wine.

"Siora Lucia," I said with my best formal bow.

"You have been a stranger," she said, putting down the basket. An apple tumbled from it, and I scooped it up deftly as it rolled across the floor and returned it to her with another bow.

"Thank you. Agile as ever," she said.

"And you are as graceful as ever," I said, feeling absurdly thrilled by her trivial compliment.

"So all is as it ever was," she said, still smiling.

"I hope so," I said, and tried not make it sound too mawkishly fervent.

"We must not be strangers," she said. "That would be too sad."

Her father put in a word. "Alvise has been very busy, he tells me."

"Of course," she said. It was evident that she was hesitant about asking me what I had been busy at. Instead she returned to her first question: "What is the good idea?"

Her father answered easily enough, "Alvise has heard about a *salotto* in the city and is curious about it."

"Which *salotto* is this?" she asked.

"One run by Noblewoman Isabella Venier-Querini."

"Ah," she said with interest. "I've heard of this. They say that it is the gathering to attend if you have any interest in the classical world. Sior Alvise, you must go, if you can."

"I fear that as a mere *cicerone* I might not be welcome."

"No, no," she said. "I've heard that it's open to all who have a genuine interest in Greek culture – and I know you do."

"Yes, I hear you persuaded your father to buy back my lost translation of *The Iliad* from a *sbirro* the other day." I pulled the book from my pocket to show her.

"I'm so glad you've got it back. Perhaps you'll tell us how you came to lose it."

Her father intervened once more. "Sior Alvise was apparently set upon by *bravi* and then rescued by *arsenalotti*."

"Goodness," she said. Her tone was immediately rather wary, as if she was wondering whether she really wanted to hear any more details.

I saved her from embarrassment: "It was nothing really. Just some drunken fools." I decided not to tell her that I had been one of them.

"You weren't hurt?"

"Nothing serious," I said. "Just the injury to my pride. And to my Homer, of course."

She smiled with relief, probably more at the fact that the conversation had been steered away from any distasteful matters than at any serious concerns for my safety, or so I suspected. She said, "It's clear that this *salotto* would be ideal for you."

"Yes, but I'll need an introduction."

"That is true," she said with a slight frown.

"I can arrange that," said Fabrizio. "My friend Filippo Madricardo will be happy to sponsor you. I've heard him mention Isabella Venier as an acquaintance. He usually visits the shop around five o'clock."

"Do you think I really have the credentials?"

"You can tell them all about English translations of Homer," said Fabrizio, "and your friend the good Alessandro Pope."

"Of course," said Lucia. "People will be fascinated to hear how Greek culture is perceived by barbarians from the northern wastes."

"Barbarians who are now becoming the wealthiest nation in Europe," I said.

"Wealth is not all," she said with a smile. "I see that its sons have not yet learned to wear wigs."

"I'm not actually a son of England," I said, touching my bare hair self-consciously.

"An adopted son," she said, "without any doubt. And don't worry: it may be barbaric but it suits you."

"Thank you," I said. "My friend Pope calls that 'damning with faint praise.'"

"How does that sound in English?" she said.

I quoted the lines in English:

"Damn with faint praise, assent with civil leer,
And without sneering, teach the rest to sneer;
Willing to wound, and yet afraid to strike,
Just hint a fault, and hesitate dislike."

"Too difficult for me," she said with a laugh. "But I like the music of it."

"I'm glad," I said. "And nothing could be less barbaric than the poetry of Pope. Some might even say he is too civilised."

"Goodness me," she said. "How strange a concept."

Perhaps this little exchange was itself all too civilised. I wondered if I should just swoop down on her and press my barbaric lips to hers . . .

But probably not in front of her father.

"I'm glad to hear your cultural interests are still thriving, Sior Alvise," she said. "Not having seen you pass this way for so long. Perhaps he has given up reading, I said to Father just the other day."

"But you none the less guessed that the Homer belonged to me."

"Yes," she said. "And perhaps the curious way it reached us was also a clue." Her tone as she said this was light, I was glad to note.

I was about to try to respond with equal lightness when the door of the shop was opened.

Lucia turned to face the door with a welcoming smile. Fabrizio looked up from the diary with his usual mild curiosity. I, however, stared in blank dismay. The man standing in the doorway, gazing around with an expression of fastidious distaste, was Marino Basso, last seen in the library at Sant'Elena.

9

A burly man with a Nicolotto cap askew on his large bristly head was standing behind the unwelcome visitor. While Basso, as usual, managed to give the impression that, despite his meagre height, he was raised above us by sheer superiority of deportment, his companion towered over the whole shop by dint of mere physical bulk. I looked back at Fabrizio, wondering if there was any way I could signal to him to thrust the diary into his drawer, but he was already addressing Basso courteously. "Good morning. Do come in and look round."

"Thank you," said Basso, and he peeled off his gloves and handed them to his companion, who took them with a grunt and shoved them into his coat pocket. "I have no intention of robbing you of your valuable time," he went on, still addressing Fabrizio. "My business is with this young man." He waved his ungloved hand at me, in a gesture clearly intended to offend.

I took a conscious decision to remain clear-headed and cool. "And what business might that be, Sior Basso?"

"I think you know perfectly well, Sior Marangon."

"Not at all," I said. "We met yesterday at Sant'Elena and concluded any business that we might have had there."

"Not exactly," he said. "Because I have discovered that you were not fully honest with me."

His companion gave another grunt, as if shocked at such a revelation.

I moved towards Basso, with the sole intention of blocking his view of Fabrizio's desk. However, he took my action as hostile and lifted his cane in a warning fashion. His companion instantly stepped forward as well, his bristling jaw thrust out like a battering ram. I spoke as mildly as possible. "I don't know what you are referring to."

Basso lowered his cane. "You told me you had not found Padoan's diary."

I heard a slight rustle of movement behind me, and spoke quickly to draw attention away from Fabrizio and his desk. "It was perfectly true. You even searched me."

Lucia spoke up. "Excuse me, sior, I don't know who you are, but this is a bookshop. If you are not interested in looking at our books I must ask you to leave." I cast her a grateful glance but then looked away at once. Her expression was firm and angry, and I guessed that some of the anger was directed at me as well as at the new arrivals.

Basso simply ignored her. "This morning we found the man who had rowed you to the island. He told us that on the way back to the city you were reading a hand-written notebook."

I cursed my impatience. Why could I not have waited those few minutes to examine my findings? I should have known how thorough the Inquisitors' agents were. The exchanged grunts between my boatman and Basso's gondolier should have been enough to tell me that they knew each other. I should have foreseen the possibility that Basso might question my man.

I tried to bluster my way out. "And what does that mean? I was just consulting my own diary, making sure I had not forgotten any appointments."

Lucia was now fuming. "Sior, I have asked you to leave. You clearly have no intention of buying—"

Basso turned to her. "I am here on business for the Inquisitors. You will kindly not interrupt me."

There was a faint creaking noise behind me, and I realised Fabrizio was opening his drawer. Unfortunately Basso heard him. "Please leave that where it is." He pushed past me and picked up the notebook. "I think this is what we were looking for. Am I correct?"

I saw no point in further prevarication. "That is Sior Padoan's diary."

"You admit you lied to me, then?"

"No. When we spoke I didn't have it – as you yourself were able to ascertain. I found it in the chapel of Sant'Elena after we had spoken."

"And although you knew I was looking for it on behalf of the Inquisitors you appropriated it for yourself."

"No, for Sior Padoan's sister. She has a right to it."

"Then what is it doing here? I rather doubt that Sior Padoan's sister is a client of this establishment."

"Let's just say I was curious and wanted an idea of what was in it. It's written in Greek and my friend Sior Fabrizio is the only person I know who reads Greek."

"I see," said Basso. "We searched your apartment this morning after speaking with the boatman."

"You what?" I said, angered but not surprised. Well, at least it would provide Siora Giovanna with a topic of conversation other than my bare head for a few days.

He went straight on. "And then our knowledge of your regular habits suggested it might be worth coming here."

"Sior Alvise is no longer a regular visitor here," said Lucia. Her voice was cold and hard.

"It's true," I said. "I haven't called here for some weeks."

"Then we will just have to congratulate ourselves on our good fortune," said Basso. "You will now forget all about this business. You will certainly not make any report to the Missier Grande." He looked at Lucia and Fabrizio. "That goes for you as well. If you have read this diary, you will cancel from your minds all that you have found there."

"I know nothing about it," said Lucia, still very coldly. "And I'm sure my father will be happy to do as you suggest."

"I'm very glad to hear it. My apologies for disturbing you."

He turned round, holding out his hands imperiously towards his companion. The latter pulled out the gloves, handed them to Basso, and then they both left.

It would not be an exaggeration to describe the silence that followed as an awkward one. It did not last long, however.

"Sior Alvise," said Lucia. Her voice was quiet but firm; her dark eyes had a steely glitter.

"Siora Lucia," I said, not sure whether to try for airy nonchalance or grovelling humility. In the end I just sounded confused, which was fair enough.

"You haven't visited us for several weeks and now that you do come you bring spies from the Inquisitors upon us."

"My dear," said Fabrizio, "that is a little harsh."

"Is it, Father? Was it just a social visit?"

"Alvise simply asked me to—"

"To inspect a document that he was trying to keep from the Inquisitors' spies."

I winced, but I could not actually fault this description. "I had no idea those people would come along. I am extremely sorry."

"You had no idea. That's clear enough."

"The diary was really not anything—"

"I would rather not know about it," she said. "I'm going upstairs to prepare our meal. Thank you for calling, Sior Alvise. Please do not call again until you can be sure that you won't be followed by *sbirri* and spies." She picked up her basket, gave me a formal bow and proceeded up the stairs in the corner of the shop that led to their apartment.

Another awkward silence. Then Fabrizio said, "Lucia is very protective of me."

"I understand that," I said, "and I honour her for it."

"She's angry now," he said, "but these moods pass with her."

"I'm glad to hear it," I said. "I'll stay away for a while." Perhaps a dogeship or two.

"Do you still intend to visit this *salotto*?"

"I'm afraid I have to," I said.

"Are you sure it's sensible?"

"I really have no choice. I don't think I'll be safe until I find out what lies behind this murder."

He gave a sigh and then spoke in a lower voice, with an involuntary glance towards the staircase. "Well, come round this afternoon as I said, around five o'clock. I'll find some excuse to send Lucia to the shops or something. Then you can meet my friend Madricardo."

"Thank you," I said, dropping my voice in conspiratorial fashion as well. It would have been comforting to believe that Fabrizio was getting some thrill out of this incursion into my way of life, but I couldn't really persuade myself that this was so.

I went home to see in what sort of condition the Inquisitors' men had left my apartment. I was expecting the worst and so was reasonably content to find that their search had been thorough but not brutally destructive. Of course, my possessions were not so many that a thorough search would have required any especially invasive actions. The books had been scattered widely and my few items of clothing had been rummaged through, but there was no evidence of any wanton breakage. The room had sometimes looked worse after I had dressed in a hurry after oversleeping. Giovanna told me that she had been obliged to open the door to the men; it was not the first time such a thing had happened, and I suppose she had come to expect that this was the least you could expect from a tenant who suddenly ceased wearing a wig. I made pacificatory remarks, explaining that it was all a misunderstanding about certain books I was reading. She took the explanation in her stride; I think she knew that she was unlikely to find another tenant who would be prepared to accept the customary noise levels from her tavern at night.

10

Things went as planned at the meeting in Fabrizio's shop. Filippo Madricardo was a little man in his fifties, in slightly dusty-looking clothes. He had a curious habit of repeating one's last remark before answering it, as if everything had to be carefully tested in his own mouth before it could be properly assessed. Fabrizio had told me that he was a lawyer and had literary ambitions; I imagined he liked poems with convenient refrains. It was agreed that we would call on the *salotto* that very evening, since it convened twice a week, on Fridays and Tuesdays. Sior Madricardo told me that masks were not worn at these gatherings, by special request of Noblewoman Isabella Venier Querini. That slightly put me out; I had hoped to be able to enjoy a certain anonymity, at least when arriving at the palace.

But I cheered myself up with the thought that the Inquisitors, while thorough, were also quite slow (Sior Massaro had regaled me with some highly comic – in his opinion – anecdotes about this tendency of theirs), and probably it would take them quite a while to arrange for the diary to be translated. For this reason I thought it unlikely that one of their agents would be on hand to report my presence at the *salotto*.

So, four hours later, as arranged with Sior Madricardo (I had spent the intervening hours on the windy plain of Troy), we met in Campo Santa Maria Formosa. I had dined, but only lightly, since I had no idea whether a literary *salotto* offered food for the stomach as well as for the mind; I did not want to offend, either with embarrassing rumbles from an empty stomach or with a display of ravenous guzzling. I was wearing my cleanest shirt, brightest waistcoat, shiniest shoes and least crumpled knee-breeches (although it would actually be more honest to use the comparative form of the adjective in most of these cases). My jacket was the usual one, as I had no choice in the matter; it was certainly not as neatly close-fitting as was fashionable, but this at least meant that the bulge in the capacious right-hand pocket where I kept my Homer was not too vulgarly protuberant. I had tied my hair with a neat silk ribbon at the back. Siora Giovanna had even complimented me as I left the house. I did not tell her that this sartorial display was for a gathering where we would probably talk about books, since that would only leave her gloomily expecting another visit from the Inquisitors' men.

Sior Madricardo had apparently found a clothes brush somewhere, since he looked a little less dusty by the light of the lantern that a *codega* was holding for him.

"Ah, good evening, good evening," he said. "Very good, very good. Great privilege to be visiting the palace this evening, the palace, you know."

"Yes, of course," I said. "I've done my best to dress suitably."

"Good, good. By the way, can you remind me what you wish to talk about, if Noblewoman Venier should be so good as to call upon you to speak?"

"A translation of *The Iliad* into English."

"A translation of *The Iliad* into English," he repeated, as if surprised at the very idea.

"That's right," I said. "Alexander Pope is the author."

". . . is the author." He only repeated the last three words this time, the foreign name clearly being an impenetrable puzzle. "Well, it's certainly something new. Something new. People might like it, they really might."

"Does Nobleman Querini ever attend these affairs?" I asked.

"Oh goodness no," he said. "Much too wrapped up in his antiquarian interests. And a little shy, you know, shy."

"Ah," I said, "so rather different from his wife, I gather."

"Very different," he said. "Doesn't like the public gaze. He's never really been involved in public matters. He once went on a diplomatic mission to Smyrna, I believe, but he spent his time studying the antiquities at Ephesus and forgot all about the business he was supposed to be attending to. A scholar, you know, a scholar."

We made our way towards the little square behind the church, the *codega* providing a damp luminescence in the mist to guide our footsteps. This feeble light proved unnecessary by the time we reached the little bridge that crossed the canal to the Querini palace, since not only was there a hazy glow of light from the *piano nobile* but there were a number of other people with lanterns; some were walking towards the bridge, while others were getting out of gondolas and giving instructions to their gondoliers about the return journey. Madricardo paid our *codega*, who disappeared into the fog.

We crossed the bridge with some other cloaked figures. A footman led us up the staircase to the second-storey *piano nobile*. Another footman took our cloaks from us at the top of the staircase, and we stepped into the great central hall.

It was clear that Isabella Venier was determined that nobody would ever be able to deny the suitability of the adjective "brilliant" for her *salotto*. The central chandelier glittered with countless bright flames, and brackets with extra candles studded the walls on both sides. One's first instinct was to shield one's eyes.

The noblewoman herself approached us in all her own glittering glory. She was wearing a silver gown that shimmered with reflected light from the candles; her hair seemed to be of spun gold, and gleaming pearls adorned her ears. There were a number of other people in the room, but they were merely vague shadows for the moment.

I think I let out a gasp, which evidently pleased her. She turned to Madricardo, and after they had exchanged formal greetings she said, "And will you introduce your intriguing companion?"

"Signora," he said, "this is Signor Alvise Marangon, who is here as a lover of Homer."

She turned to me and smiled. It was, unsurprisingly, a dazzling smile; it was as if an extra chandelier had suddenly dropped from the ceiling, fully ablaze. Her eyes, I noticed, were of an Aegean blue. She must have been in her mid-thirties, but her vivacity of expression was that of a young girl. "Signor Marangon, all lovers of Greek literature are welcome in this circle. Even more welcome when as young and full of enthusiasm as you clearly are." Her voice was unexpectedly low and breathy. She spoke in Tuscan Italian, although her accent was clearly Venetian.

I bowed and said, "Excellency, I don't know how young you have guessed me to be, but I hope at least to show that I merit your observation on my enthusiasm."

"Elegantly put," she remarked. "And I will now look forward to Homeric similes in your longer discourses."

"Thank you, signora," I said. "That is enough to daunt me, like a young lamb at the sight of an approaching pack of ravening wolves." Now I was just showing off, but she seemed to like it.

She tapped my shoulder with her pearl-embroidered fan and said, flashing another brilliant smile, "I can see you have already made a fair assessment of the present company. Let me introduce you to some of the pack." She made a swirling about-turn, which seemed to send shimmering sparks from all points of her dress, and indicated the company with a sweeping wave of her fan.

I now took in the other people present. They were an extremely diverse crowd, scattered around the long room in small clusters. There were probably about thirty in all. I was a little (but not very) surprised to notice that our hostess was the only woman. My first glance suggested that I had done well to put on my best clothes, since Spartan simplicity of attire did not appear to be the rule here. Everywhere lace ruffles and frills frothed forth from tightly tailored jackets, and powdered wigs took on an extra candour under the chandeliers. However, a second glance showed me that there was at least one cluster of people in plainer clothes, like pewter dishes among fine porcelain. There was even the occasional man wearing his own hair, like myself.

I recognised a few noblemen and one or two other faces, familiar to me from the Liston. They had all turned to gaze at Madricardo and myself when we entered, but we clearly had not held their interest, and they had mostly returned to their various conversations. Madricardo said a few mumbled words of valediction to me and moved towards a group of older men by the opposite wall, who opened up their cluster to absorb him. His mission had been accomplished, and I must now fend for myself.

Noblewoman Isabella Venier remained by my side, however, conducting me towards a group of young men standing by the window over the canal. I recognised one of them as Andrea Sanudo, a youthful nobleman with a reputation for rakish behaviour; he gazed at me with his eyebrows just slightly raised, as if challenging me to merit his curiosity. The other three seemed to be waiting for a cue from him before deciding how to react towards me.

Isabella Venier addressed them: "Signori, this is Alvise Marangon, who is going to address us in Homeric fashion all evening."

"Marangon," said Sanudo, repeating my surname with a kind of lazy relish.

"Marangon!" repeated a youth with a round face, capped by an over-elaborate wig. He let out a single high-pitched laugh.

I bowed. "At your service," I said.

"Very useful if we need our chairs repaired," said Sanudo with a slight yawn.

"Chairs repaired!" repeated the round-faced one. It seemed he favoured Madricardo's form of conversation.

"Now, now," said Isabella Venier. "We are not here to judge people on their names." She introduced the four young men to me, all of whom turned out to be scions of noble families: Andrea Sanudo, Giulio Tron (the round-faced youth), and two brothers, Marco Bon (a long-faced fellow with apparently little to say), and Federico Bon (a plumper and just slightly more loquacious version of his brother). Then she turned to me. "Perhaps you could tell us a little more about yourself, in Homeric fashion or not, as you wish." This time her smile was one of encouragement, particularly welcome after Sanudo's air of languid boredom. She took a seat on the divan next to Sanudo and waved her fan in mock command. "Please, Signor Marangon, tell us how you came to be interested in Homer."

"Perhaps I should first say that I cannot read Homer in the original Greek," I said.

Sanudo let out an audible sigh. Isabella Venier immediately

spoke up. "That is a pity for you, Signor Alvise. However, you are certainly not alone in that in this company."

Federico Bon said, "I can just about make out the letters. Not a great achievement after years spent supposedly reading the stuff at the university. Hoping to improve on that by coming here."

"Myself, I can't even read the letters!" said Giulio Tron with a squeaking laugh.

Isabella Venier continued, "We are all drawn together by our love of things Greek, but we have different relations to the Greek world. There are those like myself who grew up on a Greek island and speak the language as well as I do Tuscan Italian and Venetian. And there are those, like my husband Marco Querini" – she made the vaguest of gestures skywards, which I presumed did not mean that he had left this world for a higher realm but that he was otherwise engaged this evening – "and many others here, whose ties to the lands of the Eastern Roman Empire go back centuries, even though they themselves have never lived in those lands; such people preserve historical and familial memories even if they do not have mastery of the language."

"The language is not the point," said Sanudo. "It is the ties that count." And he stared at me, as if challenging me to deny this.

"Certainly I have no family ties with Greece, Excellency," I said, taking care to give him the respect due to his rank. There was little point in arousing resentment here.

"I have no doubt of that," he said.

"It is a cultural bond I feel," I said.

"Cultural bond," he said, slowly and deliberately. And immediately Giulio Tron took up the two words with his high-pitched giggle: "Cultural bond!"

"And what is this 'cultural bond' between you and Greece?" Sanudo said.

"A literary one," I said, "due to my own rather eccentric education."

"Tell us more," said Isabella Venier. "I'm always intrigued by eccentricity."

"So long as eccentric is not a mere euphemism for meagre," said Sanudo.

Giulio Tron squeaked a repetition of the last word of this sentence, possibly the only polysyllabic one he had understood, and the two Bon brothers indulged in sardonic smiles as well.

"Signor Andrea," said Isabella Venier, "that is entirely uncalled for. This is my *salotto*, and all my guests are to be treated with courtesy."

"It was a generalisation," said Sanudo. "I did not say it applied to Signor Marangon." He spoke my surname with careful deliberation.

She rapped her fan against his elbow, but in an archly playful fashion. She seemed determined to keep the tone light. She then turned to me. "Signor Alvise, forgive my friend. His devotion to the lands lost to the Ottomans sometimes makes him forget his manners."

I bowed, but took care to direct my bow to her and not to Sanudo. "I have not had the benefit of a university education," I said.

"Really?" said Sanudo, in evident mock surprise.

"And I grew up in England, with a number of different tutors."

"In England?" said Isabella Venier. "This is intriguing. But your accent is pure Venetian."

"My mother was pure Venetian," I said. "An actress who found fortune in England."

"An actress," repeated Sanudo. His habit of repetition was entirely different from that of Madricardo, or from that of his round-faced friend. He managed to make the words he repeated carry completely different meanings. Giulio Tron clearly caught the new meaning at once and squeaked the word with salacious delight.

"An actress," I repeated, firmly and icily.

"How very intriguing," said Isabella Venier. "And have you inherited her theatrical skills?"

"I may have done," I said. "But perhaps you will be better equipped to judge later on this evening."

"So what are you proposing to do?" she said.

"Yes," said Sanudo, "are you going to give us a full performance of a Greek tragedy?"

"I didn't come with the intention of performing but of participating in a cultural discussion. But if performance is required, I won't hold back."

"And what will you perform?" said Isabella Venier.

"Well, I came with the idea that I might talk, if required, on how Homer has been translated into English. If necessary I can give you some lines from the best translation." I pulled my volume of Pope from my pocket by way of demonstration.

"Lines that no one but you will understand," said Sanudo, as I replaced the book.

Suddenly his friend Federico Bon spoke up. "I say," he said. "I've seen you."

"Indeed?" I said.

"Yes, you were with an English visitor in the Piazza. You're a – you're a—"

"I'm a *cicerone*," I said with a bow.

"Good God," said Sanudo. He gazed at me with sudden added disgust.

Isabella Venier spoke up: "How very resourceful of you. And do you always act as *cicerone* to English visitors?"

"That is certainly my speciality," I said.

"Well, I suppose they're the ones with the money," said Federico Bon. He seemed a little more thoughtful than his companions.

"There are certainly some wealthy English visitors," I said.

"And I expect you take them to all the best *casini*," went on Federico Bon. "You can probably get a good cut like that."

"I confine myself to the places of cultural and historic interest," I said. "My clients don't seem to need any guidance with regard to gambling and other entertainments." I sounded insufferable even to myself.

Sanudo let out a sardonic laugh. "Cultural and historic interest, I'm sure. I've never seen a milord who wasn't drunk – unless he was whoring." I detected an added bitterness to his tone and wondered if he had any particular reason for this animosity against the English aristocracy.

"Signor Andrea," said Isabella Venier, "perhaps it depends on where you have been observing them."

I wished I had come out with that. Of course, if I had done so he would not have reacted quite so mildly. He merely gave her a forced half-smile with the faintest indication of irritation in his eyes. Tron let out a high-pitched laugh, and Sanudo's eyes flashed on him with full fury, causing Tron to break off with a nervous squeak.

"I think perhaps I should introduce you to some more of our guests," said Isabella Venier, getting to her feet, "before we begin our general meeting. You will be interested to encounter our Greek thinker, I'm sure."

"Most interested," I said, giving a bow to the four young men, who acknowledged it with degrees of courtesy ranging from the formally correct (the two Bon brothers) to the blatantly contemptuous (Sanudo) by way of the stridulously flustered (Tron).

Isabella Venier led me across the room. On the way she paused to give instructions to one of the servants, and while she was talking to him Madricardo came up to me and spoke in a low voice. "I thought I had better just say a word of warning, of warning."

"What about?"

"Do be careful not to antagonise Sanudo, Sanudo, you know, don't antagonise him."

I thought of saying that it was too late but instead asked, "Why do you say that?"

"He's Noblewoman Venier's *cicisbeo*, her *cicisbeo*."

"Ah," I said. It was certainly useful to know that Sanudo filled the role of semi-official gallant and possibly her lover.

At that moment Isabella Venier returned to my side and led me towards the group of people I had noted earlier because of their plainer attire. This group too had its clear leader – or, at least, its clear focal point. This was a man in his late thirties, who seemed to have chosen his clothes and hairstyle in deliberate opposition to those of his hostess; apart from a loose off-white shirt, everything about him was dark, from his gleaming black shoes to his glossy black hair, left loose and flowing around his dark-complexioned face. His dark eyes gazed with a faint glimmer of curiosity at me as Isabella and I approached. The other people around stepped aside, clearly aware that they were not the point of attraction here. They included, I now noticed, a bearded priest in the garb of the Orthodox Church and two other young men whom I also guessed to be of Greek extraction.

"Signor Komnenos, this is Signor Alvise Marangon," said Isabella Venier with her dazzling smile, apparently impervious to the gloom emanating from the man.

And then came the transformation. Suddenly he too smiled, a flash of white teeth, as if determined to match his hostess's display of brilliance. We both bowed.

"Signor Alvise is a *cicerone* for English visitors," she went on.

"The newest barbarian invaders," he said with just a trace of a foreign accent. It was an attractive voice, and I could imagine how this man had charmed the company.

"They come here in order to be civilised," I said. "It would be cruel to deny them the possibility."

"I'm not sure that everyone is capable of being civilised. Nor that this is the best place to do it." He said this casually, with only the faintest hint of a smile, and everyone was clearly delighted by the insult to their city. A grizzled man in a shabby grey jacket nodded his head and beamed; a couple of scholarly-looking men, with old-fashioned long wigs, looked at each other with expressions of satisfied complacency, as if glad that they had not wasted their evening. The priest nodded with fierce conviction.

I said, "You don't see Venice as the heir to Constantinople, then?"

"Venice is the spoiler and predator of my city." The same light tone, as if he had made a remark about the foggy weather.

Again the heads all around nodded in agreement, the priest's head moving with twice the vigour of everyone else's.

I persisted. "But can't we consider it fortunate that something of your city's greatness has been preserved here? Not all has been lost to the Ottomans?"

The mention of the Ottomans seemed to bring everyone together in a general murmur of opprobrium, but it was not clear that my overall sentiment had been approved. They all seemed to be waiting for Komnenos to supply their lead.

"The Ottomans are not are our only oppressors," he said after quite a long pause. It was something of an anticlimax, I thought, but those around us did not seem disappointed. Bewigged heads bobbed up and down in sage but lively agreement; I wondered how many of them knew exactly what they were agreeing about.

"Ah," I said, "I suppose not." I didn't point out that he had not answered my question. Here too I imagined there was probably no advantage in assuming an antagonistic stance. I would have liked to ask him about Padoan, but not in front of all these people.

"I speak for my fellow Greeks," he said, waving a hand at the two young men I had guessed to be compatriots and the Greek priest. All three nodded, although I was not sure they fully understood what he was saying. He introduced them to me; the priest was Father Giorgos, currently staying at the Greek church, and the two young men were Dimitris and Alexis (I never caught their surnames), who were working as mosaic-restorers at Saint Mark's. This last piece of information allowed me to make some vague remark about the fruitful interchange of artistic skills between the former Eastern Roman Empire and Venice, at which the young men nodded (uncomprehendingly, I think), while Komnenos said, "Very fruitful: you steal our works and when they're broken we come and repair them for you."

Noblewoman Venier, the practised hostess, broke in. "I think it might be time for us all to move into the next room where wine and biscuits will be served."

I was glad I had not come with an empty stomach. As I was close to the door she was indicating I passed through it to the next room in time to see a man with grey hair look up in alarm from a desk in the far corner; he had been gazing at a small bronze statue in an absorbed fashion. He instantly realised that his privacy was about to be disturbed. He picked the statue up protectively and scuttled towards the door at the opposite end of the room, like a startled animal. The spaniel that loped along beside him seemed less agitated.

I heard my hostess heave a sigh. When I glanced at her, she gave me a wry smile and said softly, "My husband, poor man. I had warned him there would be company."

I was rather surprised that she should speak to me so familiarly of her husband, whose noble rank was as certain as her own, and she flashed another smile at me. "You seem as startled as my poor husband. Please understand that there are no distinctions between any here on these occasions."

I was about to ask her if she had informed Sanudo of this, but fortunately held back for at that moment he came up to us and ostentatiously moved between me and her. I stepped back compliantly; the role of *cicisbeo* was his, after all. However, she gave him a reproachful tap on the shoulder with her fan and said, "I will accompany Signor Alvise this evening. It is his first time here."

"I think he can find his own way to a chair," he said.

"That is not the point, Signor Andrea," she said. "I wish to make him feel at home."

He stared hard at her and then at me. For one moment he seemed tempted to make a scene and he actually jostled against me; then, as if realising how undignified such behaviour made him look, he moved away to re-join his friends.

"Thank you," I said.

"It is my pleasure," she replied.

The whole company had now entered this smaller room, on three sides of which, framed in gilt wood against red velvet, hung life-size portraits of prominent members of the Querini family, in black and scarlet robes, with here a bright cardinal's hat, there a gleaming flash of symbolic armour, and everywhere thick creamy wigs. Chairs were placed against the walls underneath the portraits, and one hesitated to move them, since the painted decorations around their curved backs subtly matched the ones that ran along the base of each picture-frame.

People seemed to know where they were going to sit, and I noticed that the already formed clusters tended to remain consistently close. Isabella Venier took her seat in the middle of the left-hand wall, beneath a canvas of a lip-curling, scarlet-clad procurator, and with an imperious wave of her fan bade me sit next to her. Andrea Sanudo and his three friends deliberately sat opposite us, from where Sanudo stared at me, apparently trying to mimic the facial expression of the painted face above my right shoulder.

For a while we simply sat there, while three servants brought round glasses of Cypriot wine and *buranelli* biscuits. The conversations begun in the other room continued in a low buzz until the servants had retired, and then they gradually petered out, and faces turned expectantly towards Isabella Venier.

"Friends of Greece," she began, "friends of the Eastern Roman Empire, thank you all for joining me here once again." Her voice, although audible to all, seemed to be as low and intimate as ever, so that I had the impression (and I suspect I was not the only one) that she was speaking directly and personally to me alone. "As on previous occasions we will divide our encounter into two separate parts; in the first part we will discuss what practical moves can be made towards a recovery of those territories lost to the Turks."

This took me by surprise. Was this motley group of languid aristocrats, bored scholars and aggrieved Greeks planning to reopen hostilities with the Ottoman Empire, thirty years after the Peace of Passarowitz?

I looked around and saw no one raising any objection or even a single eyebrow. Komnenos had a faint smile on his lips, as if the idea of Venice's undertaking any bellicose activity was self-evidently absurd (and I could not disagree with him), while the others all nodded thoughtfully.

Isabella Venier went on, "And then we will continue with our usual cultural activities: some poetry from our friend Kostantinos Komnenos . . ." – he gave a leisurely nod, as if to say that he might be so gracious as to bestow upon us a few lines – "and perhaps a word or two from our newest arrival, Signor Alvise Marangon, a lover of Homer."

"And a *cicerone*," said Andrea Sanudo, arousing a murmur of puzzled curiosity; this seemed to disappoint Sanudo, who had perhaps been hoping for a roar of derision.

I lifted one hand, to identify myself, but did not speak.

Isabella Venier talked on. She certainly knew how to hold the attention of the audience; she talked of her own love for the island on which she had grown up, the role Kythira (or Cerigo, as the Venetians called it) had played in the expanding Venetian empire. She acknowledged how fortunate she had been to divide her time between the mother city and an island that had never come under Turkish dominion. She spoke of the sorrow she knew so many of the others must have experienced, either directly in having been expelled from their families' lands (and here she obtained the assent of some older people, who I later learned had been expelled from the island of Tinos and from the Morea in 1715), or from having grown up knowing the tears of nostalgic grandparents or the sad tales passed down from more distant ancestors, driven from the isles of the Cyclades or from Crete or from Cyprus (and this aroused widespread nodding and a general murmur of recognition). Sanudo himself was one of the most vigorous assenters. I learned later that the Sanudo family had established themselves, with the acquiescence of the Venetian Republic, as dukes of Naxos in the thirteenth century and had held semi-piratical sway over the Cyclades for centuries, until being driven out by the Ottomans in the sixteenth century.

I glanced at Komnenos. He was listening to this recital with the same expression of mild amusement, as if watching a room of children attempting a mathematical problem too difficult for them. I was a little puzzled by the high regard given to this man, who seemed to have so little sympathy with the troubles of the company he was in. However, when Isabella Venier stopped speaking and a general discussion was launched, I began to get an inkling of why Komnenos was so readily accepted. For what followed was not, as our hostess's opening remarks had half led me to expect, a series of proposals for military action against the Turks, but instead a litany of protests against the city's inaction, inertia and indifference. It all became gradually clear to me. These people had come here to grumble, and the target of their grumbling was the Venetian state. And so this Greek castigator of Venetian greed and tyranny was far from out of place. The fact that what they were mourning for was a product of an equal greed and tyranny did not seem to strike them as a contradiction. He, in his own charming way, was grumbling and so were they; that was enough for them. And he did it in a delightful foreign accent as well.

So on they grumbled. One by one they lifted their hands and recounted a story of recent humiliation or described their ever-increasing woes. Nobody cared about them. Nobody listened to their stories of former glories. Nobody was interested in their bereft state, least of all the city's authorities. Certainly nobody had ever compensated them for their losses.

In all their complaints the speakers were careful not to name any specific authority; not a word was said against the Doge, or the Inquisitors, or the Ten. It was an unspecific plural "they" that was held responsible for all their grievances. If I had been there as an agent of the Inquisitors (and it was all too likely that someone in the company was), I would not have been able to make any definite accusations of treasonous talk.

It was mostly the older people who spoke. Sanudo and his cronies listened and nodded along with the others but were clearly not going to contribute any specific complaints themselves. I wondered why they were here; perhaps it was Sanudo's tie to Isabella Venier that brought him here, and his friends felt obliged to tag along with him. Sanudo caught me looking at him at one point, and his expression changed to one of sudden defiance, which caught me off guard. I looked away with a touch of embarrassment, just as Isabella Venier announced the start of the second half of the evening's "entertainment" (she used the French word *divertissement*, to the disapproval of one or two).

Komnenos had already risen to his feet; he pushed his thick black hair back in a theatrical gesture and then stood there, his hands on his hips, almost as if he were a defiant brawler in a tavern affray. Perhaps that was how he saw himself and us.

Isabella Venier gave a few introductory remarks and then Komnenos began. He made no announcement of what he was about to recite but simply began speaking, in a low but resonant voice. It was clearly a long poem and it was all in Greek.

I caught a number of refrains and thought that Madricardo would be happy, maybe. In fact, I glanced across at him and saw he had fallen blissfully asleep.

The refrain was repeated in a louder voice each time and eventually Komnenos was almost shouting. Madricardo gave a nervous jolt and started awake. It was difficult to tell how many people understood what they were hearing. It was clear that Isabella Venier herself did; her lips moved in time with the refrain. At a certain point Komnenos's eyes fell on her, and he gave the faintest sardonic smile as he saw her lips moving. I glanced across at Sanudo. He too was watching both Isabella and Komnenos, and his expression was grim. Then he caught me watching him, and his grimness momentarily became fury; he got a grip on himself and I noticed, with some surprise, that the next time he looked at me his expression was one of smug pleasure.

That unsettled me, and I fell back to looking at Komnenos. Whatever drama he had been recounting was clearly winding towards its conclusion; I had no idea whether this envisaged perpetual bliss for all concerned or a resolutory bloodbath. Komnenos's sardonic expression was difficult to read; however, whatever was happening was doing so noisily now. The final refrain was actually shouted, and then he sat down, mopping his brow and sweeping his hair back in one single flamboyant gesture.

We all applauded, Isabella Venier most of all. She was clearly very moved. She began to turn to me. I put my hand to my pocket to bring out my volume of Pope – and felt a sudden jolt of panic. The pocket was empty.

II

It only took me an instant to understand what had happened. My eyes darted straight to Sanudo. I remembered that awkward moment of jostling as we entered the room, which had seemed partly clumsiness and partly a wish to offend me. It had actually had a strictly practical purpose. I now understood that expression of smug anticipatory pleasure I had seen on his face a few minutes earlier. He was gazing at me with a smirk of sheer triumph; he was not even bothering to disguise it.

I knew that the last thing I must do was get flustered. I must not be reduced to a panicky display of desperate rummaging through my other pockets or a floundering search around my chair. And obviously I must not level an accusation of an act of petty pilfering against a nobleman. That was probably what he was longing for me to do.

I put my hand down from my pocket as calmly as possible. So, I would not have the book to read from or to consult. That, I told myself firmly, was not a tragedy. I had spent the few hours before my encounter with Madricardo getting by heart the opening lines of Pope's translation; I knew just how much more effective it was to recite poetry by heart than to read it from a book. I had always learned verse with relative ease; it was a skill I had picked up in my childhood days playing about backstage in various theatres around England. And I had noticed that a few lines dropped casually into conversation when showing clients around the city (passages from *The Merchant of Venice* or from Ben Jonson's *Volpone*, for example) never failed to impress, particularly if the clients did not know a line of verse themselves. It had not been difficult to learn the opening pages of Pope's *Iliad*; the lines, with their elegantly clicking couplets, were designed for easy memorability.

I gazed back at Sanudo with what I hoped was an expression of calm indifference. I could see that it unsettled him.

Now I listened to what Isabella Venier was saying: ". . . a young man who has come to join us and to share his love of Homer, a love acquired not in the academies of Italy but in a distant northern land, a land possibly unknown to Homer himself".

I got to my feet and gave a slight bow. I thanked my hostess and said a few words to explain who Alexander Pope was and how his translation was generally considered to be the finest of the day. I said that I realised that most people present would not be able to follow the words, but I suggested that they should listen out for the rhymes; Pope was a supremely melodious poet, and he had attempted to find an equivalent for Homer's unique music in the very different but equally harmonious music of the English language.

I gave a quick glance at Sanudo and saw him staring at me with a mixture of puzzlement and annoyance. Then I looked away and began to recite, taking great care not to look at him again. I did not want to be distracted. I wanted simply to yield to my love for the verse. I took care not to become too dramatic, but I also made sure that I laid suitable stress on the rhymes, so that those who knew no English would catch them easily. I did not exaggerate the different voices of Agamemnon, Chryses and Achilles, but I did attempt to distinguish them. I had the impression that one or two people who knew *The Iliad* well were managing to follow the story, even if they did not understand the words.

I could not deny to myself that I also wanted to impress Isabella Venier. When I came to the final lines of the passage that I had by heart, the closing words of Achilles' first speech ("So Heav'n aton'd shall dying Greece restore, / And Phoebus dart his burning Shafts no more"), I stopped short, stood in silence staring at the ceiling for five seconds and then bowed my head (I had borrowed this histrionic trick from the last performance I had seen of *Henry V*). As applause broke out I risked a glance at our hostess. She was clapping with great energy and brightening the room with another radiant smile. An ideal audience.

When the applause had died down, I said, "Thank you. I had brought a copy of Mr Pope's translation, but I appear to have mislaid it. If anyone sees it lying around I would be very grateful to have it returned to me."

People began to look around themselves in a desultory fashion. Sanudo gazed at me with an expression of utter scorn. His friends, who did not appear to be in on his little prank, joined in the pointless search. Isabella Venier now stood up and thanked me. "I had no idea English could be so musical," she said.

"I think all languages have that capacity," I said, "when played on by a skilled master, such as Alexander Pope."

"So if the language is the instrument and the poet the musician, I'm not sure what role you are supposed to have played, but you did it superbly."

"Thank you," I said. It was an elaborate compliment, in what I had come to see was the rather formal style of this *salotto*, but I couldn't help feeling pleased.

Isabella Venier brought the evening to a close with a few more suitably chosen pleasantries, and people began to get to their feet. Madricardo reawoke with another start (I think he had missed my entire performance). Servants weaved in and out, removing glasses and bottles. We were gradually ushered towards the *portego* where we had first assembled. Just as I was about to step out – acknowledging compliments to left and right with gracious bows – Isabella Venier tapped my arm with her fan.

"Sior Marangon," she said. She now spoke in Venetian, presumably to indicate a rupture with the more formal part of the evening.

"Siora," I said.

"Please stay in here."

"If you say so," I said, a little puzzled.

I could see Sanudo bearing down on her. She turned to him with a smile, but it struck me as being a less radiant one than usual, as if she had extinguished a few candles on the chandelier. "Sior Andrea," she said, "you may leave with your friends." She was speaking in Venetian again.

"But – but –" He was clearly flustered. I could see Tron behind him, with a vacant smile on his round face, and the two Bon brothers remaining at a cautious distance. Clearly they knew better than to interfere between their companion and his lady.

"I don't require your services this evening," she said lightly. "Now don't be a bore. Run along with your friends and have a pleasant evening on the town. I'm sure you all have your masks with you."

"Yes, but—"

"Well, go out to the theatre or to the *ridotto*. I'm asking Sior Marangon to stay back for a while. He's lost his copy of *The Iliad*, and the least I can do is help him search for it."

He stared at her, clearly infuriated but unable to see a way out that would not be personally humiliating.

"I'm sure it won't take you long to look," he said at last, through clenched teeth.

"Who can tell?" she said. "Now please, do run along. If there's one thing I can't bear it's people who take ages to make their farewells." She gestured towards the main doorway out of the *portego*. I couldn't see from where I was, but I could imagine the bustling crowd of people there, ruffling through the cloaks that the servants would be holding, looking for their hostess in order to pay final elaborate compliments to her, and generally not yet leaving.

I carefully looked away from Isabella and Sanudo and pretended a great interest in the nearest portrait. Eventually I heard their voices fade into the general buzz as they moved across the *portego*.

So now I was alone. What should I do? Break open the nearest desk and rummage for papers revealing the identities of the Four Horsemen? Unhinge the portraits to find secret crannies containing hidden assassins?

Or just stand there looking and feeling bewildered?

The last, of course.

The door at the far end of the room opened and in walked the grey-haired man I had seen scuttle out in such an undignified fashion earlier. The spaniel was loping by his side again. He stared at me in blank dismay.

"I'm so sorry, Excellency," I said. "Noblewoman Venier told me to wait here."

"I thought you'd all gone by now," he said in a plaintive tone.

"Yes, everyone is leaving," I said. "But I was asked—"

"Well, never mind, never mind. I'll get on with my things over here." He made towards the desk I had seen him sitting at earlier. He seemed determined simply to ignore me, which was fine by me. He was clearly not dressed for company, being wigless and wearing a rather shabby old jacket, in marked contrast with the splendidly berobed figures of his ancestors on the walls all around us.

I returned to gazing at the nearest portrait, that of a Querini admiral in a scarlet coat, gold cloak and silver breastplate. The situation reminded me of my morning spent in the library at Sant'Elena, with the monk pointedly taking no notice of me while I scanned the bookshelves. I gave a glance back at Nobleman Querini. He was sitting at the table and staring at me with a sulky expression, quite unlike the defiant gaze of his ancestor in the painting. In his hands he was holding another little bronze statue; it looked like a miniature figure of Hercules with a club. The dog was sitting by his side, also gazing at me with big reproachful eyes.

"I'm really very sorry, Excellency, but as I said . . ."

"It doesn't matter, it really doesn't matter, but why she has to have these things here . . ." His voice faded into incomprehensible mumbling.

At that moment the same door opened and a small elderly woman appeared. "Ah, there you are." She had an imperious voice which more than compensated for her size. She was dressed in far more formal clothes than Querini. I realised she was talking to him, rather than to me. She was clearly a little short-sighted and had not even noticed me.

"Yes, Mother," he said. "Where else would I be?" His voice sounded resigned.

"Well, I don't know. With your wife taking over the palace like this. You might have been driven into the attic. What I want to know is why are we renting that casino for her over by Sant'Angelo?

You must put your foot down, Marco. You can't just lock yourself up with your sculptures and your paintings."

"Mother . . ." he tried again.

"This is the Querini family palace. We have a certain position to keep up. If she wants to consort with orientals of all sorts, with heretical priests and actors and singers, then you must tell her that she can do so in the privacy of the casino."

"Mother . . ."

"Don't keep bleating 'Mother' like that. Are you going to tell her or are you going to leave it to me?"

"Mother, we are not alone in here."

"Ah, has she come back? Well, I'm not afraid to speak my mind, even if you are." She peered around the room and eventually spotted me. "Ah. You, what are you doing here?"

"I'm very sorry, signora, I was asked to wait here by Her Excellency Signora Isabella . . ."

"Oh, were you indeed? And why?"

"That I'm afraid I can't answer, signora," I said, as respectfully as possible. "However, I'm sure she will be joining us in a moment. Once she has taken leave of the rest of the company."

"So you were with them, were you?"

"Yes, signora. It was my first evening."

"First time in a nobleman's palace as well, I'll be bound."

"Mother," said Querini, in feeble protest. "The gentleman is a guest here. The least we can do is treat him with respect."

I bowed. "Thank you, Excellency. I'm sorry if my presence is causing any inconvenience."

"You don't need to apologise to him," said the old lady. "Nothing inconveniences him, so long as he can find a corner where he can pore over his old statues –" She suddenly realised this was inappropriate and turned back to her son. "Are you going to speak to her?"

"Mother," he said. He sounded exasperated, probably because he was still embarrassed by my presence; however, the word came out in a petulant whine, like that of a child who has been told he must put away his toys. He was, I suppose, in his early fifties.

"It's time you took your responsibilities more seriously. You are the head of the household. You can't spend all your time with your dusty old antiquities." She had clearly decided that the best way to deal with an embarrassing problem, like my presence, was just to ignore it. I imagined Querini spent quite a lot of time uttering that petulant "Mother".

"Ah," said the far more attractive voice of Isabella Venier from the other doorway. "I see you have met each other."

"We have not been introduced," said Signora Querini with cold dignity. "The gentleman had just been left here, like an abandoned . . ." She clearly didn't know how to finish this sentence in any way that wasn't excessively offensive, and so just came to a sudden halt. She managed to make even that sound decisive rather than awkward.

"I just asked Signor Marangon to wait while I bade farewell to the other guests. It was a question of a minute or two." She sounded quite calm.

"So they have all gone, then," said Signora Querini. "Including that – that –" She made a dismissive gesture with one hand.

"If you are referring to Nobleman Sanudo, he too has left."

I could see that the role that Sanudo played as *cicisbeo* was not to everyone's taste. In some cases a *cavalier servente* became an accepted member of the family; not here, it seemed. However, glancing at Querini I had the impression that he probably had no problems with having Sanudo around the house; it presumably made it all the easier for him to concentrate on his dusty antiquities.

"And this gentleman?" said Signora Querini.

"This is Signor Alvise Marangon, who recites Homer in English most delightfully."

"Does he?" she said coldly. It was clearly not something she had ever felt the need for.

"Yes. But sadly he lost his book. I said he could stay and look for it."

"I'm sure we can ask the servants to do that," said Signora Querini.

"Yes, we can. However, they are now busy with other things. But, signora, there is no need for us to trouble you with this search.

If it is anywhere, it is in the *portego*. We will look there and leave you here to talk to my husband."

Her husband did not appear to think this a happy prospect. "I'll help you, my dear," he said with pathetic eagerness.

"I don't think it's necessary. I'm sure your mother has things she wants to talk to you about." There was no defiance or hardness in her tone. She was quite calm and reasonable – which clearly infuriated her mother-in-law.

"And when might we hope to have the use of the *portego* back?" Signora Querini's voice trembled just a little with suppressed anger.

"I'm sure it will only take us a minute or two, and then you can use it for whatever you wish. For your habitual evening stroll, perhaps." This was said with perfect gravity, but I guessed that the old lady was not in fact accustomed to perambulate in the *portego*, which was why she seemed unable to reply. "Come, Signor Marangon."

I made a quick and only slightly embarrassed bow towards mother and son and followed the silvery gleam of Isabella Venier's retiring figure.

The *portego* was no longer so brilliantly lit. A servant was standing on a stepladder extinguishing all the candles in the central chandelier. Two other servants were rearranging the furniture against the walls. Isabella went straight towards the end of the room, where the tall windows overlooked the canal and the little *campiello*. Her dress, still shimmering with the light from the remaining candles, made her a ghostly figure against the blackness of the windows.

"Excellency," I said, "I really don't think it's necessary to look for this book."

"No, of course it isn't," she said at once.

"You know what happened?"

"I can guess. Andrea Sanudo thought it might be amusing to see how you would cope without it."

"Yes. At least I'm fairly sure that's what happened. Of course, I couldn't accuse him."

"Of course not. What an absurd idea. You coped very well. In fact, you coped brilliantly."

"Thank you, signora."

"I think I'd like to hear some more Homer in English."

"Now?" I said, slightly taken aback.

"No, of course not now." She always replied without hesitation and she didn't seem to worry if her remarks might seem curt.

"So when?"

"Tomorrow evening. But not here. As you may have noticed, not everyone is over-delighted to have visitors here. We can meet at my casino."

"Ah, yes. I heard your mother-in-law mention it," I said.

"No doubt she was asking why I didn't use it for this evening's meeting."

"Well, yes, she did say something along those lines."

"And undoubtedly my lion of a husband sprang to my defence."

"Well . . ."

She laughed; unsurprisingly, it was a silvery sound. "Don't worry, Signor Marangon. I know my husband. He has many endearing qualities, but the ability to stand up to his mother is not one of them. He has spent his life among books and antiquities and would probably have been happier as a monk."

"A monk?"

"Well, somewhere where he could have spent his time in a library. I had thought that a literary *salotto* might be to his taste, but it seems he prefers to converse with the dead through their books rather than with living people who are interested in the books."

"I see," I said. "So he is a scholar." The Italian word was *studioso*.

She frowned. "I doubt one could say that exactly. I'm not sure he actually *studies* the books. He likes them as beautiful objects. Just as he likes ancient sculptures and images. Yes, he does like beauty."

"I can easily believe that," I said.

She looked at me quizzically. "Was that a compliment, Signor Marangon?"

I think I probably blushed. "Well, I, that is . . ."

"Please don't apologise for it," she said. "That *would* offend me. We are agreed then to meet tomorrow. At my casino. Nine o'clock would be suitable." She gave me instructions to reach it.

"Signora," I said, "do you think you will be able to retrieve my lost book?"

"Ah," she said. "Delicate point. I'll see what I can do."

"I could just ask Nobleman Sanudo for it directly myself," I said.

"That would be very foolish."

"I know he took it. He knows that I know he took it. And you know that he took it . . ."

"Yes, yes, all very clear and logical. But Andrea is not a man who acts on the basis of logic. He is driven by impulses. Sometimes very foolish impulses. But even when he has acted foolishly he never likes to admit a mistake. It would not be sensible for a man in your position to challenge him. And I think you know that."

I nodded. "Yes."

"You are clearly a good deal more sensible than Andrea."

I was struck by the way she casually used his first name when talking about him to me. "Then I will have to rely on your diplomatic skills, signora."

"Oh, I'll manage it. But it may take a day or two. I trust you can be patient."

"I'm a *cicerone*," I said. "I often spend whole days waiting for clients at Fusina."

"I, on the other hand, never like to be kept waiting. So I will expect you at the casino punctually at nine tomorrow."

"Of course, without the book I won't be able to recite very much Homer. I haven't learned the whole epic by heart."

"Then we will have to find other ways to pass the time, Signor Alvise." She said it very simply, her eyes resting on me for just a moment before darting towards the window.

I found my heart beating a little faster. "I see," I said. "At least, I think I do."

"I'm sure you do, Signor Alvise. You are not a fool, as I've already said."

"Until tomorrow then," I said.

"Oh, and do watch out for Andrea. He has a dreadful temper."

"I'll try to do so," I said. "May I ask . . ." My voice petered out.

"What?"

"It's nothing."

"If you were going to ask why I tolerate a person like Andrea then you were wise to stop."

I remained silent. She had, of course, guessed correctly. She was probably also right to have rebuked me.

She added nothing more. She gave me a formal bow, and I made my way to the door. This was the strangest lovers' assignation I had ever been involved in. But then my experience was fairly limited.

12

As I stepped out of the palace on to the little bridge I drew my cloak around me. The fog was thicker than ever, and I regretted my hatless state. I clearly should have listened to Siora Giovanna.

I could also have done with a *codega*. There was a little light from the open windows above me, but once I had taken a few paces towards Campo Santa Maria Formosa I was in total darkness. I wondered whether it was worth trying to summon a *codega* by the traditional method of clapping my hands and calling out. I tried it, but no welcome glow appeared from the gloom.

Well, I knew the way home. And once I got on to the narrow Ruga Giuffa, there was usually a little light from unshuttered windows.

Black shapes appeared out of the dark mist in front of me. Men in cloaks, with tricorn hats pulled well down over their heads. Their eyes must have been more accustomed to the dark than mine because they were walking unhesitatingly in my direction, while I faltered, putting my hands out in preventive fashion. "Good evening," I said.

They uttered not a word but just surrounded me. Four of them. Or at least four that I could see. There could have been a whole army lurking in the fog.

One of them had drawn a sword, and I found its blade touching my chest.

"What do you want?" I said.

"A quick lesson in manners," said the figure holding the sword. It was said in a whisper and the mask further muffled the words, but I had no doubt this was Sanudo.

I stood completely still. I didn't think he was going to run me through, but it was not worth provoking him. How many people had warned me against doing that so far?

"I'm always willing to learn," I said. I was glad my voice didn't shake; perhaps I'd picked up something from speaking in Achilles' voice.

We all stood completely still and silent for a few seconds. I wondered if Sanudo had not actually thought this little scene through. It would fit in with what Signora Isabella had said about his impulsiveness.

And then a voice came from behind the four dark figures. "Can I help? Do you need a light?" Even more welcome than the voice was the glow of hazy light that accompanied it.

The four figures swirled round, and the sword was removed from my chest. The light grew stronger, and as it did I realised that I recognised the voice. It was Komnenos. He now emerged from the fog, holding a lantern in his right hand. Dressed in black though he was, he struck me as a dazzling angel of salvation.

"Signor Komnenos," I said, "how kind. I would greatly appreciate it. Which way are you going?"

"I can go whichever way you need," he said. "I'm in no hurry. And these other gentlemen?"

The cloaked figures made non-committal noises.

Komnenos said, "A drawn sword? I'm sure it's not really necessary. This is not a dangerous city, you know."

Sanudo returned the sword to my chest and said, still in a whisper, "We can teach two people a lesson just as easily as one."

Komnenos said, "I expect so. But how about four against four?" He clapped his hands and two more figures emerged from the mist. They were his two young companions, Dimitris and Alexis, and they were both holding long knives. They came and stood beside Komnenos, their weapons held out challengingly. Their blades were not as long as the four men's swords, of course, but they looked as if they knew how to use them.

There was complete silence for a few seconds. Eventually Sanudo lowered his sword. Still keeping up his absurd attempt to disguise his voice, he said, "We have no intention of starting up a vulgar brawl with foreigners. Just remember, Sior *Cicerone*, that you have encountered the Four and may well do so again."

"I'm not likely to forget the encounter," I said, "although I still haven't understood its meaning."

Sanudo made no attempt to answer this. He put his sword back in his scabbard and then stood there for a second or two. I suspect he was trying to come up with a suitably menacing parting line. His three companions were obviously getting embarrassed and were preparing to depart, but they still waited for a sign from their leader. Eventually Sanudo turned round, making a clear effort at a dramatic cloak-swirling swivel, and stalked off in the direction of Saint Mark's. The other three followed, less showily but clearly with relief.

"Thank you so much, Signor Komnenos," I said at once.

"I usually carry my own lantern," he said, "and I had a feeling that you might need company. I saw that Sanudo and his friends did not leave the square and I suspected trouble, so I decided to wait round the corner with my companions."

"That was brave of you," I said.

He waved his free hand. "I don't think bravery comes into it. They are braggarts, not warriors."

"Yes, but they're four braggarts with four swords, and you're one poet and two mosaic-restorers with just two knives. Thank you." I bowed to the other two men as well, who returned the bow and sheathed their blades.

"It is my pleasure," said Komnenos. "I am actually going in the direction of the Greek church, as perhaps you have guessed."

"I've made no guesses," I said. "But that's my direction too. I live close to Sant'Antonin, so I'll gladly accompany you."

"My companions live near the Rialto, so we'll bid them goodbye."

We did so. Dimitris made an effort to say "*Arrivederci*" in tolerable Tuscan, while Alexis bade farewell in Greek. They set off in the direction of the Rialto while Komnenos and I started walking towards the bridge that led to the Ruga Giuffa.

"I was impressed by your recital," I said after a pause. "Although I'll confess I didn't understand a word."

"How convenient. We can pay each other exactly the same

compliment. But of course I knew what story you were telling, and I suspect the same was not true for you."

"No, you're right."

"I was reciting my version of a traditional kleftic ballad."

"A what?"

"Well, I suppose I would have to call it a ballad of a bandit. You may know that under the Ottomans many who do not wish to serve the Turks have taken to the mountains, where they live difficult but free lives. As klefts. Which literally means thieves, but bandits sounds more attractive. And they have developed their own songs, which recount their lives and their heroic deeds."

"And what are these deeds?"

"Oh, sometimes they're purely mythical. Legends that go back to Homer, but often overlaid with Christian themes. But the songs are very energetic and have become very popular."

"But you yourself are not exactly a bandit," I said. "I understand you served under the Ottomans."

He swung the lantern to gaze at me quizzically. "You know a good deal about me for someone who came to this *salotto* for the first time this evening."

"I was curious and I asked around before I came. You know, Venice is small . . ."

"I know there are a lot of spies in Venice."

I tried to react lightly to this. "People often say that. I think it's just that Venetians like gossip."

"So what is the gossip about me?"

"Someone told me you were a Phanariot."

He acknowledged this. "I have lived in Phanar. And I have had humble roles in government administration."

"As an interpreter, I was told."

"Your partners in gossip are very well informed. I have something of a gift for languages, as you may have noticed."

"Your Italian is very good." He spoke Tuscan Italian, not Venetian, but I had noticed earlier that he had no problems understanding both.

"Thank you. I should perhaps return the compliment on your English, but of course I have no means of judging that."

"Well, English is my first language," I said. "So if you like you can compliment me on my Italian and Venetian."

"Consider it done," he said.

"So you recite poems about bandits," I said.

"Songs composed by bandits but rearranged by me into more formal poetry for a more sophisticated audience. Yes, I can see the objection . . ."

"I've made no objection."

"No, but you are thinking it. Here I am, clearly a man from an educated background, who has worked for the Ottomans, pretending to be a wild rebel ready to cut their throats."

"Is that what was happening in your poem?"

"The refrain said '*Adelfia to maheri vastate kopteron / Nan' etimo na kopsi tyrannou ton lemon*', which is to say, 'Brothers, keep your knife sharp, so that it may be ready to cut the tyrant's throat.'"

"I see," I said. "And yet you approached Nobleman Sanudo who had a drawn sword with nothing but a lantern in your hands."

"So there is the contradiction," he said. "But while I sing the bandits' songs I do not claim to be one, merely to let people know what these people think. I bring the voice of those who dwell in the mountains to those who dwell in the city. And sometimes I improve the rhyme-scheme, since city-dwellers are particular in matters like that."

"Yes, I caught the rhymes."

"As I did your Mr Pope's. What wonderfully symmetrical experiences we have had. As perfectly balanced as his own couplets."

His tone was as light as ever, but I glanced at him. I wondered if he was referring to something beyond our aesthetic experiences of each other's poetry. I decided to wait before asking that, however. Instead I said, "I also heard about you from a man who had met you, I believe, at the monastery of Sant'Elena."

"Ah, the little man with the funny walk. Padoan. I remember him well. And I remember he died tragically. And you knew him?"

"Only slightly," I said. "He lives – or rather lived – very close to the gondolier I work with."

"And what did he have to say about me?"

"He was very impressed by you. As they all are, clearly."

We had reached the little square of San Severo. There was more light here from the windows of the Palazzo Zorzi, with its white façade overlooking the canal. Komnenos stood still for a while and nodded. "Yes, they are." He smiled. "I am the latest fashion, I believe. Perhaps next month they will want Armenians. Or Russians. But while I am in vogue I will continue to enjoy it."

"Paolo Padoan was obviously rather frightened by something that happened to him at the *salotto*," I said. It was probably time for a more direct approach.

"Yes, I thought perhaps he was."

"Oh really. What was it?"

"Did he not tell you that?"

"Not very clearly," I said. "He talked in a very confused way about – well, about a group he called the Four Horsemen."

"Ah." Once again I had caught his attention.

"Until a few minutes ago," I said, "I had no real idea who they might be, but having heard Sanudo's parting line I wonder if I've discovered them."

"It seems possible," said Komnenos. "In fact, I'm sure he could tell you more about this."

"I'm just a little puzzled by the notion that Padoan was frightened to death of Sanudo," I said.

"When you say 'to death', do I understand you are speaking literally? I understood he fell off his roof."

"No, not literally. But there are some puzzling elements about his death."

"Are there?"

"Well, let's say some people have even questioned whether it was an accident. But why do you think Sanudo might be able to tell me more? Excuse my asking you, but it's not a conversation I can easily imagine having with him."

"No, I can see that. Let's just say that Sanudo and his friends seem to have decided to play with Padoan."

"To play with him?"

"Signor Padoan was clearly out of his depth in circles like these. Oh, he had the classical learning, and he knew far more about the history of Constantinople than anyone else there. He got quite excited when he met me at Sant'Elena and learned my surname, but I had to disappoint him by telling him I was not a direct descendant from the Komnenos dynasty of emperors. I think quite a number of people at the *salotto* have never heard of the Komnenos emperors. So Padoan's awkwardness in fitting in had nothing to do with intellectual deficiencies. It was a social awkwardness. He was not used to society. Certainly not the society of a *salotto* run by a noblewoman."

"And Sanudo played on this awkwardness?"

"It was nothing crude. He didn't make fun of Padoan's shabby clothes or his table manners. After all, he had probably seen far worse from me."

"Because of course you're just a mountain bandit," I said drily.

He laughed. "All right, I'm performing again. But it's what they want from me, after all. In any case, Sanudo didn't openly jeer at Padoan. In fact he and his companions seemed to go out of their way to welcome him, to try to bring him out, encouraging him to speak up on obscure points of history – precisely because they knew his tedious manner would irritate everyone and he himself would get flustered."

"And they sat back and laughed?"

"Oh, again, nothing as crude as that. I'm sure they laughed among themselves afterwards. But Signora Isabella put a stop to it after a while. Quite severely."

"I'm glad to hear it."

He swung his lantern again, in order to look at me as he spoke. "I imagine you are," he said. "I would just suggest . . ."

"What?"

"No, nothing." He moved the lantern aside to light the way forward. We passed through the archway that led to the Rio dei Greci. To our right we should have seen the leaning tower of the church, but the mist was too thick.

"It was after she stopped it that their playing took a different form, I think. They began to talk to Padoan after the *salotto* had broken up for the evening. They flattered him that he'd been taken under their wing. And I think it was then they started telling him stories about some mysterious secret society."

"The Four Horsemen?"

"Something of the sort. They had all gone to a tavern afterwards, and I happened to drop in as well. He was clearly very flattered – and very flustered – to be drinking with four noblemen."

"So it was just a story made up to frighten him."

"I really can't say any more than what I've already told you. I was not privy to their private conversations. I simply overheard a few stray remarks on that one occasion."

"And did he ever talk to you about finding the tomb of Emperor Constantine XI?"

"Oh, that." He laughed. "It was clearly an obsession with him. He talked about it one evening at the *salotto* and everyone clearly felt very uncomfortable. Some flippant remarks were made and that, I think, greatly disappointed him. Sanudo and his companions pretended to take it seriously. Maybe it was then that their games with him began."

We crossed the bridge. To the right was the Greek church and the various buildings connected with it.

"So you live here," I said.

"For the moment. The priests are very generous."

"I saw that one of them came with you."

"Yes, Father Giorgos. He doesn't talk a great deal. His Italian is not very good."

"So you make up for it."

"Words are my calling, after all." Although he answered lightly enough I could tell that my remark had irritated him a little. Perhaps he really would have preferred to be a bandit. He made a clear effort to keep the tone light. "You can continue on your way by yourself without falling into any canals?"

"Certainly," I said. "This is my area. If I feel in any danger I'll just call on Saint George." There are numerous images of the saint in the quarter.

"Well, yes, between us and the Slavs round the corner," he said, gesturing in the direction of the little school of Saint George of the Slavs, "we have rather set his mark on this corner of the city." Then he added in a slightly more serious tone, "But don't only rely on saintly protection."

"Are you warning me against Sanudo? Or the Four Horsemen?"

"I think we can leave the horsemen to poor Padoan's fevered imagination. So, yes, I am referring to Sanudo. But not only."

"Oh?"

"When I mentioned the symmetry of our experiences, perhaps you guessed I also meant something else."

"You mean Signora Isabella."

"Yes."

"So you too ..."

"I, too, have entered her graces momentarily."

"I see. And what do you mean by a warning? Sanudo's jealousy?"

"Yes, that too. But beware the lady herself."

"And you mean ... ?"

"What I said. Good night."

And with one last smile he turned round and walked towards the church. I made my groping way back home through the fog, mulling over all I had seen and heard that evening. I will have to admit that one of the last things I thought of before I went to sleep was the dazzling smile of Noblewoman Isabella Venier Querini.

13

Next day, which was as foggy as ever, I called in at the Missier Grande's office. Sior Massaro greeted me with a woeful expression.

"Sior Alvise, what a disaster."

"Is it as bad as that?"

"It's fairly bad, fairly bad. The Missier Grande was summoned to report to the Inquisitors yesterday. He came back looking very grim."

I didn't point out that he was never a chuckling harlequin. "He was reprimanded?"

Sior Massaro looked at me reproachfully. "Sior Alvise, does that seem a word to use about l'Illustrissimo?"

"Sorry. Do you think they expressed reservations about his inquiry?"

"Strong reservations. Very strong ones."

"You mean they told him to stop."

Again he gave me a reproachful look but he didn't actually deny it. "Missier Grande has temporarily suspended the investigation."

"So I must stop."

"It would be better."

"Just when I was beginning to learn something about the Four Horsemen."

Sior Massaro was obviously dying to ask me what, but with an agonised expression he said instead, "Well, you'll have to keep it to yourself for the moment."

"Would we have any information about the Sanudo family?"

This time he actually winced. "One of the present Inquisitors is a Sanudo."

"Ah." Given the usual age of Inquisitors I imagined this would be either the father or an uncle of Andrea Sanudo.

"It would not be advisable to look into any files concerning the Sanudo family just now."

"No, I can see that."

At that moment the door behind Sior Massaro's desk opened and the Missier Grande entered. I stood up immediately.

He gazed at me for a few seconds without saying anything, his blue eyes unusually meditative. Then he said, "Sior Marangon."

"Illustrissimo."

"I expect Sior Massaro has informed you that we are to put the investigation in abeyance for now."

"Yes, Illustrissimo."

"Good. I'm sure you understand what that means."

"Well, yes," I said, surprised.

"I expect you to take account of these orders in your usual fashion."

"Yes, Illustrissimo," I said.

"In your usual fashion," he repeated. Then he simply nodded and turned round and went back into his room.

Sior Massaro was clearly a little puzzled by this, but he said to me, in as categorical tone as possible, "Well, there you have it. From the Illustrissimo himself."

"Yes," I said thoughtfully. "There we have it."

I made my way to a hat shop in the Merceria puzzling over the Missier Grande's words. If I remembered rightly, in the first case I had been involved with he had led me to believe (after it was all over) that he had instructed me to stop investigating precisely because he had guessed that this would only spur me into further action. Our relationship had altered since then, having been put on an entirely official level, with much signing and countersigning of stamped documents in which I committed myself to total obedience and to total secrecy. None the less, it was difficult to see any other reason for the particular formula he had used just now.

Of course, it was always possible I was interpreting things this way because I wanted an excuse to go on investigating. Perhaps I was just an incorrigible busybody, as Lucia clearly suspected.

No, I suddenly said to myself, as I passed under the clock-tower, it wasn't just that. There was the undeniable fact (as I now saw it) that someone had murdered poor Paolo Padoan. Crazy fantasist though he may have been, he at least deserved to have his own murder investigated. I would not stop.

I did not answer the other accusatory voice, which was telling me I just wanted an excuse to go on that assignation with Noblewoman Isabella. After all, it would be discourteous not to . . .

And so at nine that evening, wearing my new tricorn hat (the anonymity it guaranteed had been spur enough to buy it, even without Siora Giovanna's admonitions), I made my way towards Campo Sant'Angelo.

It scarcely needs saying that it was still foggy. Wherever one went one heard the grumbled word *caigo*, usually with prefatory adjectives. Some old people said that it never used to get so foggy; others that the month-long fogs that had wrapped the city when they were children were much worse. People from the mainland said that this was nothing compared with the thick fogs that swathed the countryside all the way to Bologna and Milan, while housewives complained that drying anything was impossible in this weather. Jokers recounted stories of people not seeing the canal-edge because of the fog. Sailors and fishermen told of inexperienced sailors and fishermen who got hopelessly lost in the featureless wastes of the lagoon. And tales abounded of a surge in street crime, as robbers took advantage of the possibility to evade all pursuit.

From Campo Sant'Angelo, as instructed, I took the broad Calle dei Avvocati and walked along it until I reached the fourth door. I groped in the darkness and found a bell-pull, as she had told me. Before pulling it I did what had now become almost routine with me and checked the surrounding area; I had come to realise that being disadvantaged in terms of swordsmanship (not owning a sword was the first handicap) and sheer brute strength, I was well advised to know all possible exit routes from any unknown place I visited. I found the nearest *calle* that led to a canal, and walked down it to see if there was a boat moored at the end of it (I had learned how valuable this could be from my experience at the Remedio tavern); if I lost my licence as a *cicerone* I could probably get a job as a cartographer. The alley was unpaved, just beaten earth, which turned to a muddy slime towards the water. As so often with such alleyways, the local residents had found it a convenient place to leave unwanted items of household furniture. At the water's edge there was a heap of what appeared to be broken chair-legs and some smashed jars and pots; a rat scuttled out from beneath the heap as I prodded it. There was also, to my satisfaction, a boat.

I returned to the door and pulled the bell. A few seconds later the door opened, the latch being lifted by a string from the first floor. I made my way up the stairs, which were lit by a glow from an open door above.

I expected a servant to receive me and was surprised (and not at all disappointed) to find Isabella Venier alone. This was clearly a noblewoman of a very independent kind.

She stood beside the door, the candlelight behind her so that her face was in shadow. Her dress was dark this evening. However, her smile still gleamed.

"Good evening, Excellency," I said with a bow.

"Good evening, Signor Alvise."

So we were still on fairly formal terms, it seemed.

And then she grabbed me and kissed me, long and hard.

I had been telling myself all the way to this appointment that I was going there in order to see precisely what Noblewoman Isabella wanted; I was going to try to question her on matters related to the Four Horsemen; I was going to expound my frank reservations about the appropriateness of a relationship between myself and a noblewoman; I was even going to mention that my heart was engaged elsewhere, although that particular path seemed problematic at the moment; I was only going to yield to my desires if I got satisfactory responses to the points I had raised.

As it turned out I yielded immediately.

After our lips disengaged, she said, "I never see any point in delay."

"No," I said, rather huskily. "So I see."

"We both know what we want."

"Yes, I suppose we do." It was becoming all too evident what I wanted – or, at least, what my body wanted.

"Follow me then," she said, taking me by the hand.

I had only the vaguest impression of the apartment. It was clearly furnished at some expense, with gilded furniture, tall mirrors and small but elaborate chandeliers. These were lit, as were fires in the main room and the bedroom, and I wondered in passing whether she had done this by herself or had had a servant do it.

The bedroom was decorated mainly in dark red, with gold for the frames of mirrors and paintings (mythical scenes with plenty of glowing flesh on display), and scarlet curtains. There was a welcome flickering glow from a fire opposite the bed, which made removing our clothes quite a natural act.

Where her shimmering dress yesterday had dazzled me, her softly glowing flesh this evening had a different but equally powerful effect. It looked as if I was going to have to postpone my discussion about the appropriateness of this relationship.

14

Some time later we lay back on the sheets, the blankets pulled up around us. I looked at the nearest mythological scene on the wall: Jupiter up to one of his tricks with a swooning female. Prompted by the classical suggestion I said, "And now for some Homer?"

She laughed. "That's the first time anyone has suggested a poetry reading on such an occasion."

"Well, it was the official excuse for the meeting."

She waved one bare arm in dismissal of all excuses. "We can have a Homeric feast, if you like." She gestured in the direction of the room we had passed through on our way to the bed. "It is laid out in there. I had been half in doubt as to whether you would be a pre- or post-prandial love-maker."

"I hadn't even noticed the food," I said.

"I thought as much. Perhaps it is some time since you . . ." She paused.

"Since I made love."

"Yes."

"I hope I didn't seem out of practice."

"Not at all," she said. "There was just an added eagerness that was rather charming."

"Oh," I said. "Thank you – I suppose."

"Now don't start getting all embarrassed. You were really very good. I enjoyed it."

"Well, you did give that impression," I said, slightly mollified. "Shall we go and eat, then?"

"Certainly." She got out of bed, found a pair of slippers and strode towards a wardrobe. She appeared superbly unconscious of her nakedness – probably because she was all too conscious of how superb it was. Although she was certainly ten years older than me, her body remained that of a twenty-year-old girl. I was sorry when she wrapped it in a long casual gown from the wardrobe.

I got up as well and made an awkward scrabble for my clothes. There was a washstand towards the window, and I took advantage of that before getting dressed again.

It was strange that I had not noticed the meal that was laid out on the table. It had certainly done nothing to hide itself. It was set out for two people, with fine Murano glasses, Vezzi porcelain dishes and bowls, and embroidered lace napkins. The bowls, when the lids were removed, contained razor clams, squids cooked in their own ink, small octopuses, raw oysters and crisp rosette buns. There was also a dish of grilled fish of various kinds, set on a tripod near the fire to stay warm, together with a steaming slab of white polenta.

"Probably not exactly the way Achilles would have set it out," I said, "but Homeric all the same."

"You can thank my maid Arianna for this."

I looked around the room for a startled second until she said, "She has gone back to the palace. She is extremely efficient and the soul of discretion. She's been with me since I was a child."

"So she's Greek?"

"Yes, of course. She still speaks very little Italian, which is not a disadvantage."

"For you, I suppose," I said.

She looked at me. "I suspect a criticism. But yes, I mean for me. Does that surprise you?"

"No," I said frankly.

"Good. It means you understand me. I like it when people understand who I am and how I behave. It saves a lot of time."

"I certainly wouldn't want to waste your time," I said. I waited till she had sat down and then took my place opposite her. "Shall I pour the wine?"

She nodded, and I poured a glass of white wine for her and one for myself.

"So far it has not been time wasted," she said with a smile, raising her glass towards me.

"Thank you," I said. "I'm glad to hear that."

"And for you, Sior Alvise?"

I answered in English: "'There want not Gods to favour us above; / But let the bus'ness of our life be love: / These softer moments let delights employ, / And kind embraces snatch the hasty joy.'"

"And that means?"

"Paris to Helen, Book Three," I said. I translated.

"I see. What he said to her when he should have been out fighting Menelaus on the battlefield. Not everyone would approve of such sentiments. Perhaps you yourself are already feeling guilty?"

She was extremely acute, I realised. I made warm protestations as I helped her to oysters. She merely smiled.

"While we are showing off our classical learning," she said, "it might help assuage your guilt to know that you had little chance of resisting my charms."

"I made no attempt to resist," I said.

She ignored this and went on, "You see, I'm descended from Venus."

"I have no doubt of it," I said. I wasn't being totally insincere.

"As you will know, after the Crusaders had taken Constantinople in 1204, the Venetians were declared lords of a quarter and a half-quarter of the Roman Empire; they promptly seized many of the Greek islands, including Cerigo, or Kythira, as the Greeks call it. The Venier family declared their own right to rule this island, birthplace of Venus, since the family descended from the goddess, the proof being in the name itself."

"Well, obviously," I said.

"So I was taught as a child," she said, lifting an oyster on a bright pin, "and so I have chosen to go on believing." And the oyster slid sensuously through her provocatively pursed lips.

"I believe oysters themselves are aphrodisiacs," I said.

"Why do you think I like them so much?" she said.

"However, I thought Cyprus was Venus's island," I said.

"Never say that to anyone from Cerigo. And particularly not to me."

I was reminded of the abbot at Sant'Elena making his claim for the real body of the saint. "Far be it from me to attack a local tradition," I said pacifically.

"But now let's hear some more about yourself. In particular the real reason you decided to join my *salotto*."

"The real reason?"

"Yes, Sior Alvise. The real reason. You don't really seem to me to be a natural *salottiere*."

"Did I make some foolish gaffe?"

"No, you were perfectly delightful. But I can't imagine you would have come along of your own accord. Is there some young woman who wanted you to improve your mind? Or your social standing?"

I felt myself blushing and hoped the flickering light from the fire concealed it. "If there were, do you think I would be here with you now?"

"Remember I am Venus," she said blandly. "And you mustn't think this little episode need in any way interfere with your personal relationships outside this apartment."

"So it is just an episode, then," I said, not sure whether I felt relieved or disappointed.

"I think you knew that before you allowed yourself to yield. Which is not to say that there might not be a second episode."

"That's good to know," I said, feeling it was only polite.

"Perhaps it will depend on how many oysters we eat. However, you still haven't answered my question. If it wasn't a young woman, what was the motive?"

I decided not to deny or confirm the presence of the young woman. "I heard about the *salotto* from a neighbour of a friend of mine. The friend is the gondolier I work with, who lives out in eastern Castello."

She had probably heard that such an area of the city existed, but I doubted she had ever visited it. "I see. And who was this neighbour?"

"A former schoolteacher with an interest in classical studies – or more particularly in the Eastern Roman Empire. His name was Paolo Padoan."

"Ah yes, the little man with the curious walk. Didn't he die?"

"Yes, he fell from the roof of his house."

"Poor fellow," she said. It was said simply but perhaps sincerely.

"I was talking to Komnenos yesterday evening. He actually rescued me from your friend Sanudo and his companions."

"Oh dear. What were they up to?"

"Sanudo told me he wanted to teach me a lesson. It involved a sword, it seemed. I, of course, have no sword so was at something of a disadvantage as a pupil."

She sighed. "I'll speak to him. He can be very tiresome. I've tried to make it clear to him that he has no exclusive right over me."

"That isn't something people often want to hear," I said.

"Well, I hope you at least have understood it."

"Have no worries there," I said. I speared an oyster myself with a pin.

"Hmm," she said. "Spoken almost too quickly. Now I might get offended – but I'll take comfort from the fact you've eaten an oyster."

I swallowed it and licked the salty fingers with which I had helped it to my lips. "Anyway, Komnenos told me something about Padoan and his time at the *salotto*."

"This, however, was after you had attended your first evening and so cannot be part of the motive that spurred you to join us."

"No, that's true. But what Komnenos told me confirmed some of the concerns I had had about Padoan and his experiences with your friends."

"And what were these concerns?"

"I know that Padoan had some rather eccentric ideas, but he was a perfectly decent old man. He attended the *salotto* because he was thrilled by the idea of being in contact with people from the Eastern Roman Empire."

"Which collapsed three hundred years ago."

"But was still alive in his imagination. He probably had rather unrealistic expectations of the *salotto*, and it seems Sanudo and his companions did all they could to confound those expectations."

"Yes," she said, "I can imagine that. But I'm sure it was harmless fun."

"Well, maybe. Until he fell to his death, anyway."

"Oh come now, Sior Alvise. What on earth can Sanudo and his friends have had to do with that?"

"I'm not sure," I said, quite honestly. "But there was definitely something strange about the fall."

"Well, now you are being as eccentric as your friend Padoan. I refuse to believe there was any connection between his death and the behaviour of my friends at my *salotto*. If you persist with this nonsense I will take serious offence."

"I'm talking about Sanudo and his companions, not about you."

"Yes, and please remember you are talking about members of the Venetian nobility. What you are suggesting is a serious slur on all our reputations." Her blue eyes were icy now.

"I remember you telling me that at your *salotto* there were no distinctions between people."

"I was not giving you licence to slander my friends."

"I'm sorry if that's how it seems to you. I'm merely puzzled by what I've heard. It seems Sanudo and his cronies taunted him with talk of some mysterious society known as the Four Horsemen."

She was momentarily taken aback. "Who told you this?"

"Komnenos. He thought they were merely making up stories to frighten him, but I'm not so sure. Does the name mean anything to you?"

She did not answer straight away. She took another oyster, as if it were the slippery passage of this delicacy that was delaying her. Once it had gone down her throat she said, "In the old Venetian territories of the east there have been rumours of a group by that name. Perhaps associated with the four horses of the basilica."

"The bronze horses?" I said. The coincidence of the numbers had occurred to me, but I had not been able to make any real sense of it.

"The bronze horses brought to Venice from Constantinople."

"I see," I said.

"Perhaps you do," she said, "but more probably you don't."

"Thank you."

"There's no need to be offended. The horses have a meaning to us of the overseas territories that they cannot have to Venetians born and raised in the city."

"Well, I was not raised here."

She waved her hand dismissively. "Your years spent with Angles and Saxons are irrelevant. You can't know what the horses mean to those who have lived under the constant threat of the Ottomans. Set up on the front of the basilica of our city, they make it clear that Venice is the true heir of the Roman Empire. And therefore to us they are a symbol of Venetian power and protection."

"And so an anti-Turkish symbol?" I said.

"That's one way of thinking of them."

"And would that mean that the Horsemen, whoever they are, are an active force of resistance against the Turks?" I was thinking of the recent petty acts of hostility that had been committed against Turks in the city.

"I really can't answer that. As I said, I have only heard rumours of such a group. Probably the same rumours that Sanudo recounted to your friend."

"Rumours that apparently terrified the poor man."

"That was probably embroidery by Sanudo; I imagine he just wanted to satisfy the man's craving for excitement."

"How very thoughtful of him," I said.

"Sior Alvise," she said, "I have warned you already that I will not tolerate criticism of my friends. We will change the subject."

"Shall we go back to Homer then?" I said.

"That seems safe enough. Of course, if you've had enough oysters we can always see if their reputation stands up to scrutiny." All frostiness had disappeared from her gaze, and to my surprise I found desire growing within me again.

She stood up and let her gown slip to the floor. It would clearly have been the height of ill manners to stay sitting over my meal. I rose to my feet as well and followed her back to the bedroom.

The oysters lived up to their reputation.

Some hours later she shook me awake. "Arianna will be coming soon to clear up."

I gazed at her in sleep-befuddled puzzlement. "You mean I have to go?"

"Yes, please."

"Your maid will be scandalised otherwise?" I said.

"Let it suffice that I wish you to leave before she comes," she said.

Delicate creatures, the maidservants of Venus, it seemed. I got into my clothes and dashed some water into my eyes from the wash basin. She stood still while I made my preparations for departure. Then we passed into the next room where our scarcely touched meal was still laid out. I hoped Arianna was hungry.

There was a clock in this room. I saw by the light of the one candle still burning that it was just after four o'clock.

Isabella saw me looking at the time. "Arianna rises early. She likes to do her cleaning before she visits the Rialto market. She always goes at around seven to buy fresh fruit for me. She is a lover of routine."

"I see," I said. "Well, I certainly don't want to upset anyone's routine."

She accompanied me to the door. "Sior Alvise, *addio*."

"*Addio?*" I asked. It seemed rather final.

"I suspect you have no intention of repeating this visit," she said.

"Well," I said awkwardly, "I – that is –"

"Please do not lie to me," she said. "We enjoyed ourselves."

"I hope so," I said.

"We did," she said firmly, "but it was an episode. I advise you not to return to my *salotto*."

"Not even to retrieve my Homer?"

"I will see to that. Where would you like it delivered?"

"Sior Fabrizio's bookshop in Calle dei Fabbri," I said after just a moment's hesitation. I guessed that it was unlikely she herself would make the delivery.

"I know the shop," she said. After a pause she said, "I believe Sior Fabrizio has an attractive daughter."

"I believe so," I said.

"Sior Alvise," she said, "have no fear that she will ever hear of this night."

I said nothing.

"Please go now," she said. "Take care on your way home."

"I will," I said.

"And perhaps take care of yourself for a while. It might be worth avoiding places where Andrea Sanudo is likely to be."

"I see," I said.

"But then I suspect you do not usually frequent the same places."

"Probably not," I said.

"This has been an interesting exception," she said with a smile, which was clearly one of farewell.

I made her a formal bow, but she then leaned forwards and gave me a long lingering kiss. "Go, my northern songster, and captivate others with your sweetly barbarous verses."

There was no answer to that, so I just gave her a final wave and set off down the dark stairs.

I stepped out into the clammy mist, my head reeling with a fuddled mixture of drowsiness, perplexity and melancholy-tinged elation. It was still dark, but the open space of Campo Sant'Angelo at the end of the *calle* offered a hazy illusion of light, so I moved in that direction.

And as I did so I heard footsteps. Perhaps Arianna hurrying to wash her mistress's dishes?

But no, these were at least two sets of footsteps, and they were heading towards me. I stood completely still, making sure that I had detected the direction correctly. Then I turned and headed towards the alleyway I had checked out earlier, which led to the canal.

As I turned into it I glanced back and could make out dark shapes blundering towards me through the mist. There was no way to distinguish any features; in any case, they would almost certainly be wearing cloaks and masks.

I ran down the alley, hoping the earthy surface was not too treacherously uneven. I came to a panting halt beside the heap of broken chair-legs and shattered pots; I grabbed a handful of the short stumpy poles and threw them down the alley behind me, where they thumped and clattered on the earth. Seconds later I heard the first of my pursuers grunt as his foot skidded on one of them; I could hardly see anything, just a floundering black shape. Then he let out a curse and there was a louder thump, followed by another one, as the man behind him cannoned into him.

I was fairly sure I recognised the style of these two. It seemed they had not learned much from their previous experience. I didn't stop to enjoy the confused noises of their predicament but stooped down and scrabbled amid the rubbish heap until I found a sharp-edged shard of a broken pot, and then stepped down on to the boat. It was a simple *sandolo*, and I guessed it was moored at the front end. It rocked drunkenly as I clambered forward. The shard would serve to cut the rope, if not for any more drastic purpose.

However, just before I put the shard to the cord I heard ominous noises from the alley and swivelled. One of the men had reached the water's edge and paused, ready to leap on to the boat. As he did so I spread my feet wide apart and set the boat rocking even more drunkenly, so that when he crashed down on to the boards he immediately stumbled, keeling over towards the side, his hands flailing for support; from one of them dropped a dark object. I leaned forward and grabbed the nearer hand, supplying the extra momentum needed to tip him completely off-balance and into the water, which he entered with a gratifyingly turbulent splash.

I stooped and snatched up the object he had dropped: a cudgel.

His colleague now appeared and stood hesitantly at the water's edge. I crouched in what I hoped was a menacing position, swinging the cudgel. The boat rocked again, this time as the man in the water grabbed at the side.

I said to the man above me, "Come down here and help your friend if you want. But leave me alone – or I'll break his fingers." I gestured with the cudgel towards the hand that was clutching the side of the boat a few inches away from me.

The man in the alley said, "All right. I'm going to get into the boat. No tricks." His voice was muffled; he was wearing a mask, as I had suspected.

He stepped down. He, too, was holding a cudgel.

"Drop your cudgel," I said.

"You too," he said.

"No," I said. I lifted it over his friend's hands again.

"I'm putting it down," he said. He bent down and laid his cudgel on the planks and then straightened, showing me his empty hands.

"Who are you?" I said.

His friend was spluttering now. "Help me!" I imagine his sodden clothes were impeding his movements. The boat continued to sway as he tried to pull himself out.

"Can't tell you," said the man in the boat.

"I can guess," I said, moving warily down the boat towards the alleyway. However, it seemed the second man was now more concerned with his colleague than with whatever violence he had been paid to inflict on me. It was touching to see such solidarity among *bravi*.

I was able to heave myself out of the boat unimpeded, and I ran briskly down the alley, listening to the splashing and scrabbling and cursing behind me. I thrust the cudgel into my breeches and made my way towards Campo Sant'Angelo.

I knew where to go next. Even at this time of night.

15

I arrived at the casino in Corte Contarina about five minutes later. There was a torch ablaze beside the door, and I could see lights in the rooms on the first floor. As I approached the door a large man stepped out and blocked my way.

"Yes?"

"I'd like to play some faro."

"You got an invitation?"

"Yes," I said. "Sior Boldrin himself asked me to come along."

"So you'll know the password then," he said.

"He must have forgotten to give me that," I said.

"Well, you'll just have to come back another time after you've reminded him to give you it." He folded his arms in a decisive, conversation-ending fashion.

"Well, you could go and ask him to come down."

"I suppose I could, but I'm not going to. Goodbye, sior."

"Oh, I think I'll hang around and wait for him."

"That's up to you, sior. It could be a very long wait."

"Well, I'll find a way of filling the time. Perhaps I'll recite some poetry."

"You go ahead, sior. Whatever you feel like."

I stepped away from the door and strolled to the opposite side of the courtyard. I looked around. Apart from the lights in the casino, all the other windows had their shutters closed, as one might expect at this time of night. Presumably the good citizens of Corte Contarina were getting their well-deserved rest. I imagined there was occasional tension with the casino hosted in their midst, which kept rather different hours; presumably those running the casino did their best to keep the noise level down. Such establishments were actually illegal but were generally tolerated so long as no significant complaints were lodged.

I leaned against the wall and coughed. Then I began to recite the same lines that I had aired the previous evening, but this time rather more loudly: "'Achilles' wrath, to Greece the direful spring / Of woes unnumber'd, heavenly goddess, sing!'"

I gave the last word an unearthly shriek. As I embarked on the next couplet the man at the door said, "Here, cut it out," and moved menacingly forward.

I pulled the cudgel out and swung it nonchalantly as I recited in a bellow: "'That wrath which hurl'd to Pluto's gloomy reign / The souls of mighty chiefs untimely slain . . .'"

He paused for a moment and then pushed his sleeves back purposefully and continued to walk towards me. "Look, sior, we don't want any trouble. Just stop that noise."

I kept reciting, beating the cudgel in the air in time to the metre. He paused a few feet away and said, "You are asking for trouble, sior, and my job is to give it to you."

"Declare, O Muse! in what ill-fated hour
Sprung the fierce strife, from what offended power
Latona's son a dire contagion spread,
And heap'd the camp with mountains of the dead."

He lunged at me and I leaped back, waving the cudgel wildly as I gasped the last line. I certainly had no intention of striking him, but of course he wasn't to know that.

There was a sound of other voices and also the scraping noise of a shutter being pushed open.

"What's going on?" It was a sharp voice that I recognised and it came from the open doorway. I turned and saw Marco Boldrin. His wig was a shimmering white in the torchlight. For once he wasn't smiling – or, at least, he wasn't displaying his gleaming teeth.

"Can't stop him," said the doorman. "I think he's crazy."

I put my cudgel away. "No, not crazy," I said, addressing Boldrin. "I just wanted to talk to you."

"Who – oh, it's you. What do you want?"

A voice from an open window called out, "Some people have to sleep, you know."

Boldrin's teeth were immediately brought into service as he turned his face upwards with a conciliatory smile and made an apologetic fluttering gesture with his hands. "So sorry," he said, in a rather absurd attempt at a loud whisper. "We'll deal with this at once."

I said loudly, "Well, it's really your master Sior Molin that I want to talk to."

"I don't know that he wants to see you," he snapped, still determinedly whispering.

"I'll just go on reciting Homer very loudly until he does," I said calmly.

Another shutter was opening above us, and he stared upwards in flustered irritation. Then he said, "Very well, come in."

"Sior, he's got a cudgel," said the doorman.

"Hand it over," said Boldrin.

"You'll have to make me," I said, "and although you might be able to I will make a good deal of very loud noise while you try to do so. But don't worry: I don't intend to use it. I just want to show it to your master. He will be interested to see it."

His face twitched in annoyance, and then he said, "Follow me."

We went up the stairs together, the doorman standing aside with a very surly expression.

We entered the main gambling room, where about fifteen people were clustered round two tables. Those at the tables were mainly men, but a few women in bright dresses were looking on from close by. They were all wearing masks, and the faces below the masks were shiny in the candlelight. Hardly anyone looked up from the cards as we entered; presumably they had not heard the altercation below. At the nearer table I could see a man in a nobleman's cloak whose hunched figure betrayed intense anxiety; the parts of his face that were visible were shinier than anyone's – shinier even than the impressive pile of coins that lay before the man sitting opposite him. There was very little noise; just the flipping of the cards and an occasional sigh or muttered exclamation. I could only presume that it was concentration on the game that had prevented them from hearing my Homeric performance.

Boldrin gestured me towards a door behind the tables. A man in a servant's livery standing beside the door looked questioningly at Boldrin, and at a sign from him knocked at the door. A sharp voice called out, and the servant lifted a hand, instructing us to wait.

We all stood there, listening to the muted sounds of play behind us. There were some faint scuttling sounds beyond the door, and a feminine squeak. Half a minute later, while Boldrin grew increasingly agitated, there came the sharp bark of a summons, and the servant opened the door.

Boldrin and I stepped into a smaller room. It was a good deal darker than the gaming room, with just a couple of candles in brackets on opposite walls. A large man with a bald head sat at a desk in front of us. There was no pretence that he had been working; the desk contained nothing but a large plate of biscuits, a flask of wine, a tumbler and a wig. The man just glared at us; I had the impression that he was buttoning his breeches behind the desk. I saw another door to my right, which was slightly ajar, and I imagined that someone, presumably the person with the feminine voice, had hastily passed through it.

"Well?" His irritation was clear and, perhaps, understandable.

"Sorry, sior, but this man insisted on seeing you," said Boldrin, in a nervous, placatory voice.

"Who is he? What does he want?" Sior Molin's voice was quiet but peremptory. This was a man accustomed to being obeyed. He brought his hands up from below the desk and put one to his head; he suddenly realised its uncovered state, reached out for the wig and thrust it on.

"My name is Alvise Marangon," I said. "I think you've heard it."

"Yes," he said. "You're the *cicerone* who insulted me." He gave no indication of surprise or indignation.

"I said nothing about you at all," I said. "And for no reason at all your hired *bravi* attacked me viciously, instigated by this man." I jerked my head at Boldrin and made no attempt to conceal my contempt.

"Why did you let him in?" Molin said, addressing Boldrin in a cold flat tone.

"He was creating a disturbance below," said Boldrin. "We can throw him out if you like." He gave his automatic smile, but he sounded too eager to please.

"I will create an even bigger disturbance if you try any such thing," I said.

Molin stared hard at me. "How many drunken idiots do you think I've had thrown out of here?"

"A good many, I'm sure," I said. "But I'm not drunk. And I'm not an idiot." Well, the first of these was true at least. I was hoping I could now prove the second as well.

"I can have you trussed and gagged and rowed to an island in the lagoon just like that," he said, giving a flick of his fingers.

"Not before I make an enormous row," I said, pulling out the cudgel.

"Do you think that will intimidate me?" he said, flicking his fingers again, this time in the direction of the door behind me. I heard it open and someone enter – presumably the servant. I did not turn round to look.

"I'm not intending to use it," I said. "Just to tell you where I got it."

"Where?"

"Off your hired *bravi* this evening. They both attempted to attack me again."

"I know nothing about that," he said in a bored tone. He raised his hand and beckoned, and I heard the servant coming up behind me. I still didn't turn round, and I tapped the palm of my left hand with the cudgel. I braced myself for a sudden assault.

"I brought this one with me," I said, attempting to sound completely calm, "but I have put the other in a safe place." This was the first lie, and I had to make it convincing. "Your men are not especially good at their job."

"Their job is simply to protect my interests." He was gazing curiously at me now, and so the servant remained still, waiting for an order.

"And that's what they are not doing," I said. "In particular when they attacked me a second time, after having been given specific orders not to do so by the Missier Grande himself." I allowed a hint of the customary awe to affect my utterance of this name.

His face showed just a flicker of irritation. "I don't believe you."

"What don't you believe? That the Missier Grande gave specific orders?"

He waved his hand impatiently. "I don't believe my men attacked you again tonight."

"I can prove it," I said. "And I can prove it to the Missier Grande as well."

"You can prove it, can you?" He said it with a sneer, but there was obviously curiosity in his voice as well.

"Yes," I said.

"Sior," said Boldrin, "this man is bluffing. We can deal with him for you." He knew that he had made a mistake in disturbing Molin and was eager to make amends.

Molin made an impatient dismissive gesture, just a flick of one hand as if driving away a fly. Boldrin fell silent.

I went on, "I can prove it with this cudgel."

"Are you threatening me?" It was said with cold disdain, certainly not with a trace of fear.

"Not in the way you think. I know cudgels like this," I said. "You see, I'm an agent for the Missier Grande."

This clearly caught everyone's attention. I had no doubt they believed it; few people were likely to boast of such a thing. Molin, however, did his best to disguise any reaction, merely raising his eyebrow a fraction.

"And as an agent I've had occasion to investigate the spread of such weapons in the city." This was true. "This is not a home-made object; it's been made by a professional, someone who knows the right weight to give such a thing, who knows how to achieve the right balance between the business end and the handle, how to make the handle easy to grasp, and even puts a little personal finishing touch to it." I pointed at the polished metal ring round the end of the handle, which had a small dolphin engraved in it. "This was made by Filippo Contin, in his workshop near San Leonardo.

He also makes handy daggers and poignards. And curiously he has a sideline in picture-frames."

"And so?"

"He keeps strict records of everyone he sells these things to. He has to. And he will be able to tell us who this cudgel belongs to. And of course the same goes for the other one. So when I report that I have been attacked again, and I show the Missier Grande the weapons that were used . . ." I paused and simply tapped the cudgel on the table. I hoped my argument sounded as convincing as the thwacking sound of wood on wood. I had completely invented the strict records kept by Filippo Contin. But I knew it was the kind of thing that people would believe.

"Keep off my table." Molin said nothing else for a moment or two. Then he spoke to Boldrin. "Leave us alone."

"Are you sure?"

"Get out."

Boldrin and the servant both got out. Molin stood up and stared at me for a moment. He wasn't a tall man and had a large belly; however, he still bore himself with a natural sense of authority. I noticed that his breeches were properly buttoned.

He walked to the side door and closed it firmly. Then he returned to his seat and sat down and stared at me again.

"So where are you saying they attacked you?"

"That's an interesting point," I said. "They were waiting outside a private house I had visited. It would be good to know how they knew they would find me there."

"I didn't send them." He said it very flatly.

"No," I said. "I didn't think you did. But they were your men. I recognised their – well, let's call it their style."

"They're blundering idiots. Boldrin hired them."

"So are you saying Boldrin ordered them to attack me?"

"No, of course not. He'd never dare. Certainly not after what happened last time."

"I presume he thought he was doing what would please you," I said. I had no idea why I felt spurred to defend his hapless assistant.

Perhaps because he was so hapless and hopeless, for all his gleaming teeth.

"Yes, he makes a lot of mistakes like that. But after that first time he wouldn't have done it again."

"So," I said, "are you really telling me you don't know who ordered this attack?"

"No," he said. "I have an idea." And he took another biscuit and chewed it, still staring at me.

"Are you going to tell me?" I said.

He kept chewing and staring. I think he was trying to keep up the pretence that he was in command, but he was also thinking hard.

"Well, if you don't, then I will," I said.

"Go on then," he said through his half-chewed biscuit.

"Like so many *casini* of this sort, you have a partner who's a nobleman."

He gave a half-shrug.

"You need a nobleman to bring in the other noblemen. And to offer a certain amount of protection. Your partner is a young member of the Sanudo family."

He poured himself a glass of wine. And then, after a moment's deliberation, he said, "Do you want some?"

"Thank you," I said.

He reached towards a shelf behind him and took down another glass. He said, "Sit down."

So now we were drinking mates. I sat down, giving a glance towards the door to our right which he had just closed.

He gave one of his characteristic dismissive waves. "She'll wait," he said, and handed me the glass he had just filled.

"Sorry to have, em, disturbed you," I said.

He gave a shrug. "These things happen." He sipped his wine. "So, young Sanudo . . ."

"Yes, young Sanudo," I said. "It seems he doesn't like me." I remembered the sudden extra animosity Sanudo had shown on discovering I was a *cicerone*; presumably he had recalled the story he must have been told about an arrogant *cicerone* who had turned down an offer to bring rich Englishmen to the casino in which he had a vested interest. It had given his spite an added financial motivation.

"He can be hot-headed," said Molin.

"So I've been told," I said. I sipped my wine. It was very good.

"But there's no reason for you to connect this in any way with this establishment."

"Those two men are in your employ, I believe," I said.

"Generally speaking, that is true. But on this occasion they were acting quite independently."

"But presumably paid for by your partner."

"But not on behalf of the business. I have no idea what's between you and his Excellency . . ."

"No, and I'm not going to tell you."

"I'm not asking. But whatever it is, it has nothing to do with our establishment. You know how young noblemen can be when they feel offended."

"Yes," I said. "But I want it to stop."

"Well, of course you do. Bit difficult for me, though, to give orders to a nobleman."

"Yes, I can see that," I said. "But you can help me put a stop to it."

"Oh yes?" He sounded wary.

"I just require clear proof of your good will in this matter."

He threw wide his arms, in a gesture of total affability. I was beginning to realise he was something of an actor. In front of Boldrin and his other servants he was a laconic bully; with me he had now become the genial and willing host.

"Just say the word," he said.

"I'm in a similar situation with regard to Sanudo," I said. "I certainly can't challenge him openly. What I need is some information that I can hold against him if necessary."

He frowned. "Are you asking me to inform on my partner?"

"No, not that exactly. But I do need to have some idea of what he might be planning."

"With regard to what?"

"Well, that's the point. I don't know exactly. But I think he's mixed up in some dangerous business. And if you know anything about it you won't be helping him by keeping quiet about it."

He stared hard at me for a few seconds. All the affability had gone from his face. Then he took another sip of wine and forced a smile back to his lips. "I wish I could help, but I'm not sure I know what you mean."

"But I think you do," I said quietly. "And remember, although Sanudo himself may be an impulsive fool . . ."

He winced. Such direct talk about a nobleman was clearly going too far.

". . . his family are not. And his father will certainly not be pleased if it turns out that anyone knew what his son was up to and did nothing about it. Oh, and his father is currently an Inquisitor."

Another wince.

"I don't really know anything," he said. "Just rumours. Things I've heard him talking about with his friends."

"Tron? The Bon brothers?"

"Yes, I think so. One of them laughs a lot."

"So what have they been laughing about?"

"I can't really say for sure," he said. "They don't talk openly about it. But they use the private room next to this one." He gestured to the right. "Don't think they realise that there's that grating up there." He pointed to a grille high up in the wall by the ceiling. "I had it put in to keep an eye on things. And an ear. Well, I sometimes overhear some of their conversations – without meaning to, of course."

"Of course," I said.

"And I've heard them mention the Turks."

"The Turks. Any specific Turks? The Sultan?"

"Not really sure. They don't like them, though."

"Well, that could be said about quite a few people in Venice."

Boldrin made one of his fly-whisking gestures. Clearly he had no such prejudices. I wondered if he had occasional Turkish clients. "Perhaps," he said. "But these people, Sanudo and his friends . . . They had lands out east, I believe. Anyway, I've heard them mention the Fontego a few times."

"The Fontego?" He was clearly referring to the Fontego dei Turchi, the ancient palace on the Grand Canal towards San Zan Degolà which had been given to the Turkish community back at the beginning of the previous century; it was used as both a residence for visiting Ottomans and a warehouse for their goods. There was even supposed to be a small mosque inside it; there were certainly tempting exotic smells that came from the building at mealtimes.

"Yes. Don't know what they're thinking of doing."

"They're not planning to attack it, do you think?"

"Attack it? What for?" He clearly found the idea ridiculous.

"Well, not for financial reasons, obviously," I said. "A gesture of some sort?"

He made another of his sweeping dismissive gestures; they were obviously the only kind he understood.

"You must have heard of some of the provocative things that have been done recently against Turkish visitors and merchants," I said. "Perhaps by these very people."

He thought about this. "It's possible, I suppose. Can't say I've heard anything specific."

"Anything else you can tell me?" I said.

"Well . . ." He lowered his voice. "You might want to have a look at the little place he has on the Giudecca."

"What sort of place is that?" The long island of the Giudecca is sparsely inhabited; there are some monasteries, a number of *palazzi* along the waterfront and a great many cultivated fields and orchards towards the southern side. It had once been fashionable for noble families to have small houses with gardens there for summer retreats, but nowadays people of means had villas on the mainland for such purposes, usually along the River Brenta.

"I don't know exactly. I just know the family has a place near Sant'Eufemia. I've heard him mention it to his friends. They're doing something there."

"But you have no idea what."

"No." He was finding it harder and harder to keep up the pose of the affable host, happy to share his knowledge with his new friend.

"I will have to ask you to be very discreet in the way you use this information."

"Yes, of course," I said. "We're called confidential agents, you know."

"Because of course I'm doing this for Sanudo's own good. He probably does need reining in, but . . ."

"You don't want to be known as the one pulling on the reins."

"Exactly." He had another swig of wine. "Do you want some more?"

"No, thank you," I said. "Just one last question. Have you ever heard any talk of an organisation called the Four Horsemen?"

He looked blankly at me. "No. Who are they?"

"It doesn't matter," I said. "I just wondered."

"I think I've answered enough questions. I'll ask you one."

"Please go ahead," I said.

"Now that you've had a chance to see our establishment, are you going to reconsider our offer and direct your clients towards it?" He clearly wasn't sure whether to make this request in an all-friends-together-now tone or in an assertive business-like one. He made a compromise, delivering the question firmly but then adding a friendly leer at the end. It didn't work.

"I'll certainly consider it," I said neutrally.

"Something in it for you, you know," he said, and the leer became more pronounced.

"Yes, so I was led to believe," I said, remaining vague.

"Anyway, now I have other matters to see to." He gestured to the side door, and the leer turned from affable to frankly lewd.

"Well, I'll leave you to it," I said. "Do you want me to send Sior Boldrin in?"

"You can tell him that if he so much as knocks at the door I'll rip him apart."

"It'll be my pleasure," I said.

When I stepped into the main room I found Boldrin and the serving-man still standing beside the door. "Well?" snapped Boldrin.

"He gave me a message for you," I said, and repeated Molin's last words. It was a pleasure to see the expression on his vindictive little face.

He glared at me. "I suppose you think you're so clever."

"Just well informed," I said. "I now know that the decision to set those *bravi* on me the other day was your own, and it was a mistake. Did you know what they were doing this evening?"

"No," he said, and then he clearly regretted having even deigned to give me a reply. "Whatever you and Sior Molin may have said to each other in there, I'm sure he doesn't want you on the premises a second longer."

"And I have no desire to stay a second longer," I assured him.

"Well, get out then." He prodded me with a manicured finger. He was obviously delighted at having found a way to use the insulting words that his master had addressed to him just a few minutes earlier, and he even raised his voice to do so. One or two of the players turned round in some irritation, including the hunched figure of the man in the nobleman's gown, whose demeanour seemed even less cheerful now; the mask he was wearing did not fully conceal the sheen of sweat around the lined sides of his face. Not a young man, I saw; probably another noble family on the brink of ruin – or, at least, of shameful exile to the cheap accommodation provided for such broken figures near San Barnaba.

I looked away from the gaming table and stared down at the intrusive finger still touching my chest. I refused to move until Boldrin had removed it. Then I left, resisting the temptation to whistle an aria from Pergolesi as I did so. There is such a thing as overdoing it.

16

I returned home and decided to catch up on some sleep. It was not until mid-morning that I was again abroad. I was glad to see that the fog had still not lifted; this was a perfect day for a discreet visit to the Giudecca. And I decided I would ask Bepi to take me.

I had already had to tell him that I wouldn't be able to go to Fusina the next day to look for English travellers, since there was no way I could fit in my half-job as *cicerone* with what was becoming my full-time job as agent. So the least I could do was offer him some hired work as my own gondolier. I just hoped he wouldn't have already found someone else to replace me.

I walked across Saint Mark's Square, glancing up at the four horses as I passed by. Their bronze bodies gleamed with a sleek lustre in the damp air. It was good to know they were watching over the city. People were making their way into the church for High Mass; the bells rang with a muffled solemnity through the fog. I promised myself that I would catch up with my devotions later that day.

Bepi fortunately was at his usual place at San Moisè; with the persistent fog he and his mates had moved inside their little wooden cabin by the canal. The dice clicked just as merrily indoors as outdoors.

He glanced towards me as I looked in through the doorway. "And so?" he said in his characteristic greeting.

"And so," I said. "Even if we can't go to Fusina tomorrow, would you take me out now? Usual rates?"

He got up and came towards the door to discuss it privately.

"Usual rates for a foreign visitor?" he said.

"Usual Venetian rates," I said. "But a whole day's worth."

"Sounds good," he said. "You paying?"

"Yes," I said.

"And just you travelling?"

"That's right," I said. "Who were you thinking of?"

"No one," he said. "Just I heard . . ."

"What?"

"People said you were moving with the nobility now."

"What people?"

"Oh, you know . . ." He gestured to his companions behind us. They were all looking curiously at us.

"Did anyone say which branch of the nobility?" I said.

He stroked his chin and looked sideways at me. "Venier?"

"My goodness," I said. "Word gets around very quickly."

"The lady has a certain reputation," he said.

"But how on earth did anyone . . ."

"Oh, nothing. It just seems you were one of the last to leave her *salotto* the other evening. One of my mates was working for the Tron family. He just mentioned it to me."

"There's no more to it than that," I said. "She wanted to help me find a book I'd lost during the evening, and so she kept me a little later than the other guests."

"Oh yes?"

"Yes," I said firmly.

"If you say so," he said. "So where do you want to go now?" He started walking towards his gondola.

"The Giudecca."

"It'll be tricky in this fog," he said.

"Yes," I agreed. "Though I don't mind the fact that we won't be noticed."

"Is this for – for your other job?"

"Yes," I said. "Hope you don't mind."

"Well, just so long as we keep quiet about it."

"Yes. That is always part of the bargain."

We got into the gondola. As usual I stood outside the cabin, resting my hands on its roof, so that I could chat with Bepi as we moved off towards the Grand Canal.

"You heard the news?" he said.

"What news?" I said.

"Well, it's not actually news, I suppose. Just rumours. Something strange happened up the other end of the Canal." The Canal always meant the Grand Canal for gondoliers.

"What sort of strange?"

"Seems a gondola disappeared."

"Disappeared? You mean vanished into the air?"

"Well, into the fog."

"Whose gondola?"

"It worked for the Fontego dei Turchi—"

"What?" I said it so loudly and so immediately that Bepi almost lost his balance as he unmoored the boat. He looked round at me in curiosity. "Why is that so interesting?"

"I'll tell you in a moment. But first tell me what happened."

"I'm not sure of all the details. It seems the gondola set off from the Fontego with some passengers, and just a minute or so after it had left, the two gondoliers who were supposed to be rowing it were found in another boat, drifting down the Canal. They said they'd been waiting outside the Fontego and this boat had come up and three men had jumped out and attacked them; they tied them up and threw them into the boat they'd come in and took over the gondola."

"Who were they?"

"They didn't know. They were wearing masks. They didn't speak a word. One of them stayed in the boat with them and rowed down the Canal, and then another boat came up and he got into it and just left them drifting."

"So how many were there in all?"

"I think four, if I got the story right. Three in the first boat and then another man who came up in the other boat."

"And were they gondoliers?"

"Well, they knew how to row."

That didn't rule out Sanudo and his friends. There had been a brief fashion a few years earlier for competitive rowing among young noblemen. It lasted until they realised just how hard it was, but there was no doubt that one or two had acquired some skill at it.

"Did they row well?"

Bepi shrugged. "Don't think anyone was really taking any notice of that." His tone suggested a hint of disapproval of this failure on his colleagues' part; he couldn't imagine any circumstances in which he would fail to notice such an important fact. He set us moving towards the Grand Canal with his usual apparently effortless skill.

"So who were the passengers that got kidnapped?"

"That's not clear. All I can tell you is what the gondoliers said. They'd been told to be ready to take some passengers somewhere, but they didn't know who."

"Where?"

"They hadn't been told that yet. Seems they were never very chatty, the people who gave the orders. Paid well, though."

"Anyway, they were Turks."

"Well, yes, of course."

So at the very least a major diplomatic incident had been provoked. I sighed and gazed towards the hazy shape of the Salute church, whose great dome disappeared into the mist above us. Bepi steered us across the canal towards the tip of the wedge-shaped customs building that stands at the threshold of the Grand Canal.

"When did this happen?"

"Early this morning. Before the first bells for Sunday Mass."

"I see," I said.

He said in a voice that he was clearly trying to keep casual, "Is this trip anything to do with that business, then?"

"Well, possibly," I said.

"And it's just the two of us," he said.

"We're just going to inspect a place," I said. "That's all."

"What place?"

"A private house owned by the Sanudo family, near Sant'Eufemia."

"Where they're keeping the people they kidnapped?"

"I don't know that at all," I said. "I didn't even know about the kidnapping until you told me about it."

"No, but you got very interested in it. Look, is this a good idea, just the two of us?"

"I don't know," I said honestly. "But at the moment I don't know who else to ask to come with us. If you want the full truth, Bepi, I've been told to stop investigating this matter. I'm not doing this for the Missier Grande or for the Inquisitors."

"All right then," he said.

He didn't stop rowing. We had now rounded the tip of the Customs House, with its swivelling gold statue of Fortune, and were rowing across the Giudecca Canal. The Giudecca itself was invisible; there were few other craft out at the moment, just a long barge laden with poles being rowed down alongside the Zattere. The voices of the bargemen sounded muffled in the fog. Somewhere a fog-bell was tolling steadily. Otherwise the canal was grey and featureless, merging in the distance into the trailing mist.

After a minute or so, he asked the obvious question: "So who are you doing it for?"

"Well, it might sound stupid, but I suppose I'm doing it for Venice."

He didn't answer at once. After a few more strokes, he said at last, "It does sound a bit stupid."

"Thanks."

"But I suppose I'm a bit stupid myself," he said. "So all right."

"Thanks, Bepi." I wondered whether he had actually found it easier to agree once he had heard that the Missier Grande was not involved.

"What is this place, then?" he asked.

"Just a house or a casino that the Sanudo own. That's all I know. We'll have to ask once we get there."

"Hope they'll understand us," he said. "Funny people, the Zuechini." He used the dialect name for the inhabitants of the Giudecca.

"I don't know any Zuechini," I said.

"No, don't think they get out much. Too busy digging their aubergines."

I gathered that Bepi didn't know any Zuechini either. The stately white façade of the Redentore church began to emerge through the mist. A few people were climbing the steps to enter it.

We made our way down the canal, past the various palaces and warehouses that stood along the water's edge, until we reached the wide canal that splits the Giudecca in two and is spanned by a rickety wooden bridge known simply (and aptly) as the Long Bridge.

"So what do you think Sanudo is up to?" said Bepi, after a long pause.

"Well, if you really want to know, I think he's involved in some absurd plan to provoke the Turks."

"Provoke them?"

"He comes from a family that's never got over the fact that it lost lands to the Turks."

"Well, he's not the only one."

"No, but he's a particularly bitter one. And he's got three idiotic friends, a Tron and two Bons, who seem to be at his bidding." I thought of something. "Didn't you say that one of your friends works for the Tron family?"

"Yes, my friend Lele."

"Has he ever said anything to you about Sanudo? Or about the Four Horsemen?"

"The what?"

"The Four Horsemen. I think they imagine themselves riding the four bronze horses against a Turkish horde."

"Venetians have never been much good at horse-riding," said Bepi. "Maybe best to start with bronze ones."

"Do you know if young Tron can row?" I asked, prompted by a hazy association of ideas.

"Well, funny you should say that," said Bepi. "Lele told me just the other day that his master asked him for a lesson, out over by the Fondamenta Nuove where no one would see him. Told him to keep quiet about it, of course."

"And so he told you."

"Well, we gondoliers tell each other things, but they don't go any further."

"No, of course not," I said with an ironic smile.

"If I'm telling you now," he said sharply, "it's because you said it's for Venice."

"Yes, of course. Sorry," I said. I meant it.

"So there are going to be four of them," said Bepi.

"Possibly," I said.

"And there are two of us."

"Yes."

"Now, you know I like an occasional gamble?" he said.

"Yes."

"Well, I wouldn't stake too much on our chances."

"We're not going to fight them," I said.

"Right." He paused. "You've been in this business for a while now, haven't you?"

"If you mean my work as a confidential agent, a few months, yes."

"Have you ever thought of getting a few lessons in, I don't know, fencing? Or buying yourself a pistol?"

"What kind of agent do you think I am?" I said.

"I'd have thought those skills could always come in useful."

"Yes, perhaps. Only I don't think they're my kind of skills."

"Right." Another long pause, as he revealed his kind of skill in swinging us to the right around an approaching *sandolo*. "And your kind . . ." he said eventually.

"All right, this is not going to sound impressive . . ."

"Yes . . ."

"I'm quite good at improvising in a difficult situation."

"I see," he said.

"And I do notice things. Things other people don't notice."

"I see," he said again. "Still . . ."

"Yes?"

"A pistol would always come in handy."

"Well, actually . . ." I said, and I pulled out the cudgel.

"Well, it's something, I suppose," he said, after giving it a glance.

"Can't imagine ever using it, mind you," I said.

"That makes it a bit less handy," he said with a sigh.

We arrived alongside the church of Sant'Eufemia. The front of the church gave on to a side canal, and Bepi manoeuvred us into it. An old lady dressed in black was sweeping the ground in front of the entrance. Bepi edged us to the canal-side, and I clambered out and approached her.

"Excuse me, siora," I said.

"What do you want?" she said. At least that is what I presume she said; the fact that she had hardly any teeth and spoke in a very thick dialect did not help. I had thought I understood all the dialects of the lagoon, but it seemed that the Giudecca had its own unique variety.

"I'm looking for the house of the Sanudo family," I said.

"Who?"

"The Sanudo family," I said, wishing I didn't have to shout it.

In fact she at once said, "You don't have to shout, I'm not deaf." I followed this by intonation, rather than by any specific consonantal sounds.

"Sorry," I said.

"They don't live here," she said.

"I know that, siora, but they have a house here."

"Well, it's not really a house," she said.

"No," I said, "I suppose not."

"So why did you say a house?"

"I was misinformed," I said.

"House indeed," she said with a scornful laugh. "I suppose you'll be wanting them to give you a bed for the night." I was getting better at interpreting her spluttering outbursts, or perhaps she was taking more care at enunciating her words, having grasped that she was dealing with an idiot.

"No, no," I said.

"Well, good thing. You'd be sorely disappointed."

"Yes, I realise that. But I don't want . . ."

"Bed for the night indeed," she said. "You'd be in a pretty fix." She laughed again. I imagine she didn't get many opportunities for jocular conversation.

"Yes, siora. I don't want a bed. I just want to know where their house is – or casino or whatever it is."

"Well, everyone knows that," she said.

"Not quite everyone," I said. "I don't."

She looked at me with contempt; she had never come across

such ignorance. "Go down this *fondamenta*, past the church of Saints Cosma and Damiano, you'll see the gardens of the convent, go beyond them, in the field just before you reach the lagoon you'll see a small house – only it's not a house, just a large cottage, really, near some hazel trees . . . Used to be a house, but it's falling to pieces now." This was all remarkably clear.

"Thank you, siora," I said, "you've been very helpful."

"But they can't give you a bed for the night, remember. I warned you . . ."

"Yes, I realise that. Thank you."

I went back to the gondola, leaving the old lady to shake her head over my stubborn refusal to take her word about the lack of available hospitality.

Bepi rowed us down the narrow canal. We passed the large classical church dedicated to the two martyr saints on our left, and then the open spaces of the Giudecca's fields and orchards revealed themselves, the rust-coloured autumnal trees looking damp and bedraggled in the mist. A solitary building gradually became visible in this flat landscape; it was a square single-storey construction in crumbling brick with arched windows and a steep tiled roof. It looked several centuries old and one side was propped up with dark wooden beams. There was a single door at the front and a man in a cloak and a tricorn hat was standing outside it. Oddly (and ominously), given the rural context, he wore a mask. His blank face turned in our direction.

"That must be it," I said. "What would the Sanudo family be doing with a place like this?"

"It was probably just a hunting lodge," said Bepi. "I know other noble families that have places like this on some of the other islands."

"Hunting?" I said.

"Well, birds. Someone once told me there were even rabbits."

"Keep going," I said. "We can't stop here." I gave another glance at the man, who took a step or two in our direction but then seemed to think better of it.

"I think I know who that is," I said. "It's your friend's master."

"Tron?"

"Yes. I think I recognise the way he walks: small indecisive steps. That might make things a little easier. Tell me anything you know about him from your friend. Anything at all; it doesn't matter what."

"He's got a lot of gambling debts. He tried to court a girl from the Loredan family but got turned down. He studied half a year at Padua but then gave up. His father is always shouting at him. He never gets up till midday – you sure that's him?"

"Maybe he hasn't been to bed yet. Yes, I'm sure. Keep going."

"He tried to get into business importing *malvasia* but got cheated and had to ask his father for money. He was once accused of cheating at cards by a man from Florence and was supposed to fight a duel but got out of it by apologising. He's got a mistress in Castello who's a singer at the San Giovanni Crisostomo theatre; she once pretended to be pregnant to scare him. He went to Corfu to get out of that. He's written a lot of bad poetry about her." Bepi paused for breath.

"My goodness," I said. "I don't know why the Missier Grande hires people like me."

"We pick things up," said Bepi.

I decided not to ask what his mates knew about me. Instead I asked, "Tell me about the gambling debts. Who with?"

"Mainly with Molin, in Corte Contarina. I think one of his friends gets him to play there."

"Yes," I said, "Sanudo. Maybe I can do something with that."

We were now approaching the open lagoon on the south side of the island. A clump of trees concealed the house from us.

"All right," I said. "Let's moor here. I'll go and check things out."

"I'm coming with you," Bepi said.

"Thanks," I said. "You don't have to."

"No, but I think it wouldn't be a bad idea. Just until you've learned how to use a cudgel."

I smiled. "Perhaps you'd better take it," I said, pulling it out of my cloak.

"Maybe you're right," he said. "Handier than an oar." He steered the gondola towards the bank, coasting alongside a convenient tree.

He clambered out and secured the boat, and I followed him. I handed him the cudgel, which he slipped inside his jacket.

We were in an uncultivated field, which sloped down towards the lagoon. There was almost complete silence, just the faintest lapping noises from the water and an occasional cry from a seagull. The house was a dim shape through the mist; there was no sign of Tron, who had been standing on the opposite side of the building.

We began to trudge towards it. The ground was soft and mushy, and we were able to walk almost noiselessly. We came up to the back of the house, and there was still not a sound. There was a single window on this side, which had a dark wooden shutter across it. However, it had a crack down one side, which allowed me to peer in. There was complete darkness. Bepi stood dead still by my side.

Then I heard a faint rustling sound, as of someone moving inside the house. I listened hard. The noise was repeated; it sounded like something or someone sliding, or attempting to slide, across the floor. There was also a strange muffled whimpering. I listened for another few seconds, then turned to Bepi.

"There's someone in there, and I think they're gagged," I whispered.

Bepi simply nodded.

I listened again, trying to decipher the whimpering sounds.

"I think it's a woman," I said.

Bepi's eyebrows went up, but again he said nothing.

"Listen," I said, "I'm going to speak to Tron. But I think it's best if you don't show yourself, unless I get into serious trouble. Wait here."

He scratched his cheek doubtfully but nodded. I walked around the side of the house, making no attempt to silence my footsteps. Before I reached the end of the wall the man in the cloak had stepped out to face me. Prepared though I was, the blank gaze of the white mask was disconcerting.

"Ah, good morning," I said, making my tone sound as casual as possible.

He said nothing. He had, however, drawn out a sword and held it just slightly raised.

"Sanudo sent me," I said.

The sword wavered slightly. "Sanudo?" He was whispering, but I recognised Tron's high-pitched voice.

"Yes," I said. "He said we have to move her." Even as I said it I realised I didn't know whether it was one person or more.

"Move them? Where?" He had not even spotted my slip. He was clearly agitated.

"He told me Molin has got a useful place. Somewhere on Murano."

"Molin? You mean he knows about this?" He was not even bothering to disguise his voice in his agitation.

"Yes, but don't worry. He's got too much money tied up with Sanudo to let anything slip. And then there are your own debts. He certainly doesn't want to lose his chance of getting those paid."

"Oh my God," he said. "And why did Sanudo send you?"

That, of course, was the weak point. "Don't worry about that. Sanudo and I have made things up. Isabella Venier made him see that we're on the same side." I could only hope that he had little insight into Sanudo's character.

"So what are you going to do with them?"

"I've got a gondolier, entirely trustworthy. He and I will take care of them. We'll hide them in the *felze* and deliver them to Molin's place on Murano. I think Sanudo is going to be there to receive them. And the other Horsemen, I expect."

"All right," he said. He pulled a key out of his pocket, and we approached the door to the house. I realised that the only possible reason it had been so easy to deceive him must be because he desired nothing so much as to be rid of his captives. This was a Horseman who could not wait to dismount.

The door scraped open, and we stepped into the gloomy interior. There was just a single large open space; it might have been divided originally into separate rooms, but any interior walls that had once existed had been removed to transform it into a broad barn-like space. The walls were just bare brick, and the windows were all shuttered. The floor was mainly hard earth, although there were traces of a former tiled surface around the edges. There were dim shapes of farming implements on the right, but my eyes were drawn at once to two dark recumbent figures against the opposite wall. They stirred as we approached them, and as my eyes became accustomed to the gloom I saw they were trussed and gagged. They were clearly female figures and were dressed in long dark garments. They made whimpering noises as we came nearer, and I felt a burning rage rising inside me. I knew I had to be very careful not to give this feeling free rein.

"Can they walk?" I said in as casual a tone as possible.

"Walk? Of course they can." His voice was rising to an agitated pitch. He knew just how terrible his present role was. "We haven't hurt them."

I said, "No, I suppose not."

They both had traditional Turkish headscarves and veils; I expected to see their eyes at least, probably glazed over with fear, but then I realised they were blindfolded. It was actually something of a relief.

"How long were you planning to keep them here?" I asked, as if out of mild curiosity.

"I don't know. It's Sanudo who planned all this."

I was on the point of asking where Sanudo had gone when I remembered that I was supposed to have come from him. "Have they behaved well?" I asked.

"The younger one's been all right. The older one has done nothing but whimper, even with the gag on. It's been awful."

I wondered if he expected me to pity him. I merely grunted something inarticulate. Then I said, "I'll call my gondolier. He'll help me get them into the boat."

"All right," he said.

And then we both heard approaching footsteps and a murmur of voices. My heart sank.

There was an exclamation, presumably as they saw the open door, and the footsteps became swift and urgent. Seconds later three figures appeared in the doorway, pausing on the threshold for their eyes to adjust. They were all wearing long cloaks, tricorn hats and masks, just like Tron. It was quite intimidating.

17

"What's going on?" came Sanudo's sharp voice.

"He said you'd sent him," said Tron, in an automatically defensive tone.

"Who?" The figure of Sanudo advanced into the dark space; he had already drawn his sword. "Oh, you." It was said with venomous intensity.

"Yes, it's me," I said. "Before you run me through, I'm not alone. BEPI!" I yelled.

He had already appeared in the doorway behind them, the cudgel held firmly in one hand.

"So there are two of you," said Sanudo. "That's not a problem. Two low-life rats."

His companions had drawn swords as well but were looking to Sanudo rather than at us. Tron had lifted his sword in a rather unconvincing fashion.

"I think it's more of a problem than you suspect," I said. "I have no doubt you can run us both through eventually, although my friend Bepi will probably cause some damage before he goes down . . ."

"Just a little," he agreed, swinging the cudgel demonstratively.

"But then what do you do? Are you going to bury our bodies out here? The Missier Grande knows I came out here, by the way, so don't think there won't be questions. I suppose you could take the bodies out and sink them in the lagoon, but you'll have to go a long way to find a deep enough part to be sure we won't re-emerge . . ."

"These are our problems," Sanudo snarled. "Don't worry on our accounts." And he came towards me with the sword outstretched.

"Well, you feel like that, I suppose, since you have some personal grievance against me, but I'm not sure that your companions do." I turned away from Sanudo and addressed the two Bon brothers.

"I know your friend can be very persuasive. But ask yourselves if you really want to run the risk of a trial for murder just because he's a hothead. At the moment you haven't yet committed any really terrible crime." This was yet another lie I was forced to tell, one that was clearly disproved by the presence of the two women lying there, terrified out of their wits. "It can even be hushed up. I can take these two women back to the Fontego on my own initiative, and I won't need to say anything about where I found them."

"He's lying," said Sanudo. "He's a spy. He'll rat on us."

"You know as well as I do," I said, "that the authorities will want this whole story hushed up. Everyone will be very glad if the whole thing is quietly forgotten. And I can certainly help you there."

"We don't want it to be forgotten," said Sanudo, his voice quietly furious. "We did this to make a mark; we *want* people to remember it. We particularly want the Turks to remember it."

"So you plan to rape these women and send them back to the Fontego shamed and humiliated?"

He did not deny it. "It's no worse than what happened to our people in Cyprus, in Crete, in Negroponte . . ."

"All right. But now you will have to rape them and then kill us. Or kill us first and then settle down to your rape. Whichever is easiest, I suppose." I turned again to the other men. "Do you still go along with this plan?"

One of the Bon brothers spoke at last. "I never wanted to do this at all. Not the rape. I didn't mind an attack on the Fontego. Like the other things we've done."

"You filthy traitor," spat out Sanudo. He seemed about to turn his sword on the backslider.

I spoke up: "So let's get these women into our gondola and then it can all be forgotten."

Sanudo suddenly lost control and rushed towards me with his sword upraised for a slashing attack. Even as I reared backward I saw something fly through the air and crash into him, knocking him sideways. Still crouching defensively I swivelled and saw Bepi straightening up. He had hurled the cudgel and perhaps saved my life.

"Come on," I said to Tron. "Let's help these women to their feet."

Tron gave a curious whimper himself, looking nervously to his fallen companion.

"He can get up by himself," I said.

I moved towards the recumbent figures. One of them was trembling uncontrollably while the other was rigid. I bent down and spoke in as soothing a voice as possible. "Siora, I'm here to help you."

I put my fingers to the blindfold.

"No!" said Tron, clutching at my hand. "They mustn't know where they are."

I looked at the two Bon brothers, who were kneeling over Sanudo. They had their masks turned towards us, but I could tell they were equally agitated. I realised I would have to humour them on this if I wanted to get these women to the gondola quickly. I tried to rationalise it in my mind: what difference did another couple of minutes of blind terror make for them, after all? But I did not feel good about it.

Bepi had joined me, after retrieving his cudgel. I said to him, "We'll have to do what they say, leave them blindfolded till we get them to the boat."

It took us another minute or so to get the women sufficiently calm to be raised to their feet. It became clear, even without uncovering their faces, that one of them was just a girl, perhaps only fourteen or fifteen, while the other was middle-aged. Mother and daughter, I guessed.

Bepi and I walked them to the door, touching just their arms to guide them. They stayed as close to one another as possible, leaning inwards, away from us. Their arms were still trussed behind their backs, and I decided it would be best to leave them like that until they were safely in the cabin.

As we reached the doorway I allowed myself one last remark, turning and addressing all four men. Sanudo was sitting up; his mask had come off and his face was twisted in pain and anger. I said, "Sorry to have robbed you of your fun."

The three other men did not answer. Their heads were bent downwards. Sanudo just spat on the floor.

Once the gondola was moving in the direction of the Giudecca Canal (I will spare you the complicated and heart-wrenching details of getting them, blindfolded and trussed, aboard the boat) I put my hands to the blindfold of the girl and removed it as gently as possible. A pair of dark eyes, startled and fearful, stared at me. I mouthed the word "Sorry" and turned to the other woman; I had to put a hand to either side of her head to get her to stop trembling enough for me to be able to remove her blindfold. The eyes thus revealed were rolling in crazed fear.

I said, "Sorry" and then took off the gags. For a while both women did little more than pant. Then the older woman pulled her veil down over her face and began to recite a sing-song litany. I imagined she was praying. The girl looked at the older woman and pulled down her own veil. She did not join in the litany, however.

"Sorry," I said again. I had no idea, of course, whether they could understand the word. I just hoped my tone was sufficiently soothing to tell them they were no longer in any danger.

Of course, I should also have untied their wrists; however, I was worried that they might attack me. It would not have been wholly unreasonable on their part.

I said gently, "We are taking you back home. Home." I was still sitting next to the older woman and so I tried to communicate to her by gestures that I would untie her wrists; it would involve some obviously unwelcome contact, and I wondered for a moment whether it would be worth asking the old woman from the church to come aboard for a moment. But then I saw that we were already out in the Giudecca Canal, and so I put aside the idea.

The woman clearly did not understand what I was trying to convey to her and began to grow even more agitated. The girl said something calming to her and then twisted herself on her seat so that her wrists were towards me.

"That's right." I leaned across the cabin and looked at the rope: the knots were painfully tight and would be very difficult to untie. I said, "One moment," and stepped out of the cabin. "Bepi, you always carry a knife, don't you?"

He was looking particularly grim-faced as he rowed. We had hardly exchanged a word since we left the building with the two women; our conversation had been limited to quiet and, we hoped, soothing remarks as we somehow got the women to pass into the cabin. Now he said, "Yes," and reached inside his jacket with one hand. He passed it down to me. "Better be careful how you show it to them."

"Yes," I said. I had realised this. I put it inside my cloak and stepped back into the cabin. The two women were talking quietly and urgently. I gave them a smile and hoped it looked reassuring rather than crazed. Then I gestured to the girl's wrists again, and she obligingly turned herself. I drew out the knife. A sudden gasp came from the older woman, but I put up my free hand reassuringly and then as gently as possible slid the blade between the girl's wrists and the rope. Seconds later the rope parted and she rubbed her wrists with relief. Her mother's agitated gasping slowed down and eventually she turned round so that I could do the same for her.

They did not attack me. None the less, I decided it would be best to leave them alone for the moment. They were probably not used to being in the presence of unknown men.

I stepped out of the cabin and handed the knife back to Bepi.

"How are they?" he said.

"Still terrified. Particularly the older one."

"And we're just going to let those shits go free?" he said with sudden asperity.

"Bepi, they're all noblemen. I'm a *cicerone* and you're a gondolier. And those women are never going to testify."

He said nothing for a few seconds. He clearly realised the grim sense of what I had said.

"We can just be thankful we got there before . . ." My voice trailed off.

"They really were going to do that?"

"That was certainly Sanudo's intention. And the others probably would never have found the guts to go against him."

"I would never have guessed it from the way Lele described Tron."

172

"He'd have done it out of pure weakness," I said. "Or, at least, he wouldn't have stopped Sanudo from doing it."

"And what was it all for?"

"Don't ask me. Perhaps they thought it would provoke another war and another Morosini would rise up and retake the Peloponnese. And Crete. And Cyprus. And another Dandolo would retake Constantinople even . . ."

"They're just shits," said Bepi.

"Yes, that sums it up quite well too."

We could now see the Zattere. Bepi was heading straight towards the canal that led towards the church of San Sebastiano. I had only the vaguest idea of the geography of the canals in this western corner of the city, but I presumed Bepi was going to wiggle us up through Dorsoduro and Santa Croce to the far end of the Grand Canal, where the Fontego dei Turchi is situated.

After a pause he said, "See what you meant about your kind of skills. You did pretty well."

"And so did you. Thanks so much for that use of the cudgel. Unusual but effective."

"Well, you have to work with what you've got."

"Exactly."

"Does this mean you've finished this case?" he asked.

"I don't think there's ever such a thing as finishing a case. Not completely."

"No, but bringing these two lasses back to the Fontego must count for something."

"Yes, you'd think so," I said. I had been wondering, of course, how we were going to do that. If the Missier Grande were around it might help things, but I had no idea whether that was likely to be the case.

We were now passing up the canal in front of the church of San Sebastiano. I thought of the splendid ceiling canvases by Veronese depicting the story of Esther, slave-girl raised to the status of queen and saviour of her people. One of the three canvases celebrates the triumph of her cousin Mordecai, who rose to his position by thwarting a conspiracy against the king. It was a painting that had grown dear to me in recent months; it was, after all, the only great painting I knew that paid tribute to a confidential agent.

"I'm afraid," I said, "that we might not be able to get the credit we deserve for this."

"That's all right," said Bepi. "That's not why we did it, is it?"

"No," I said. "I just hope we don't actually get into trouble. If we can't report the real perpetrators we have to come up with some explanation of how the women come to be in our gondola."

As the church slipped past us to our left I recalled the fact that Mordecai's triumph consisted in riding on a splendid white horse, formerly used by the king himself. I thought of Paolo Padoan, who had, according to Fabrizio, been terrified of four very different horsemen. Could it really have been Sanudo and his feeble accomplices who had instilled such fear into the poor man? Something told me that the case was not over.

Ahead of us was the marvellous tracery of the windows of Palazzo Ariani, like a little offshoot of the Doge's palace in this western corner of the city. Bepi swung us to the right along the Rio dei Carmini. This was a busy canal, and Bepi had to exercise great skill in weaving amid the various *sandoli* and gondolas, especially since we were now in Nicolotti territory and his red cap marked him out as a Castellano. A gondolier wearing the dark cap of the Nicolotti called out to ask him if he was lost; he merely smiled ironically and rowed on. We passed the Campo dei Carmini and a short while later encountered the Rio di Ca' Foscari, which swung right and became the Rio Malcanton, or Bad Corner.

"You know your way around this side of town very well," I said.

"I've got an aunt who married a Nicolotto; she lives near Anzolo Raffaele," he said. After a pause he added, "Some of them aren't so bad once you get to know them."

"I imagine not," I said.

"Maybe the same is true of Turks too," he added philosophically, glancing down at the cabin.

"Probably," I said. "Mind you, I don't think we're going to have much chance of getting to know these two."

"No," he said. "Probably best to leave them to themselves."

We continued to move northwards, swinging westwards briefly along the Rio del Gaffaro and then proceeding north again past the church of the Tolentini. The church of Santa Croce, with its tall bell-tower, partly lost in the fog, marked the entrance to the Grand Canal.

"So what are we going to do with them?" said Bepi.

"I think we'll have to see when we get there," I said.

"You mean we're going to improvise again," he said with just a hint of scepticism in his voice.

"I don't think the cudgel is going to be much use this time," I said.

"No, but we could, say, leave them nearby, point them in the right direction and row off."

"It sounds good," I said, "but I think they need to be delivered to their doorstep. I don't think they're in any condition to go wandering in the fog."

He was silent. "I suppose you're right," he said eventually.

We passed by the church of Santa Lucia, the church of the Scalzi, and then the great mass of the church of San Geremia, where the Cannaregio Canal joins the Grand Canal. As ever this part of the waterway, even on a Sunday, was full of jostling traffic: barges, gondolas and *sandoli* somehow making their various ways without colliding, even if with a certain amount of caustic commentary and the occasional curse.

The Fontego appeared through the mist on our right, with its long line of slender arched windows. It had presumably once had an equally elegant ground floor, with a line of wider arches along the canal, but a ramshackle set of smaller shed-like buildings had been untidily stuck on to the façade; the entrance was now by a side door in the broad *calle* to the right of the palace. There were several gondolas moored here, and there was a group of people standing in front of the doorway. They were mostly Venetians, but there were at least two people in Turkish garbs. Animated conversation was under way.

There was still room for our gondola among the ones already moored by the *bricole*. Bepi steered us in delicately. Two gondoliers were standing close by and watching the crowd around the door.

Bepi addressed them as he tied us up to the nearest *bricola*: "What's going on?"

"The Inquisitors have come," said the one with a red Castello cap. "They're in the building."

"Yes, but why?" said Bepi.

"You haven't heard? A Turkish ambassador, his wife and their daughter were kidnapped."

An ambassador. I winced.

"How did it happen?"

It took a while, since each man wanted to make it clear that he knew that extra little fact that was the key to the whole story ("and it was my friend Piero who saw the boat drifting with the gondoliers who'd been tied up", "yes, but my friend Marco spoke to them straight afterwards . . ."), but eventually we got a clearer picture of what had happened. The gondola had contained the ambassador and his wife and daughter, and they had been intending simply to go down the Grand Canal to see the Piazza from the water, since there was no other way for the women to get an idea of the city; moments after the gondola had left, the ambassador was attacked by the usurping gondoliers and thrust out of the boat at Campo San Stae; the gondola had then disappeared into the mist and no trace of it had been seen since. The moment the ambassador had got back to the Fontego the alarm had been raised; the real gondoliers had then been discovered, tied up and drifting down the canal in a boat, and they had recounted their side of the story. The Turks immediately summoned the authorities, and the whole place had been swarming with *sbirri* and agents ever since. However, it was not until the three Inquisitors had turned up that any of them had been allowed into the Fontego. Orders had been given that no one must speak of what had happened. Anyone found recounting the episode was liable to arrest ("They say they'll have their tongues ripped out," said one of the gondoliers with gusto; Venetians love to spread wildly exaggerated rumours about the hideous cruelty of their rulers). Of course, that didn't apply to gondoliers, who could be relied on to keep things to themselves. (One of the gondoliers had given a slightly nervous glance at me at that point, but Bepi had raised a reassuring hand: as a friend of a gondolier I was automatically to be trusted.)

All the while the story was being recounted I found myself continually glancing back at the door to the cabin, nervously expecting the women to appear at any minute, but for the moment they remained secluded.

Looking towards the entrance to the Fontego I suddenly saw a small man leave the group and walk towards us. I at once recognised the self-important strut of Marino Basso, pigeon-chest thrust out, pointed chin raised as if he were balancing a glass on it. His burly assistant followed close behind. Basso raised his silver-topped cane in an imperious summoning gesture towards me.

"Marangon!" he called.

"Sior Basso," I said, in as coolly courteous a tone as I could manage.

"What are you doing here?"

"My friend Bepi Zennaro just wanted to chat to some friends," I said.

"I will have to ask you to leave," he said without even glancing at Bepi. "I am here with the Inquisitors on important state business, and we cannot have our investigations in any way impeded by people who have nothing to do with the matter."

"Perhaps I can help," I said.

"Sior Marangon," he said in a pitying tone, "I think you are rather out of your depth here. This is not a matter for mere gossipmongers."

This was certainly not how had I had planned it (if I had indeed planned anything), but it was impossible to resist the provocation. I said in my mildest tone, "I understand you are looking for two missing Turkish women."

"Silence," he snapped. "This must remain absolutely secret." He now acknowledged the presence of the lowly gondoliers and addressed them severely. "Not a word of what has happened must get abroad. The penalties will be most severe."

The gondoliers, including Bepi, all lifted their hands, as if shocked at the very notion of their letting slip a word on the subject.

I said, "Well, it may have to remain secret, but I still say that Bepi and I can help you."

"For goodness' sake. I have no time to waste . . ." And then his irritated voice died away, for I had leaned over, opened the cabin door and gestured towards the interior; the girl's veiled head had appeared there for an instant before she retreated nervously into the gloom.

"Who . . . How . . ."

I thought to myself that even if I were to be sent to the galleys for this little trick, it would have been worth it for the expression on his face at that moment.

"I think," I said, "these are the women you are looking for." I lifted a hand as Basso tried to board the gondola. "No. They've had a severe shock. I think you must summon someone they know from inside the building. They can't be subjected to any further indignities."

He glared at me but after a few seconds clearly saw the sense of this and strutted back in the direction of the building. His hefty shadow lumbered after him.

"So now what do we tell them?" said Bepi. He had already put up a hand himself to bar the other gondoliers from boarding. I'm sure they were already picturing themselves in the tavern that evening, outdoing each other with first-hand details of the story of the day. "No," he said to them. "As my companion said, these women need protection."

"I don't think we've much choice," I said in answer to his question. I lowered my voice so that only he could hear. "Something as close to the truth as possible but without giving any names. One of the Inquisitors is Sanudo's father."

"Oh, Christ," said Bepi. "That's all we need."

"This is the story," I said, quietly and firmly. "You and I went to the Giudecca to hunt rabbits because your brother told you they could be found close to the lagoon . . ."

"Which brother?"

I was about to explode that it didn't matter when I realised that it did; it was exactly the sort of question they would ask. And then they would ask the brother in question. "All right. You'd heard it from someone in a tavern."

"Which tav—"

"You decide. It doesn't matter to me. And we were walking round the back behind Saints Cosma and Damiano and we heard cries from this house . . ."

"Sanudo's house."

"It's just a ruin. They can make what they want of it. Sanudo will probably deflect all inquiries at that point. And we found these two women tied up and we brought them back to the city. They're clearly Turkish, so we brought them here. That's all we know."

"The women will tell it differently."

"I doubt the Turks will allow the women to be interrogated. Anyway, it'll have to do for now. Remember that we have the advantage of knowing that they won't want the truth to come out, so they'll be happy to go along with our story."

Bepi looked doubtful but gave a shrug of assent.

A group of people were heading in our direction, led by Basso, whose strutting march had become more self-important than ever; his upturned chin led the procession like a precious relic. No doubt he had told them that he had single-handedly extorted the truth out of us before we made a break for it. I saw that the group included a number of people in Turkish robes. One of them, a bearded man in a white turban and red robes, looked especially agitated; I guessed him to be the ambassador.

This turned out to be the case. He was the first to board, and Bepi and I stood respectfully aside as he crouched down and entered the cabin. There was an explosion of voices, which gave way to sobbing and wailing. A minute or so later the ambassador led the two women out, the older woman visibly quivering, the younger silent but defensively hunched in on herself. Bepi and I stood aside as other Turks came forward to assist the women in disembarking. Then they all made their way swiftly towards the entrance of the Fontego, the two women in the centre of a tight protective cluster of billowing garments and turbans.

And then began the questioning.

18

The Inquisitors requisitioned the priest's house at the nearby church of San Degolà, and there Bepi and I were interrogated together and separately for at least an hour. As usual the Inquisitors were never introduced by name; the awe induced by their role would be diminished if one could imagine them as specific individuals with relatives and friends and dependants. None the less, I was able to identify Sanudo's father quite easily; there was not only a strong family resemblance, but there were also clear worry-lines around the man's mouth and eyes, fully understandable for any man with such a son. As I had foreseen, the moment I mentioned the ruined house on the Giudecca Sanudo took charge of the questioning and carefully steered it towards the condition in which we had found the women and what we had done next.

When I was questioned on my own, Marino Basso was sitting behind the Inquisitors and at a certain point he leaned forward and whispered something into Sanudo's ear. A few seconds later I was asked about my relationship with the Missier Grande.

I said that I had carried out investigations for him on various matters but that this had nothing to do with the present case. It was all a question of rabbits. And, no, we hadn't found any rabbits. Quite possibly my gondolier friend had been misinformed. And, no, I didn't know a licence was required for the hunting of any wild animals in the lagoon. And of course I would be sure to apply for such a licence before attempting such a thing again.

No, we hadn't been able to communicate in any way with the two women, since not only were they in no state to answer any questions but they didn't speak Tuscan or Venetian. We had had no idea who they were, just that they were clearly Turkish, and so naturally we had brought them here.

After swearing to keep total silence on the whole affair I was eventually allowed to leave. It turned out that Bepi had been dismissed a while back, and I was going to have to walk home. Possibly I could have got a passage from one of the gondoliers we had talked to earlier, since they would certainly have loved a chance to extract the full story from me for later retelling at their favourite tavern, but choosing between them might well have led to an unseemly fracas. And besides, I was glad for the moment to abide by my promise of silence.

I felt a strong temptation to go to the Missier Grande's office (he was often there on a Sunday) but decided I would have to resist it. It was quite probable they would be watching the building. I just had to hope that things were now over. Even if Sanudo and his cronies had not been arrested, it was likely that the Inquisitors would make sure that they were rendered incapable of doing any further harm. Perhaps they would all be sent off on missions to their beloved Greek world . . .

But even as I crossed the Rialto Bridge and returned to the side of the canal where I always feel more at home I felt a return of that worrying premonition that things were not over. The figure of Paolo Padoan and his terror of what he had discovered kept returning to me. Certainly Andrea Sanudo and his friends had shown a capacity for evil, but even so I found it hard to believe they were what had terrified Padoan.

Well, time would tell, I told myself.

Late afternoon, having eaten at my usual *furatola* in Corte dell'Orso, I made my way homewards, passing naturally enough through Campo Santa Maria Formosa. I was gazing rather aimlessly at the window of an antiquarian's shop in the square when I became aware of a man hovering indecisively by my side. I took my eye from the heterogeneous collection of gilded picture-frames, miniature bronze statues and battered marble fragments that could be glimpsed through the shop window and saw a stooping elderly man looking doubtfully at me. It took me a second or two to recognise Nobleman Marco Querini, since he was, if not elegantly dressed, at least wearing a wig and a nobleman's cloak, albeit both a little tattered at the edges.

I hoped my embarrassment was not immediately visible. I knew that conjugal fidelity was not considered of prime importance among most members of our city's ruling class, where marriages were usually based more on questions of familial convenience than on amorous attachment; none the less, to encounter him so shortly after my night's intimacy with his wife was disconcerting, to say the least.

"Excellency," I said, stammering a little.

"It is you," he said. "I thought it was."

His tone was reassuring; it was not that of a man about to challenge his cuckolder to a duel.

"Alvise Marangon, at your service," I said, managing to get my tongue at mine. I made a courteous bow.

"Yes, yes. You're the fellow my wife took up the other night."

"I – er – that is, I suppose you could . . ."

"Oh, don't worry about it," he said affably. "My wife is always taking people up and then dropping them."

"Oh, is that right?" I said, wondering whether I should be offended or reassured by this.

"Yes. Seems to like novelties. You're foreign, aren't you?"

"Venetian, Excellency, but brought up in England."

"Ah, that will explain it. She likes collecting strangers. There's that Greek fellow."

"Komnenos," I said.

"Yes, that's the name. Tells me he's a poet. He does go on, I know that. Always hearing his voice. Still, if it makes her happy, why not?"

"Certainly," I said.

"I know she gets a little bored in the *palazzo*; she was used to a good deal more – well, I suppose a good deal more space back in Cerigo, you know. Not been there myself but I believe it's beautiful. Birthplace of Venus, you know."

"Indeed?" I said, and I could feel my cheeks flaring.

"Yes," he said. "She's always joking about that. Maybe she wishes

I were a little more ardent." There was a slightly wistful tone to his voice, as if he were dreaming of sweeping his wife off to some rocky cave by the Ionian Sea.

"Em . . ."

He clearly realised the inappropriateness of his last remark. "Sorry, I was just, um, just . . ." He didn't know how to continue this and so started on a new tack. "Are you interested in antiquities?" He gestured at the shop.

"Well, to a degree," I said. "I'm a *cicerone*, so I feel I should know a little about most things."

"A *cicerone*, indeed? I did wonder. My wife's evenings seem to bring together all sorts of people. I think she hoped I would become involved, given my classical interests. But then I found people mostly wanted to talk politics . . . Not my thing."

"I see," I said.

"So I left her to it. She seems to know what she's doing, even if my mother doesn't approve."

"No," I said. "I did get that impression."

My assent clearly reawoke his sense of the proprieties, and he changed direction once again. "No, antiquities are my thing. Were you wanting to buy something here?"

"No, no," I said, "just looking."

"Ah, pity," he said. "I could have got you a fair price, you know. I know the owner well. And he's often here even on a Sunday."

And as if to prove the point the door of the shop opened and a small man with an ingratiating expression appeared there, his head bobbing up and down eagerly, as if pre-emptively agreeing with whatever we might want to say to him.

"Excellency," he said, "are you intending to buy or sell today?"

"It depends on what you have, Sior Visentin. This young man is a *cicerone*, he tells me. You might want to cultivate him rather than me." He said it with a kind of forced jocularity; it was clear that banter was not his style.

"Certainly, Excellency," said Visentin. He at once turned to me, his head still bobbing convulsively. "And your clients . . . ?"

"Mostly English," I said. "Young noblemen on the Tour, you know."

"Yes, of course, of course. We deal quite frequently with such clients. We certainly know their tastes. Perhaps we can come to some arrangement?"

"Yes, perhaps," I said, leaving things a little vague. I was not in the mood for such considerations at that moment.

Querini must have sensed my embarrassment. He said, "Sorry, didn't want to rush you into anything. Sior Visentin is always very eager to do business. Doesn't realise that it's not everyone's prime concern."

Sior Visentin at once waved his hands apologetically. "Do excuse me. I certainly didn't mean to be too forward . . ." His head stopped bobbing and started waving from side to side. I wondered if he ever got giddy.

"No, no, I perfectly understand," I said. "But some other time, perhaps."

I was in fact quite touched by Querini's helpfulness – and not a little embarrassed. I wondered whether it was his method of dealing with his wife's amorous propensities. Making it fully clear that he bore no resentment was one way of preserving some shred of dignity, perhaps.

"Of course, of course," said Visentin.

Querini gave him a gentle pat on the shoulder, as if to indicate that he need not despair, and the man retired into his shop again, after one last burst of deferential bobbing.

"I understand that you might have reservations about committing yourself," Querini said, "but there's really nothing underhand about it."

"No, no," I said. "It's just I prefer to consider these things carefully first."

"I see," he said. He gave a little sigh. "Good to see a young person who isn't impulsive. Very rare, very rare. I myself have my own regrets . . ." And he gave another sigh.

I was beginning to wonder whether perhaps the final aim of this little conversation was simply to cause me to die from embarrassment. But no, I thought, it was clear that he really was just musing to himself, and not necessarily on his matrimonial troubles. Or so, at least, I tried to convince myself; I just wished there was not such an infinite melancholy in his tired eyes.

We exchanged a courteous goodbye, and he disappeared into the shop (which, I suppose, was blessedly free of mothers and wives) while I proceeded on my way towards the Ruga Giuffa.

The only consolation I could find lay in the thought that I had agreed with Isabella that we would not be renewing our tryst. This, of course, was not something I could say to him, though he would find out soon enough, I imagined. And then maybe I could take up his suggestion and work out some deal with his antiquarian friend – and try not to feel too guilty about it.

I decided I needed a moment of pure evasion from all such thoughts, which could be provided by attending the latest Goldoni play and then enjoying a good night's sleep.

The former was accomplished successfully, and I made my way back home from the Teatro Sant'Angelo that evening with the best lines still resounding in my head. The latter was successful only up to a point: a point that was marked by a sudden agitated knocking at my door in the early hours of the morning.

This was not the first time such a thing had happened to me, but it was the first time that my heart had leaped in quite the way it did this time in response to the noise. Or rather, in response to the accompanying noise, which was an urgent female voice. In fact, to be more specific, it was Lucia's voice.

I will admit that being visited in bed by Lucia was something I had occasionally (oh, all right, often) dreamed of, and so one might imagine that my immediate feeling would be one of eager delight. However, dreams are one thing and reality another. And it did not take me much longer than a confused two seconds to realise that Lucia had not come out of an irrepressible craving for my body, or even my conversation. The next two seconds were given over to dismay that she would see the squalor in which I lived. And then the time between tumbling out of bed, grabbing a cloak to cover my tawdry nightgown, shoving the chamber-pot out of sight and making my way to the door was given over to a host of other feelings and worries and thoughts. Absurdly (or perhaps not so absurdly) the overwhelming feeling was of guilt.

It was a kind of generic sense of guilt when I fell out of bed but by the time I was turning the door handle it had taken on the very specific form of guilt over Isabella Venier. By the time I had opened the door I was almost expecting to see the aristocratic lady standing next to Lucia. Perhaps naked.

Of course, there was just Lucia. That should have been a relief, but when I saw her dark troubled eyes and her agitated face I began to take in the words that were spilling from her trembling lips.

"Oh, Sior Alvise, thank God. You must get dressed; you must get away from here. You must . . ."

"What on earth is the matter, Siora Lucia?" I said. I stood in the doorway without inviting her in. It would, of course, have been most inappropriate for me to do so, and in any case I couldn't have borne her seeing the twisted tangle of my dirty clothes, the accumulated dust, the remains of last night's fishy supper . . .

Of course, it was already inappropriate – or, at least, highly unconventional – for her to have come all the way up to my door unescorted. I began to think beyond the confines of my embarrassment and my guilt, and a sense of fear began to steal over me.

"Sior Alvise, listen carefully." She paused to catch her breath. I realised that she must have run all the way here. Probably she would have had to ask for directions at some point, since she rarely came to this part of town.

I felt forced to say, "Would you like to come in and sit down?"

She just waved her finger negatively. She did not seem shocked by the proposal, but I took no comfort from that; it was clear that she was far too agitated to be thinking about the proprieties. After a pause she said, "Sior Alvise, there has been a murder and they will come looking for you."

"For me?" I said in bewilderment. Then I added the obvious question: "Who's been murdered?"

"It's a man called Boldrin."

"Boldrin?"

She caught my intonation and said, "You know him? You knew him, that is?"

"Yes. But how . . . when . . ."

"Sior Alvise," she said, "get dressed and meet me somewhere nearby and I'll tell you everything. I think they'll be coming here very soon."

Her urgency was catching. I told her to go to the church of San Giovanni in Bragora, which was just a couple of minutes away, and I would join her there.

19

Minutes later I was descending the stairs. I had put a few spare clothes and other items into my old satchel for all eventualities. As I stepped out into the street, Giovanna looked out from the tavern. She gave me a roguish smile: "I just saw your lady friend leaving, Sior Alvise."

"Ah, yes, she came to call on me . . ."

She smiled indulgently. "You don't have to pretend with me, you know. She looked a very nice young lady."

"She is very nice, but she isn't my . . ."

Giovanna tapped her nose and winked. "Oh, Sior Alvise, I'm not your mother, you know."

I gave up. "Very well, Siora Giovanna."

"I'm so glad to see you've got some company. And maybe she'll persuade you to get another wig. She looks like a lady with some sense."

"I'll be sure to ask her about it," I said. "Anyway, I must be off. If anyone asks about me, I'm leaving town for a few days."

"Taking her somewhere nice, I hope."

"Yes, certainly," I said. Should I indicate a destination, like the Barbary Coast or the Americas? I decided to leave it vague. "To see relatives," I said.

"Ah," she said, looking a little surprised. Despite her facetious reference to my mother I think she had never really thought of my having any family. I was just the lone Anglo-Venetian who didn't complain too much about the noise and occasionally had some unusual visitors.

Almost out of instinct I set off in the opposite direction from Campo San Giovanni in Bragora. If anyone did come to see me, the first person they would question would be Siora Giovanna. I crossed Ponte Sant'Antonin and headed in the direction of the Greek church. Before I reached it I turned left and doubled back on myself, crossing the little bridge that led towards another entrance into the *campo*. Then I crossed the square and entered the church.

It was not only my parish church, and the one that I attended when I remembered to do so, but was also one of my favourite. Small, intimate and with some striking works of art. Lucia was standing in front of the altar steps gazing at the luminous painting of the *Baptism of Christ* that hangs above the high altar. With a veil pulled over her hair and a rapt expression on her face, she looked like a saint from a *quattrocento* painting herself.

But I'd never longed to kiss one of those saints, as I did Lucia at that moment. And all the time I couldn't force out of my mind the real but treacherous kisses I had exchanged with Isabella Venier.

She turned to face me. "What a beautiful painting," she said.

"Cima da Conegliano," I said.

"It's very calming," she said, "which is what I need."

"Indeed," I said. "Look at the ducks."

She did so, and the faintest trace of a smile appeared on her face for just a moment. Then she looked back at me, and the expression of deep concern returned to her face. She gave a quick glance around the church, confirming that we were more or less alone (the sacristan was extinguishing candles in a side chapel). "Sior Alvise, they will be coming to question you. I thought it best to give you warning so you can prepare yourself."

"Tell me exactly what has happened," I said. "And if you get agitated, look at the ducks."

She flashed a quick smile but returned to full seriousness immediately. "They woke me and my father very early this morning. It was before the Marangona and it was still dark." The Marangona is the bell on the campanile of Saint Mark's that marks the beginning and end of the working day.

"Who?" I said.

"The *sbirri*. And an examining magistrate. I don't know his name. They didn't tell us what had happened. They just wanted to know about that book of yours."

"Which book?"

"The translation of Homer."

"Ah," I said. "It keeps turning up."

"Yes," she said, "and this time it had turned up next to a dead body."

"I see," I said, quite untruthfully. "What did they want to know?"

"Well, if you remember it was brought to us by a *sbirro* after you had lost it. Well, the same *sbirro* was helping the magistrate with the murder, and he recognised the book. He told the magistrate about it, saying that he had sold it to us, and so they came to ask about it. Of course, they didn't tell us what it was all about. They just asked us what had happened to the book."

"And what did you say?" I said with an uneasy feeling.

"Fortunately Father answered, and he just said that he couldn't remember. And then when they pressed he said he thought he had sold it to an English visitor but he couldn't be sure." She looked hard at me. "Father doesn't usually tell untruths, but he had a bad feeling about this affair. He told me afterwards that he had immediately suspected something very bad had happened and he didn't want to send them on to you until we had had time to find out more about it."

"That was very considerate of your father," I said. So now I had Sior Fabrizio's descent into untruth on my conscience as well.

"After they had gone," she went on, "we found out from the neighbours that they had found a dead body not far from our house. In Corte Lavazzera. He had been stabbed, several times. Apparently it was a dreadful sight." She swallowed. "A boy had slipped as he came out of his house to go to the bakery where he works, and he found it was blood he had slipped on."

"Oh, goodness," I said, as much concerned by the troubled expression in her eyes as by the story itself. I wondered whether to tell her to look at the ducks but decided it would sound too flippant.

She made a great effort to get a grip on herself and continued. "He gave the alarm, and they found this poor man huddled in a corner of the square, in what they called a pool of blood. Whoever had done it had been in some kind of rage, they said. He had stabbed him over and over again, continuing even after he was dead. They didn't find the knife, but they did find a book, which they say must have fallen from the murderer's pocket in his fury. So then the *sbirri* came and one of them recognised the book, as I said. They came immediately to ask us about it."

"So they don't know your father gave it back to me," I said.

"No," she said, "but I don't think it will be long before they work it out. They know it was originally yours. And they know that you are our friend."

"Thank you," I said.

She looked a little surprised. "For what?"

"For calling me your friend."

She waved her hand dismissively at this. "Of course you are, Sior Alvise. The fact we've had some moments of – of misunderstanding, well, that doesn't mean anything."

"But also thank you both for thinking of how to help me now."

"You really did know this man, then?"

"Yes," I said. "I did. And unfortunately the last time I saw him we exchanged some angry words. In front of quite a lot of people."

"Where was that?"

"At a gambling house in Corte Contarina where he worked," I said.

"I see," she said. "That's not good."

"In case you're worried about my frequenting gambling houses," I said, "I should say—"

Again she waved a dismissive hand. "Don't be foolish, Sior Alvise. Of course that's not why I'm worried." She gave a half-smile. "You know there are aspects of your life that do give me some cause for concern, but it's never crossed my mind you might be a gambler. At least not a gambler of that sort."

"I don't like to think I'm causing you concern," I said, "but I can't deny I'm touched by it." And I wondered whether, by way of proof, I should put my hand out and touch hers. But even as I thought so I remembered the touch of Isabella Venier's skin, and that wave of guilt washed over me again. My hands did not move.

"So what will you do?" she said.

"I will have to speak to the Missier Grande," I said. "He is the only person who can offer me any kind of protection."

"And where will you stay?"

"Well, I'm hoping that the Missier Grande will be able to help me there too," I said.

"And you have no idea who could have committed this murder?"

I shook my head. "Boldrin did not live in a very pleasant world," I said. "I have no doubt he will have had enemies. But I can't think of anyone who would behave with that kind of ferocity." A thought struck me. "Nobody mentioned seeing or hearing a Neapolitan anywhere nearby?"

"A Neapolitan?" she said. "Why?"

"Just a thought," I said.

She was frowning. "As it happens, we had a Neapolitan visitor in our shop just yesterday."

"Oh really?" I said. "Did you notice anything about him?"

"He wanted to buy a copy of Ariosto," she said. "He didn't seem to be a very, well, a very literary sort of person. But Father chatted away, telling him he had been to Naples once as a young man, and that he thought it was a very beautiful city . . . The man himself didn't say very much."

"Nothing else about him?"

"I think he was lame," she said.

"Ah," I said.

She looked at me. "Does that tell you something?"

"Yes," I said, "but I'm not sure what to do with the information."

"Tell it to the Missier Grande," she said. It was the first time she had ever referred to my employer, and she did it without visible distaste.

"I will do so," I said.

"Sior Alvise," she said, "I know you can have had nothing to do with this terrible crime." She looked straight into my eyes as she said this. Her own eyes were lucent with tears.

"Siora Lucia," I said awkwardly, "I don't like to see you distressed."

"Don't worry about me," she said. "It's you who are in trouble, and I wish I could be of more help."

"You've done more than enough in running all the way out here," I said. "I'm so sorry for all the worry I've brought upon you and your father."

She forced herself to give a smile. "It seems we are going to compete in our apologies. I was too harsh on you the other day. I should have been more understanding." She turned away. "Now I'll have another look at those ducks."

"There's another painting by Cima," I said, gesturing to the right. "At least there should be . . ." I stared in some uncertainty at the right-hand wall. There was a gap on the plaster, with the clear marks of a missing painting.

"That's strange," I murmured.

"What is?"

"The other painting by Cima has disappeared."

"Oh, really?" She was only half interested, which was understandable enough.

However, I was definitely intrigued. I crossed over to the sacristan, an elderly man with white hair and a benign expression; there were parishioners who claimed that his benignity of appearance helped him in the sideline he had established of selling used wax to local taverns. "Excuse me," I said, "can you tell me what's happened to the painting of Constantine and Helen?"

"Oh, that," he said, "Father Marco thought it might be better to keep it in the sacristy for the moment."

"Why?"

"Well, you know it shows Constantine and Helen standing by the cross."

"Yes," I said.

"Well, there you are. That's why."

"Sorry," I said, "I really don't follow you."

"You've heard of all these other items that have been stolen over the last few months," he said.

"Well, vaguely," I said vaguely.

193

"We lost Saint Spiridion a few weeks ago," he said, gesturing to a nearby altar. "You know we have the guild of *sabbionai* who attend the church?"

"The what?" said Lucia in puzzlement.

"The sand-carriers," he repeated. "You know, people who carry sand."

She looked as if she were about to ask where or why but then thought better of it. The sacristan went on, "Their altar had a reliquary of Saint Spiridion, who's their patron saint. It had come from the East, a fine piece in silver, and it just disappeared. Well, Father Marco had been talking to other priests and it seems that it's only Greek items that have been disappearing like that. So he thought, what with Constantine being Greek . . ."

I was about to object but then thought better of it.

". . . he said we had better keep it somewhere safe until this business is cleared up. You can come and see it, if you like."

"Another time," said Lucia firmly. "I'm afraid we're in something of a hurry now."

I realised that Lucia was right. There were more urgent things to think about.

"Thank you, sior," I said. "It's very worrying. Unfortunately we have to go now."

"Certainly," he said. "You don't want to light a candle first?"

"Yes," Lucia said at once. "Let's say a prayer before we go."

"Let's say it to Saint John the Alms-giver," I said, leading her to the altar dedicated to this saint in the right-hand transept. "He was bishop of Alexandria, and when the relics of the True Cross were captured from Constantinople by the Persians he set out for the capital to bless Emperor Heraclius on his mission to recover them."

"Goodness," said Lucia. "You're beginning to sound just like my father."

"Remember I'm a *cicerone*," I said, "and this is my parish church. Naturally I've read up on the stories associated with it. Anyway, I've a feeling I need the protection of a saint who can help in the recovery of precious things." I was not entirely sure what I meant by that, but it felt right.

She humoured me, and we lit a candle in front of the altar, where the saint's remains lay in a rich urn. There was also a painting devoted to him, which Lucia studied with some care.

"By Jacopo Marieschi," I said. "It was painted five or six years ago."

"He looks kindly," she said, presumably referring to the saint rather than the painter. "I hope he can help. But now you had better go."

"I'll try to speak to the Missier Grande," I said. "I'll get word to you later."

"Don't come to the shop," she said.

"No, of course not. I'll find a way to send a message." I gestured towards the door of the church.

"You go first," she said. "I'll say another prayer."

"Thank you," I said.

"I didn't say it would be for you," she said with a smile.

"No, that was presumptuous of me."

"But it will be. You certainly seem to need it." On a sudden impulse she held out both hands to me, and I stooped and kissed them, my lips lingering no longer than was courteous. For those few instants I managed to put Isabella Venier out of mind.

"Go now," she said. "And be careful."

"I will," I promised.

20

I stepped out into the grey morning air. I realised that with the urgency and panic of the last quarter of an hour I had had no time to roll my eyes up at the tedious inevitability of yet another day of *caigo*. Still, I could not really complain. Anything that made it easier for me to remain anonymous was welcome.

As I made my way towards the Riva I wondered if this meant that I was condemned to a life forever yearning for fog. I thought of my ex-colleague, Paolo Padoan, and wondered whether he too had found himself most at ease in misty weather – until that fateful day when he had taken advantage of the blazing sun to hang his washing out.

As usual, the crowds thickened as I approached Saint Mark's Square. I wrapped my cloak more closely around myself. It was too early in the day to be wearing a mask, I realised, without arousing suspicion. I would just have to rely on the crowd, the fog and my carefully angled new tricorn hat.

I walked a couple of times up and down past the door that gave on to the private staircase to the Missier Grande's office, carefully but discreetly looking out for anyone who might be watching. I realised it was an impossible task. The coffee houses were milling with people, many of whom had little else to do than watch the people going by. It is a Venetian pastime. And some of us have turned it into a profession, if a slightly unseemly one.

I would simply have to run the risk, I decided, and I walked as casually as possible towards the door before running swiftly and lightly up the stairs. There was no one in the outer office, which was unusual but not unheard of at this hour in the morning, and I walked straight through to Sior Massaro's office.

He was sitting at his desk, quill in hand as usual. The moment he saw me his mouth opened in astonishment. Then he made a series of pantomimic gestures, dropping his quill and putting one finger to his lips, and waving the other hand as if to indicate that I should immediately crouch down on the floor, or possibly search for a handkerchief he had lost; when that left me bewildered, he flipped the hand over and waved it urgently in a shooing gesture. All the time his other hand remained close to his mouth, with that one upright finger tapping his pursed lips frenziedly in a plea for silence.

I wondered whether to answer with my own series of harlequin-like gesticulations, indicating my total inability to understand what he was trying to communicate, but in the end I took the course that seemed most likely to be the one he wished me to follow and backed out of the office as quietly as possible.

Seconds later he followed me, making a great show of shutting the door secretly behind us.

"Sior Marangon, you must flee, you must flee," he whispered, his hands making flapping gestures again.

"Flee?" I said. "Can't I see the Missier Grande?"

"It will do no good," he said, his round face a picture of dismay.

"No good?" I said. "He's my only hope."

"He is no more." This time he raised both hands to his face as if he were afraid it was going to peel off like a carnival mask.

"No more?" I gasped. "Is he dead?"

"He is no more the Missier Grande." He somehow forced these words out. It was clear that this was the end of Sior Massaro's entire world.

"He's been dismissed?" I said, aghast.

Sior Massaro just opened his arms out, as if a verbal answer was too painful.

"So where – what . . ."

"The Inquisitors' men are removing all his files at this moment. That's why you must flee. I know they're looking for you too."

"You're telling me to go on the run?"

His face, usually so comforting in its serene roundness, was painful to watch. Although sceptical of the competence of some of the higher authorities in the city, he had probably never before in his life suggested breaking any of the city's countless laws and regulations. But at last he said, "I think it would be best. And I know the Missier Grande would counsel it."

"Where is he?" I asked.

"At his family home in Campo Sant'Agnese."

I had never imagined him having such a thing. "And what's he planning to do?"

"I don't know," said Sior Massaro disconsolately.

"And do we know why this has happened?"

"No one has said anything."

This was standard procedure, so I was not surprised.

"But," he went on, "I have to say I think it is connected with your activities." And the reproachful expression on his face was awful to see.

"Ah," I said, not attempting to defend myself. I had already guessed as much. Something struck me. "So why are you telling me to flee? Why not hand me over to the authorities?"

He glanced back over his shoulder. "Well, that would have been my instinct," he said, "but there's something the Missier Grande said before he left the office . . ."

"What's that?"

"He told me to say to you, 'Don't give up.'" He looked at me with some curiosity, to see if this meant anything to me.

"Don't give up," I repeated. "I see."

There was a stir in the room we had just left, and he returned to his Harlequin mode, making urgent flailing gestures. "Quickly," he said. "Run for it. Don't go down the stairs. You can go on up to the roof and then . . ." He paused, thought for a moment and then said, "No, better go down the stairs."

I went down the stairs. I could hear him making loud and clearly artificial remarks to cover the sound of my retreating footsteps. Before I reached the door at the bottom it opened and I saw the silver pommel of a cane enter, followed by the tip of a raised chin – and then, of course, by the rest of Marino Basso, closely followed by his hulking companion. I had the advantage of being above them in the gloom and so, after just a split second in which I wondered whether the roof would have been a better option, I kept on walking determinedly downwards. I had already passed them before Basso recognised me and squeaked, "Marangon!"

"Good day to you," I said.

"Stop him!" he shouted to his companion.

I dodged the lunging hand and headed for the *sottoportego* that led out of the square. I could hear several voices yelling "Stop him!" Faces were turning towards me, so I yelled "Stop him!" myself, pointing agitatedly forward in the direction of a group of gondoliers lounging beside the canal. This created enough of a confused distraction for me to run unimpeded down the narrow alleyway that led towards the Frezzeria. After a few more abrupt twists and turns I reached Campo San Paternian, and I was able to pause, feeling reasonably sure that I had outrun all my pursuers.

So now where? "Don't give up," I said to myself. Don't give up what? Well, it could only mean the investigation into the Four Horsemen. The murder of Boldrin was almost certainly connected. But it was difficult to see how I could investigate his murder as a fugitive. I needed assistance, and there were only two people I could think of who were likely to be willing or able to provide it. I just had to get a message to them.

It didn't take me long to work out who would be the best messenger. It took me a little longer to reach him.

21

Half an hour later I was among the boatyards of eastern Castello. I found Lucio, Marco and Piero busy scraping barnacles from an upturned boat. It turned out this was actually a paid job, rather than one of their countless inventive ways of turning their surroundings into an endless playground.

However, Lucio was willing enough to take a break; this involved a little mathematical dispute, as they worked out how to divide the eventual pay for the boat-scraping, taking into account the length of time he would be absent, but this was soon settled (rather to Lucio's advantage, as it seemed to me, but I knew better than to interfere).

I gave Lucio clear instructions on how to reach the bookshop. As I described the approach to it, via Saint Mark's Square, the eyes of the other two boys began to grow round. "The Piazza!" said Piero, as if he were Marco Polo speaking of Kubla Khan's summer palace at Shangdu.

"When I get back I'll tell you all about it," said Lucio; and maybe that's what Marco Polo had said to his family as well.

"Next time we'll come too," said Piero, scrubbing fiercely at a particularly adhesive and all too allegorical barnacle.

"I'll show you around," said Lucio.

I gave him the message in the form of a folded piece of paper, telling him to make sure that no one else saw it; I didn't need to tell him not to read it himself, since I was aware that he could not read. "Give it either to the man who owns the bookshop, Sior Fabrizio, or to his daughter, Siora Lucia."

"Fabrizio or Lucia. Which would you prefer?" he said, looking sharply at me.

"It doesn't matter," I said.

"I'm guessing Lucia," he said, putting the folded paper inside his shirt. He darted a quick smile at me.

"If you say so," I said.

"Is she pretty?"

"Yes," I said. "And clever."

He shrugged at that. I imagine he had never thought of cleverness as either a likely or a desirable quality in a female.

I gave him the agreed sum (one *lira*), and he set off, swaggering slightly as befitted an adventurous traveller. Then I bade farewell to Marco and Piero, who stood gazing wistfully at their friend as he disappeared into the mist, and set off myself.

An hour or so later I was sitting near the door in a tavern in Campo SS Giovanni e Paolo. I had already eaten a plate of fried fish and drunk a glass of wine and had paid for them, so that I could leave at a moment's notice. I saw Fabrizio and Lucia approaching and went out to meet them before they could enter.

"Not here," I said. "People will remember us. Let's walk towards the Fondamenta Nuove."

They said not a word but walked on either side of me as I set off across the square; perhaps they thought they had to act as bodyguards. As we passed the statue of Bartolomeo Colleoni I gestured towards it.

"The only great horseman in Venice," I said.

"Quite," said Fabrizio. "Though not a Venetian, of course."

I realised it was the first time I had talked to Fabrizio outside his shop. He noticed me looking at him.

"Surprised to see me out and about?" he said.

"Well, not accustomed to it," I said.

"I don't get out as much as I should," he admitted. "Although Lucia knows that I often go for long midnight rambles."

She nodded. "And when I was a child you used to take me all over," she said. "We even went to Torcello and Burano once." She turned to me. "That was a bright boy you sent."

"Lucio?" I said. "Yes, he's clever."

"I don't think he'd ever been in a bookshop before," said Fabrizio. "He seemed fascinated."

"He loved the gold bindings," said Lucia.

"I'm sure he did," I said. "And I'm sure he'd love their contents if someone could just teach him to read."

"I told him that," said Lucia, "and he just looked at me as if I were mad."

We passed the corner of the great marble façade of the Scuola di San Marco, under the eyes of its stern white lion, and started walking down the *fondamenta* alongside the Rio dei Mendicanti.

"But none of this is to the purpose," said Fabrizio. "What are we going to do now?"

"I've got to find out who killed Sior Boldrin," I said.

"Yes," they both said, though in rather doubtful tones.

"You don't sound very convinced," I said. "I'm hoping it's not because you think I did it."

"Of course not," said Lucia at once. "But who do you think did do it? And why?"

"Well, I believe it may well have been that Neapolitan who came to your shop."

"What makes you think that?" said Fabrizio. "Not just a general belief in the murderous tendencies of Neapolitans, I trust."

"No," I said. "I'm quite sure he's a hired killer. I've read a file on him."

"Goodness," said Lucia. "Where did you read that?"

I made a slightly impatient gesture. "At the Missier Grande's office, as I'm sure you guessed."

She was silent.

"Sorry," I said, "But you are going to have to accept that my work as a confidential agent is part of this whole story. I never chose the role, but that's what I've been doing for the past few months."

Sior Fabrizio said, "We understand that. Just go on. Why did this Neapolitan kill Boldrin?"

"Well, this is the part that you might find hard to believe. He did it, I think, for the sole purpose of incriminating me. I'm sure he had nothing against Boldrin at all."

"It seems a little excessive," said Fabrizio. "If he's a killer and he wants you out of the way, why doesn't he just kill you?"

"Father!" said Lucia.

"I'm not advocating it, my dear," he said. "Just pointing out that it would have been a much easier solution to his problem."

"Well," I said, "there are two answers to that. One is that Antonio Esposito apparently specialises in murders that look like accidents."

"That's certainly not the case of Boldrin's murder," said Fabrizio.

"No, but if the real intended victim was not Boldrin but me, since I would of course be executed when found guilty, then you could say the crime still shows something of the same deviousness of approach. But more important, there's the fact that using this method he would succeed not only in eliminating me but also in discrediting me totally. If I'm the kind of person who viciously and vindictively murders a man because he threw me out of a gambling house, then I am certainly not the kind of person whose views on anything are worth considering."

"And what are these dangerous views?" said Fabrizio.

"That's the problem," I said. "I'm not sure. But I think that whoever hired Esposito believes I know something of vital importance. It's the same person who hired Esposito to murder Paolo Padoan."

I glanced at Lucia. She nodded. "Yes, Father has explained that part of the story to me. The poor old classics teacher. I remember him, you know."

"So why do you think Esposito came to our shop?" said Fabrizio.

"I'm not sure. I imagine that whoever hired him had just told him to look into all possible ways of getting rid of me. And we are known to be friends."

"Oh, *cospetto*," said Fabrizio. "And the book? How did they get hold of it?"

I told them about Sanudo's trick at the *salotto*.

"So Sanudo was the last person to have it," said Lucia. "And he obviously hates you. So doesn't that make it clear?"

"I have thought of that, of course," I said. "But I'm still not sure that he would have the wit or the connections to hire a killer like Esposito."

"So who else knew Sanudo had the book?" asked Lucia.

I could already feel my cheeks flushing. "Well, I did mention it to Noblewoman Isabella Venier. She detained me at the end of the *salotto* and I explained to her what had happened."

"Goodness me," said Lucia. "She must have been shocked. But you're surely not suggesting that she—"

"No," I said, perhaps too hastily. "But she might have informed someone else."

"Or Sanudo might have given it to someone else," said Fabrizio.

"I am presuming," I said, "that this all has something to do with what Padoan was investigating when he was killed. The Four Horsemen."

We came out on to the Fondamenta Nuove; there was no view of San Michele, Murano or any of the more distant islands, just the flat greyish-green expanse of lagoon merging murkily into the rolling mist. A gondolier strolled up to us and asked if we wanted to be taken to Murano. We declined and began walking to the right, in the direction of Santa Maria del Pianto.

"Father has told me something about that," said Lucia. "Have you any more definite ideas of who the Horsemen are?"

"Well," I said, "yes and no."

"Let's begin with yes," said Fabrizio. "That sounds more likely to take us somewhere."

"It seems that Sanudo and some of his companions chose to frighten Padoan with stories of some secret society, so Komnenos told me. And I presume that was the Four Horsemen. And I have since discovered that Sanudo and his companions – three of them, as it happened, making four in all – had indeed formed a secret society, with the aim of carrying out little acts of revenge against the Turks. You may have heard of some of them."

"You mean the various indignities against the Turkish merchants?" said Fabrizio.

"Yes, and something far worse that happened yesterday." I gave a brief account of the kidnapping of the two women. My audience was suitably shocked by the crime and gratifyingly impressed by my role in thwarting it, off-handedly though I recounted it.

"Well," said Lucia when I had concluded, "what are you so puzzled about? Isn't it obvious that there are your Four Horsemen? And now they've been discovered and so presumably that's an end of it."

Fabrizio paused, gazing out at a seagull perched on a pole. "I heard some curious rumours of some such business yesterday. But nobody seemed certain what had happened. And then Madricardo told me that he had heard that Sanudo was being sent off to Corfu by his father. Family business was the excuse. Now I understand."

"So if that is the case," I said, "why was Boldrin murdered last night?"

"To stop you telling the full story," said Lucia. She seemed relieved to have got to the bottom of it all.

"Maybe," I said, "but maybe not." I turned to Fabrizio. "Can you remember anything in Padoan's diary that might be helpful? Particularly towards the end, I imagine."

"There were some things that puzzled me there," said Fabrizio. "He began to make some strange classical references. He mentioned Hephaestus a couple of times – just the name, which he circled."

"Hephaestus?" I said. "The armourer of the gods – Vulcan to the Romans. And lame. That must be a reference to Esposito."

"It seems possible," admitted Fabrizio. "And he referred a couple of times to having found the thread of Ariadne but didn't make it clear what he meant."

"The thread of Ariadne?" I said.

"Yes," Lucia said, "I'm sure you know—"

"Yes," I said, a touch impatiently, "the thread she gave to Theseus to help him find his way through the labyrinth."

"Sorry," she said. "I certainly didn't want to impugn your knowledge of classical myths."

"I'm sorry too," I said, at once embarrassed. "Always too sensitive on matters to do with my education."

"And I'm always too ready to tease you on it," she said with a frank smile.

I didn't reproach her. A touch of light relief was welcome, in fact.

I turned to Fabrizio and said, "And he gave no clue as to what he meant by this thread?"

"No. He just announced it, in the very last page he wrote. He seemed to be sure that he was going to see something important. Presumably at the end of the thread."

"See something?"

"Yes, that was the verb he used."

"Ariadne," I said. "Definitely Ariadne?"

"Is there anyone else who has a thread?" he said.

"No," I said, "but there are other Ariadnes."

"I'm sorry?" said Fabrizio.

"Siora Isabella Venier's Greek maid is called Arianna. Which, I presume, is just the Italian version of Ariadne."

"Indeed?" said Lucia. "How do you know her maid's name?"

"She mentioned it to me," I said, trying to sound casual. "And she also mentioned the fact that she speaks hardly any Tuscan or Venetian."

"And so?" said Lucia.

"I think it very likely that Padoan, visiting Siora Isabella's *salotto*, would have loved the chance to try his Greek out on someone who could only communicate in that language."

"Perhaps you're right," said Fabrizio thoughtfully.

"And very possibly Ariadne was gratified to find someone she could talk to."

"And she gave him a thread," said Lucia.

"That's what we have to find out," I said.

"How do we do that?"

"We speak to Ariadne ourselves," I said. "Or rather your father does."

"Oh dear," he said. "I hope she will understand Homeric Greek."

"Please, Sior Fabrizio," I said. "It's all we have to go on."

"Very well," he said in a resigned tone. "Tell me what I have to do."

"Well, I think we're going to need help from our bright messenger boy," I said.

22

Next morning Fabrizio and I sat in one of the small taverns in the Erbaria close to the Rialto market. All around us the market men – porters, bargemen, street-cleaners, stall-holders and assorted beggars and urchins – were taking their first refreshment of the day, some after several hours already spent carting goods to the Rialto and setting them up on the stalls, others in preparation for a long day to be spent out-bawling their neighbours in the advertising of their wares, or displaying their crippled bodies and ragged clothes behind their begging bowls. Red wine was the refreshment of choice, although some were taking small mugs of *grappa*. People had run out of comments to make on the *caigo* and instead were chatting loudly and amiably about the prospects for the next regatta or the success or failure of the latest Goldoni play. There was some light-hearted banter between Nicolotti and Castellani, but it was all clearly part of an established routine.

Fabrizio and I were probably the only strangers there, but no one bothered us, for which I, for one, was grateful. I had not slept well, having spent the night in an empty apartment near the church of the Madonna dell'Orto which I knew about from an earlier investigation; it had once held a gambling den owned by a Friulian schoolmaster, who had been banished from the city once it had become clear that his nocturnal activities were taking a toll on his diurnal duties at his place of employment (he kept falling asleep during lessons); the authorities had not yet worked out to whom the apartment belonged, and so it had remained empty for a couple of months now. I had expected to have the place to myself but had been disturbed in the middle of the night by the incursion of a local prostitute and her drunken client. Once they had got over their shock at finding themselves with company, they had been most insistent that I should feel under no constraint to leave, and having no alternative I did in fact remain, doing my best in the adjoining room to ignore their clumsy efforts to carry out their business discreetly; I was astonished at the man's ability to persist in his endeavours while his partner made constant shh-ing noises every time he uttered any sound of either desire or satisfaction.

All in all it had been something of a relief to get up very early and make my way through the damp dim streets to the Rialto. Crossing the Rialto Bridge at that hour and gazing at the long line of majestic palaces fading into the *caigo*, while barges and *sandoli* and gondolas, their lanterns twinkling feebly in the grey light, wove swirling patterns in the water, made me realise just how intensely I yearned to remain a part of this city, even if it were to mean skulking around corners, hiding under porticoes and wrapping myself in my cloak at the approach of *sbirri* and watchmen for the remainder of my days.

I found Fabrizio already seated at a table by the door, a glass of red wine and a volume of Virgil in front of him. He looked remarkably bright and cheery. I began to suspect he was enjoying the novelty of this investigative life.

After a few remarks of greeting we settled down to a companionable silence; he returned to his book, and I kept an eye on the passers-by.

At last I spotted Lucia making her way through the crowd. She had a cream-coloured shawl over her head and shoulders, and this helped me to keep track of her as she walked into the bustling confusion of the stalls. She was gazing very fixedly ahead of herself, keeping an eye on her quarry. Since she didn't know what Ariadne looked like, she had been obliged to wait outside the Palazzo Querini to spot her as she set off on her usual shopping expedition (to the Rialto market at seven o'clock, as her mistress had helpfully informed me).

Now I saw Lucio weaving along beside Lucia, his bright red Castello cap flickering in and out of the bustling crowd.

I got up from my seat and said, "It's started."

"Ah." Fabrizio put down his Virgil and gazed vaguely at the market. "I can't see . . ."

"Just wait here," I said. I set off after the intermittent flickers of Lucia's bright shawl and Lucio's cap.

The two of them had halted, and so I presumed had their quarry. I made my way to the right, close to the Grand Canal, and saw they were both gazing at a small woman in a dark dress with a grey veil over her head. She had a large shopping basket on one arm and was standing by a fruit stall, pointing with a determined finger at a mound of pears. The vendor, clearly used to her miming mode, made no attempt to speak to her. I saw a certain amount of haggling going on, all in mime, with upraised fingers and shaking of heads, until a deal was reached to the satisfaction of both; this, it seemed, was all part of a well-established routine. The process was repeated for grapes, oranges and apples, and eventually, with a final wave of her hand, she turned away.

At that point Lucio darted forward and grabbed at her basket, giving it a determined yank. The woman shrieked and released it, and Lucio immediately ran off, leaving a trail of scattered fruit as he did so. I loomed up before him, yelling, "No you don't!"

I grabbed him by the arm as he attempted (at least apparently) to swerve past me. He dropped the basket and bent his head and bit my restraining hand. We had rehearsed this the previous afternoon, but it was clear that the actual performance brought out a greater sense of realism in him, and I let out a yelp that was entirely unfeigned. I let go of him at once (I couldn't risk anyone else's grabbing hold of him), and he disappeared into the crowd, flashing a quick apologetic smile at me. I picked up the basket and made my way towards Lucia and Ariadne. The latter was leaning against the stall and panting, while Lucia comforted her, together with a crowd of other shoppers and vendors.

I held up the basket reassuringly, and people congratulated me; I ruefully exhibited the deep-set imprints of Lucio's teeth on my wrist and received sympathetic expressions of commiseration. Lucia put her arm round Ariadne's shoulder and led her towards the taverns that lined the side of the square, making soothing noises. I could tell that Lucia was not at all happy with this part of our stratagem, but as I had pointed out to her it would have been very difficult to find another way to persuade her to sit down and talk to an unknown man.

I could hear Lucia saying "My father, my father" as Ariadne let forth a seemingly endless stream of frantic Greek, interspersed with sobs.

Fabrizio stood up as they approached and said something reassuring. Ariadne looked a little wary but was eventually persuaded to sit down at the same table. I came up and put the basket of fruit down by her side, and she looked at me and said breathily, "*Efcharistò, efcharistò.*" Lucia sat down next to her father and held Ariadne's hand.

Fabrizio began to speak to Ariadne in slow and careful classical Greek. After a moment's puzzlement she responded with a few short words. Fabrizio talked on. It was not clear how much she was understanding, but his voice is always very calming. It's possible he was simply reciting selected passages from Euripides, but in any case she appeared to be happy to hear him. She was persuaded by Lucia to take a glass of *malvasia*.

I hovered nearby without sitting down. I thought it best that my role in the whole business should be relegated to the background; there was always the possibility that she might recollect having seen me at the Palazzo Querini at some point, or that the story of our little scuffle might reach the ear of a *sbirro*, in which case it would be best if I were not the first person to be spotted.

Eventually I saw that Ariadne was actually smiling in answer to something Fabrizio had said. He looked suitably gratified. She gained confidence and began to talk. As she chattered away rapidly I saw Fabrizio gently indicate that she should slow down. She nodded and started up at a slightly slower pace, but after a few seconds was already cantering and clearly heading towards a full gallop again. It took Fabrizio a minute or so to get her to appreciate that the only chance she had of being understood was if she spoke to him in ponderous fashion, word by slow word. After a while she seemed to enjoy doing this, treating Fabrizio as if he were a slow-witted child, and he played along, clearly with equal enjoyment. Lucia looked on, her expression of anxiety gradually fading as she saw that Ariadne had recovered from her moment of shock.

At a certain point I saw Fabrizio lean forward and point to something hanging round her neck, presumably a medallion or a crucifix or some such ornament. This led to further animated conversation, during which she clearly talked with some enthusiasm about the thing, touching it with affectionate pride. At a certain point Fabrizio glanced towards me with an enigmatic smile, which I interpreted as meaning that something useful had emerged from their talk. I gave him an appreciative nod and stepped away, looking warily around the market square. Nobody was paying any attention to us any more, fortunately, and the market was its usual noisy, bustling self.

I glanced back and saw that Fabrizio had risen to his feet. He was gesturing to Ariadne and telling her to stay where she was. Lucia put a restraining hand on her arm as she began to rise, and she sat back down again.

Fabrizio came towards me. He was looking quite pleased with himself.

"It took me a while to get used to the vowel sounds," he said, "and there were quite a few words that got past me completely, but I think I followed most of what she had to say."

"And is it helpful?"

"I think it may be. But you had better be the judge. It was very fortunate that I spotted the medallion of Constantine XI she was wearing. That provided the perfect cue for what I really wanted to ask."

"Yes," I said, "I can imagine it might have been useful."

"I told her that I had had a friend who was a great admirer of Constantine XI, a former schoolteacher called Paolo Padoan, and she immediately told me that she knew him. She seemed quite excited. It turned out that Padoan had asked her about her devotion to Constantine, and she had become very fond of him. He spoke Greek, even if it was the same antiquated version as mine (she was really quite indulgent with me), and he admired Constantine. Two ways to her heart. In fact, she had become so fond of him that she had offered to show him something special. And at that point she suddenly seemed to think she had gone too far, and she stopped. I said I had a friend who was very interested in Constantine and I expect he would like to hear about it too. That's you, by the way."

"I see," I said. "And I just happen to be here in the market as well. The person who saved her basket of fruit."

"Don't worry about that," he said. "She is not naturally suspicious. I suppose if our young friend who made off with her basket were to turn up as well she might become a little wary, but so long as we're all warm-hearted people who love Constantine I don't think you need worry."

I allowed him to lead me back to the table, where she recognised me as her fruit-saviour and again expressed her gratitude profusely and incomprehensibly, while I simpered modestly. Then Fabrizio drew my attention to the little medallion she had round her neck; it was a charmingly stylised portrait of the emperor, shown with crown and halo, and holding a bejewelled cross. I murmured suitable appreciative remarks, and she beamed. She then evidently made up her mind and leaned forward and said something in a low voice to Fabrizio.

I turned to him inquisitively. He translated: "She says that she can show you an even better image of the emperor. But you must promise to tell no one."

I immediately made elaborate gestures promising total discretion, and she smiled. She spoke quietly again, and Fabrizio translated: "Come to Campo Sant'Angelo this afternoon after the Marangona and she will meet you."

Given the meeting place, it seemed she was going to show me something in Isabella Venier's casino. I nodded. The *tesserae* were beginning to come together, but I didn't like the overall picture that was being created. None the less, I nodded and agreed to meet her there.

She finished her wine, bowed and thanked us all again profusely, picked up her basket and set off through the crowds.

"I hope she's got over the shock," said Lucia. "It was a shameful trick."

"Yes," I said, "but how else could we have done it?"

"Yes, yes, I know, but even so . . ."

Fabrizio said, "It is remarkable that after just one meeting she's prepared to reveal to you something that is obviously so secret."

"It's not so remarkable," said Lucia.

"Because of my irresistible charm?" I said.

Lucia gave me a dutiful but commiserating smile. "Because she is clearly a very lonely woman."

"Ah yes," I said. "I suppose so."

"It's obvious. She probably never gets a chance to speak to anyone except her mistress day in, day out. So when she is able to speak to people who understand her, who have helped her in a moment of crisis, and who share her own religious devotion – or claim to share it—"

"Siora Lucia," I said, "you understand I'm not doing this just for the fun of it."

"I know, Sior Alvise, I know. I just wish there were some other way."

"So do I," I said. "But I can't think of one."

"Well, in any case," said Fabrizio, "it's fortunate I spotted that icon. I had been thinking of other ways to engage her in conversation. I had wondered about talking about Cerigo, and its devotion to Venus, but then I thought she might take that the wrong way."

"Yes, Father, I'm glad you didn't do that."

"Because of course you know the Venier family claim to have a link to Venus, because of the name," he went on chattily.

He was looking at me as he said this, so I replied, "Really? No, I didn't know that." I could hear the hollow sound of my voice even as I spoke.

"Yes," he said. "I remember reading somewhere that they even put up a little temple to Venus on an island they own in the lagoon."

"Oh really?" I said again, looking as uninterested as was compatible with good manners. I had the feeling that Lucia glanced at me rather oddly, but I did not dare to look. Fortunately at that moment a diversion occurred.

"Alvise," said Fabrizio, "I think you had better leave now. I think I see *sbirri* on the other side of square."

I turned to stare in the direction he was looking. There were familiar oafish figures with thick beards and suspicious expressions making their way through the crowd; no one was making any effort to offer their goods to them. It was possible that someone had reported the little fracas. I bade a hasty farewell to my friends and set off in the direction of Campo San Cassiano.

23

I had plenty of time to kill between now and the appointment with Ariadne. I found my feet taking me in the direction of the Fontego dei Turchi. I certainly had no definite plan in mind; I just had a vague inkling that I might find something there. Perhaps if all else failed I could ask the Turks to take me in.

I made my way through the narrow streets and small squares of the Santa Croce district. I paused on the bridge that leads towards Campo Santa Maria Mater Domini to admire the splendid view of the curving side of Ca' Pesaro, its white wall gleaming phantom-like in the mist to the right. There was something suitably melancholy and mysterious in the dematerialisation of its massive marble essence.

This is, after all, a city where even in clear weather it makes no sense to talk of being down to earth or having one's feet on the ground; how much more evanescent are all one's certainties in vaporous weather like this? Perhaps if the mist never did clear up I'd find myself growing convinced that I must have killed Boldrin myself. How could I be sure I hadn't? How could I be sure of anything? Two days ago I'd been convinced I loved no one but Lucia . . .

As I continued on my way through the small but charming square of Santa Maria Mater Domini I realised that this conviction at least had not really changed. And I would do well to keep it firmly in mind – and in heart. That way I'd have at least one clear point of reference.

The accompanying guilt was just something I would have to find a way to deal with.

I began to wonder whether it really was a good idea to be heading towards the site of a serious crime, given the fact that I was being sought as the committer of a serious crime myself. But I assured myself that it was unlikely that there would still be investigators or *sbirri* hanging around. The Turks themselves would not appreciate the attention.

I made my way down the broad road that led to the side entrance to the Fontego. As I approached the end, where the street gave on to the Grand Canal, I saw two young men in Turkish robes standing near the entrance; they were clearly there as guards or watchmen. I could not recall ever having seen such figures before. They eyed me curiously as I approached. I did my best to avoid looking at them, without, I hoped, appearing to do so too obviously.

As the road ended in the Grand Canal, I either had to hail a gondola or stand and admire the view for a few seconds, pretending like all people who have walked down the wrong street that that was precisely what I had come to do, and then return the way I had come. I decided on the second option; I could not afford to leave traces, and you cannot enter a gondola without being duly noted and, sometimes, interrogated (in the most friendly fashion, of course).

So I feigned an interest in the hazy view of the unfinished façade of the church of San Marcuola on the opposite side of the canal and then turned to make my way back, with the nonchalant air of one who has taken a wrong turning but has no regrets, having enjoyed a splendid view I would otherwise have missed. At that moment the door of the Fontego opened and a man stepped out into the street. He was dressed in black, and as I stared at him he pushed back his glossy black hair in a gesture I recognised, before positioning a tricorn hat. It was Kostantinos Komnenos.

My instinct was to step back and turn away, but it was too late. His teeth flashed white in his dark-complexioned face, and he raised his hand to me. I acknowledged his greeting and would have proceeded on my way, but he was already striding towards me. Did he know about the murder I was suspected of?

It seemed not. He said, "So you've discovered my little secret."

"What's that?" I said in some confusion.

He turned and gestured towards the Fontego. "I imagine you did not expect to see me coming out of there."

"Well, no," I said.

"And yet you knew I was a Phanariot. I remember you saying so during our little walk the other evening."

"I understood you had worked for the Ottomans but had given it up for your poetry."

"Would that it were so," he said with a light smile. "I'm afraid singing about banditry is not quite so remunerative as actual banditry. So I still take on occasional jobs as translator and interpreter for my former employers. It seems there has been something of a diplomatic crisis in the last couple of days, and I was asked to lend a hand. Which way are you going?"

"Um, back to – well, in this direction," I said, gesturing along the broad street. "You're not taking a gondola?"

"No. Even with occasional work like this I still find it more advantageous to use my own legs. As you appear to be doing yourself. Shall we walk together?"

It was impossible to refuse, and we began to stroll down the street. He seemed to be in no hurry, so I accommodated my gait to his.

"And what is the crisis?" I asked.

He glanced sidelong at me. "Do you really not know? I thought the networks of Venetian gossip were all-extensive."

"Well," I said, "yes, I do know something about it. But I thought it would be good to hear it from the Turkish point of view."

He gave a sharp intake of breath. "Are you being deliberately provocative?"

"I thought you could tell me what the Turks are saying about it," I explained, in as bland a voice as possible.

"I see. Well, first, what do you know? Because in theory I am bound to silence on the subject."

"Yes, of course," I said. "As we all are." I took a swift decision and decided I would have to forgo the pleasure of bashfully revealing my role in the affair; if he were to grow curious about it, he might extend his enquiries and discover the later story I was involved in. As a general rule there is no point in arousing unnecessary curiosity. "I heard something about an outrage against two Turkish women. And I heard our friend Sanudo may have been involved."

"Ah," he said. "So that has got out, has it?"

"I don't know how widely it's known," I said. "Just something I heard from a gondolier."

"Ah, the gondoliers. I understand that they once recited verses from Tasso. Now it seems they confine themselves to local gossip."

"Not all gondoliers," I said. "Some can be remarkably reticent. But is it true about Sanudo?"

"Your gondolier was well informed," he said. "I believe the family has already found urgent business for the young man in Corfu. I'm sure it will be very beneficial for him. Not so sure about the Corfioti."

"I wonder how Noblewoman Isabella Venier will take it," I said casually.

"I hardly think she will be devastated," he said. "But I would advise you not to build too many hopes on that assumption."

"Don't worry," I said. "I have no aspirations in that direction."

He looked at me again; I think he was trying to see how seriously I meant that.

"Very wise," he said after a brief pause.

"But how have the Turks taken this affair?"

"How do you imagine?"

"Well, I really have no grounds for imagining anything. I have never had any dealings with any Turks. I just know their popular image. Comic figures in Goldoni's plays. Terrifying conquerors in the annals of history." I paused and gestured back in the direction of the Fontego. "And always worth trading with."

"Spoken like a true Venetian. But to answer your question, there is deep, deep anger. There is a desire for revenge. But there is also an unwillingness to allow this to disturb normal relations between the two powers – if powers is still the right word for either of them."

"I would advise you not to say that last bit too loudly – to either of them."

He smiled. "I'm caught between the two and know full well how to soothe them – and how to provoke them, should I so wish. I now have to speak to the Procurators and inform them how matters stand at the Fontego. I will be playing this non-poetic role for a few more days, I believe."

"A peacemaker rather than a bandit."

"That's one way of putting it. Which way are you going?" he asked as we reached the end of the street.

I guessed he would be heading towards the Rialto and so indicated the opposite direction. He bade me farewell with a dramatic sweep of his hat, followed by another toss of his thick black hair, and strode off.

24

After a day spent slinking around the quieter corners of the city, thinking about all I had seen and heard, wondering what the *sbirri* would have done to my room this time, and counting my money (I needed to make plans for an eventual flight to safer shores), I made my way to Campo Sant'Angelo for my appointment with Ariadne. She was there, standing by the well on the north side of the square, close to Calle dei Avvocati.

I had the distinct impression that she was already regretting her decision but didn't know how to back out of it. I firmly thrust from my mind all considerations of what Lucia would have advised in such a situation and determined to go ahead as planned. And so I bowed to her and smiled, and gestured that I was ready to follow her lead.

She proffered a weak, nervous smile in return and started walking towards the casino. She gave an agitated look over her shoulder as she inserted the key in the lock and then beckoned me to follow her quickly. I did so.

We mounted the stairs and entered the familiar rooms. She found a tinderbox and lighted a candle, and I glanced around. There were, of course, no signs of the sensuous feast from my previous visit. The chairs were set back against the walls, and the table was covered with a dark cloth. She led me through the bedroom, whose neatly made bed had an air of crisp and pristine innocence, to another smaller room beyond it. She put her finger to her lips as we entered it. I guessed this room must be reserved for herself on occasions when her mistress decided that she needed her maid on hand all night. It was furnished very simply with a plain bed, a single straight-backed chair and a tall dark wardrobe. She walked over to the wardrobe, and then, with another nervous look behind her as if other people might have slipped into the apartment in the last ten seconds, she turned a key in the wardrobe door and opened it. I could see nothing but long hanging dresses; she put the candle down on the chair and parted the skirts. From the deep recesses of the closet she brought out an icon, about a foot high, of the emperor saint. It was set in a silver frame with precious stones at top and bottom. She held it towards me with nervous reverence, and I put down my satchel and lifted the candle to inspect it.

It was a fine work, and I had the clear impression that I had seen it before. My *cicerone*'s mind was turning over image after image, and at last it came to a halt on a sharply defined one: I could see the icon on the cluttered wall of a Venetian guildhall, the Scuola dei Calegheri, in Campo San Tomà. Why the shoemakers should have paid homage to Constantine the Great I had no idea; it was quite possible that one of their number had simply inherited the artefact from a crusading ancestor (it was clearly Greek in origin) and donated it to his guild. And it had disappeared a few weeks earlier. What on earth was it now doing in this woman's wardrobe?

"Very beautiful," I said. "*Poly kalò*," I added, a few words coming back to me from the two or three lessons I had once had in ancient Greek somewhere in England before my mother's professional engagements had resulted in a move to yet another part of the country.

She nodded with fierce agreement, and took it back from my hands and replaced it in her wardrobe, crossing herself several times after she had done so. She put her finger to her lips to inform me that it was a secret.

"Are there any others?" I asked. "Others?" I repeated the last word, feeling it was one she might have come across.

She looked warily at me. I think there was a flicker of understanding in her eyes, but seconds later she clearly decided it was safest to feign a total lack of comprehension. She waved her hands helplessly and shook her head.

At that moment we heard a noise from the direction of the entrance to the apartment. In an instant Ariadne's face turned from wary to terrified. She gazed aghast towards her mistress's bedroom. She seemed frozen with fear.

I moved swiftly to the door and closed it noiselessly. There was nothing else that could be done. There was no way out of this small room except via Isabella Venier's room.

We could now hear people approaching. I recognised the low but distinctive tones of Isabella's voice, even though I could not make out any words as yet, and then came a male voice, equally distinctive: Komnenos. They came into the bedroom.

Ariadne gestured frantically towards the wardrobe. Was I really going to get in there? This was like a scene from a Goldoni play. But there seemed little choice. I tiptoed towards it. Fortunately it was still open, and I was able to step inside without making any noise. For a moment I wondered whether Ariadne was going to get in after me, which would have added to the overall embarrassment and general absurdity; I think she hesitated for a second or two, but then she quietly closed the door on me, leaving me in the musty darkness on my own.

The cupboard was tall enough for me to stand upright, even if I was hemmed in by dresses, at least one of which gave off a distinct smell of sweat. I couldn't see it, but from the feel of the coarse texture I assumed that it was Ariadne's, rather than her mistress's. Fortunately the wooden wardrobe was old and full of cracks; even with the muffling effect of the clothing, I was able to make out words and even whole sentences of what was being said in the next room, particularly by him, as his voice was slightly louder. I prayed hard that Ariadne and I were not going to have to listen to a scene of passionate love-making. Quite apart from all other considerations, it would be very embarrassing for us both – and might lead to all sorts of depressing comparisons. But the voices did not sound like those of aroused lovers. They were business-like and brisk.

Komnenos: No, it's not completely without risks, but nothing is in this world.
Venier: (*inaudible*) but how will you persuade the . . . (*inaudible*).
Komnenos: It only needs one, and that's already done. He obtains the . . . (*inaudible*) from the other two. They don't all have to be

there. In this case we have specifically asked for as small a delegation as possible. To preserve the . . . (*inaudible*).

Venier: When you say "we" . . .

Komnenos: My employers. Or so it must seem.

Venier: It just seems a little precipitate. I thought our plan . . . (*inaudible*).

Komnenos: I'm taking things as they come. Your friend Sanudo delivered this beautifully into our hands.

Venier: That was partly the idea. But I didn't know that he and his friends would take it . . . (*inaudible*).

Komnenos: It has made me indispensable to both sides, but discreetly so: that is the beauty of it. And I have insisted on this desire on the part of the ambassador for immediate reparations to his wife and daughter. They haven't questioned it.

Venier: (*light laugh*) What else do they expect Turkish women to be interested in?

Komnenos: That's what I calculated on.

Venier: (*inaudible*) be sure there won't be anyone else?

Komnenos: That's what I mean by the beauty of it. There is an intense desire for secrecy on both sides. I just take advantage of it. It helps too that the Missier Grande is out of the picture. I'm sure he would not have allowed it to go ahead without more thorough checks.

Venier: And you have all the necessary . . . (*inaudible*)?

Komnenos: Those have been ready for weeks.

Venier: Well, you know what to do afterwards. It can all be concealed there, for weeks or months if necessary.

Komnenos: I hope it won't be necessary to wait for months.

Venier: No, but it never hurts to be cautious. And it's our own goddess who will be protecting it (*light laugh*).

Komnenos: Of course, we will respect the usual pact. One quarter . . .

Venier: We can sort out those details in future weeks. Now I suppose you had better go.

Komnenos: Yes.

Venier: Kiss me one last time . . .

(*Long silence*)

I prayed that the length of the silence was not an indication of the transformation of the salutary kiss into something more passionate. However, there were no further noises indicative of intimate contact, and eventually they resumed talking. I could hardly distinguish any words now, as their voices had become much quieter. Presumably they were standing closer together.

However, despite the softness I could detect a nervousness in their tones. I surmised that despite their intimate knowledge of one another there was not complete trust. And at the moment they were both very much on edge. Clearly something extremely important was about to happen, and it was overwhelming all other considerations.

Their voices faded as they passed back out of the bedroom. I remained completely still; I could now hear Ariadne breathing hard. She was presumably releasing tension. Then Isabella's footsteps could be heard returning, and Ariadne caught her breath again.

There were faint noises from the bedroom as Isabella pottered around. I thought I detected the rustling sounds of clothes being removed. And then the door to the inner room was opened.

There was a second of silence, and then Isabella's voice spat out a single vituperative syllable. It sounded like "si", but I guessed it must be Greek for "you".

Immediately Ariadne's voice responded, in a babbling torrent of apologetic words. Isabella cut her short with a few more explosive syllables. And then there was another second of silence during which Ariadne merely whimpered. I could hear Isabella moving across the room and suddenly light hit my eyes as the wardrobe door was flung open. Isabella Venier stood there, wearing only her undergarments and holding my satchel in one hand.

25

She was clearly astonished. I could only imagine that she had expected to find some humble lover of her maidservant: a local porter or a stall-keeper, whom she could have freely tongue-lashed.

However, it took her only a couple of seconds to recover her poise, which cannot have been easy, dressed as she was. Of course, the absurdity of my position must have helped.

"This is embarrassing," I said, quite unnecessarily.

She let out a burst of laughter. It was not merry, but it was real enough. I stepped out of the wardrobe and tried to smile myself; it seemed only courteous.

"Well, Sior Alvise," she said, "let us hear your explanation for this." It was striking that she made no move to cover herself up.

I did my best not to look at the superb curves of her body. Such a distraction would not help.

"I foolishly panicked," I said. "I knew I should not be here."

"Am I to understand that after your assignation with me you conceived a passion for my maidservant?"

I noticed that she did not deign to glance at Ariadne, who was gazing at her mistress with a piteous expression of contrition and fear on her face. It struck me that it would be best for the safety of both Ariadne and myself if I allowed Isabella to think along those lines, damaging though it would be to my dignity (not to mention Ariadne's).

I opened out my hands in a helpless gesture. "What can I say?"

"As little as possible," she said. The contempt in her voice was total.

"Please don't blame Ariadne," I said. "I took advantage of her—"

"I really don't want to hear any of this," she said. "Just get out."

I took my satchel from her hands and moved towards the door.

She must have been struck by a sudden thought because she stopped me with a sharp "Wait!"

I turned round. She was staring hard at me. "Were you listening to our conversation earlier?"

"Siora," I said, "I was inside a wardrobe, surrounded by thick dresses. I could hear voices, but I certainly couldn't make out any words."

She continued to stare hard at me. I gazed back, as guilelessly as possible. After a while her expression changed to one of contempt and she said, "After you had had this," and she gestured to her own body, "could you really crave that?" And she jerked a scornful thumb at her maidservant cringing pitifully by her side.

I was tempted to say that there was certainly more human warmth in her servant but guessed that this would not do the poor woman any favours. I simply shrugged and said, "Siora, I was weak."

At that moment there came a thunderous pounding at the front door of the casino. Isabella Venier pushed past me into her bedroom, where she snatched up her dress, which was lying across the bed. Ariadne, clearly eager to make amends, hurried to help her. The next moment we heard the front door being opened and urgent footsteps crossing the entrance hall.

"Who on earth . . . ?" began Isabella Venier, her voice furious again, as she thrust the dress into Ariadne's hands.

The door opened and Lucia stood there, her face determined and stern.

Even as I stared at her, in the full consciousness that I had fallen into a convoluted plot scripted by Goldoni at his most farcical, I could not help thinking how enchanting she looked, her dark eyes flashing with fiery determination. And then the full awfulness of the situation was borne in on me.

"Just who are you?" said Isabella, once again refusing to be embarrassed by her state of near nakedness.

Lucia spoke with breathy urgency. "I was worried about my friend." She refused to look at me.

"And so you came breaking into my apartment without permission?"

"I'm sorry, but I thought something bad was happening." She said it with a kind of resolute calmness. "The door was unlocked. But I see I've made a mistake, and I apologise."

"If this is your friend," said Isabella, "I think you have probably made a bigger mistake than you know."

"I'll leave," said Lucia. The fire had passed from her eyes into her cheeks, which were now blazing.

"Please take him with you. I certainly have no use for him."

Lucia did not answer but turned and walked towards the door. I gazed after her but did not move.

"Please leave," said Isabella to me. As I followed Lucia towards the door she called after me, "If that is your friend from the bookshop you've made an enormous mistake yourself."

"I know," I said. And I meant it. I wasn't sure what Isabella meant, but did not think it the right moment to ask. But the mention of the bookshop did remind me of something I had to ask her. I stopped walking and turned to face her. "Signora Isabella, before I go, can you tell me what happened to my book?"

Her blank stare suggested that the Homer had quite gone from her mind; it also suggested that she had not yet heard of the murder, which was slightly reassuring. After a moment's pause she clearly recollected what I was referring to and said, "Do you think I've had time to think of that?"

"My apologies," I said, and headed for the door again. As I reached it I glanced momentarily back at Ariadne, thinking that from common courtesy if nothing else I should make some kind of acknowledgement to her. However, she was standing with her head bowed, holding her mistress's dress with as much penitent reverence as if it had Constantine's face blazoned on it. I felt that I had done as much as I could to protect her from her mistress's wrath. Probably silence would now be the best strategy. I walked swiftly after Lucia.

She was making her way down the stairs as fast as the darkness allowed. I called after her, "Siora Lucia, wait."

"Please leave me," she said. "I need to be alone."

"You've misunderstood the situation," I said, realising even as I said it that while technically true it was not the whole truth.

"I'm not sure I've understood anything at all," she said, pulling open the door into the street. There was a catch in her voice.

I followed her into the open air. She had paused for a moment, as if uncertain which way to go.

I said, "Siora Lucia, Noblewoman Venier came into the apartment with Komnenos, and when I heard them I made the foolish mistake of hiding in Ariadne's bedroom." I could not quite bring myself to say that I had been in the wardrobe. "When Komnenos left she must have decided to change her dress, or perhaps she wanted to lie down on her bed. And then she found me. That is the story." I had been intending to say "the whole story" but at the last moment could not bring myself to do so.

She lifted her head and gazed up at me. Even in the darkness I could see the lucent moisture of her eyes. "Sior Alvise, I only know ..." She paused. "I only know that I feel deeply humiliated."

"Please, Sior Lucia ..."

"It's probably my fault. I followed you to the *campo* because I was worried about your appointment with Ariadne, and I saw you enter this house with her. And then when I saw the noblewoman go in with that other man I was at a loss as to what to do. Then he came out, and I had all sorts of thoughts. Suppose he had killed you ..."

"Killed me?"

"Why not? People have been killed for less. So I entered the house myself. Now I wish I hadn't."

So did I. But that, of course, was the last thing I must say. The only way out at this point was a complete change of subject.

"I'm extremely grateful to you for your solicitude," I said, not completely untruthfully. "But there are other urgent matters to talk about. I heard a very significant conversation between Noblewoman Venier and Komnenos. And it suggests to me that something important is going to happen soon. Perhaps even this very night." I started walking in the direction of the square.

"Are you sure you want to talk to me about this?" she said.

"Siora Lucia, I have no one else I can turn to. No one."

"Dear me," she said with utter simplicity. "You are in a wretched situation."

"I know it," I said. "But I will be eternally grateful for your help."

She was silent for a few seconds before saying, "Then come with me."

That surprised me. It sounded as if she was taking the initiative. "Where?"

"To your gondola."

"To my what?"

"Well, your friend's gondola. Bepi. He's waiting in Rio San Luca."

"Why?"

"I just thought it might be prudent. I didn't know what was going to happen after your meeting with Ariadne, but I thought transport would always be useful. You might have had to escape to the mainland, and you would obviously need a friend to help you to do that. So I went and spoke to Bepi, and he agreed at once."

"Siora Lucia," I said, "I don't deserve your friendship." And that *was* the whole truth.

"Maybe not," she said. "But that's not the point right now. Let's go. Oh, and my father is waiting with Bepi."

"Your father?"

"Yes. The moment I mentioned my plan I couldn't stop him. If nothing else I have to be grateful to you for that: you've got him out of the shop twice today."

"Well, I'm glad to have been helpful in that at least," I said.

We were now walking along the Calle de la Mandola, which leads towards the Rio San Luca. There were a couple of taverns from which light, laughter and cooking smells emerged enticingly. I felt a sudden yearning for a carefree social life, where one could sit down in a tavern without checking it first for killers or *sbirri* . . .

We did not speak again until we reached the bridge over the canal, which leads into the narrow Campo San Paternian. To the left of the bridge I saw the dark shape of the gondola, with a single lantern at its prow. Bepi and Fabrizio were both sitting at the front of the boat, outside the *felze*, their cloaks wrapped tightly around themselves, playing dice on a small board which was balanced on Bepi's knees.

"Sior Bepi," called Lucia, "I trust you are not leading my father into bad ways."

Bepi looked up at her and smiled. He had always been fond of Lucia and had difficulty in understanding the seeming lack of development in my relations with her. (He expressed it a little more simply than that.)

"Siora," he said, "it was your father who wanted to try."

"Yes," she said with a sigh, "I can believe it."

Fabrizio was still gazing intensely at the two dice on the board; he now looked up with a slightly abstracted expression. "I'm intrigued by the infinite permutations of chance that these tiny objects represent. And yet my friend Bepi seems to have some system that allows him to foretell the odds."

Bepi shrugged. "It's not a system," he said. "It's just my nose."

"I would never have thought that I could become so interested in so seemingly insignificant an object," Fabrizio mused on. "I begin to understand the reason so many people become fascinated by games of chance."

"Bepi," I said, "how much have you taken from him?"

"We've only been playing for *bagattini*," he said. "Just to introduce him to it."

"I'm so sorry, Alvise," said Fabrizio. "My new pastime has made me forget my manners." He rose to his feet, setting the gondola rocking, and made a welcoming gesture towards me. "Has all gone well, my dear?" he said to Lucia.

"I don't know," she said. "Sior Alvise will tell us."

Bepi helped Lucia to climb aboard, and I followed her. At this point we had to enter the cabin, since there was not enough room outside. Lucia and Fabrizio passed through the door, while I remained outside for the moment. Bepi unmoored the boat and scrambled around the outside of the cabin to take up his post at the stern. "Where to?" he called to me. "Are we heading for the mainland?"

"Not yet," I said. "Perhaps the Fontego again . . . but stay on the opposite side of the canal."

"All right," he said. He did not sound fully convinced of the wisdom of this destination but pushed off none the less.

I bent down and passed into the cabin. Lucia and Fabrizio were sitting side by side on the two chairs opposite me. She had clearly been saying something quietly to him, and his face, in the dim light from the lantern, looked rather perturbed. But he turned to me and said with forced lightness, "Well, then? Have you found your thread?"

"I don't know," I said. "I do know that I could use some help. As I've already told Siora Lucia, I overheard fragments of a conversation between Noblewoman Venier and Komnenos and I've been trying to make sense of it. The fundamental point is that Komnenos works as interpreter between the Turks and the city's authorities. And it seems that he has managed to work out some kind of immediate reparation to the ambassador, but one that must remain secret on both sides. And it will serve also as reparation to the ambassador's wife and daughter." I paused.

"That's not enough information," Lucia said.

"No," I said, "I know. But it's all we have to go on."

Fabrizio said, "What did Ariadne show you? I thought that was supposed to be the point of your visit."

"Ah yes," I said. "She showed me a very fine Greek icon of Constantine, which used to be in the Scuola dei Calegheri in Campo San Tomà."

"What? Did she tell you that?"

"No, I recognised it. It's one of a number of such things that have been stolen over the last few months. You may have heard about it. All religious items. Nearly all Greek or Eastern in origin."

"And you think Ariadne has been doing this?" Fabrizio said, sounding very doubtful.

"No, of course not. It's almost certainly been Komnenos and his cronies. With, I think, the assistance of Isabella Venier."

"Why?" said Lucia.

"Komnenos more or less boasted of it the other evening. He's a bandit. Or, at least, he sings bandit songs."

"Against the Turks, as I understand it," said Fabrizio.

"Well, not only," I said. "And in fact if the Four Horsemen mean anything—"

"I thought Sanudo and his band were the Four Horsemen," said Lucia.

"Yes, so did I. Now I'm not so sure. Maybe they thought they were too."

"This is making no sense to me," Lucia said.

"Nor is it to me," I admitted. "At least not entirely. However, if the Four Horsemen are connected with the four horses of the basilica, then from the Greek point of view the real thieves are not the Turks but the Venetians."

"I see," said Fabrizio. "You are referring to the Fourth Crusade."

"Exactly," I said. "The never-forgiven crime of the sack of Constantinople."

"This is not making things any clearer to me," Lucia said.

"Come, my dear," said Fabrizio. "You've heard of the Fourth Crusade."

"Well, yes," she said, "I've heard of it. Was it a crime?"

"Well," Fabrizio said, "that entirely depends from which point of view you consider it. From the Venetian point of view it's always been considered one of the high points of our history. It was then that the Doge declared himself lord of a quarter and a half-quarter of Romania – which is to say the Eastern Roman Empire." He paused and added reflectively, "So very mathematically precise. You can tell we have always been merchants at heart."

"But the Greeks have always considered it a crime," I said.

"That is so," Fabrizio said. "From conversations I've had with Greek scholars, the year 1204 for them is no less grim a date than 1453. They have really never forgiven the West for what it did on that occasion. A chronicler of the city described the Crusaders as 'heralds of the Anti-Christ' who tore out the jewels from chalices and used them as drinking cups, hurled sacred relics into the latrines, raped maidens and nuns, and set up a harlot on the Patriarch's chair in Santa Sophia . . . And, of course, the leading force in that assault on the city was Venice itself. Essentially we made ourselves the new Constantinople from that date on. And even when a new dynasty of Greek emperors, the Palaiologos family, returned to Constantinople in 1261, ousting the Crusader intruders, they never regained their former glory."

"Nor all the booty," I said. "Including the four horses."

"Indeed not," said Fabrizio. "You know, I did do a little research after our conversation about these mysterious horsemen. I couldn't find any definite data, but there are rumours of a mysterious society that took that name. Something that arose in the aftermath of the Fourth Crusade, probably in the territories that fell under Latin rule."

"Latin rule?" asked Lucia.

"That was how the crusading powers from the West were known," Fabrizio explained. "They were called either Franks or Latins. I believe that even today the Greeks and the Turks often refer to western Europeans as Franks."

"But this secret society," I said, "who were they?"

"Well, it's very difficult to find any definite documents, but it seems there was a close-knit group of Greeks who were determined to avenge the crimes of the Fourth Crusade. And they took the name, as you surmised, from the most significant item of plunder on that sad occasion. I presume they also liked the hint of apocalyptic doom that the name gave them."

"This is rather different from what Isabella Venier said to me," I said. "She talked about the Horsemen as having adopted a name that was symbolic of Venetian power, something that could comfort those under the Ottoman yoke."

"When did she tell you that?" asked Lucia.

"Oh, the other evening," I said awkwardly, hoping the sudden flare in my cheeks was not visible in the lantern-light. I attempted to deflect the subject. "Of course, the horses now *are* a symbol of Venetian power – and a clear political statement."

"Yes," Lucia said meditatively, "it's difficult to see any religious significance in them."

"Indeed not," said Fabrizio. "In fact, they were originally set up in front of the Arsenale. Fine horses like that were nearly always symbols of Roman triumphalism. And so by setting them up on the front of our most important church we were essentially declaring that we were now the new Rome. I can well imagine that it might offend the sensibility of some Greeks from the old Eastern Roman Empire."

"Yes," I said. "And I think Komnenos is one such Greek."

"So," said Fabrizio, "this society, devoted to avenging crimes committed against the Greeks, has either survived down through the centuries since 1204 or has been revived, perhaps under the leadership of Komnenos."

"Well, he doesn't exactly make any mystery of his feelings about the crimes of the West," I said.

"Not such a very secret society, then," said Lucia ironically.

"Well, I don't know," I said. "I'm beginning to suspect it's all part of his strategy. And quite a successful one."

"How so?"

"Well, in Venice we always lay the emphasis on secrecy. Our whole system of government is based on it. Secret councils, secret sessions, secret denunciations placed in lions' mouths . . . the Three, the Ten, the Forty . . . No names, just the mysterious numbers."

"I suspect it's all a little exaggerated," said Fabrizio. "I know it impresses foreigners."

"It impresses many Venetians too," I said. "We love to think that our rulers move in mysterious ways. And then we're always looking for secrets ourselves."

"Some of us," said Lucia, a little sharply.

"Yes, I know that I'm talking about myself as much as anyone. And about the work I do for the Missier Grande – work that I have to keep secret. But the point is that when someone comes along and openly talks about his anger at the Venetians for their crimes against his people, and openly professes his admiration for bandits, we naturally suspect nothing. His very openness disarms us. He even manages somehow to work as an intermediary between the Turks and the Venetians without arousing any suspicion. Perhaps precisely because he is so open about his allegiance to the Greeks. We assume he can't be up to anything bad because he apparently isn't trying to hide anything."

"I wish I had met him," said Lucia. "You make him sound intriguing."

"You would find him completely charming, I'm sure," I said. "He has clearly charmed Noblewoman Venier."

"Is that very difficult?" she said.

"Perhaps not," I said. "She is always looking out for distractions."

"And that is why you think she has been helping him to steal these valuable items?" said Fabrizio. I wasn't sure whether he was aware of a slight tension as Lucia and I talked of Isabella Venier, but I was certainly grateful for his intervention. It also helped to redirect the conversation to the essential point.

"It's the only explanation I can find," I said. "She is a wealthy woman, married to an elderly and rather tedious nobleman, whom she clearly doesn't love . . ."

"You've found out a good deal about this woman," said Lucia.

"I've surmised a good deal," I said. "But I think it's accurate."

"Oh, I trust your judgement on her," she said. She was looking steadily out of the window as she made these remarks, refusing to catch my eye. "We're in the Grand Canal. Where are we heading?"

"To the Fontego dei Turchi," I said. "Purely on the basis of those fragments of conversation I heard."

"An act of reparation for the ambassador," said Fabrizio thoughtfully.

"Yes. And one that must remain secret." I laughed.

"What's the joke?" Lucia said.

"I think Komnenos has understood how to make the Venetian love of secrecy work for him in every possible way. I'm suspecting that he has devised something that neither the Turks nor the Venetian authorities have completely understood but which is going to serve his purposes."

"And those purposes are . . . ?"

"Well, I suppose what he's been doing all along. Stealing items of

Greek art in order, presumably, to restore them to his people." Another fragment from the conversation returned to me. "There's something else. At a certain point Siora Venier laughed and said something like 'What else do they expect Turkish women to be interested in?'"

Lucia repeated the words to herself. She said thoughtfully, "I imagine the idea is that we just think of Turkish women as being locked up in harems, with nothing to think about but their fine clothes and their jewellery."

"Fine clothes and jewellery," I repeated thoughtfully.

Fabrizio coughed. "This may seem absurd, but if we're talking about precious items of Greek workmanship, there is one obvious place where a great many such things can be found."

I said slowly, "The treasury of Saint Mark's."

26

"Well, unless he's planning to steal the four horses themselves, I can't see a more obvious target," said Fabrizio. "Many of the finest pieces in the treasury are loot from the Fourth Crusade, just like the four horses."

"And I should have thought they would be equally difficult to steal," said Lucia.

"Yes, and so they would be in normal circumstances," I said. "But Komnenos has managed to create some exceptional circumstances." Another part of the conversation came to me. *It only needs one, and that's already done. He obtains the . . . (inaudible) from the other two. They don't all have to be there. In this case we have specifically asked for as small a delegation as possible.*

"Usually a visit to the treasury is a very public occasion," I said. "Distinguished visitors are granted access, and they are surrounded by all sorts of officials. In particular, there have to be three Procurators because the treasury has three locks and the keys are held by three separate Procurators. However, it is possible for one Procurator to obtain the keys from the other two, and this is quite often done. The important thing is that all three Procurators must have agreed to grant access."

"Goodness," said Lucia, "how do you know all this?"

"From my work as *cicerone*," I said. "Although I have to admit I've hardly ever managed to obtain access for any of my clients. I don't know any Procurators. Komnenos, it seems, does. More important, he has managed to persuade the authorities to grant the ambassador a private visit with his wife and daughter . . ."

"Because of course there's nothing women love so much as looking at shiny objects," said Lucia drily.

"Well, certainly that will have sounded convincing to the authorities. And they will be desperate to do anything to mollify the

Turks at this point. So what better than to offer them an exclusive private visit to the great treasures of our basilica? And, specifically, it must be private. No word is supposed to have got out about the crime committed against those poor women and so the fewer people present on this occasion the better. Therefore, presumably, it will be a night-time visit, with as few authorities and guides as possible. Probably just one Procurator with all three keys. And the Turks themselves won't want to advertise their wish to see a collection of infidel treasures just to satisfy the cravings of a couple of women, so my guess is that there will just be the ambassador, his wife and daughter, and perhaps one or two guards."

"And then?" said Lucia.

"I don't know," I said. "But I'm sure something like this is what is planned. And Komnenos will be part of the delegation, to act as interpreter."

"And then he'll spring out, snatch all the booty and make a dash for it," said Lucia.

"Yes, I realise it sounds rather unlikely, but it makes sense of some of what I heard. I know that Komnenos does have followers. They will be with him. In fact, I know that he has had friends or followers working in the basilica for weeks now, working on the mosaics in the baptistry. Perhaps they'll find a way to hide inside."

"So when is this going to happen?" said Fabrizio.

"I don't know. I had a sense they were talking about something imminent. I'm hoping that if we go to the Fontego we might be able to find out something."

"You propose to call at the Fontego and ask when the secret trip to the treasury is?"

"Not exactly in those terms."

"So what is your plan?" asked Lucia.

Was this the right time to tell them both that my specialty was improvisation, not long-term planning? I remember it hadn't greatly impressed Bepi – at least, not until he had seen the skill being deployed. Perhaps I should call him as a witness to my abilities in this area.

"Let's see when we get there," I said.

We fell silent for a while. I stepped outside to talk to Bepi. We were passing under the Rialto Bridge at that moment, and I waited until we had cleared it and swung round the curve of the canal before I spoke.

"Bepi, do you know the gondoliers who work for the Turks?"

"The ones who were beaten up the other day? I know one of them a bit. At least, I know his cousin, who works for the Loredan family."

"Are they back at work, do you know?"

"I imagine so. Can't think why they wouldn't be. There weren't any bones broken."

"Well, if they are there at the Fontego, perhaps we could have a word with them. Only I think it would be best if you could talk to them by yourself."

"Yes, all right."

"I mean, we were both interrogated yesterday by the Inquisitors, but you haven't been accused of a brutal murder in the meantime."

"No, not so far as I know," he said. "I see your point. What do you want me to ask them?"

"As casually as you can, see if you can get them to tell you if they've been booked to take a delegation to Saint Mark's, and if so, when. And see if you can find out who'll be in the delegation."

"All of this, just casually."

"Yes. The way you managed to slip in the subject of dice-playing to Sior Fabrizio."

I could see his teeth flash in a grin. "It wasn't so difficult, you know. He's a curious old fellow. All right, I'll do my best. If there's anyone there to talk to."

We agreed that Bepi would find somewhere to moor not too far from the Fontego, and Lucia, Fabrizio and I would go and find a tavern to have something to eat. Bepi would join us as soon as he could.

We turned off the Grand Canal into Rio di San Zan Degolà and moored there. I remembered a *furatola* in Campo San Giacomo dell'Orio, which was just nearby; it served simple food and although it wasn't allowed to serve wine there was a nearby *malvasia* where we could get a glass of Cyprus wine, before or afterwards (or preferably both). I led the way, while Bepi, after tying up his gondola, set off towards the Fontego.

Lucia had never been in this area before, and so I was able to bestow upon her some of my *cicerone* eloquence as I told her of the treasures held within the church of San Giacomo, whose buxom apse protrudes into the square (as so often, the façade looks on to the nearby canal, rather than the square itself). She thanked me and wrapped her cape about herself as we entered the *furatola*; it was not a place that women of her class usually entered, and Fabrizio put a protective arm around her as we made our way to a table. Obviously I would have liked to provide the same protection on the other side but realised that this was not the right moment. And I was not the right person.

The other clients, who were mainly intent on their food, paid little attention to us. I had the impression that this was not somewhere people went for elegant conversation or even for company. It was a strictly practical place providing cheap, solid (and not entirely fresh) food.

A rather surly waiter brought us a board with a selection of cheeses, cold meat, some coarse bread and a few leaves of lettuce and red *radicchio*.

Fabrizio gazed around with curiosity. "A long while since I ate out," he said.

"Perhaps we'll find somewhere a little more genteel next time," said Lucia.

"I apologise," I said. "But I think it's the most convenient place in the area. And certainly the least expensive."

"I hope so," said Lucia, lifting a hunk of bread and picking some of the mould out of it.

"Come, my dear," said her father. "We mustn't be fussy. It's all part of the adventure."

She smiled at him. "Dear Father, you always manage to see the bright side of things."

"I try, my dear. Perhaps Sior Bepi will let me have another game of dice when he comes back."

"I have no doubt he will," she said.

We set to eating. The cheeses and meat were quite good and the bread acceptable, once the more colourful elements had been removed. We did not talk for a while; I was sitting opposite Lucia and her father, and I noticed that she carefully avoided catching my eye.

After a while Fabrizio spoke. "You haven't said where you think the murder of that poor man comes into the story."

"No," I said. "Because I'm not sure."

"If, as you have indicated, this Greek person is responsible for the thefts and is planning something more ambitious now, logic would suggest that he was behind it."

"Yes," I said, "logic perhaps. But I still find it hard to believe."

"I've a feeling you rather like this Komnenos," said Lucia suddenly.

"Well, let's say I find it hard to dislike him entirely."

"Even if he's planning an assault on the city's most sacred treasures?"

"I certainly don't approve," I said. "And I hope we can prevent it. But . . ." My voice trailed away. I wasn't sure what I wanted to say.

"But you can't help admiring him as well," she said. Her voice wasn't gentle and it wasn't hard. She was merely stating a fact.

"Perhaps," I said. I realised that, as was so often the case, there was something in what she said. "Maybe it's not exactly admiration. It's just that I think I understand him. I've a feeling perhaps we're similar in certain ways."

"You too feel that the Venetian state has oppressed and enslaved you?" she said. This time her tone was definitely sardonic.

"No, it's not that. It's more an attitude to life. A need to take advantage of things as they happen. Which probably also means I'm not as good as I should be at making long-term plans."

"Yes, that seems a fairly accurate picture of you," she said. "Of course, I have no idea how true it is of your friend."

"He's not my friend," I said at once. "I hardly know him."

"Well," said Fabrizio, "since long-term plans are not your forte, perhaps Lucia and I should give some thought to them." He lowered his voice. "For example, what are we going to do about the fact that you've been accused of murder? We seem to be forgetting all about that."

"Forgetting is perhaps overstating it," I said. "But one thing at a time."

Lucia sighed. "There we go again."

"No," I said, "I'm not just putting it off. But first I think it essential to find out what Komnenos is up to. There are clear indications that it must be linked with the murder, so one thread will lead to another, I'm sure."

"So we return to Ariadne," said Lucia. "Let's hope she really can get us out of the labyrinth." Her eyes had taken on a distant look. She was clearly remembering the scene with Ariadne's mistress.

It was something of a relief when Bepi arrived some quarter of an hour later. He had prudently taken off his red Castello cap and he looked around the uninviting locale rather warily. "We do these things better out in the east," he said as he sat down at our table, gazing unenthusiastically at the food before him.

"Remember we're all Venetians," said Fabrizio mildly.

"It just seems a place where there are unlikely to be too many *sbirri* or agents," I said.

"Too high-class for them," said Bepi.

I ignored this and got to the point. "Did you manage to speak to the Fontego gondoliers?"

"Yes," he said. "I found them in a *magazen* not too far from San Zan Degolà. They didn't mind talking, once I told them I had an aunt at Anzolo Raffaele. Turned out one of them knew her – or, at least, his cousin knows someone who lives just next door—"

"Yes," I said, a little impatiently. It is impossible for two Venetians to meet without finding mutual acquaintances, and I knew that if I allowed him to expand on the subject we would be lost in an unending labyrinth of linked friends and relatives, without an Ariadne's thread to extricate us. "But what did they say about the visit to San Marco?"

"Well, it took me a little time to work that into the conversation," he said with mild reproach. "First I had to hear all about his cousin and his wedding next month; I used that to ask if he would be ferrying guests. And he said yes, so I said I hoped he could get time off from the Fontego. And he said it wouldn't be a problem. Just so long as he told them in time. So I asked if they let him know things in advance. Because I'd heard of some foreigners who expect you to be on hand all day and night, and never give you any indication of their plans. You know, my cousin, who works for the Germans . . ."

"Yes, yes," I said, "I know." I had indeed heard a good deal of this cousin and his troubled relationship with his Teutonic employers.

"Well, he said that although they're heathens, they're not bad as employers. They don't always tell him ahead about their plans during the day, but they always let him know if they're going to need him at night." He took a bite of cheese at this point, and his eyes expressed surprise that it was not as bad as he had expected.

"And so?"

"So I asked if they often went out at night. I'd not seen many Turks out in the Piazza after the Marangona, I said. And he said, oh, they did occasionally. In fact, just tomorrow evening . . ."

"Ah," I said.

"Yes, just tomorrow evening he and his mate have been asked to be ready to take a party down to the Piazza. Around nine o'clock, he said. And he was to keep quiet about it."

"Good to know he's loyal to his employers," said Lucia.

"Well, you know," said Bepi, "among gondoliers . . ."

"And we're now honorary gondoliers," she said with a smile.

Bepi smiled back and nodded. "I'd be honoured to think so."

"You are a true *cortesan*," said Lucia, bestowing on him the term Venetians often use to indicate a gentlemanly man of the world. He bowed his appreciation.

I felt a slight and entirely unwarranted pang. She had never used such a term to describe me – but then why should she? "So tomorrow evening," I said in a business-like fashion.

"That's what they said."

"So we have time to plan this properly," said Fabrizio.

"Yes," said Lucia. She turned to me. "Perhaps you had better leave this to us then?" She said it with a slightly ironic inflection.

"Naturally I'll be glad to have your help," I said politely.

"We could think about turning to the appropriate authorities . . ." Fabrizio left this thought hanging in the air.

"Yes," I said. "The authorities that are trying to arrest me for murder."

"Sior Alvise," said Lucia, "I remember when your English friend was arrested for murder, you didn't advise him to try to escape. You told him to trust in Venetian justice."

"Yes, I know," I said. "But a rich Englishman is rather different from a – well, from a low-life spy. Especially now that I have lost my protection."

"Don't belittle yourself," she said sharply. "It's not dignified."

She was right. There was no point in self-pity.

"And remember the story of the poor little baker's boy," said Fabrizio.

I knew the story he meant and had often recounted it to my clients. However, I wasn't sure I liked where it took me. "As I remember, Sior Fabrizio, the little baker's boy was beheaded for a murder he didn't commit."

"Yes, but the point of the story," Fabrizio said, "is that ever since then the Venetian magistrates have been much more careful before issuing a death sentence."

"Well," I said, "let's see if we can gather some evidence to help the authorities avoid a wrong sentence."

"How shall we do that?" said Lucia. "Follow Komnenos around? I don't even know what he looks like."

"No," I said thoughtfully. "The authorities do, though. They know him well."

"What are you trying to say?"

"I'm not sure," I said. "I'm just thinking of his very recognisable face. Certainly much more so than the Turks' . . ."

"Why are we talking about his face all of a sudden?"

"It's not his I'm thinking of," I said. "It's theirs."

"Whose?" she said with justifiable impatience.

"The Turks.'"

Fabrizio spoke up. "Sior Alvise, if you don't express yourself more clearly I fear you will lose some of our sympathy."

"Sorry," I said. "It's just that I'm working things out as I speak. Which is very much what I think Komnenos does as well. As I said, no long-term planning."

"Go on," he said calmly, as his daughter began to show signs of intense irritation.

"No long-term planning," I said again. "Tomorrow evening for someone like Komnenos is a long way away."

"And for you too, I gather," said Lucia.

"Yes, exactly. I'm sure Komnenos has no intention of waiting till then. He's going to act tonight."

27

"But I thought the whole point was that he was going to act when this delegation visits the treasury," said Lucia.

"Yes," I said. "And that will be tonight."

"Are you saying the gondoliers were lying?" she asked.

"They weren't," said Bepi at once, as if offended at such an outrageous suggestion.

"No," I said, "they weren't. The Turks and their gondoliers are all planning to visit tomorrow night. But Komnenos is going to do it tonight."

"All on his own?" Lucia said.

"No, together with what will appear to be a delegation of Turks. That is to say, the ambassador, or someone standing in for him, the ambassador's wife and their daughter. Both the women, of course, veiled."

"He will never get away with it," she said.

"In normal circumstances, certainly not," I said. "And he certainly wouldn't get away with it if he waited until tomorrow. Then people would have time to reflect, to carry out checks, to make the whole procedure much more formal and official. He is relying on a sense of urgency – and, of course, on the need for secrecy on both sides."

"How can you possibly know this?" said Lucia.

"I don't *know* it," I said, "I strongly suspect it. From what I have gathered of his character. And from the situation."

"And because it's what you would do," she said.

"Yes, perhaps," I said, "if I were a bandit."

"I'm beginning to think you wish you were one," she said.

"I may end up being one, of course," I said. "But for the moment I'm still mainly on the side of the law."

"But if this is so," said Fabrizio, "then we must act. At once."

"Yes," I said. "Without too much long-term planning."

"Just the way you like it," said Lucia.

"Just the way the situation demands," I said.

"You want us to go straight to San Marco," said Bepi, taking things in with his usual phlegmatic calm.

"Yes," I said.

"No more cheese," he said. "And no glass of *malvasia*."

"Maybe a quick one before we set off. We might need some stimulation."

"I'll need it," he said, putting another piece of cheese into his mouth and getting to his feet.

And so, after settling our score (I insisted on paying, and my offer was accepted), we all had a glass of wine at the nearby *malvasia* and then made our way to Campo San Zan Degolà, where the gondola was moored.

"So who is going to play the part of the ambassador?" asked Lucia, as we clambered into the *felze*. "Don't they know him?"

"Not necessarily," I said. "And possibly Komnenos will explain that the Ambassador was unable to come and so this other person, whoever it is, has had to take his place. I don't know the details, obviously, and maybe I'm completely wrong. But I think it's worth going to check."

"And the fact that the date is different?"

"That's the easy part," I said. "Remember, Komnenos acted as interpreter between the two sides, and he simply told them two different dates for this excursion. I know that it was he who arranged things with the Procurator."

"Can it really be that simple?" said Fabrizio. "I thought the whole point of people like – well, people who do the job you've been doing all this while – was to ensure the city's security."

"Yes," I said. "And one thing I did hear Komnenos say to Isabella Venier was that the whole matter was greatly simplified by the fact that there is no Missier Grande at present. I have no doubt that his plan would never work if the Missier Grande were overseeing things. But if things are left up to people like Marino Basso . . ."

"Who's he?" asked Lucia.

"He's the man who came to your shop the other day and took away the diary."

"Oh, him," she said with great distaste.

"Yes, him," I said. "He's revelling in the downfall of the Missier Grande. I strongly suspect that he took it upon himself to oversee the security for this entire affair."

"Now you're making me want Komnenos to win," she said.

"We don't need to go that far," I said. "We just need to show Basso that he can't manage things by himself."

Lucia peered out of the cabin window. "Where are we now?"

"We're going down the Rio di San Zan Degolà," I said. "It'll take us past Sant'Agostin and then San Polo, and then we'll re-join the Grand Canal."

"So we're not going back the way we came," she said.

"No," I said. "This is much faster, since it cuts out the great loop of the Grand Canal – leaving aside the fact that Bepi couldn't turn the gondola round in this one."

"No, I suppose not," she said. "Not even Bepi. Do you think we'll make it in time?"

"It all depends where Komnenos started from. I was presuming he would set off from the Fontego, but of course there's no reason why he would do that. He just has to turn up at the quay by the Piazzetta in a suitably dignified gondola to be taken seriously as an official delegation. I have no doubt that he can arrange that. But with this fog he could have started out even from a place as close as the Salute church and no one would be any the wiser."

"And who will be helping him?" Fabrizio asked. "He obviously can't do all this by himself."

"Well, no," I said. "I think we can presume there will be at least three other people."

"The Four Horsemen," said Lucia.

"Yes," I said. "The real Four Horsemen."

"But we're also talking of probably two gondoliers," she said, "two people posing as the wife and daughter, the ambassador or someone similar, and I imagine some kind of guard. Does he have all these people at his beck and call?"

"He has followers," I said. "How many will be closely involved, I don't know. There's a priest from the Greek church who I suspect will be on hand. Maybe he'll even play a part as a member of the delegation. Anyway, we'll soon see."

"If you're right," she said.

"If I'm right. Let's get to the church and see if we can work out what's happening. And then . . ."

"And then we'll make a plan," she said calmly.

We emerged into the Grand Canal and Bepi steered us to the left, towards the Rio di San Luca, from which we had come about two hours earlier. There were now fewer other boats around, but Bepi none the less took care to call out the traditional "Òhe" as we veered into the narrower waterway. With a growing sense of impatience and anxiety I stepped out of the cabin. Bepi, a dark shape against the tall buildings that loomed from the canal, seemed as unflappable as ever.

"You want me to wait by the quay?" he asked.

"I suppose so," I said. "Though I'd rather have you with me."

"It might be better to know you can get away quickly," he said.

"Yes," I said. "I think you're right."

I marvelled at the way he guided his gondola down the canal in almost total darkness, our little lantern at the front providing just a faint yellowish glimmer, enough to illuminate the few inches of black water directly ahead of us. Occasionally another gondola would glide past us in the opposite direction, its own lantern emerging as a vague glow from the fog and then flickering into the gloom as the sleek black shape slid alongside us. Bepi would generally exchange a brief salutation at the closest point of encounter. At times there were sounds of mirth or festivity from the closed cabins, but for the most part it was a quiet journey, with just shushed slapping noises from the disturbed water and the occasional echoing sounds of footsteps from nearby bridges or alleyways. The canal grew wider after we had passed Campo San Paternian, our starting point that evening, and soon the familiar sight of Bepi's own station, Campo San Moisè, slid past us. There were more lights here and Bepi raised a hand in greeting to one of his colleagues in the little wooden shed by the water. And then, after another warning "Òhe" from Bepi, we emerged again into the Grand Canal, the great bulk of the Salute church rising in the mist before us.

Bepi steered us to the left, and soon the lights of the Molo flickered into hazy brilliance ahead of us, illuminating the still lively Piazzetta, where people were parading on the Liston.

Other gondolas were off-loading passengers at the various landing stages, and we had to wait for a minute or two before Bepi could steer us towards one.

"See if you can find out any news," I told him.

"You mean ask if anyone's been spotted running off with the *pala d'oro*?" he said, referring to the basilica's most treasured possession, the great bejewelled gold panel that stands above the high altar.

"Well, casually," I said, "as you know how." I took my mask from my satchel and put it on. In the Piazza in the evening one is more noticeable without a mask at this season.

"Piero!" Bepi called to a young gondolier sitting by the landing stage, who was playing cards with an older colleague who had the smug smile of one who holds all the best hands. Not surprisingly, Piero didn't seem to mind the interruption.

"Ciao, Bepi," he called back. "Haven't seen you round here for a while. You still with that *cicerone*?"

"Say no," I whispered urgently as I stepped out of the gondola. I put on an exaggerated act of gawping at the impressive buildings like a newly arrived traveller.

"No," said Bepi aloud to his colleague. "Haven't seen him for a couple of weeks."

Lucia looked out of the cabin. She had heard the exchange between Bepi and the other gondolier, and she did not call my name. "I'm coming too," she said quietly.

This was clearly not the moment to draw attention to ourselves by arguing, so I offered my arm as she stepped out. She accepted the assistance, but as soon as she was safely landed she detached herself from me.

Her father had followed her out of the cabin. "Don't worry; I'll stay here," he said.

"Certainly, Sior Fabrizio," I replied.

"No dice games," said Lucia.

I winced at the idea. A gondolier playing dice with his client would not fail to arouse attention in this most public of places.

"Don't worry," said Fabrizio. "I'll behave impeccably." He retreated into the cabin.

Meanwhile Bepi had got into conversation with his friend Piero. "Anything happening this evening?" he said. "A friend from up by the Rialto told me there was some visit to the basilica by some foreigners or others this evening. You seen anything like that?"

Piero considered. "Ah, that was what it was. Nothing special, though. Not like when the French ambassador called last month. That was ten gondolas in all. Procurators and magistrates and what have you all lining the Piazzetta. And jabbering away in French."

"Nothing like that this evening, then?"

"No. It was just one gondola. But there was a Procurator waiting. And there were two *Mahometan* women in the gondola. You know, all veiled and scarved. And off they went."

"When was that?"

"Oh, about twenty minutes ago."

"We'd better go and see," I said quietly to Lucia. "Bepi, will you wait here?"

"Of course," he said. "Although if I'm stopping for a while I may have to moor over there." He indicated the poles further along the Molo, in front of the library.

I nodded, bade him farewell and set off with Lucia. We walked across the Piazzetta, moving to the right-hand side, towards the Doge's palace, so as not to get caught up in the parade on the Liston. I gestured towards the four porphyry statues on the corner of the treasury. "Earlier horsemen, they say."

She gave me a quick, tight-lipped smile. She apparently knew the legend.

The doors at the front of the basilica were all closed, as was usual at this time in the evening. We rounded the far corner and headed towards the north-western door, the one that was generally used for private visits to the church after hours.

A custodian was standing there; I recognised him as the usual night watchman for the basilica. Years of standing in the doorway in all weathers refusing entrance to hopeful visitors had given him an expression of perpetual dismay. His voice, as he told us that the church was closed, seemed laden with all the cares of the world.

I put on my most commanding voice. "We have come with an urgent message for the Procurator. The Missier Grande has sent us." I was gambling that the news of the Missier Grande's dismissal would not have reached so lowly an official as this. I was also hoping that he would not recognise me as one of the more persistent *ciceroni* who contributed so greatly to his woes.

"Well, I think you'll have to wait while I go and fetch him. I've been told no one is to enter."

"Has anyone left?" I demanded sternly. I turned to Lucia. "Siora, take note of his answer."

She gave a firm nod of acquiescence.

"Left?" he said, slightly flustered. "Not yet. Just the workers."

"Which workers?" I snapped.

"You know, the ones who have been working on the mosaics in the baptistry."

"When did they leave?"

"Just a few minutes ago," he said. "They seemed to have a lot of tools tonight. They took a whole chest of things with them."

"Why were they still in the church during this private visit?"

"I don't know," he said, getting even more flustered. "In fact, I didn't even know they were there . . . there must have been a mix-up when Luigi and I changed over. He didn't tell me they were working late."

"This is the kind of incompetence the Missier Grande has been complaining about. How many workers were there?"

"Four," he said. "Two more than usual, but that's happened before."

"Which way did they go?"

"Over there." He pointed in the direction of the Rio de la Canonica, the canal that flows under the Bridge of Sighs.

"I see," I said. I moved towards the door. "Let us in."

"But, sior, my instructions—"

"Have been over-ruled," I said, waving a piece of paper I had taken from my pocket for this very purpose. (It was a sheet on which I had tried to work out my drinks bill at the Remedio tavern.) "Come along, siora."

He made a half-gesture, as if about to try to restrain us physically, and then allowed it to collapse into a helpless shrug.

"Thank you," I said. "Oh, and I'll borrow your lantern." I took it off him, and Lucia and I stepped into the narthex.

At once the festive noises from the Piazza died away. The light of our lantern flickered on the shimmering golds and scarlets of the mosaics above us. We climbed the steps to the inner entrance door and pushed it open.

Ahead of us a light burned in front of the image of the Madonna Nicopeia. I whispered to Lucia, "At least they haven't taken that." It was, after all, one of the most precious images that had been taken from Constantinople. But perhaps the fact that it was placed on an altar had deterred them.

"I've never been in here when it's empty," Lucia whispered back.

"Are you frightened?"

"Yes. But it's magnificent."

We moved cautiously across the church. There were a few candles lit here and there, but otherwise the only light was our lantern. It helped us across the splendidly decorated but uneven floor, but it was not sufficient to illuminate the vast golden domes above us.

"Is there anyone there?" I called, my voice a little hoarse. Reverence for the place prevented me from shouting.

We heard faint scuffling noises ahead of us, from the direction of the right transept – and the treasury. I suddenly remembered the rustling noises I had heard two days earlier from the barn on the Giudecca. I suspected we were about to make a similar discovery.

We approached the great iron door to the treasury; our lantern brought out the glittering shapes of the two mosaic angels that stood above the doorway, set within the elegant curves of a Moorish trefoil arch. The door itself was slightly ajar and we could see a glow of light from within.

"Hello?" I called out again.

More scuffling noises.

Lucia touched my arm, as if involuntarily, and I gave her what I hoped was an encouraging smile. We passed through the doorway and turned right into the first room. The light came from a chandelier with numerous lighted candles. On either side of us cabinet doors were hanging open, displaying a gleaming collection of wonderful objects – bejewelled reliquaries, chalices, crucifixes, crosiers – but there were clear gaps in the array, and one or two of the cabinets were completely empty.

Lucia gave a gasp. "It's happened," she said.

We heard further scuffling noises from the next room and passed rapidly on. There were more cabinets here, but our eyes were immediately drawn to the figures lying against the far wall. A number of people, all with their hands tied behind their backs and gags over their mouths. One or two of them were making desperate writhing gestures, their eyes glaring furiously up at us. In one corner was a pile of colourful robes: presumably the discarded Turkish disguises of the men who had then left the basilica dressed as simple workmen.

"Oh my God," said Lucia.

I ran my eyes over the prisoners. A quick survey told me there were two guards, one Procurator, one other official and two women in Turkish garb. It was both the puzzling aspect of this last discovery and, I would like to think, a certain sense of chivalry that induced me to direct my attention immediately to these two. Lucia helped me remove the gag from one of them.

The torrent of Venetian curse-words that at once assailed our ears made it clear that these women were neither Turkish nor Greek.

"Calm down, siora," I said. "We're here to help you."

". . . never been so filthily treated," she said. She pulled the veil back from her head, revealing a face that was not young but bore the traces of former beauty. At the moment it was contorted in anger. "Just a bit of carnival fun, the man said it would be. That was all."

Lucia had removed the gag from her companion, who added her quota of curses. Lucia said mildly, "Siora, we are in a church . . ."

"We certainly haven't been treated like people in church," spat out the other woman. "Last time I go with a foreigner, no matter how much they pay."

I turned my attention to the Procurator, whose white-bearded face was twitching urgent signals to me.

"Just one moment, Excellency," I said. I had recognised the sharp chin and furious little eyes of the man squirming beside him.

"Sior Basso," I said, bending over and removing his gag. Once I had done it I lifted my mask off my face so he could see me.

"I might have known you had something to do with this," he spat out.

"Actually, I think the phrase you are looking for is 'thank you'," I said. "I imagine it was you who made the arrangements for this debacle."

"Sior Alvise," he said venomously, "you are already under suspicion of murder. It looks as if we're going to have to add treachery, blasphemy and theft . . ."

"Oh, I've had enough of this," I said, and thrust the gag back into his mouth.

Lucia gave a gasp. "Sior Alvise, what are you doing?"

"I'm going after Komnenos," I said. "I haven't time to stay and answer these people's questions. I'll leave you to deal with them."

"Thank you very much," she said drily.

"Sorry, Sior Lucia," I said, "I don't want to seem selfish, but you heard what this man said. I'm still under suspicion. I think it will be far more profitable for me to follow Komnenos than get myself thrown into a prison cell while they run round in circles looking for the wrong people."

She bent over the nearer woman and started to undo the rope binding her wrists. "You're probably right. Go, then. Oh, and send my father in here, will you?"

"I'll be happy to," I said. "You might want to help the poor Procurator over here before he bursts a blood vessel. But I wouldn't remove the gag from Sior Basso's mouth until you absolutely have to."

"Leave me with them," she said. "I think I can cope."

"Thank you so much, Siora Lucia. As ever, I don't know what I'd do—"

"Just go. No more flowery speeches."

"No."

"And Sior Alvise – be careful."

I left her, infinitely grateful for those last two words.

28

As I made my way back through the church I heard a spluttering outburst which suggested she had not followed my advice about Sior Basso's gag. Well, that was now her responsibility.

When I reached the outer door the little custodian looked at me, his face twitching with conflicting expressions of guilt, concern and dismay. I said, "My friend could do with some help. In the treasury."

"My lantern?" he said, pointing at it in my hand.

"If you don't mind I think I'd better keep it for the moment. Plenty of candles inside."

I strode off. He called a feeble "Hey" behind me, but in the end he must have decided that he had better see what was happening in the church, because when I glanced back he was no longer there.

I walked swiftly back to the gondola. Bepi had moored by one of the poles opposite the Zecca and was looking out for me.

"They've done it," I said.

"You mean . . . ?"

"They've looted the treasury. They took it all off in a chest towards the Rio de la Canonica. They must have had a gondola waiting for them there."

"And so where do you think they've gone?"

"I think Sior Fabrizio might be able to help." I moved towards the gondola and called his name.

Fabrizio peered out of the cabin, his face peering up at us in mild curiosity. I wondered if he had been taking a nap.

"Sior Fabrizio, you must go and help Siora Lucia in the church."

Mild curiosity gave way at once to intense concern. "Is she all right?"

"She's fine," I said. "But she's looking after the people who were assailed by the thieves."

"So you were right," he said.

"I'm afraid so. Now I intend to go after them."

"Where?"

"I want you to tell me," I said.

"What?"

"Sior Fabrizio, do you remember telling me that the Venier family had built a temple to Venus on an island in the lagoon?"

"Yes, of course. You didn't seem very interested."

"I was agitated at the time," I said. "But now I've remembered something I heard Isabella Venier say to Komnenos. She said the 'stuff' would be watched over by their own goddess."

"Oh really? How interesting. So the Venier family keeps up this legend of Venus, then."

"Well, yes," I said, perhaps a little brusquely. "But do you see what it means? That's where they will be hiding the booty. So can you remember where this island is?"

"Oh, goodness," he said. "You know, I did go out there once with friends. Just to see what this temple was. Over beyond Burano. North of Sant'Ariano."

"Bepi, are you listening?"

"Yes," he said. "You're suggesting we go out in the fog to the northern marshes and look for an island with a temple."

"Yes," I said. "That's what they're doing. So it is possible."

"Oh, it's possible," said Bepi. "But of course they know where they're going."

"Well, we do too, more or less. Sior Fabrizio, how big is this temple?"

"Oh, it's just a little round thing, an imitation of the temple of Vesta in Rome. Of course, it's absurd to conflate the two goddesses, but I don't think they were greatly concerned with classical exactitude. There used to be a little statue of Venus inside, but I suspect that has gone."

"But we should be able to see it, even in the fog."

"Oh, I should think so. The island is not very big; not much bigger than, say, the island of Sant'Elena. Some of it is just *barene*."

He used the Venetian word for the marshy terrain that constitutes a great portion of the lagoon. "There's also a little wooded part. The temple is right in the middle, but it stands out."

I turned to Bepi. "Is that helpful?"

He nodded. "I know where he means. I've been out there with my brothers once. We were duck-hunting. I can find it."

"Good," I said with slightly artificial jauntiness. "So we're prepared."

"I suppose so. I've still got that cudgel."

"Right."

"You haven't got hold of a pistol in the meantime?"

"Goodness me," said Fabrizio, "what are you suggesting, Sior Bepi?"

"Just a thought, you know," he said. "Of course we might need some other kind of protection when we pass Sant'Ariano."

"What's Sant'Ariano?" I asked.

"It's the bone island."

"The what?"

"Where they take the bones when the cemeteries fill up. There's nothing else on it. Just bones. Four or five feet deep, I believe."

"Well, should be easy to recognise," I said. "That'll help us navigate."

I gave my hand to Fabrizio as he climbed out of the gondola. "You'd better go to Lucia now," I said to him. "And if you can, try to convince the authorities that they need to come out to Venier's island. But knowing the people you'll be dealing with, I suspect that will take some time. And it probably won't help if you say that I asked you to tell them."

"I see," said Fabrizio. "Well, I'll do what I can."

"You'll need to enter by the Porta dei Fiori," I said.

He set off towards the basilica, at a faster pace than his usual gait.

"Come on," I said to Bepi. "Let's start. Are you sure you don't want any help with the rowing?" This was a question I asked him every other month or so, always eliciting the same negative response. The fact that he would first have to teach me to row was, of course, the major stumbling block.

259

"Not if we want to get there before daybreak," was all he said this time.

We set off, heading eastwards. Bepi then swung to the left and we entered Rio dei Greci. We passed the Greek church with its leaning tower. Bepi said, "Perhaps they've stopped here for the night. That would save us a little time."

"Not very likely," I said. "This time Komnenos has burned all bridges with Venice. As have his cronies. They're going to be on the run for ever."

"What do they think they're going to do with the stuff?"

"Good question. I think it's more the gesture that counts. I didn't have time to look very closely back in the treasury, but I did get the impression that they had only taken stuff that once belonged to Constantinople. I think they didn't take any items that were made by Venetians – at least, not knowingly."

"I suppose we can be thankful they left the horses."

"Oh, if they get away with this, I expect they'll be back for them at some point."

We passed Campo San Lorenzo and then turned right towards Santa Giustina.

"There's where we started as a team," I said, pointing to the Teatro Santa Giustina.

"Ah yes," said Bepi, a touch of nostalgia in his voice. I remembered that it had taken him a while to recover from the heady experience of being on a stage, even without an audience. "Good days."

The canal broadened. The darkness seemed to have acquired an extra layer of density ahead of us; it was the open expanse of the northern lagoon, shrouded in even thicker fog. After a few strokes there was nothing around us but the clammy darkness. It was as if the whole of the rest of the world had suddenly been wiped out, leaving just Bepi's gondola and the feeble glows of our lanterns to indicate that there had ever been life on Earth. The only noise was the faint sloshing of water and the regular creak of the oar in the *forcola*.

"You're sure you know the direction?" I said. Instinctively my voice had lowered to a whisper.

"Yes," he said. "I've been to Burano enough times. It's beyond Burano I'm a bit less certain of." After a pause he added, "Perhaps we'll hear the clacking of the bones."

I didn't answer this, even with a laugh. I was all too ready to believe it possible.

"I'm heading for Murano," he said, "and then I'll follow the Canale San Giacomo. Otherwise we could get stranded on the *barene*."

It is almost impossible to go anywhere in the lagoon in a straight line. There are great stretches of water that are too shallow for even the lightest of craft, and there is often no clear demarcation between lagoon, *barene* and mudflats; they merge indistinguishably. That is why the deeper canals are carefully marked out with poles.

I was waiting for Bepi to ask the obvious question: what was the plan? I wouldn't be able to answer. My mind was like the *barene*: a marshy mishmash with no clear-cut canals of purpose or design. As ever, it would probably not be until our boat crunched into the pebbles of the island that my brain would start operating usefully. At least I hoped it would.

We coasted past the dim shapes of the kilns and furnaces of the glass factories of Murano and began following the regularly placed poles that marked out the navigable canal leading towards Mazzorbo and Burano. Occasionally a seagull would rise from a pole ahead of us with a shriek, its belly and wings flashing a ghostly white in the light from our lanterns. There were no other boats. If one had passed this way before us it must have done so some considerable time earlier, to judge from the unruffled dark surface of the water that lay endlessly ahead of us.

Probably ninety minutes or so later we made our way down the canal between Mazzorbetto and Mazzorbo, the houses all shuttered and silent on both sides of us. I imagined that the fishermen and lace-workers of those islands had to rise very early.

Bepi then steered us in the direction of the island with the oldest buildings in the lagoon, Torcello. However, before its eleventh-century basilica became visible to us, he turned into the canal along the island's eastern flank, and we made our way into the boggy innards of the Dead Lagoon.

"This is where it gets tricky," muttered Bepi. "It's all *barene* and mudflats from here on."

I thought Bepi probably didn't need to be told that it was, indeed, on account of the ever-increasing bogginess of this part of the lagoon that the inhabitants of Torcello had begun to abandon it from the fifteenth century on, so that all that remained of the once lively city was just a cluster of small houses scattered loosely around the magnificent basilica. Malaria had also contributed, of course, to the exodus. This part of the lagoon was a very unlikely place to build a temple to the goddess of love, but probably the area had been very different when the Venier family had first acquired their island. Almost certainly their nearest neighbours had not then been skeletons.

Some twenty minutes later, after much skilful twisting and turning, Bepi said quietly, "That's Sant'Ariano on the left."

I peered out. I could only see the dim dark shape of a brick wall rising from the water.

"No bones," I said, trying to sound breezily disappointed.

"Climb up on that wall and you'll see them," Bepi said. He freed one hand from the oar and crossed himself.

We fell silent, and the gondola continued to thread its way along the narrow canal between the marshy banks.

"Now I think we have to make our way up here to the left," Bepi muttered a little while later, when the canal split into two diverging branches.

"Do you think we should put out the lanterns?" I asked.

"And then how do we get there?"

"I don't know. I'm still trying to think what . . ."

". . . what we're going to do *when* we get there," concluded Bepi.

I smiled. "You do know me."

"Anyway, it's along here, I'm fairly sure." The gondola pivoted to his command, and we nosed our way along an even narrower canal, flanked by reeds and spongy terrain.

Some considerable time later, during which we saw and heard nothing but the muted melancholy sounds of the marsh, a more solid shape appeared ahead of us. Bepi began to row more slowly. "Now might be a good time to douse the lanterns," he whispered.

I extinguished the lights and we paused for a moment, allowing our eyesight to grow accustomed to the almost total darkness. Then he slowly urged us forward. We began to distinguish the shapes of low trees ahead of us to the left and the jagged shape of some kind of tumbledown building to the right. Straight ahead there slowly emerged in the mist the outline of a more elegantly shaped building with a low conical roof, which had to be the temple.

There was a gently sloping, shingly shore right in front of us. No lights could be discerned anywhere and there was not a sound of life.

"Do you think they've already left?" I whispered.

"Possibly," he said.

"Well, shall we go and see if they've left the treasure?" That would certainly make things a great deal simpler.

He manoeuvred us towards the little beach, and with a slow hissing, crunching sound we came to a halt. We both clambered out. There was nothing to moor the boat to, so Bepi and I simply dragged it a little further up the beach.

"We might as well light a lantern again," I said. I was still instinctively whispering.

He found the tinderbox and got one of the lanterns alight. With this in my right hand we made our way along a very rudimentary path that seemed to lead in the direction of the temple. There was a good deal of brambly undergrowth on both sides of the path, and to the left this undergrowth became, after a few yards, a fairly thick wood. Ahead of us the temple took on greater solidity, a little round structure surrounded by a circle of marble pillars supporting a conical roof. The whole thing stood on a miniature mound, to which ascended a flight of six or seven steps. At the top of the stairs was the black oblong of an open doorway leading into the interior of the temple.

"If they've just left it in there for us," I said, "then we can go straight back." But my heart was hammering as I climbed the steps. I somehow knew it could not be that simple.

I raised the lantern and we peered into the musty interior together. Seconds later we both let out something between a gasp and a yelp.

29

It had taken us those few seconds to understand what we were seeing on the floor of the temple. But it was only a visual comprehension. For the moment our minds could do no more than reel in shock; they certainly could not make sense of what our eyes were telling them.

The floor was apparently covered with an old fishing net, thrown down in a snarled, bunched tangle. After a few seconds it became clear that the bunches were caused by the sprawling objects that lay beneath the net, and another couple of seconds told us what those objects were. They also explained the dark glistening sheen that coated much of the net.

Underneath the net lay hacked, gashed bodies, with twisted limbs and battered heads. The blood was still flowing in places.

"My God," said Bepi, "my God . . ." He was staggering back.

I forced myself to take another look, holding the lantern high, and tried to make sense of what I was seeing. I could see three heads, two still attached to bodies, and the third gorily free of its neck, lying with its eyes rolled upwards to the dark heights of the ceiling. Above the clotted mess of the stump and through the slimy interstices of the net I recognised the bearded face of Father Giorgos. I guessed the other two must be Dimitris and Alexis. I realised the lantern was shaking in my hand, which explained why the bodies seemed to be moving beneath the net, as the light flickered over them.

"Let's go," said Bepi in an urgent whisper, tugging at my arm.

"Yes," I said, "you're right." I realised I had no breath. I stepped back and turned round, extinguishing the lantern as I did so.

"Over here!" came a voice from the wood, hissed and urgent.

"Oh shit," said Bepi. He began to run down the steps, and I followed him. He was running blindly, and suddenly I saw him trip and sprawl ahead of me. I leaned over him.

"Are you all right?"

"I don't know," he whispered, trying to scramble to his feet. I saw his face contort with pain as he rose. "I've twisted my ankle." He leaned on me.

The voice came again from the bushes: "Over here, quickly!"

"Oh, God," said Bepi. "I don't think I can run."

There was a rustling amid the bushes, and we saw a dark shape emerge.

"Quickly," said Bepi. "Let's get to the boat."

"It's too late," said the dark figure, still moving towards us.

"You can't scare us," said Bepi. "We're ready for you."

That would have sounded more convincing if he had not been leaning heavily on my arm and his voice had not been choked with pain.

"I'm Komnenos," said the figure, and now I recognised both the voice and the dark outline of the man approaching us.

"What do you want?" I said, bracing myself for I knew not what.

"Come with me into the wood. It's too dangerous here."

"We're going back to our boat," said Bepi.

"You won't make it in time," Komnenos repeated.

"What do you mean?"

"He'll attack you while you're trying to launch it."

"Who is he?" I said.

"I don't know. A maniac with an axe. Come with me."

We had little choice, so we followed Komnenos back into the bushes, Bepi limping painfully.

"And you're not the maniac?" I said, feeling someone had to say it.

"I am not," he said simply.

We were now pushing aside damp brambly branches and kicking our way through clingy undergrowth. After a few yards Komnenos came to a halt in a small clearing. "He can't see us now," he said in a whisper. Bepi gave a sigh of relief; steadying himself on a tree trunk, he lowered himself to the ground. Komnenos and I also crouched down.

"What's happened?" I asked, whispering as well.

Komnenos took a breath. "You presumably know that we've retaken possession of our treasures."

Now was not the time to start a discussion about rights of ownership. I just said, "Yes. We've seen the treasury."

"So the four of us – Father Giorgos, Dimitris, Alexis and I – came out to this island with the treasures."

"Who was rowing?" asked Bepi. It was the natural question for a gondolier to ask.

"We'd hired two gondoliers to take us from San Marco. They had no idea what we were doing. They rowed us to the Fondamenta Nuove where we had our own *sandolo* waiting for us. Dimitri and Alexios are skilled oarsmen – *were* skilled oarsmen." He corrected the tense with something very close to a sob. "And they rowed us out here."

"Where's your boat?" asked Bepi.

"It's no good," said Komnenos. "He's smashed it up. I heard him do it."

"But where is it?"

"We always leave it on the other side of the island. Can't be seen there." He sank down to a kneeling position, and I did the same. Bepi was sitting on the ground against the tree trunk, one leg stretched out in front of him, and the other crossed awkwardly over it.

"So you've been here before," I said.

"Of course," Komnenos said.

"The island of Venus," I said.

He didn't respond to this but went on, "I stayed to secure the boat while the other three took the chest to the temple. Then I heard screams, sounds of fighting – and then just silence. It was the silence that was most terrifying." He fell silent himself, and we all found ourselves listening hard to the new silence that hung over the island. For a few seconds there was scarcely any noise at all, just the intermittent sound of dripping from the fog-soaked vegetation around us. Then Komnenos started whispering again, the syllables coming out in an urgent, breathy rush.

"I ran to the temple and saw a man come out; there was still some light from the lantern they'd taken inside. He was holding an axe and I could see . . ." he faltered, "I could see it had blood on it. So I ran into these bushes. He must have seen me, but he didn't follow. Then I heard him smashing the boat."

"Did he limp?" I asked.

"Yes. How did you know that?"

"He's a hired killer," I said. "A man from Naples."

"He was waiting for us," said Komnenos. "He knew we were coming."

"Obviously," I said.

"There's been treachery," he said. His voice was quite level, without any audible rancour. But as we were all still whispering, it was not easy to judge.

"So you were the Four Horsemen," I said.

"Yes." And this time I detected a rather forlorn note of pride in his voice.

Bepi spoke. "So what do we do now?"

"There are three of us," I said, "and one of him."

"He has an axe," said Bepi.

"Yes," I said, "but he can't attack us all together. He was only able to do it with those three because he had prepared a trap with a net."

"Is that what he did?" said Komnenos.

"Yes," I said. "This is a man who prepares things. But obviously he didn't plan for you not accompanying your friends to the temple. Nor for our arrival."

"So what's he doing now?" said Bepi.

"Waiting," I said. "And hoping that we get frightened and make some stupid mistake."

"Well, there's no point pretending we're not frightened," said Bepi. "I know I am." Probably for the first time ever I could hear fear in his voice, unless it was pain.

"Yes," I said. "Obviously we all are. But that's not a reason to behave stupidly."

"He must be hiding in that ruined building," said Komnenos. "I would have heard him if he were in the bushes here."

"I think he's going to go on waiting," I said. "He's a professional killer. He's used to this. He knows we're not."

"Well, *I'm* not," said Bepi.

"Nor am I," said Komnenos.

"The Four Horsemen have never done anything violent?" I asked.

"Not under my leadership," he said.

I returned to the subject of the killer. "So he's sure that sooner or later one of us is going to panic, try to run to the boat or something, and that'll be his chance."

"I'm not going to run anywhere," said Bepi ruefully.

"No, but he doesn't know that."

"And how do you know what he's thinking?" asked Komnenos.

"Obviously I don't *know*, but I'm trying to imagine. As I did with you. Which is how we come to be here now."

"Unfortunately," said Bepi.

Komnenos was quiet. I think he was realising he could not agree with Bepi's adverb. But such a thought would take him down very difficult paths. Eventually he said, "So you imagined yourself as me."

"Yes," I said.

"And you had no help from our mutual friend." His tone was recognisably bitter this time.

"No," I said. I was certainly not going to tell him that I had been hiding in a wardrobe while he spoke to her earlier this evening.

"Did she hire this man?"

"I don't know," I said honestly. "I sincerely hope not."

"What are we going to do?" said Bepi, breaking into our dialogue to raise a more immediate problem.

"Turn his tactics on himself," I said.

"Wait until he panics?" Bepi said, clearly sceptical.

"Well, remember there are three of us and one of him, so the idea is not totally absurd."

"He's still got the axe," Bepi said.

"Yes," I said. "But it's not a practical weapon for attacking three people who are prepared for you."

"It's better than anything we've got."

"So far," I said.

"What else is there?" said Komnenos. "Shall we snap off a twig, or some brambles?"

"As I said, we can use his tactics. There's the net."

This was met with silence from both Bepi and Komnenos.

"It's our best chance," I said after a long pause.

"How are we going to get it?" said Bepi.

"We'll have to work that out," I said. I was trying to sound much calmer than I felt. I knew that only by forcing myself to concentrate on the problem from a purely logical point of view could I avoid collapsing into a state of helpless, gibbering panic. It probably made me seem unnaturally phlegmatic, but that was the least of my worries.

My tactic seemed to have a calming effect on the other two as well. Their breathing had become more measured, and their whispered words came out less jerkily. We actually had a two-minute conversation devoted to purely practical matters, and three minutes later I was sidling my way towards the temple, remaining as far as possible amid the bushes and trees.

After another minute or so I was about twenty yards from the temple, gazing from the bushes at the rough path that led towards the steps that rose to its entrance. There was complete silence. I could feel sweat breaking out from my every pore, as if in soggy sympathy with the mist that swathed the whole island. I stared up at the dark gap of the doorway and wondered whether I was really going to be able to force myself through it to the horrors that lay beyond.

I tried to encourage myself with the thought that also beyond that door lay a chest containing some of the finest works of religious devotion in the world: votive crowns with enamelled medallions of saints and martyrs, silver and sardonyx chalices that had belonged to emperors, alabaster patens with bejewelled handles, gold monstrances, the bejewelled panel with the enamelled bust of the Archangel Michael, the gem-studded silver reliquary of the True Cross . . . objects created by artisans and artists under divine inspiration, for the greater glory of God.

Or, to put it in another way, loot from the heinous sack of the Holy City of Constantinople. It was not the first time, I thought ruefully, that these shiny objects had lain alongside hacked and bloody corpses. Perhaps I should not place too much confidence in divine protection for what I was about to do.

It struck me, rather irreverently, that if I was going to pray maybe I would get better odds from Venus, who, in *The Iliad*, showed great skill at concealing her often undeserving favourites in convenient clouds at moments of great peril.

Of course, all these abstruse thoughts were just a know-it-all *cicerone's* way of fending off fear as I waited for the signal.

At last it came. To my right there broke out a sudden sound of thrashing and scuffling amid the bushes and some deliberately cryptic cries as Bepi and Komnenos set up the necessary distraction. They were hurling a small pile of stones that we had gathered for this very purpose into the undergrowth some thirty or so feet from where they lay in hunched concealment; and they were making odd whooping noises, at irregular intervals, with the sole aim of unsettling the killer.

I jerked forward and ran as noiselessly and as unobtrusively as possible (I was running with my body bent almost double in a painful crouch) along the path towards the temple. The noises continued behind me as I reached the dark doorway, my heart pounding.

I had thought that the lack of light would be a relief but of course it was not. I could still dimly perceive the lumpish shapes and the glistening sheen – and, to my horror, I could smell the blood. I did my best to shut my mind off from what my senses were telling it and bent down to get a grip on the portion of netting closest to me. Fortunately the piece I gripped was dry to the touch. I jerked it hard – and it resisted my tug. I had the horrific notion that the corpses were pulling against me, and I think I even let out a pathetic whimper. I gave another jerk, and there was a tumbling, thumping sound that I did my best not to interpret, and the net shifted a few inches in my direction. I squatted lower in order to pull it horizontally and braced myself for my next tug, listening to the noises outside. The thrashing in the undergrowth continued, as did the staccato whoops and yells. I could hear no other sound.

I gave a brisk vigorous jerk and the net came suddenly free, so that I staggered back, almost falling. I managed to straighten myself and pulled the freed strands of net towards me; parts of it were viscously sticky under my scrabbling fingers and I found myself whimpering again. Once I had recovered from my revulsion I realised that all I held was a scrappy torn-off corner section of the net, hardly enough to cover a person's head.

And then I heard the footsteps. They were coming at a swift, if irregular, pace in my direction. I moved to the doorway, and saw a thickset dark figure walking jerkily along the path to the temple. He had an axe held firmly in both hands. This was a professional who knew a distraction when he heard it.

30

My instinct was to retreat into the dark recesses of the temple, despite the horrors it held. I told myself that when he climbed the steps would be the best moment to rush out and attack him, but then I fell back on instinct; even standing above him I would still be at a disadvantage with nothing more than a sticky scrap of net to wave against his axe. I should place more faith in instinct; it had worked for me in the past.

As long as it was instinct and not just panic . . .

I tossed the scrap of net aside and worked my way round to the right of the pile of cadavers, staying close to the wall. My mind was working feverishly to wrest some kind of advantage from the situation.

Well, there was the fact that the man was lame and I was not. It suddenly struck me that I was going to have to do the unthinkable: use the corpses as a battleground. On that uneven heap I would have the advantage of two steady limbs to support myself against his unbalanced ones.

I saw the dark outline of his body appear at the entrance, both hands still gripping the axe, which was raised in a threatening way. He stood still for a moment, his head turning slowly as he sought me out.

I remained equally still, my arms lifted at a tense angle from my body. My right hand flexed itself in preparation for whatever was going to happen next – and my fingers touched something wooden.

I instantly realised it must be the chest containing the treasures. I went with my instinct again and bent down to fumble at the wood. I found it had a single leather-covered handle on the top and I was able to lift the whole thing up with one arm. It was not quite as heavy as I had expected and it did not rattle as I had thought it might; presumably the items had all been carefully wrapped before they were loaded.

He saw me immediately and charged forward, swinging the axe above his head. There was nothing for it but to match charge with charge. I held the chest out to my right as I moved. We instantly found ourselves trampling over the mound of broken bodies, the net tangling with our feet. Instead of continuing my rush forward I halted as soon as I found a secure perch, my left foot planted on what I guessed was someone's stomach and my right on a tangled knot of netting, and braced myself. I saw him make a sudden sweep towards me with his axe, but it was clear that he was by no means as secure in his position as I was; I was able to rear back, clear of the slicing blade (though I felt the rush of displaced air against my face), and yet remain steady, while he tottered forward. Before he had time to straighten up I smashed the chest on to his outstretched arm and then instantly jerked it upwards towards his face. There was no impact, but he fell backwards as he swayed to avoid the blow, and released the axe.

I dropped down, letting go of the chest and groping for the handle of the axe. My hand clutched instead at the hair of someone's head, which moved sickeningly under my fingers. Instead of dropping it with revulsion I snatched it up – it must have been the head of Father Giorgos and was much heavier than I expected – and hurled it in the direction of the killer's own head. I heard a satisfying thump followed by a grunt of pain. I scrabbled around on the floor again and this time found the axe and scrambled to my feet, doing my best to get a firm grip on it.

And now what? Was I going to split him in two? I suspected I wouldn't be able to do it – but I certainly didn't want him to know that. I stepped cautiously backwards, towards the free area of floor, still gripping the axe firmly. He was slowly heaving himself up; I could make out his dark shape, becoming vertical and massive before me, even though not tall. Then he spoke.

"You know you can't do it." It was a surprisingly sharp, shrill voice, with a thick Neapolitan accent.

"What makes you think that?" I said, keeping my voice as flat and steady as I could.

"You're not the rough kind," he said. He was trying to sound reasonable, as if all we needed to do to sort out our differences was have a chat.

"You'd like to think that," I said, "wouldn't you?"

"I can tell," he said. "I can always tell." He was now lurching his way forward, slowly and deliberately trampling over all obstacles. The creaking and crunching noises under his feet were perfectly horrible.

"I'm a confidential agent for the Missier Grande," I said, "and have killed twelve enemies of the Republic to date." I guessed that a precise figure would sound more convincing. Then I added, "Thirteen, if we include an accidental victim when I burned the French ambassador alive in his apartment. I'll be happy to make you my fourteenth. I'll even claim fifteen, if I split you in two."

"You think you're funny," he said. Clearly he intended to sound contemptuous, but I could tell that my banter had unsettled him. It was vital that he should not discover that it was the only weapon I knew how to use.

"I just tell things as they are," I said. "Come any closer and I will hack off any part of you I please."

He paused, still undecided whether to risk a sudden charge.

I gave the axe a few gentle waggles. I didn't know whether he could see the movement or not, but at least it gave me the illusion of being ready to hack him to pieces.

Then he charged. It happened so suddenly that I was taken completely by surprise and found myself instinctively falling backwards. This time, of course, the instinct was wrong. I knew it at once, as I found myself unable to swing the axe forward in a counterbalancing move; I couldn't tell whether the inability was due to weakness of character or just the physical laws of gravity. In any case, it was sadly clear that I was not the rough kind.

I found myself lying helplessly on my back, and seconds later he was scrabbling for the dropped axe beside me. This was clearly the end.

And then there came a strange thumping noise, and he jerked forward and collapsed in a sprawling heap beside me.

I twisted my head to the door, and saw a man who was bent

forward in the attitude of one who has just hurled something. Next to me the Neapolitan was making a sputtering noise and his fingers were scrabbling at the floor. I could now make out the distinct shape of a knife buried deep in his back.

The figure at the doorway said a few words in Greek.

"Thank you," I managed to say, although my voice was hoarse. I pulled myself away from the Neapolitan, who continued to twitch and sputter.

"It was my pleasure," Komnenos said. "And I mean that literally." There was a kind of bitter joy in his voice.

"You didn't tell me you had a knife," I said. "Not that I'm complaining."

"I don't always say everything," he said. "I think you should have learned that by now."

"I suppose I should have," I said.

"But don't you remember: 'Keep your knife sharp . . .'?"

"Yes," I said. "I remember." I realised now that the Greek words he had uttered earlier had been the refrain from the kleftic ballad he had recited at the salotto.

Komnenos had now made his way round the edge of the temple to where the Neapolitan was lying. He bent over and pulled the knife from the man's back, and then in one sudden decisive action he pressed one knee to the man's back, wrenched his head up and placed the knife at his throat.

I made a gasping sound of protest. Komnenos paid no attention. With a sudden savage jerk he slit the throat and jumped back as the blood spurted.

"My God," I said. "My God . . ."

"'So that it may be ready to cut the tyrant's throat,'" said Komnenos, throwing the knife down beside the still quivering body. He sounded quite calm.

I forced myself to my feet, if only to avoid the spreading pool of blood. My legs were shaky but still able to support me.

"Let's get out of here," I said. Then I remembered what still lay among the mangled bodies. "The treasure . . ."

Komnenos leaned forward and grasped a corner of the chest. He gave it a jerk and got hold of the handle.

"You take it," he said. "I have no further use for this."

"I'm glad to hear it," I said. I took it from his hands.

"Too much blood," he said simply.

We made our way out of the temple. When we reached the open air I saw Bepi painfully limping his way towards us. Even in the dark I could see the sudden brightness of his smile as he recognised me.

"Alvise," he said simply. "I thought . . . I thought . . ."

"Komnenos saved me," I said.

"Sorry I wasn't there."

"Well, you are now. And I've got the treasure here." I put the chest down on the ground.

"Well, that's useful," he said, and promptly sat down on it with a relieved sigh. Then he asked, "So what happened to – to him?"

"I killed him," Komnenos said.

"Oh, ah, right," said Bepi, a little disconcerted.

"And now I'm going to leave you," Komnenos said.

"Leave us?" I said. "How?"

"That man came here in a boat. I imagine it's over there." He gestured in the direction of the tumbledown building. "It's the only place to conceal a vessel."

"And where are you going?" I said.

"That need not concern you," he said. "I gather you are an agent of the Missier Grande."

"I was," I said. "And by the way, if you were listening, I've never killed anyone."

"Oh, I knew that," he said.

I felt rather annoyed at this – and then, just seconds later, perturbed. Why should I ever want to be taken for a killer? I tried to reassure myself that my annoyance derived only from the blow to my self-esteem as a skilful improviser.

"And neither had I," he went on, "until just now."

"So what you said about the non-violence of the Four Horsemen was true."

"I don't know about the original organisation," he said. "There are ballads about some of their deeds which suggest they could carry out some cruel actions when necessary. But we're talking about wilder times."

"So you didn't inherit your position in the Four Horsemen from your father or an uncle?" I asked.

"Good heavens, no," he said. "I came across references to them in manuscripts in a monastery in the Morea, while I was looking for old ballads. And in the same monastery I met Father Giorgos and persuaded him that they might be revived. He persuaded two young novice monks to join us, Dimitris and Alexis, who hadn't yet taken their vows. You are probably aware that the Venetians are as unpopular as the Turks in parts of the Morea, so it wasn't so difficult to persuade them. And so we came to Venice to reclaim what was ours. That's the full history of the new Four Horsemen."

"And Sanudo and his cronies?"

"Find out for yourself," he said. "I've had enough of the whole story."

"What were you going to do with that?" I said, indicating Bepi's perch.

"Restore our pride," he said simply.

"And now?"

"Find a way to recover my own pride," he said. "Back home."

"Phanar?"

He didn't answer. Presumably he was thinking of my role as agent.

"Don't worry," I said, "I'm not going to inform on you. My only concern was to recover the treasures of San Marco."

"The treasures of Constantinople," he corrected me.

"Let's not argue about that," I said. "They're no use to you now."

"Agreed," he said. "But one day . . ."

"You'll be back for them. And for the horses too. Well, good luck – wherever you're going."

"Roumeli," he said after a short pause.

"That's a big area. I won't ask any further questions."

He bowed. "Farewell, Signor Marangon. Congratulations on accomplishing your mission. Do what you like to our mutual acquaintance. I have no wish to know any more about her."

"I understand," I said.

"You can tell your Missier Grande that you fought me bravely and I used some underhand oriental trick to escape your clutches. Otherwise you would have consigned me to the prison I undoubtedly deserve." He turned to Bepi. "Goodbye, Signor Bepi."

"Goodbye," said Bepi.

He gave one last wave of his hand and then made a cloak-swirling turn. He did it much better than Sanudo. He strode off towards the tumbledown house. Seconds later he had rounded the jagged wall and disappeared.

31

"He took his time in going," said Bepi.

"He's a performer," I said. "That last bow is always the most difficult. Well, I hope he gets away." To his new life as a kleft, I thought to myself. Well, it would add authenticity to his poems.

"He'll be heading for the mainland, I suppose," said Bepi.

"Yes. I think he's done this before. I imagine they've used this island as a place to stow booty before it makes its way eastwards."

"Then we'd better take these things back to the city," he said, patting the wooden chest beneath him. "Before someone comes to call for them."

"Yes. Can you row?"

"I'll have to," he said. "But I'll probably need to rest occasionally."

"We'll hire someone at Torcello or Burano," I said.

"Maybe you're right," he said. "We've certainly got the means to pay for it." And he tapped the chest beneath him again.

"I hope they'll ask a more reasonable price than that," I said.

"Not when they hear we're Venetian," he said gloomily.

It was, in fact, not easy or cheap to find someone ready to row us across the lagoon at that time of night, but eventually we were able to intercept a fisherman on Burano who was preparing his boat to go out before dawn and said he had a brother who would do it for a ducat. It was an outrageous sum, but we had little bargaining power, and I felt it was important to get back to Venice as soon as possible.

The brother was roused. He was a small but sturdy man with the impressive black moustaches of a true Buranello; these details, at least to my rather befuddled mind at that hour, inspired confidence. He did his very best to make it clear just how inconvenient this trip was for him and how much he wished he were still in bed – until Bepi growled that he was not sure he really wanted to entrust his oar to someone only half awake. At this the man became immediately invigorated and displayed an almost revolting liveliness; even his moustaches seemed to perk up.

"Don't watch him," was my advice to Bepi, knowing that having to leave his precious boat in the hands of a stranger was torture to him. As it turned out the pain of his ankle induced him to take a seat inside the *felze*, and thus the Buranello was able to row undisturbed by Bepi's severely judgemental gaze; Bepi limited himself to the occasional wince and intake of breath whenever the gondola pitched an extra unwarranted inch to the left or right.

The chest was wedged between myself and Bepi, giving us very little legroom. There was certainly not enough space to open it to inspect its contents, as we would both have liked to do. And we didn't want to do it outside the cabin, under the eyes of the oarsman. We remained silent for the most part; I was trying to keep my mind focused on the exquisite beauty of what I knew was inside the trunk, in order to blot out the horrific images that would otherwise fill my mind. I cannot say that I was very successful, and so I was not surprised when Bepi broke the silence with a simple question: "Why an axe?"

"I think it was just practical reasons," I said. "He knew he would have to conceal the bodies and they would fit into a smaller hole if suitably chopped up."

Bepi emitted a sharp wincing noise, and I was left to wonder whether it was caused by the image I had evoked, a sudden stab of pain in his ankle, or a perceived error of oarsmanship. Eventually he said, "He could just have dumped them on Sant'Ariano."

"Then he would have had to flay them first."

Bepi fell silent again. A little while later he asked, "Where do we go now?"

"Campo Sant'Agnese," I said.

"Why?"

"It's where the Missier Grande has his family home. That's where he is now, since being pushed out of office. He's the only person we can trust with this thing." I tapped the chest.

Our Buranello oarsman, being unfamiliar with Venice, needed advice on the best way to Sant'Agnese. We directed him down the Rio di Santa Giustina, returning along the way we had come hours earlier. By this time it was beginning to grow light and there was even a slight thinning of the fog. When we emerged from the Rio dei Greci the church of the Salute was hazily visible, and there was even the faintest hint of a daub of sunlight towards the top of the dome. I told him to steer to the left of the Customs House and follow the line of the Zattere.

Ten minutes later we had reached the church of the Gesuati and I told him to moor there. We could, of course, have turned into the Rio Sant'Agnese itself, but instinctive caution warned me against that. It was always possible that the Missier Grande's house was being observed.

I told Bepi to wait in the gondola with our Buranello friend while I went to find the Missier Grande's house. I stepped out, hoping that Bepi would not now embark on a litany of his colleague's errors, and made my way underneath the *sottoportego* that led into the square. It was a quiet place, flanked on its north side by the church of Sant'Agnese, on the west side by the canal of the same name, and by fine *palazzi* on the other two sides. In the centre was an ornate hexagonal well. At that early hour there was just a boy aged about twelve or thirteen sitting on the edge of the well and playing with a bucket. I guessed that he was hired by the local residents to bring them water.

I went over to him and asked how much he would charge for a single beaker of water. He eyed me for a couple of seconds, making a quick estimate of my probable wealth and intelligence. His assessment was more flattering to the former than the latter, since he demanded two *soldi*. I did not demur but fished in my pocket for the coins. Before handing them over I said, "Do you happen to know where Sior Carraro lives?" It was perhaps the first time I had ever uttered the Missier Grande's surname, and I felt a tingle of daring even as I did so.

He didn't hesitate but pointed immediately to the street that led out of the square at the south-eastern corner. "Down there, under the *sottoportego* at the end by the canal, first door on the left."

I handed him the two coins and he gave me the water, which I drank gratefully. It made me realise that I hadn't eaten or drunk anything for many hours now. Well, soon I would reward myself with a large meal at the nearest tavern. I walked along the street and found the archway he had mentioned. I was a little surprised at the shabbiness of the entrance door, which was actually underneath the archway itself; I had imagined the Missier Grande in a light-filled palazzo looking on to Campo Sant'Agnese on one side and the Giudecca Canal on the other; that at least would be some compensation for having had to move from Saint Mark's Square. However, in Venice it isn't uncommon for unimposing entrances to lead into splendid interiors, so I pushed open the door, which was slightly ajar, without worrying too much about it. I was extremely tired and just anxious for the whole thing to be over.

I found myself in a dingy, clutter-filled room, with no sign of a staircase leading to the upper floors. I took a few paces into the room, waiting for my eyes to adjust to the gloom. The only light came from a small grilled window high up on the opposite wall. I realised that this was a storeroom probably used by a number of local residents; there were old pieces of furniture (a tilting wardrobe, some broken chairs, an upended table), old picture-frames, piles of wooden boxes and a general smell of mustiness. I guessed that the boy had given me the wrong directions and turned to go out.

Even as I was turning I heard the door click shut. I then made out the dark shape of a figure by the door, someone who had presumably been standing quietly in the shadows close by.

"Good morning, Sior Alvise." I instantly recognised Isabella Venier's quiet tones.

She was dressed in dark clothes, a long black cloak covering her from head to foot. Her golden hair was concealed by a grey shawl. There was just the silvery voice to recall her customary coruscating presence.

"Good morning," I said, keeping my voice as calm as possible while my mind raced in an attempt to understand what was happening.

"This is a little less embarrassing than our last meeting," she said, "although no less difficult."

"We are both dressed at least," I said. Before she could answer that I said, "So the Missier Grande does not live here."

"No. But I see the boy was convincing."

"There's also the fact that I haven't slept all night," I said. "So my mind is not at its sharpest. How did you know I would come here?"

"I didn't know for certain. But last night after I saw you set off from the Piazzetta with your gondolier friend I thought it might be a possibility. The old Missier Grande is, after all, the only person who still believes in you. And I imagined that you would probably not know the exact house where he lives. He isn't the sort of person to give out his address to all and sundry."

"I see," I said. "So you thought you would intercept me."

"It was worth trying. This door to this place was not locked, so it seemed a good place to wait. And I found that helpful boy by the well and paid him to direct you here."

Her guess had been a shrewd one. In Venice, unless you have actually been to someone's house, you rarely know any address more precise than the nearest *campo*; you then have to rely on local people to point you to a specific house. Given the quietness of Campo Sant'Agnese she could be fairly sure I would turn to the boy, who by the nature of his job would be bound to know all the local residents.

"So you were on the Liston last night," I said.

"Of course. Did you think I would fail to oversee events while my Greek friends were risking their lives in their attempt to recover their dignity?"

"Siora, are you aware of what happened to your Greek friends, as you call them, on your island?"

"I am now, because my husband has told me. But you must believe me when I say that I had no idea what he had planned for them."

"They were hacked to pieces by a hired killer with an axe."

She gave a slight gasp.

"I saw their mutilated bodies," I went on. "I saw the blood."

"Please," she said, "please stop. I had no idea. My husband just told me he had arranged for them to be – to be silenced."

"All except Komnenos," I said.

"He's alive?" There was a sudden note of excitement in her voice. I began to think she might be sincere.

"Yes," I said. "And he killed the killer."

"I'm glad," she said with a sudden fierce intensity.

"Because it will save your husband having to pay him?"

"That is cruel."

"Nothing like as cruel as what your husband did, with your assistance."

"Not with my assistance," she said. "Please. You must believe that."

"All right," I said. "I'm not in the mood to argue over this. It really doesn't matter whether you knew or not. The fact is that a number of people have been killed to fuel your greed. Or your husband's greed. Or both. We'll have to leave it to the Inquisitors to find out the full truth now."

"No," she said. "That does not need to happen. Please, Sior Alvise. For the sake of what has been between us . . ."

And I realised she was moving towards me, her face lifted in supplication, those Aegean-blue eyes gazing tenderly up at me. She pushed back the shawl so that a few strands of golden hair caught the light.

"Siora," I said, "it's over."

"I'm not trying to seduce you," she said, ceasing to move forward. "I know that would be a mistake. I know you have your own lover. And if necessary I can explain to her that she is mistaken in believing there was ever anything between us."

"Unfortunately she isn't mistaken. That can't be undone."

"She can be made to realise that one small slip in fidelity does not mean you don't love her. Especially when you explain that I had all the powers of Venus on my side." She attempted a smile here, providing another momentary hint of incandescence amid the dinginess.

"Siora, what are you suggesting that I do?" I was genuinely curious.

"If you have managed to save those treasures, then you can return them to the Procurators, explaining that you were able to pursue the thieves because you had been investigating the Four Horsemen. That will restore you to favour. But you don't need to bring me or my husband into it. And I will make sure that he leaves Venice, never to return. For someone like my husband who loves this city that will be a real punishment."

"Are you aware of just how many people have been killed on his orders?"

"It's terrible – but they were all in their own way criminals themselves."

"Paolo Padoan? Just a poor retired schoolteacher?"

"Oh, him. That was unfortunate. I had no idea at the time. But he was meddling in things that did not concern him. And he misused his relationship with my maidservant shamefully. As did you."

"I'm sure you know now that I had no amorous relations with her."

She let out a light laugh. "That was embarrassing. But I soon discovered that you had been asking about the painting I had been foolish enough to give her. It was then that I began to realise you were something more than just a naively amorous busybody. My husband discovered you were a known agent of the Missier Grande. As that man Padoan had been. And my husband told me that Padoan, after being shown that particular painting of Ariadne's, had realised it was one of a number that had disappeared from various churches and other places."

"The Scuola dei Calegheri, in that particular case," I said.

"I see you must be a very good *cicerone*," she said.

"What was the agreement you and your husband had with the Greeks?"

"With Komnenos, not with the Greeks as a whole," she said. "And I arranged that."

"I had guessed that," I said.

She smiled. "He was a very attractive man. And a very good lover. Quite as good as you, if not so charmingly eager."

"Siora, I told you that it is no good trying to seduce me."

"No, but there is no harm in reminiscing. And I'm glad to know I can still reminisce about dear Constantine without having to mourn him."

"I very much doubt he will ever forgive you."

"I can imagine that too," she said. "It is a pity, but . . ." She sighed. "Well, you can't have everything."

"So what was the agreement?"

"He came here to Venice, he attended my *salotto*, he came to my bed, we talked. I found out about his dreams of restoring the dignity of the Eastern Roman Empire. And I offered to help him. He had this plan of re-appropriating stolen works of art, as he termed them. I believe he had a friend in the Morea who had promised to store them until such time as they could be openly displayed. But obviously it would not be easy. I said that with the help of my husband, who was a collector and knew some of the best dealers in artworks in Venice, we could finance his operations. If he and his team would give us just one out of every four of the works they stole, we would make sure they had all the logistical assistance necessary. A certain Sior Visentin, who has a shop in Campo Santa Maria Formosa, knows a number of people who specialise in transporting art clandestinely when necessary. And I was able to offer my family's small island in the northern lagoon as a very safe storage place for items that had to be taken out of the lagoon."

"And why did you offer this help?" I said. "Was it just because Komnenos was so good in bed?"

"There's no need to be insulting," she said with a sudden return of her aristocratic hauteur. Then she made a visible effort to control herself. "I apologise. It is a reasonable question, even if phrased with unnecessary crudity. It all comes down to debts. Sior Alvise, quite simply, my husband is a gambler."

"Yes," I said. "I had suspected that. In fact, I realise I must have seen him at Molin's establishment the other night. And he was clearly losing."

"As usual. He is not a strong man. And of course all around him in the family home are portraits of his glorious ancestors: successful admirals, bishops, procurators . . . And he has the incessant voice of his mother reminding him of his failings. His art collection is not sufficient consolation – especially when he keeps finding himself forced to sell the most valuable works. So it is not surprising he has looked for other possible sources of revenue. Of course, gambling rarely proves to be one of those. And so when I mentioned this new possibility to him he jumped at it. I understand he owes Sior Molin a good deal of money. I know that he was really very happy when Molin's odious debt-collector was murdered the other evening."

"Of course he was," I said. "He ordered it. And it was two birds with one stone. The debt-collector – and myself."

"Yourself?" She seemed genuinely puzzled.

"You really didn't know that he had set things up so that I would be accused of the murder?"

"No," she said. "I knew nothing of that at all."

"My copy of Homer was found near the body," I said. "If you're telling the truth then your husband must have obtained the book directly from Sanudo."

"That is perfectly possible."

"Does your husband have friendly relations with all your lovers?"

"When he thinks it might serve his purposes," she said. "He is a practical man in the end. In the case of Sanudo and his foolish friends he had what struck me as rather a clever idea."

"You mean the false Four Horsemen," I said.

"Exactly. I see you've worked it out."

"Once you had told him about Komnenos and the real Four Horsemen your husband saw the danger of the secret's getting out. After all, Komnenos was not exactly a master of intrigue and secrecy."

"No," she said with a slight smile. "That, of course, was a great part of his charm."

"And so Querini came up with the idea of creating some false Horsemen, just in case one of the city's numerous secret agents heard rumours of the real ones."

"Well, it *was* a risk," she said. "You know how many of those odious characters there are in Venice . . ." She put a hand to her lips in sudden realisation at what she had said.

I ignored it and went on, "And Sanudo and his friends turned out to love the idea. I suppose it was your husband who fed them the notion of the Four Horsemen as a secret group of Venetian resistance against the Turks."

"I imagine so. It was only Sanudo he ever talked to. They both got some perverse pleasure out of creating a strange relationship between them, almost like father and son. Something that went against the usual rules for such situations. There was also the fact that they frequented the same gambling house."

"Both petty little failures as men," I said, "who found a way to play at being dangerous rebels. And Sanudo could even play at being a leader."

"You're very harsh," she said.

"I'm an odious spy," I said. "It's my job."

"I should not have said that."

"Don't worry about it. I'm used to it. But whatever else, I am a loyal spy. I do my job for the city I love. The city of Saint Mark."

"You want me to weep and play the penitent?" she said. "I don't weep. But I am penitent."

"Because you didn't succeed," I said.

"I won't deny that comes into it," she said. "But please remember I had no idea any violence would be used. To tell the truth, I didn't think the final plan of looting the treasury would ever come about. It was something Komnenos had talked about: his great dream. He had managed to get his two friends places as mosaic-restorers inside the basilica – thanks to my husband's contacts, it must be said – but then he discovered just how strict the rules were for access to the treasury. So when he talked about it I just thought of it as his dream – a boy's dream, if you like. There is something boyish about Komnenos. And then suddenly, yesterday afternoon, he sent me a message asking me to meet him at my casino, where he told me of this wild plan to impersonate a Turkish ambassador that very evening and rob the treasury. He had already let my husband know.

In my case he wanted to bid me farewell, since he would never be able to return after this exploit. But I confess I never really thought it would work. The idea actually shocked me."

"But not so deeply that you felt you should warn the authorities."

"We had been following this path together for some time, remember. I suppose I had even been affected by his rhetoric. What right does Venice have to that treasure from Constantinople?"

"And what right do you or your husband have to it?"

"None, of course. But as I have told you, I had no idea that my husband's plan was to acquire the booty all for himself. I would never have countenanced it."

"You were happy with just a quarter of it."

"In this case I would not have asked even for that," she said.

"Very cautious of you," I said. "After all, how would you sell such famous items?"

"Oh, you'd be surprised," she said. "And some of the pieces would be worth a fortune just for the jewels themselves."

"So your husband would have simply ripped them out? Melted the gold and silver down?" Perhaps it was the *cicerone* in me, but I found this even more shocking than the notion of the theft.

"I don't know what he would have done. All I know is he was tempted by the idea of all that sudden wealth. And so he sent word to his – his . . ."

"His personal killer."

"I suppose that's not an unfair definition," she said, after a short pause. "It seems he'd had this planned for a long time, if ever the Horsemen should succeed in robbing the treasury. It was going to be the end of the whole thing. And, I suppose he thought, the end of all his financial troubles. When I told him my suspicions that you had uncovered the scheme he was terrified."

"I imagine he thought I had already been arrested," I said.

"Possibly," she said, clearly pausing to think back. "Anyway, it was then he confessed to me what he had planned. All four men would be killed, and the treasure would remain there on the island until it would be safe to go and recover it. It would be all ours. I was horrified, of course. But reason told me that there was nothing that could be done to stop it."

"Nothing?" I asked.

"It was too late to find a reliable gondolier."

"By reliable you mean one who wouldn't reveal anything."

"Yes, of course. So we just had to think of a way of limiting the damage if you should survive and return to the city. My husband thought it unlikely you would survive, of course. This man from Naples was very efficient, he said."

"I suppose he had met him on that one foreign mission to Smyrna."

"I believe so. My husband then introduced him to Visentin, and they often used his services. He was a skilful smuggler, you know, not just a killer."

"Good to know he had other lines of work to fall back on in hard times," I said. "You know he almost killed me. It was Komnenos who saved me."

"I'm glad to hear it," she said. "Two men I've loved."

"And two men your husband must have hated," I said. And then I remembered something: "Hephaestus ..."

"I beg your pardon?"

"It was something the poor schoolteacher wrote in his diary: just a reference to Hephaestus. And I thought he was referring to the Neapolitan killer, who was lame. But no: I'd forgotten."

"Hephaestus is the husband of Venus," she said with a quiet smile.

"Exactly. Cuckolded and scorned by the other gods. 'Vulcan with awkward grace his office plies, / And unextinguish'd laughter shakes the skies,'" I quoted in English.

"I presume this is your Alexander Pope," she said.

"Yes," I said. "First book of *The Iliad*, when the other gods mock him. Padoan must have seen how your husband was not a forgiving man. Like Hephaestus he stored his resentment, forging his weapons and waiting for the right moment for revenge. It wasn't only greed."

I detected a slightly agitated expression flickering across her face and wondered what had caused it. But I remembered she had probably spent some hours in this cold and dingy storeroom, waiting without any certainty for my arrival, so a certain degree of stress was only to be expected.

"So what do you want?" I said, deciding it was time to get to the point.

"Just exclude us from your account of this whole affair," she said. "My husband will depart for Cerigo at once."

"Hephaestus banished to the land of his in-laws," I said. "I can see it might be uncomfortable, but it is hardly commensurate with what he has done."

"I'm asking for myself, not for him," she said frankly. "And I can't believe you feel nothing for me." She pushed her shawl right back so that her hair was visible in all its golden glory. She gazed steadily at me, the cool blue pools of her eyes drawing mine towards them.

"And now you're demeaning yourself," I heard my voice say, a little hoarsely.

Anger flickered in her eyes for one second – and then, to my puzzlement, the agitation returned. I saw she was now looking over my shoulder, and I turned round. The door of the dark rickety wardrobe was opening: out stepped Nobleman Querini.

32

I couldn't help but utter a brief laugh. But then it stopped being funny. He was holding a large pistol, and it was trained on me.

"Thank you, my dear," he said. "You've done your best. Now you had better leave it to me."

"Was that all a pack of lies?" I said to Isabella Venier. "Were you in on the whole scheme from the beginning, murders and everything?"

"No," she said, her voice now breathy with agitation. "It was all true. I just omitted to mention that my husband . . ."

". . . was hiding in the wardrobe," I concluded. "Well, that would have been embarrassing to admit, after yesterday."

She didn't answer. Querini spoke: "'Demeaning' is the word you've just used, isn't it?" he said. "You dared to use it to my wife."

I decided not to point out to him that he had just stepped out of a wardrobe, and so the word was not exactly inappropriate for him either. It was not the right moment to antagonise him.

"A mere *cicerone*, pretending to teach deportment to a noblewoman," he went on.

"Not deportment," I said. "Honesty."

"How dare you?" His voice was shrill and intense, the voice of a weak man who had worked himself up into a fury, which he was trying to convince himself was righteous indignation. "You who come treacherously into our house, who break all the traditional bonds of hospitality . . . A mere vagabond, pretending to know about art, about the great classics . . ."

"Excellency," I said, "this is scarcely the time for a competition in artistic expertise. What exactly do you want from me?"

"Where are the treasures?"

I had hoped he was going to ask that. So long as he held on to a greedy desire to reacquire them, however mad it might be, my life was worth something to him. The moment he realised they were unattainable, he would kill me. I had no doubt about that.

"I've put them in a safe place."

"You are going to tell us where."

"And then?"

"And then you can go back to your petty little life, showing the glories of our civilisation to uncultured barbarians who understand nothing. My wife and I will retire to her properties in Cerigo." He was now making an obvious effort to calm himself and appear reasonable.

"Well, that sounds sensible," I said slowly. "Do you want to come with me and I'll show you where they are?"

"No, you will tell me here and now."

"It's a little difficult to explain," I said.

"Stop playing with me!" he snapped. I could see the pistol shaking slightly.

"My dear," said Isabella Venier, "try to stay calm." She moved towards him.

"It is very difficult," he said, apparently through clenched teeth, "when I am dealing with a wretched fool who has interfered in matters that do not concern him."

"Excellency," I said, "my only concern was for the city I love. I'm sure you can understand that."

"Do you think I don't love this city? Do you think I haven't devoted my life to appreciating its treasures? But I can also see beyond its confines; I know that the great works of art do not belong just in one place."

Ah, I thought, that was how he had rationalised his theft. He was liberating the works of art for the benefit of others.

"I see," I said.

"I doubt that you do," he said. "But, to use your own word, I demean myself by talking about such things to you. Just tell me where the treasures are. Immediately."

"Excellency, I'm sure you can understand that I would like some guarantee of my safety if I do so."

"You have my word as a Venetian nobleman."

And as a Venetian bankrupt, thief and hirer of assassins. "Well, would you mind putting the pistol down then, Excellency?"

"You are not in a position to tell me what to do," he said.

"No, Excellency, I'm asking."

"And do as you ask I will not. Now tell me where the treasures are."

"And I can only answer that I will show you. I can't tell you."

"I will not ask again. I will shoot."

"And then you will never know."

"I will shoot your leg. The pain and the blood might help you to reflect on how absurd your attitude is." He pointed the pistol downwards to make his intention clear. His hand continued to shake slightly. Without taking his eye or the gun off me he addressed his wife: "My dear, you will find another loaded pistol in the wardrobe. Please have it ready."

She did not say a word but went to the wardrobe and returned with another pistol. She held it in both hands, its muzzle pointed at the ground. She stood just behind him.

"I'll count to three," said Querini. "Then I will shoot. You do realise I don't want to do this, but you are forcing it upon me? My dear, the moment I have fired, please pass me the other pistol. We must be ready for all eventualities."

"Excellency," I said, "please consider what you are doing." Would it be worth trying to rush him?

"One," he said, very slowly and deliberately.

"Excellency . . ."

"Two."

There was a sudden loud explosion, and I reeled back. Almost instantly there was a sudden gasping cry from Querini, and he pitched forward to the ground. Isabella Venier had also staggered back, from the kick of her pistol, which was now smoking.

Seconds later I was bending over Querini. There was a great spreading stain in his back. He was still breathing, and his fingers still clutched his pistol. His face was turned towards me and was twisted in pain and shock. "What . . . what . . ." he managed to gasp.

"I've had enough, dear husband," Isabella Venier said in a flat voice. "It's all over." She made no move towards him but just stood there, the pistol pointing downwards once more.

"You've betrayed us all . . ." he gasped. "For this wretched vagabond . . ."

"Don't force me to say what I think when I compare you both," she said. Her voice remained flat and unemotional.

"My mother said you were a whore . . ." His face gave one final twitch of pain and became still.

We stood in silence for a few moments. Then she said, "Typically gracious last words."

I was unable to speak for some seconds. Eventually I managed to say, "Thank you."

"For what? For aiding a thief and murderer? For destroying your love life?"

"For saving my life."

"I wonder whether he would have ever found the courage to pull that trigger. Well, we'll never know. Now do what you must do."

"I'm not sure what that is," I said.

"Go and talk to your famous Missier Grande. He'll know. Don't worry. I won't run away. I have nowhere to run to."

"There's always Cerigo," I said.

"I hope that will be allowed me," she said. "I know that otherwise I'll be expected to join a convent."

I could not help smiling.

"Ah, Sior Alvise, I see you find that a ridiculous idea. Whatever else, I feel you do know me."

"I think so. I hope so."

"Before you go to your Missier Grande, grant me one last favour."

"What's that?"

She said nothing but laid her gun down on a nearby chair, put both hands up to my face and drew me into a long and passionate kiss. Inappropriate though it was, I could not help responding. Once again it seemed only polite.

"Thank you," she said. "That really was the last time."

"Yes," I said, a little hoarsely.

"And your bookshop lass has never had the experience?"

"No," I said.

"I would love to tell her myself that it's worth it, but perhaps that's not a good idea."

"No," I said again. Then, feeling embarrassed by my curt replies, I added, "Siora, please don't misunderstand. What happened between us was – was good, but . . ."

". . . but mustn't happen again. May I offer some advice?"

"Certainly." It was a strange moment to be exchanging tips on amatory procedures, but I was so befuddled with exhaustion and strain that thoughts of appropriateness were the last thing on my mind.

"You must tell her everything."

"Ye-es," I said, a little unconvinced.

"It is the only way. How did you explain the scene she witnessed yesterday?"

"I told her the truth, ridiculous though it was. Wardrobe and all."

She shook her head. "But of course that wasn't all, and she could see it wasn't. Was it likely that I would have been standing there so calmly and unashamedly in my undergarments if there had been nothing between us?"

I could see the truth of this. "No," I said. "You're right."

"Of course I'm right. I've lived long enough amid lies and hypocrisy to know what you can get away with and what you can't. But go now. I'll sit down and perhaps I'll even say a prayer." She moved over to the chair where she had laid the gun. She picked it up, placed it on the ground and then sat down, pulling her shawl over her hair again and wrapping her cloak about her. I decided not to tell her that in that half-light she could have been mistaken for a nun.

33

It all happened with surprising rapidity after that.

The square was a little more lively by now, with a number of people drawing water from the well. The boy was nowhere to be seen. I soon found someone who could tell me where the Missier Grande's real house was. It turned out to be a comfortable first-floor apartment which had a view over both the square and the Giudecca Canal, as I had first imagined.

I had the strange experience of seeing him for once without his wig and official robes, after the serving-woman who opened the door to me had summoned him. Despite this more homely appearance he had lost none of his dignified bearing, nor his ability to grasp the essence of a situation remarkably quickly. He gave instructions for a servant to accompany me to the gondola, first to help unload the trunk of treasures and then to assist Bepi into the house, where he was made to rest on a divan while a doctor was sent for. The Buranello gondolier was paid handsomely, and he and his moustaches set off on the long trip back to his island.

The Missier Grande then came with me to the storeroom, where we found Isabella Venier still sitting composedly beside the corpse of her husband. She rose and bowed formally to him, then corroborated what I had told him already. A message was sent to the Inquisitors, telling them that they would hear useful information on the events in the basilica of the previous evening if they should come to the residence of Sior Giacomo Carraro in Campo Sant'Agnese.

Two hours later (during which time Bepi had had his ankle tightly bandaged, we had both consumed a hearty breakfast and I had been able to wash and make myself more or less presentable), Marino Basso, looking considerably harassed (I imagined that he too had not slept all night), presented himself at the front door of the apartment, in his role as trusted confidential agent of the Inquisitors. He presumably knew who Sior Giacomo Carraro was, and so his attitude was both supercilious and distrustful; sentiments, of course, which were only exacerbated when he found me in the front room. He refused even to bow to me.

Then we showed him the treasures.

They had been taken out of the trunk and displayed, in all their splendour, on the large table in the middle of the room. It seemed as if the sun had emerged at last with the sole aim of adding extra effulgence to this one moment; the Giudecca Canal glittered below the windows of the house, and shimmering reflections of this light danced on the ceiling above the silver and sardonyx chalices, the bejewelled reliquaries, the enamelled medallions, the gold monstrances and votive crowns . . .

It was even better than the moment when I had revealed the presence of the Turkish ladies in Bepi's gondola. Amazement, resentment, anger and finally relief passed in quick succession over Marino Basso's features, and he was unable to utter a single coherent word for several seconds. Eventually, after some cursory explanations had been given, he made a deliberate effort to assume a respectful tone and declared that he would arrange for a suitable escort to take the treasures back to the basilica, where the Inquisitors would meet us.

The Missier Grande then said a few words about the corpse in the nearby storeroom, and Basso promised that this too would be handled with all the necessary discretion.

Only after he had left did the Missier Grande turn to me and say, "Thank you, Sior Marangon."

"Illustrissimo, thank you – for the encouragement."

"I don't believe that I ever did encourage you," he said.

"Not in so many words," I said.

"I see that you understand me well," he said. "I think we will continue to work together profitably."

"Sior Massaro will be immensely relieved," I said.

"Ah yes. I will make sure that he too is restored to his position."

Sior Giacomo Carraro did indeed take up his old position as Missier Grande, with Sior Massaro in the outer office. What had happened that night at the treasury never became publicly known, although rumours abounded. The corpses on the Venier island were swiftly removed; it is possible that they were, in fact, transferred quickly and silently to the nearby bone island of Sant'Ariano. The death of Nobleman Querini could not be treated quite so unceremoniously, but public scandal was averted by a declaration that he had been the victim of a hunting accident; when objections were raised that he had never been known to go hunting before, the response came back that it was precisely his unfamiliarity with firearms that had led to the tragedy. His grief-stricken widow retired to her property on the island of Cerigo, where, it was said, she devoted herself to good works among the poor. Her maidservant, Ariadne, accompanied her. The Scuola dei Calegheri never did reacquire its painting of Saint Constantine. The Querini family, meanwhile, drew a collective sigh of relief.

Nobleman Sanudo quietly resigned his office as Inquisitor. It became very clear that it had been due to pressure on his part that Paolo Padoan's investigations had been halted and his reports suppressed, all out of a misguided desire to hush up all possible scandals connected with the younger Sanudo's exploits. Of course, he had had no idea of what the real Four Horsemen had been up to, nor what Querini's hired killer had been doing.

After continuous protestation on my part Paolo Padoan's sister regained some of her lost property, including a number of Greek books, which she was happy to sell to Fabrizio, who gave her a good price for them. Padoan's diary, however, never did resurface. (And no further news was ever discovered of the location of the tomb of Constantine XI.)

My copy of Homer was eventually found among the various pieces of evidence retained by the magistrates, and I was allowed to retake possession of it. I had been worried that it would be damaged by bloodstains, which, however appropriate to the story recounted within its pages, would undoubtedly have spoiled my enjoyment of it.

Fortunately this turned out not to be the case, and Pope's couplets were preserved in pages that were only occasionally crumpled.

Bepi was forced to take an unexpected holiday for a couple of weeks, while his ankle healed. He was helped in this by receiving a reward from the Council of Ten for his assistance in "recovering some stolen items"; along with the reward came a stern warning not to reveal anything of what had happened to anyone. Bepi, firm believer in the Inquisitors' well-established custom of tearing out the tongues of garrulous revealers of state secrets, was happy to abide by this, even with regard to his mother. He spent some of his enforced holiday explaining the more intricate rules of dice to Fabrizio, who actually began to meet him regularly at a tavern in Castello for this very purpose. To the relief of Lucia, their stakes remained *bagattini*.

One evening in the bookshop, when her father had gone to meet Bepi, I gave Lucia a fairly detailed account of what had happened on the island and then in the storehouse at Sant'Agnese. When I told her how Isabella Venier had saved my life by shooting her husband her face grew serious.

"I knew that woman loved you," she said at last.

"That's a big word," I said. "She loved in the same way Konstantinos Komnenos and Andrea Sanudo."

"And did you all love her back?"

"Obviously I can't speak for Komnenos and Sanudo. I was dazzled by her. I'll admit that."

"I see."

"And in the end I was – well, I was seduced by her."

Lucia began dusting a shelf of books at around waist-level, which meant her face was turned downwards. She said, "The passive voice is a very useful grammatical tool."

"Siora Lucia," I said, "it happened after you had been angry with me – understandably so. I felt a little lost."

"I see." She straightened up and looked directly at me. "And did she help you find yourself?"

"She gave me the momentary illusion of having done so. It didn't last."

"And in any case she has gone now," said Lucia. "To the island of Venus."

I wondered if she had been doing some research of her own – and then remembered that her father had idly mentioned this legend that morning at the Rialto. Lucia had not forgotten it. I tried to make light of it. "She did play on the notion. It was a rather foolish one." I shifted tone and tried to make myself sound more serious. "Siora Lucia, do you think . . ."

"Don't ask me, please."

"Are you already saying no?"

"I'm saying don't ask me. Not just yet."

"Not yet," I repeated.

"Exactly. Now if you'll excuse me I think I should close the shop."

"Certainly. Siora Lucia, goodnight."

"Goodnight, Sior Alvise."

Not yet. It could have been worse, I thought, as I set off home.

End note

The Querini and the Venier were, of course, two of the most distinguished families in Venice. It would seem that the Venetian state managed successfully to eliminate all trace of this scandalous story from its records, since no reference can be found to a marriage between the two families in the eighteenth century, and neither Isabella Venier nor Marco Querini figure anywhere in the annals. The Querini family, perhaps because of the early scandal of their involvement in the Bajamonte Tiepolo uprising, would have been particularly keen to have any suggestion of treacherous behaviour on the part of one of its members expunged from the records. It is probable that Isabella Venier did subsequently live an entirely retired life on the island of Kythira; who knows, she may even have ended up taking holy orders.

The palace near Campo Santa Maria Formosa is now the Querini-Stampalia Museum and Library. The decoration is mainly eighteenth-century but mostly from a period slightly later than the events recounted here. However, the grandiose family portraits that Alvise describes can still be seen there.

My thanks go to Panayotis Ioannidis, who provided the rhyming couplet refrain for Komnenos's kleftic ballad, and to Ernest Hilbert, who provided information on early editions of Alexander Pope's translation of *The Iliad*.

I would also like to thank John Beaton, my agent, for all his untiring work and his continual encouragement.

Glossary

(Words that are Venetian rather than standard Italian are indicated by V in brackets)

altana (V)	a wooden structure on the roof of buildings, used for various purposes (drying of clothes, taking of sun)
arsenalotto (V)	a worker at the Arsenale
bagattino	the smallest Venetian coin, worth 1/240th of a *lira*
barene (V)	the low-lying marshy terrain of the lagoon, often submerged at high tide
barnabotto (V)	a Venetian nobleman fallen on hard times and granted cheap rented accommodation in the parish of San Barnaba
bauta (V)	White face-mask
Bondì (V)	Venetian for *Buongiorno* (good morning)
bravo	a hired thug
bricole (V)	poles driven into the mud of the canals or the lagoon to act as markers or mooring-poles
buranello	native of the island of Burano; also the name for a local biscuit often taken with wine
caigo (V)	fog
caleghero (V)	a shoe-maker
calle (V)	a narrow street
campo (V)	a city square (in Italian the word indicates a field)
campiello (V)	a smaller city square
canalazzo (V)	alternative name for the Grand Canal
casino (V)	small room or set of rooms used by Venetian

305

	aristocrats for various leisure purposes, including gambling
cavalier servente	see *cicisbeo*
cicerone	tourist-guide
cicisbeo	married woman's semi-official gallant, sometimes her lover; also known as a *cavalier servente*
codega (V)	"link-boy" (hired escorts holding lanterns)
confidente	a confidential agent
cortesan (V)	literally a "courtier" (*cortegiano* in Italian); in Venetian indicating a gentlemanly man of the world
cospetto	mild imprecation
felze (V)	the cabin of a gondola
filippo	coin, worth eleven *lire*
fioi (V)	Venetian appellation, corresponding roughly to "lads"
fondamenta (V)	road running alongside a canal
fontego (V)	(also *fondaco*); literally a warehouse, but also a residence and meeting-place for foreign communities in Venice
forcola (V)	the carved wooden structure on gondolas acting as a rowlock
foresto (V)	Venetian for foreigner
furatola (V)	a cheap tavern
guagliò	abbreviation of *guaglione*, Neapolitan for "lad"
illustrissimo	most illustrious or eminent; a term of respect generally used in Venice to address those not of noble rank
Liston (V)	in Saint Mark's Square, the area between the clock-tower and the pillars by the water-front, used as a fashionable parade ground
magazen (V)	cheap taverns, not allowed to serve cooked food
malvasia	malmsey wine; also used as the name of taverns that served such wine
marangon (V)	carpenter

Nicolotti (V)	inhabitants of western Venice (around the parish of San Nicolò dei Mendicoli); traditional rivals of the *Castellani*, inhabitants of eastern Venice
osteria	hostelry or tavern
passeggiata	stroll, particularly the evening stroll along the *Liston*
piano nobile	the first floor of a Venetian palace; containing the principal rooms.
portego (V)	the central and most splendid room of a Venetian palazzo
Ridotto	the government-owned gambling house at Palazzo Dandolo (literally "the closed-off or private room")
rio (V)	Venetian word for a canal
Salizada (V)	a broad street in Venice (one of the first to have been paved)
salotto	a salon, often understood to be a gathering-place for refined conversation
salottiere	one who attends a *salotto*
sandolo (V)	flat-bottomed Venetian rowing boat, of a simpler build than a gondola
sbirro	officer of the law; often used derogatorily
scudo	coin worth seven *lire*
scuola	literally a school, but in Venice often used to refer to a charitable institution, a guild-hall, or a meeting-place for foreign communities, usually under the protection of a patron saint
Sior/Siora (V)	Venetian for *Signor/Signora*
sottoportego (V)	archway or passage under a building
tabarro	cloak
zaffi (V)	see *sbirro*; also often used derogatorily
zecchino	the principal Venetian coin, worth twenty-two *lire* (origin of the word "sequin")
zuechino (V)	inhabitant of the Giudecca island